D0964063

Also by Maisey Yates

Confessions from the Quilting Circle
Secrets from a Happy Marriage

Gold Valley

Smooth-Talking Cowboy
Untamed Cowboy
Good Time Cowboy
A Tall, Dark Cowboy Christmas
Unbroken Cowboy
Cowboy to the Core
Lone Wolf Cowboy
Cowboy Christmas Redemption
The Bad Boy of Redemption Ranch
The Hero of Hope Springs
The Last Christmas Cowboy
The Heartbreaker of Echo Pass
Rodeo Christmas at Evergreen Ranch
The True Cowboy of Sunset Ridge

Copper Ridge

Part Time Cowboy
Brokedown Cowboy
Bad News Cowboy
The Cowboy Way
One Night Charmer
Tough Luck Hero
Last Chance Rebel
Slow Burn Cowboy
Down Home Cowboy
Wild Ride Cowboy
Christmastime Cowboy

For more books by Maisey Yates,
visit www.maiseyyates.com.

MAISEY YATES

Unbridled Cowboy

HQN

ISBN-13: 978-1-335-50321-3

Recycling programs
for this product may
not exist in your area.

Unbridled Cowboy
Copyright © 2022 by Maisey Yates

Once Upon a Cowboy
Copyright © 2022 by Maisey Yates

For questions and comments about the quality of this book,
please contact us at CustomerService@Harlequin.com.

HQN
22 Adelaide St. West, 41st Floor
Toronto, Ontario M5H 4E3, Canada
www.Harlequin.com

Printed and bound in Barcelona, Spain by CPI Black Print

CONTENTS

To my editor Flo, for being not only a story genius but also a sounding board, a panic button, an advocate and someone I am happy to call a friend. For all the books and all the years, and all the things that have happened in between. You're amazing, and you'll continue to be amazing as you take on all the great adventures up ahead. I'm so glad you're on my team.

UNBRIDLED COWBOY

CHAPTER ONE

"THERE'S NO WAY around it. I'm going to need a wife."

Sawyer Garrett looked across the table at his brother, Wolf, and his sister, Elsie, and then down at the tiny pink bundle he was holding in his arms.

It wasn't like this was an entirely new idea.

It was just that he had been thinking the entire time that Missy might change her mind, which would put him in a different position. She hadn't, though. She had stuck to her guns. When she found out she was pregnant, she told him that she wanted nothing to do with having a baby. She wanted to go through with the pregnancy, but not with being a mother. Not even when he proposed marriage. Oh, they hadn't been in a relationship or anything like that. She was just a woman that he saw from time to time.

In fact, Sawyer Garrett could honestly say that he had a very low opinion of relationships and family.

Present company excluded, of course.

But when Missy had said she was pregnant, he'd known there was only one thing to do. His dad had been a flawed man. Deeply so. He'd acted like the kids were an afterthought and all he'd really done was let them live under his roof.

Sawyer wanted more for his child. Better. He'd determined he would be there, not just providing housing and food, but actually being there.

If he could spare his child the feeling of being unwanted, he would.

And that was where this idea had been turning over in his head for a while.

The fact of the matter was, Garrett's Watch had a lousy track record when it came to marriage.

The thirteen-thousand-acre spread had been settled back in the late 1800s, with equal adjoining spreads settled by the Kings, the McClouds and the Sullivans, all of whom had now worked what was known in combination as Four Corners Ranch in the generations since.

And where the Garrett clan was concerned… There was nothing but a long history of abandonment and divorces. The one exception being Sawyer's grandparents. Oh, not his grandfather's first marriage. His biological grandmother had run off just like every other woman in their family tree. As if the ground itself was cursed.

But then the old man had happened upon an idea. He thought to write a letter to one of the newspapers back east asking for a woman who wanted to come out to Oregon and be a mother to his children. They'd had the only successful marriage in his direct line. And it was because it was based on mutual respect and understanding and not the emotional bullshit that had been a hallmark of his own childhood. He barely remembered his own mother. He remembered Wolf's and Elsie's, though. Two different women. Only around for a small number of years.

Just long enough to leave some scars.

Hell, he didn't know how he wound up in this position. He was a man who liked to play hard. He worked hard. It seemed fair enough. But he was careful. He *always* used a condom. And Missy had been no exception. He'd just been subject to that small percentage of failure. *Failure.*

He hated that. He hated that feeling. He hated that word. If there was one thing he could fault his father for it was the fact that the man hadn't taken charge. The fact that he just sat there in the shit when everything went to hell. That wasn't who Sawyer was. But Sawyer had to be responsible for his siblings far sooner than he should've had to be, thanks in part due to his father's passivity. If there was one thing Sawyer had learned, it was that you had to be responsible when responsibility was needed.

He wasn't a stranger to failing people in his life, but unlike his father, he'd learned. He'd never let anyone who needed him down, not again.

"Marriage," Wolf said. "Really."

"Unless you and Elsie want a full-time job as a nanny."

Elsie snorted, leaned back in her chair and put her boots up on the table—which she didn't normally do, but she was just trying to be as feral as possible in the moment. "Not likely," she said.

"Right. Well. So, do you think there's a better idea?"

"Reconsider being a single father?" Wolf said.

"I am," Sawyer said. "I'm aiming to find a wife."

Wolf shook his head. "I mean, reconsider having a baby at all."

A fierce protectiveness gripped Sawyer's chest. "It's a little late, don't you think?"

"Wasn't too late for Missy to walk away yesterday," Wolf said.

"Too late for me," Sawyer said.

It had been. From the moment he'd first heard her cry. The weight of… Of everything that he felt on his shoulders when this tiny little thing was placed into his arms. It was difficult to describe. Impossible. He wasn't good with feelings when they were simple. But this was complicated. A burden, but one he grabbed hold of willingly. One he felt simultaneously uniquely suited for and completely unequal to. He didn't know the first thing about babies. Yeah, he had done quite a bit to take care of Elsie and Wolf, and… He could see where he'd fallen short. Elsie was just a hair shy of a bobcat in human form, and Wolf suited his name, and, well…big, a little bit dangerous, loyal to his pack, but that was about it.

"It's not too late," Elsie said. "In the strictest sense. You haven't even given her name."

No. It was true. He hadn't settled on anything yet. And he knew there was paperwork that he had to do.

"You want me to give her back?" He shook his head. "It's not like I have a receipt, Els."

"That's not what I meant," Elsie said. "It's just… It's a hard life here."

"And I aim to make it a little less hard."

"So, you're going to… What? Put an ad in the paper?"

"Granddad did," he said.

And it had changed their lives for the better. The history of Garrett's Watch might be rich with failed love stories, but it was a marriage of convenience that had brought real love to the ranch.

Their grandmother—their real grandmother (blood didn't matter here, staying mattered)—had loved them all with a ferocity their own mothers hadn't managed, let alone their father.

She had taught Sawyer to tie his shoes and ride a bike. She'd hugged him when he'd fallen and scraped his knees.

She taught him tenderness. And he was damned grateful for it now, because he had this tiny life in his care, and if it weren't for her, he would have never, ever known where to begin.

And thanks to his grandfather, he knew what else he might need.

However crazy his siblings thought it was.

"It's not 1950," Wolf pointed out.

Though, sometimes, on Four Corners you could be forgiven for not realizing that. For not realizing it wasn't 1880, even.

Time passed slowly, and by and large the landscape didn't change. Sure, the farm implements got a little bit shinier.

On a particularly good year, the savings account got a little bit fatter.

But the land itself remained. The large imposing mountains that surrounded the property that backed Garrett's Watch. The river that ran through the property, cutting across the field and the base of the mountain. The pine trees, green all through the year, growing taller with the passage of time.

They were lucky to have done well enough in the last few years that the large main house was completely updated, though it was ridiculously huge for Sawyer by himself. Wolf and Elsie had gone to their own cabins on the property, which were also sturdy and well kept.

In truth, this whole thing with the baby had been a wake-up call. Because whether or not he could look out the window and see it, time was passing. And when Missy had asked him what he wanted to do about the baby, the answer had seemed simple. It had seemed simple because… He had no excuse. He had plenty of money, and had the sort of life that meant he could include a kid in most anything. His dad had done him a favor by showing him what not to do. They were largely left to their own devices, but it was a great place to be left to your devices. And he'd had to ask himself… What was he hanging on to? A life of going out drinking whenever he wanted, sleeping with whoever he wanted.

He was at the age where it wasn't all that attractive, not anymore.

Thirty-four and with no sign of change on the horizon. In the end, he decided to aim for more. To take the change that was coming whether he was ready or not.

Turns out not very ready. But again, that was where his plan came in.

"I'm aware that is not 1950," he shot back at his brother. "I can…sign up for a… A website."

As if he knew how the hell to do that. They had a computer. Hell, he had a smartphone. They had a business to manage and it made sense. But the fact remained, he didn't have a lot of use for either.

Elsie cackled, slinging her boots off the table and flipping her dark braid over her shoulder. "A website? I don't think people swipe on their phones looking for marriage. I think they look for… Well, stuff you seem to be able to find without the help of the internet."

His sister wasn't wrong. He found sex just fine without the help of his phone. That was what Smokey's Tavern was for.

"The way I see it," Sawyer said, speaking as if Elsie hadn't spoken, which as far as he was concerned was the way it should be with younger siblings, "marriage can work, relationships can work, as long as you have the same set of goals as the other person. It's all these modern ideals… That's what doesn't work."

"Which modern ideals?" Elsie asked. "The kind that saw every woman in our bloodline leaving every man in our bloodline all the way back to when people were riding around in horse-drawn carriages?"

"Yes," he said. "That is what I mean. People thinking that they needed to marry for something other than… common need."

He was pretty sure his grandparents had loved each other in the end. But it reminded him of something other than romance. It reminded him of his connection to the land. You cared for that which cared for you. It sustained you. You worked it, and the dirt got under your nails. The air was in your lungs. It became part of you. Of all that you were.

That was something better than romance.

Romance, in his estimation, was screaming fights and other bullshit. Punishing each other—and your children— because you couldn't figure out how the hell to deal with yourselves.

He wanted no part in it.

"And what is it you have to offer a woman?" Wolf asked, grinning. "Why exactly would she agree to leave her life behind, to marry you and take care of your kid?"

"I've got this house," he said. "A fine working ranch, cute baby."

"A lot of bad habits, cheap beer and a bad temper," Elsie said, as if she were finishing his list.

"I didn't say I was perfect," he said.

"It's not going work," Wolf said. "You are not going to find some woman desperate enough that she's going to be willing to cross the country to marry you."

"And if you do," Elsie said, "I would be worried."

Wolf slapped his palm on the table. "Good point."

"Worried about what?" He frowned. "What do I have to worry about a woman for?"

"She could be a bunny boiler," Elsie said. "The crazy jealous type. Or just plain crazy."

"She's right," Wolf said.

"I'll figure it out," Sawyer said. "You act like I'm some kind of greenhorn. I know women. And I know what I need."

"Do you? Because it seems to me you got yourself saddled with a baby mama no different than your own mother," Wolf said.

And that bit down. Hard. Right on Sawyer's neck.

Leave it to Wolf to get right to the real issue. He felt guilty as hell. Because he'd done it, hadn't he? He brought a kid in this world under the exact same circumstances that he'd been brought into it.

Though he had to give it to Missy. She'd known that she didn't want to be involved. From the beginning.

His daughter... His *daughter.*

Damn.

That still hit him. Right between the eyes every time he thought it. He needed to give her a name so he didn't have to think of her in that way. He didn't have time to be going around feeling like he'd been punched in the heart every five seconds.

His daughter wouldn't have vague memories of her mother. She wouldn't have any of her at all. And if he got himself a wife fast enough, then she would only know one mother. One that shows her. One that chose to be here.

He wouldn't repeat the same mistakes as his father. Because Sawyer was a man who knew what he was about. Sawyer was a man who wouldn't sit on his ass and let his kids pay the price for his own bad mistakes. No. He wouldn't do it.

Sawyer Garrett was going to find himself a wife.

If a mail-order bride was good enough for his grandfather, it was good enough for him.

And he was going to get started right away.

CHAPTER TWO

EVELYN MOORE HADN'T realized that her life was a Jenga tower until a very key piece had been removed from the center of it and the entire thing had collapsed around her in a heap.

She hadn't realized the way that each integral piece was connected, the way each and every component of who she was rested on another.

It was abundantly clear now. Crystal. And it was too late to do anything about it.

Actually, and in fairness, it had been *two* Jenga blocks. Two blocks that had come out at once.

Hollyn and Andrew.

And with them had come… Everything.

Even now, five days later, with her mascara gluing her eyes shut, she could clearly see the scene as it played out in her memory.

Walking through the beautiful top-floor office building with the fantastic view of Central Park, the sun streaming through the windows, across the open-plan floor, with the glass-walled offices that allowed them all to engage in the kind of team building that was important to Evelyn, Hollyn and Kioni.

Because they were all about their staff. All about closeness. All about female empowerment.

Lifting each other up.

It was how they had managed to take their organization company from social media into a high-rise building inside of five years. Building their followers from the three of them to millions upon millions.

They had celebrity clients, and there were even talks of a TV show. The book that the three of them had put together—which was mostly them giving their ideas to someone who wrote it all down and made it make sense, and a photographer who took beautiful pictures of their different projects—had made them a fair amount of money, and brought them into the mainstream. They had been profiled all across the media as SheEOs.

Women bosses who ran a different sort of company. Who broke the mold.

Which is why Evelyn had been so shocked when she had walked into the only office in the building that afforded privacy and seen her fiancé, Andrew, lying on Hollyn, thrusting away, while sprawled across her desk.

It had all fallen apart.

Right then.

She had screamed. A horror-movie scream that had alerted everyone on their floor to the fact that something was happening. She'd left the office door wide open, giving everyone who had come running a front row seat to the indignity of Hollyn and Andrew scrambling to right their clothing. And she had…

Well, she had unleashed her fury like a wave of fire, and she hoped it burned everything right to the ground.

Andrew.

He was the love of her life. And suddenly those words didn't make any sense. They didn't mean anything. Because the love of your life would never… How could he?

The man she'd felt like she'd loved. The only man she'd ever been in love with.

She wanted to build a life with him.

Have babies with him.

Oh, she really wanted a baby. She was ready for one—not like her mother, who'd made her feel the regret she had over her unexpected pregnancy for…forever. Evelyn was ready. She'd done everything right. She'd been with this man for years and they were ready. She was thirty-four and it was time.

And now she had to start over.

Above all else, that hurt. And maybe that was messed up, but it did.

She was so happy with the life she'd made, but one of the biggest things left for her was motherhood.

She'd wanted a big family. A stark contrast to the echoing silence of the family home she'd grown up in. She'd been ready for that. For a home outside the city. She'd built her career to the point where it was stable enough she would be able to do a lot of her work from home and choose her hours judiciously.

She had created the perfect tower.

She'd thought.

And when she went into the office that Kioni was in and expressed her shock to her other *absolute dearest friend* that she had known since college, the expression in her dark eyes had told Evelyn everything she needed to know.

Kioni had already been aware that Hollyn and Andrew were screwing.

"I didn't know how to tell you," Kioni said.

"Some way that doesn't involve me *walking in on it*," Evelyn said.

All she could do was stare at her friend.

Kioni and Hollyn knew her, and that was what hurt the worst. They were supposed to care for her. They knew about her past, about the way her parents had pressured her and how she'd rebelled. How she'd worked so hard at climbing out of that mess, rebuilding her grades so she could get accepted into college, rebuilding her self-confidence after it had been so badly battered.

And it wasn't just Hollyn who had destroyed their friendship when she'd touched the man Evelyn loved. But Kioni…

She hadn't defended Evelyn, or warned her or…or told Hollyn to stop. That was what she couldn't bear. One friend betraying her, her fiancé betraying her…

That would have hurt.

But to feel like all the people she loved were hiding this…

That was something she didn't know if she could survive.

Evelyn turned on her heel and walked out of Kioni's office.

"I'm sorry," Kioni said, chasing after Evelyn, down the hall and into the elevator. "I didn't feel good lying about it. I thought… I thought that he would tell you. I thought the two of you would handle it. I figured either it would stop, and he would go forward with the wedding, or…"

"You were going to let me marry someone… She was going to… You are my maids of honor. And she was having sex with him, and you were going to let me marry him knowing that."

She hadn't spoken to either of them since then. She stormed off the elevator and created an absolute scene out on the street. Crying, with actual snot dripping down her face. And it was too late to cancel… Everything. And her parents didn't want her to. All anyone seemed to care about was the brand and the fact that if it got out that this betrayal had occurred in the group it would damage the brand irreparably. Managers were calling her. All kinds of people who didn't seem to care at all that she'd been betrayed. It was just suddenly her responsibility to be okay with it. It was up to her to preserve female unity, not up to her friends to be better people.

She wasn't a stranger to starting over. She'd done it before.

But she'd never imagined she'd be in a position where she had to do it again.

One thing she loved about organization was that it allowed her to make sense of a chaotic world. To control all the things she couldn't.

When she'd been young she'd dreamed of being a ballet dancer, and her need for control had damaged her. But as an organizer, controlling the chaos was good.

Because she'd embraced chaos for a while, after leaving school, after leaving dance, and it hadn't been going anywhere good.

Except it wasn't helping her now. Not in the least.

She had reorganized her house four times in the last few days.

She turned on a TV movie channel renowned for its easy, sweet romances. She had been shamefully watching them on repeat ever since it had all happened. Locked away in her apartment—which was small, but beautiful, and had a lovely view of the city.

Something caught in her chest. She'd been ready to leave this view behind. She'd been ready for the next thing. For a home and a yard, and a place for children to play.

When she'd gone to the boarding school upstate, they'd come into Manhattan often, and she'd dreamed of living here. She'd dreamed of performing here as a dancer, but even when that dream had ended, she'd still longed for this view. And achieving it with her new business had been... triumphant.

In the end she hadn't needed to be thinner. She hadn't needed dance. She had a successful career. She was supposed to get married in just two weeks to the man she'd been in love with since she was twenty-three years old.

But now it had all...crumbled, and she couldn't see the triumph. Not anymore.

Not such a bad thing now that he insisted on living apart.

True. She was grateful for the space now. It hadn't seemed practical, because they practically lived together, but there was just some part of her that wanted to preserve her own space, and now... Well, now she was very glad about it.

She got more ice cream out of the freezer and sat down on the couch, and then she picked up a throw pillow and threw it across the room. Of course her apartment was perfectly organized. Organization was what she did. And for what? She had organized this place. It was done. So she did things for other people, showed them how to do it. But it wasn't personal. And when you became so aware that you could destroy everything by removing the wrong couple of pieces, it all just seemed...hollow.

This view, this top of the world view... It didn't even feel like anything.

She might've been turning her brain to mush with these movies, but small-town life was beginning to look better and better. If you did that with your best friend's man in a small town, then everybody would cross the street to avoid you. They would all know. The town gossip would make sure.

Her eyes were crusty, but she wasn't crying anymore, so there was that.

She'd started over before.

She'd reinvented before.

A burst of something other than sadness popped in her chest.

She picked up her phone and looked at it, and saw that there were about three hundred messages, and nearly threw it across the room.

Then she picked up her tablet, setting it in her lap, adjacent to her ice cream, starting to look at pictures of small towns while the comforting movie played.

The lead heroine on it was pretty, a transplant from the city who had gone to a small town to open up a bakery. The man was handsome and extremely smooth, in a nonthreatening way. He had small-town manners, and was always opening doors and pulling chairs out.

"And not sticking your penis in her friends," she said at the TV, lifting her bowl as if in salute.

That was a good man.

She mindlessly clicked through endless articles. The cutest small towns in the Northeast. The cutest small towns in the Southwest. Ghost towns you've never heard of. Each article led to another interesting related article, and all of it provided fantastic small-town fantasy porn to go along with her chosen movie.

A movie she was beginning to think she had actually seen before.

It didn't matter. That made it even better. Because she had positive feelings about the movie, which meant that everything had likely ended up okay. She was way too fragile to go dealing with anything too dramatic.

And then the article down at the bottom of the cutest small towns in Oregon slideshow stopped her.

Cowboy at Oregon's Largest Family Ranch Seeks Wife

She clicked it.

She was clicking things, anyway.

It was a write-up. On a man who had placed an ad on a dating website.

She started to read out loud to herself. "Sawyer Garrett, thirty-four, of Pyrite Falls, Oregon, is seeking a wife, and mother for his infant daughter."

She skimmed the article, but then clicked to the original post. And it was… She honestly couldn't believe it. It was real.

He didn't have a picture of himself, rather of a giant ranch house set on the side of a rocky hill, overlooking a river below. The scenery took her breath away. Pine trees, and a pristine river. A mountain covered in dark pines at the back of the house. There were a couple of other pictures, all of the land. And then of a baby. A little girl. She was being held in a large, masculine hand, but there were no pictures of the man himself.

Seeking a wife for help raising my little girl. I was raised by a single father, and always felt that there was something missing. I don't want that for my child. I'm seeking someone who's looking for a partner. Someone who understands commitment. And keeping promises. I have a house, and thirteen thousand acres of land. I work the land with my family, a brother and sister, and employ fifty others.

So, he was a businessman. He had to be. The place was clearly in good shape.

And for just a minute, she... She placed herself as the heroine in one of those movies. Walking into a small town as a soft backing track played behind her. Upbeat, easy music.

She laughed. But what kind of woman would respond to something like this. It would have to be somebody who wanted... Who wanted a fresh start.

Still, marrying a stranger was...

You were about to marry a man that you were with for close to ten years. And you didn't really know him.

She blinked, hard. Because suddenly the tears were back. That truth hit, and it hit true. Because she thought that she'd known Hollyn and Kioni, too. Her friends, who she'd been so certain would be on her side if something happened... And they just hadn't been. All these people who were supposed to know her. And she was supposed to know them. They had been lying to her. Tricking her. They had been willing to let her make a huge mistake, with a man who didn't really love her... For what? To preserve the business? To preserve the status quo?

She stood up and looked out the window at the view below.

All the things that she had overlooked to preserve this view. The little checks and problems that she had felt in her soul when she had thought about her future with Andrew. Because she'd really been going over all of those intensely in the last few days. Asking herself what little thing she had overlooked. And what big things. But more, she asked herself what all of them had been willing to compromise for these views. For this life.

She had started over before.

Why couldn't she do it again?

Different. Bigger.

She wasn't a rebellious teenager anymore. She wasn't going to go off and self-destruct. But she also didn't have to only want this. She'd only ever lived in New York state, never anywhere else. What if she…what if she went somewhere new, really new?

What if she changed her view? Not just a different street in the same city, but profoundly.

And she suddenly ached for the view of a river and mountains that she had never seen.

No one was stopping her. No one was holding her here.

Her parents weren't on her side, she knew that. Repairing things with Hollyn and Kioni was…impossible. Going back to her job was impossible.

Getting married to Andrew was impossible.

Her life had crumbled, so why not set it all on fire?

Why not…why not make some ashes to rise from?

"This is insane," she said to herself.

And still, she went to the couch, and looked back at the article. She stared at it until the movie finished. And then with sweaty palms, she clicked on the contact information for Mr. Sawyer Garrett.

Mr. Garrett,
I trust that you're not a serial killer.

She considered hitting the backspace and deleting that. But then she thought, *No.* She wasn't going to actually hit Send on this. So she might as well just type it out.

And anyway, if she *did* send it, she was going to say everything that entered her head. She was going to put it all out there. Because why not? He was a stranger. And she wasn't actually going to take him up on his offer. She was just curious. What kind of man would do this? And what kind of responses would he have?

If you are murderous in any way, I would appreciate you letting me know. I'm not in the market for any more surprises. My wedding just imploded and I'm considering changing absolutely everything. So what exactly do you want? And I don't mean this website write-up. I mean, really what do you want? Like how many times a week do you think you're going to have sex, and what kind of food do you like, and do you expect me to cook?

Yours,
Evelyn Moore

It was absurd. She stared at the email until the words didn't make sense. And then her fingers just felt sweaty, and suddenly it seemed like hitting Send wasn't totally unreasonable.

All she had to do was push the button.

And then she did.

And it was gone. Just vanished into the ether. Into his inbox.

She stood up and started pacing.

What she didn't expect was a response, at least not so quickly. But she realized that it was three hours earlier in Oregon, and it didn't take long for the pinging of her email to draw her back to the tablet.

I'm looking for exactly what I said. A woman who will stay with me. A woman who won't abandon my daughter. My mother left me, and my siblings' mothers left them. I don't

want the same thing for her. The amount of sex is nego-
tiable. Cooking isn't. I work a long day on the ranch, and
if I'm going to have a wife, I would like meals. I'll eat pretty
much anything.

She cleared her throat and sent off her next message. But
you would expect sex?

His response was instant. If I can't get it from you, I'd
have to get it somewhere else. So it depends on how you'd
feel about me sleeping with other women.

That made her think of Andrew. No. I don't think I would
like that.

Maybe that was a dumb response given she'd never even
seen the man.

His response was quick.

I'll tell you what. Whatever we decide, we just make sure
we're honest about it. I don't have any fear of letting you
down. You don't seem to be afraid of letting me down.
Also not a serial killer. Not even a one-time killer.

Good to know. I could have killed my fiancé when I caught
him having sex with my best friend. But managed not to.
So, I don't think I'm a latent murderer, either.

His next question was a potential problem. Any experience with babies?

She hesitated. No, I don't have any experience with babies. But I like them.

An understatement.

She wanted a baby so badly.

She had been very much looking forward to being a
mother. But she wanted to be married first. And it had taken

Andrew so long to… And she was thirty-four. And it was really time. There was no way she would have the big family she wanted if she didn't get started this year. And that was why they'd been getting married finally. It was why…

And Sawyer Garrett had a baby. And she was beautiful.

How exactly did you end up with a baby?

She sent off the message.

His response was as fast as the others. The usual way. Casual bar hookup. She didn't want her.

And *he* did.

That stuck with her.

It said something about him, a lot actually. He wasn't perfect, obviously. He'd gotten a bar hookup pregnant, after all.

She took a shower and thought about the email exchange the whole time, her body and brain buzzing.

Because for the first time in days she didn't feel like all her dreams were dead.

For the first time she felt like she could see the way forward.

She looked at the picture of the baby again.

And something in her shifted, and was just…bright and clear and certain.

She wanted to hold that child.

She wanted to be her mother.

She shut her phone screen off. The feeling was so real, so deep…it terrified her.

Evelyn put her pajamas on and curled up in bed, her mind a mix of what-ifs and hazy images of a potential future.

And when she got up in the morning she had another

message from him, sent the night before. Along with his phone number.

She waited for what she thought might be an appropriate quitting time for a rancher, in his time zone, and then called him.

"Hello?"

His voice sent goose bumps over her arms. She hadn't expected that. It was deep and rich. He didn't have a drawl. But she hadn't really known what she'd expected. A drawl, she guessed, because that article had called him a cowboy. But she didn't really know that they drawled out in Oregon.

"Hi," she said, breathless. Unbearably conscious of the sound of her own accent, which was different than his. "I'm Evelyn. We emailed last night."

"So you are," he said. "You're not the first woman to respond to the ad, but you are the first one to ask if I was a serial killer. I liked that. You can't be too careful."

She laughed. "No. I don't suppose *you* can be, either."

"No."

"So... What exactly... What if I... What if I said yes?"

"I guess I would have to also say yes," he said.

It was so crazy. So crazy to consider this. He was a stranger. She had traveled to California for different organizing projects and events, but she'd never been to Oregon. She hadn't even spent significant time on the West Coast as a whole. But right now, she wanted to hit eject on everything. Her apartment felt claustrophobic. The city felt too loud. And she was starting to hate the view.

And the picture of that sweet baby loomed large in her mind.

"I don't know anything about ranches. But I'm a good cook. I'm a professional organizer, and I can keep your house in impeccable order, I promise you that."

"Do you make meat loaf?"

"No," she said. "Why would I do that?"

"Because it's good."

"It is not."

"It's damn good," he said. "And I'm a cattle rancher."

"So, you come with a very healthy supply of steak."

"And meat loaf."

"*I* don't like meat loaf."

"I think you should cook it for me, anyway."

And there was something about the way he said it that set a strange fire off in her midsection. And she realized she'd never even seen a picture of him. And for some reason... She didn't even care.

"I want someone who's serious," he said. "My life has been full of abandonment. Do you understand? You can't come kick the tires, and get my daughter attached to you, and then... And then go. I can't have that."

And there was something about that statement that got the fire stoked even higher. The protectiveness of his daughter was... Well, it was an attractive trait.

And there was a freedom here, too, in this interaction. He was setting the tone, and it was honest. She had the feeling he was completely okay with walking away from this. That he wasn't trying to soften any edges or contort himself to get her to agree to saying yes.

It made her want to return that same honesty, especially when the life she was living now was under a cloud of lies.

"I understand that," she said. "Serious question—what if we hate each other?"

"Surely we can deal with that for eighteen years."

"Eighteen years," she said, laughing. "I'm serious."

"In my experience, only strong feelings can turn to hate.

You seem like a nice woman, but I don't have any strong feelings for you."

She thought back to that sweet movie that she had watched last night. Good feelings. And sweet, easy connections. Not all that complicated… Stuff that she had in her life here.

"Okay. That's a good point. But for argument's sake…"

"There are other houses on the property. And hell, my house is huge. There would be room. It's just… I think it can work."

Could they? Could they make it work? Was wanting a home and a family and to hold that sweet baby enough of a reason to…uproot everything?

It's uprooted already. The question is where you're going to plant yourself now.

And she had that same feeling she'd had right before she'd hit Send on the email. That reckless feeling of being on the edge of a cliff.

The easiest thing to do would simply be to fling herself out into that blank, endless space. And fall.

So, she did.

"When do you want me to fly out?"

"Tomorrow. And then you have a few days to decide."

She shouldn't have clicked that link last night. Because she was sitting there in rubble. Everything that she knew was rubble. And that made this seem…almost reasonable. Because she could see a path to that life. To a small town and a beautiful ranch, and a man she'd never met, and it seemed so much better than trying to rebuild the Jenga tower.

"I'll be out on the earliest flight."

"You probably only have one flight option, and one of us will have to come get you."

He didn't commit to it being him, she noticed. "Well, all right, then." She could not believe she was doing this. It was potentially…dangerous. And very impulsive.

Still easier than the idea of ever going back to her office, ever seeing her friends again. Contacting every person on the invite list to her wedding, look Andrew in the eye after seeing him *inside* her friend and…well, the move to Oregon sounded less and less dangerous. "Just one more question. What's the weather like there? I need to know what to pack."

"Pack like you're planning to stay."

CHAPTER THREE

"I CAN'T BELIEVE IT." Hunter McCloud practically howled out a laugh on the back of his horse, and if he hadn't been such an accomplished rider, he might have unseated himself. Sawyer couldn't deny that he might've enjoyed that. "You actually got a woman to respond to you."

"I have had *several* women respond to me," he said, adjusting the front pack with the baby in it as he resituated himself in the saddle.

"Women who weren't all there," Wolf said, tapping the side of his temple.

"And they might have *responded*," Elsie added, "but they didn't...say they were going to get on a plane. They didn't talk to you on the phone, either."

He thought back to his phone conversation with Evelyn Moore last night. Her voice was... Well, damn if it wasn't sexy. But he hadn't asked her for a picture.

Didn't seem polite.

He didn't know too much about online dating and the like, but everything he'd heard was that it involved men sending pictures of their junk to women who hadn't asked. So, he wanted to stay away from any kind of picture sharing and strange expectations that might come with it.

He hadn't asked.

But he'd liked her voice. And her opinions about meat loaf, no matter how wrong they were.

"Well, she did," he said.

"She's flying out this evening," Elsie dropped that bit of knowledge as if it might have escaped him somehow.

"Yep."

"And you're gonna marry her," Hunter said. "You are *actually* going to marry a stranger."

"Not right away," he said. "There's no rush. And anyway, we are going to have to nail down legal things."

"Right. You got a lawyer?"

"Well, no, but I figured I'd talk to Tom Pryor down at Becky's." Becky's was a small café, not named for a woman as many people often imagined, but an old miner whose full name had been Beckham who had come to seek his fortune and had instead ended up slinging hash back in the 1800s—and had probably made more than most of the actual prospectors. "He went to law school."

"Yeah, and he must've been real successful, since he ended up here." That derisive statement came from Hunter.

Elsie rode her horse around the back of his and to the other side. "Hey," she said. "We all did. What does that say about any of us?"

"I didn't set out to be a lawyer," Hunter said. "I set out to be a cowboy."

Elsie made a scoffing sound. "Pretty lousy cowboy, McCloud."

"Well, gee," he said. "If I cared one lick about your terrible opinions, Garrett, it might hurt my feelings."

"You'd have to *have* feelings. And everyone knows you don't."

"Knock it off," Wolf said. "I don't want to listen to the two of you snipe. Don't you have your own livestock to fuss with, Hunter?"

"I do," Hunter said. "But I'm borrowing Elsie tomorrow,

because she's interested in checking out the horses. Which means I'm lending a hand today."

Wolf cast Sawyer a sidelong glance. "And I wasn't consulted."

"Hey," Elsie said, "neither was I."

"I'm doing you a favor, half-pint," Hunter said. "You better be nice to me."

"I'm about half a pint of whoopass," Elsie muttered, riding down along the fence line up ahead of them all.

"Do you have to do that?" Sawyer asked, directing that at Hunter.

"I don't have a little sister," Hunter said. "I have to have my fun when I get the chance."

"Great," Wolf said.

"All this has been *fun*," Hunter said, "but are you seriously going to marry some random woman from the city?"

"I don't know," Sawyer said.

"You're acting like you aren't completely set on this," Wolf said. "And we all know that's not true. You never once set your mind to something and not gotten it, Sawyer. Hell, not getting Missy to marry you was probably the only thing you've ever been denied."

"You don't know what all I've been denied in my life, Wolf."

"Fine," Wolf said. "Let's pretend that's true. Let's pretend we haven't all been right in each other's pockets forever. By my observations, if it's in your control, you tend to get it. When you put an ad out for a wife, don't even pretend that it wasn't your absolute intention of finding one. And hell, just a few days later you've got a woman coming out here on a plane. That's you, Sawyer. Down to the ground."

"I wouldn't put out an ad if I didn't intend to have it answered," Sawyer said. "I might not know everything but I know my own mind."

"That's my point," Wolf said. "So why are you even bothering to act like you don't think it's full speed ahead."

He shrugged. "I haven't met her. But yeah. She shows up, and she's all right to look at, and the baby doesn't cry when she holds her..."

Wolf raised a dark brow.

"You're going to have a stranger look after the baby?"

That question came from Hunter, and it was one that actually got its hooks right into him. "No," he said, putting his hand on the back of her head. "I'm not going to leave her with her right away. No. I'm going to have to... Find some ways of verifying who she is and all of that."

"Good idea," Wolf said. "Because honestly, if she's willing to move across the country and shack up with you sight unseen..."

"I posted a picture of the house."

"Smart," Hunter said. "Definitely more attractive than *you* are."

"I do all right," Sawyer said, frowning.

He wasn't vain, but hell. He knew women liked him.

"Yeah, the baby is proof of that," Wolf said dryly. "I'm just saying, I know you well enough to know your hard-headed ass does exactly what it makes its mind up to do. So it's my job to say...maybe this isn't a great idea."

"And as your best friend," Hunter said, "it's my job to second that. We'll question you, since we know *you* won't question you."

"Thanks," Sawyer said. "But I'm not an idiot."

"You had unprotected sex with Missy Coulter, so I'm not exactly sure—"

"I did *not* have unprotected sex," Sawyer said, because

as much as he hated to talk about his sex life he hated bad faith assumptions more. "The condom must've broken."

"Hell," Hunter said, having the decency to recoil. "That's like something out of my nightmares. I prefer to believe that can't happen."

"Well it *can*," Sawyer said. "So, before you go throwing stones, just think about how easily it could happen to either one of you. It's not like you're discriminating."

"Not at all," Hunter said.

"You could just as easily be in this position," Sawyer said.

Wolf laughed. "Except I wouldn't be getting married."

"Then I did something wrong helping raise you," Sawyer said. "Because it's *responsible*."

"You know you can't keep calling the baby *Bug*," Wolf said.

"Says the guy named after a pack animal."

"I have no control over my mother," Wolf said. "Nor do I have a relationship with her. And Dad didn't have any control over her. So, my name isn't really my fault. Besides, at least a Wolf is intimidating. She's a little girl. You can't call her Bug."

His heart squeezed tight.

He'd put June Bug on the birth certificate. He'd figured he'd change it eventually. But it was what worked for now.

"I can call her whatever I want. Anyway, since I'm going to get her a mother, maybe her mother should have a say in the name."

"Leave it to you, Sawyer," Hunter said, "to just think you can buy a wife like something you choose in a grocery store aisle."

"I don't see why not. It's how things used to work. You

got married because you had things in common. Common goals. It just stands to reason."

"If it were that simple, it's what everybody would do."

"No," he said, "it's not. Because people like to needlessly complicate their lives. As a matter of course."

"But not you," Hunter said, clearly filled with sarcasm that Sawyer was going to choose to ignore.

"No," Wolf agreed, not being less of an ass.

"You like to keep things simple," Hunter belabored. "You're a logical man."

"Just the most logical," Wolf said.

"Screw both of you. I have work to do. I do not have time to sit around talking like a bunch of hens." Because later, he was going to meet his wife.

On that Wolf was right. He was settled. He'd made up his mind.

And once Sawyer Garrett made up his mind, there was no going back.

IT HAD BEEN a long haul. She hadn't realized that she was going to have to get a connecting flight. But there hadn't been any direct flights from JFK to a town close enough, so she found herself cooling her heels in Portland before getting on a very small plane that connected to a smaller, regional airport that was about a half hour from Pyrite Falls. It was a small plane. A very small plane.

She could not stress that enough.

So small.

She had not cared for it at all. But she'd made it, with the suitcase and… She was shocked by the size of the air-port. There was one baggage carousel, and it didn't take long for her to fish her bag off it and get out the doors of the airport. Where she knew she was being picked up by…

Well, by someone. He had been pretty noncommittal about it. He had just said that someone would be there to get her.

Would it be *him*?

Thinking about him made her feel…things. But it was just such a relief to feel something other than despair.

She had decided to have Kioni and Hollyn buy her out. Which hurt.

As much as Andrew's betrayal, if she were honest. And if it wasn't for…

She couldn't *trust* them. Not anymore. Not either of them. How could she go into work knowing they'd lied?

In the same way that thinking of Andrew as the love of her life no longer felt right or real, thinking of Hollyn and Kioni as her best friends didn't, either. How could it?

They must never have been close, not really. How did you keep these things from your best friend?

Whatever Kioni's excuses for it, she'd known that Andrew and Hollyn were cheating and hadn't said anything. And maybe it was a bad position to be in because…she supposed Kioni didn't hate Hollyn and there was probably a dramatic story about why and how they were in love and whatever else but…

Well, Evelyn didn't care.

It wasn't love.

Not between Andrew and Hollyn, not between her and Andrew, or her and her friends. How could it be when there were so many lies?

And that was what she comforted herself with as she waited.

She had no reason to lie to Sawyer Garrett about anything. And he had no reason to lie to her.

She watched every face that pulled up to the curb. There

was an older man, way too old for her, and it made her stomach freeze over. But he didn't appear to be looking for her.

It was ridiculous. She had said that she would be the blonde woman with the flowered suitcase.

And then she heard rather than saw a truck, and peered around the line of cars, only to see a big, dark blue beast headed her direction. And she just knew. That that was her ride.

But there wasn't a man at the wheel.

No.

Instead, it was a small woman, with a cowgirl hat and a long braid.

This had better not be a sister-wives situation...

Although. It might be nice to have extra help...

The woman pulled up to the curb, leaned across the cab and opened the door, interrupting Evelyn's thoughts with the rusty creak of the door.

And Evelyn could see that...the woman was barefoot.

"Are you Evelyn Moore?" she asked.

"Yes," Evelyn said.

"I'm Elsie. Elsie Garrett. My brother said that maybe I should come get you because you were less likely to think that I was a serial killer."

"Oh," Evelyn said. *"Oh."*

Well, that was better than sister-wives.

He had mentioned a sister.

The one time they had talked. Before she had committed to come out here and give serious consideration to marrying him. It only just occurred to her as she stood there on the curb to look out beyond the airport. To look at her surroundings. There were mountains all around. She had seen how green it was when the plane had landed, but it had seemed so distant and…almost surreal. But now… She was here. Her feet were touching the ground.

"Do you need help with your bags?"

"No," she said. "Should I put them in the back?"

"That works," Elsie said.

Evelyn tossed her two suitcases in the back, keeping her carry-on with her as she hefted herself up into the truck and closed the door. She had never ridden in a truck before.

And before she could fasten her seat belt, her chauffeur had taken off from the curb. "How was your flight?"

"Oh," she said. "It was… It was good."

"That's good. You came from New York City?"

"Yes," Evelyn said."

"I've never been there," Elsie said.

"Well, I've never been to Oregon before," Evelyn replied.

"Can you really just put your arm out and get a car to anywhere you want to go?"

"Yes," Evelyn said. "Though you can also use an app."

"Interesting," Elsie said. "So, why did you want to move here?"

Apparently being forthright was a family trait. She opened her mouth to say why and then it just sort of got crowded in her throat.

It felt exposing to even think of the whole thing, and not talking about it was part of why she'd left. Being honest with Sawyer on the phone had been one thing.

"I…" She cleared her throat. "Well, I was supposed to get married. Next weekend actually. And… That isn't going to happen. So…"

"You decided to marry my brother instead?"

Good Lord the girl was relentless. "I decided to investigate other options. Including getting a completely new life."

Elsie made a considering sound. "I've never thought about getting an entirely new life."

"Well. Sometimes it...sometimes it seems easier than fixing the old one."

"How come you broke up with your fiancé?"

Well, she was stuck in a truck with Elsie, so her options were ignoring the question, telling her she didn't want to talk about it or...just telling her.

She felt wary of people. But she'd chosen to go to this new place and maybe it was...time to establish new precedents.

Why hold things back?

"He was having sex with my best friend." Her words felt too stark and too honest beneath the rumbling of the truck engine and Evelyn wondered if she should have softened them slightly.

But why?

She'd seen it.

There was nothing soft about that.

Elsie let out a long, low whistle. "Wow. Yeah, that would do it."

"Yes," she said. "It did. So... Your brother..."

"He's a pain in the ass," Elsie said, then smiled. "No, he's good."

"And...the baby?"

"She's the cutest thing I've ever seen," Elsie said, suddenly softening a little bit. "I don't know anything about babies. And never been that interested in them. But I didn't really have a mother and... Well... None of us did. And I think that Sawyer just wants to make sure that she... That she has better than we did."

Evelyn blinked. She had both her parents. And in the end, they hadn't supported her. She had to admire that...

That he was going to great lengths to give his daughter the kind of support that he felt like he hadn't had.

Suddenly, her hands felt clammy. Because she realized she wasn't just about to meet a man she might marry, but she was about to meet what could very well be her child.

She wanted a baby. She wanted a house and a husband. She blinked, her eyes suddenly filling with tears. Thankfully, Elsie was paying attention to the road and didn't notice.

"You're not just a loose woman from the city that's going to hurt him, are you?"

She whipped her head toward her driver. *"A loose woman from the city?"*

"Well, you hear things," Elsie said, shrugging a shoulder. "I want to make sure that my brother isn't getting himself into a bad situation. He's had enough things go wrong. He proposed to Missy, but she wouldn't have it."

"Who's Missy?" Evelyn asked, feeling absurdly jealous over a woman she had never met, over a man she had also never met.

"The baby's mother."

"You keep calling her the baby. What's her name?"

"Well, he put June Bug on the birth certificate. Because he had to put something. I don't think I was supposed to tell anyone that. Mostly he just calls her Bug."

She didn't really know what to say to that. She looked out the window and there was just… There was a whole lot of nothing. It was beautiful. It was so green. They passed through multiple small towns, including Wonder and Elkton, both of which she thought were amusing names. She had driven through small towns on the East Coast, of course, but there was something different about this. Everything seemed a little bit wider here, spread farther apart. The roads, the buildings.

The highway followed a river all deep, wide and green, punctuated by shallower spots with rocks and white water. There were smooth round pebbles at the shore and more pine trees scaling up the side of a steep mountain. It was the mountains that took her breath away. They seemed to loom in front and behind, on all sides.

A patchwork of purple and blue glory that extended past where she could see a sign, a diamond, with a large black silhouette that didn't quite look like the deer crossing signs she had seen while driving around the country back east.

"What's that?"

"Elk crossing," she commented.

"I've seen moose crossing before. But never elk."

"Moose? Where did you see moose?" Elsie asked, clearly interested. "We don't have them this far south."

"Oh," she said. "When I've gone up to Maine or Vermont in the summer."

It had been a long time since she done that. It had been a long time since she'd gotten into a car and gone on a road trip, which was something she had once enjoyed very much.

"With your friends?"

"Yeah," Evelyn said, thinking of Hollyn and Kioni now.

"Not very good friends," Elsie huffed.

"No," she agreed.

"Were they the same ones? I mean, the same friend that… Was with your dude?"

Evelyn laughed. "My dude?"

"Yeah. You know. Well, anyway, was it?"

"Yes. She was my best friend from the time we were freshmen in college. And our other best friend knew about it. So, I guess you could say… That I lost everything."

Elsie shook her head. "I can't imagine a man coming between me and my best friend. A horse, maybe."

"A horse," she said.

"Yes. That's my first true love. Horses. We have a cattle ranch, but part of the larger operation includes horses. I'm learning more about them, more about how to breed and train them. From the McClouds."

"Who are the McClouds?"

"Oh, they're one of the families with a spread on Four Corners. Did Sawyer explain that to you?"

She thought back to the conversation she had with Sawyer. They'd... Talked about getting married. And food. And sex. Precious little else.

"Uh. No. He didn't."

"Well, combined it would be the biggest ranch in the state. But technically, there are four separate pieces. But we call it Four Corners Ranch. Ours is Garrett's Watch. Then you've got Sullivan's Point, McCloud's Landing and King's Crest. It's been in our families for generations. And everyone who wants to stay and work the land stays and works the land. I'm planning on staying."

"Are you?" She couldn't get a read on Elsie's age. Probably in her early twenties. But she could've easily been younger. Or older. She had that indefinable fresh-faced look about her, and a ready sort of energy that spoke of a life spent with no real disappointments. "Have you ever left?"

"No," she said. "I don't need to. Sawyer and Wolf... They're the best brothers that anyone could ask for. Now that it's just them everything is great."

"Who was it before?"

"Our dad. He was... I dunno. I guess you shouldn't speak ill of the dead. But it's not a real surprise he died early. He drank himself right into the grave." She was so matter-of-fact about it. As far as Evelyn could tell, the other woman didn't have a single feeling about it. Though she wondered to an extent if it was a ruse. Because she thought only a moment before that she seemed the sort of girl who hadn't been through anything. But now she wondered if she was just the sort of girl who put on a coat of Teflon when need be so that whatever she needed to could slide right off and she could keep moving forward.

Was that what Evelyn was doing?

Trying to make all this pain slide right off and continue on with her life plan?

No. She hadn't stayed in Manhattan.

But you wanted a house. You wanted a baby.

She had been willing to twist and bend and ignore a lot of unhappiness to have those things. How was this…how could this be worse?

"I'm sorry," Evelyn said. "About your dad."

"That he was an asshole or that he's dead?"

"Both," she said genuinely.

She looked out the window.

"Sawyer is not an asshole," Elsie said. "I mean, he can be one. He's my older brother. Believe me, he gets under my skin sometimes. But… He's not a bad guy. He doesn't drink too much. He's really good to animals."

"Well, I'm glad to hear that."

"He's a good dad to Bug. I mean, he does the best he can. He's not… He's not an emotional guy. But he… He gets things done. That's the thing about Sawyer. He had to keep the ranch going. My dad… Well, he just kind of gave up when my mom left. At least, so to hear tell of it. I don't really remember. Sawyer was eleven. He took care of me, he took care of the ranch… He's the best."

"It sounds like he is," she said.

She suddenly felt restless. Edgy. And then she saw a big, rickety wooden sign with faded blue letters carved into it. Welcome to Pyrite Falls. There was a crudely carved gold miner on the side, waving what looked like a pickax.

And the town was… Not a whole lot of anything. Wooden buildings surrounded by trees. A big general store with the gravel lot in front of it. A building with a sign that said Smokey's Tavern, and a tiny little diner that might as well have been set up in a shack. And yet, every single building seemed to have a sign proclaiming the presence of ice cold beer. There were cabins to rent, which mystified her.

"Fishing," Elsie said. "And hunting. Also, there's a lot of lakes. And the coast is just about an hour west. So, it's a place people like to come and stay. Little bit less expensive than beachside accommodation. Not far from the dunes if you like to four-wheel."

"I see," Evelyn said. "I just thought… You know, I thought there would be a town."

"It is a town," Elsie said.

"There's not even… Is there a school?"

"There's a schoolhouse at Four Corners. Most of the kids go there. You can bus to Elkton, or Florence. But it'd take so much time that collectively the families around here decided it wasn't worth it. Either the kids homeschool or pay what they can to support a teacher on the ranch."

"All the kids are… The kids of the ranch families?"

"And employees. Four Corners is the biggest employer out here. Other than the forest service. Still, Four Corners might win. Each spread is thirteen thousand acres. It's a massive job. Mostly its cattle and horses, but there's hay also. Hazelnuts, a few other crops. Spread out over the different pieces of land. There's a lot to do."

"Sounds like it."

"Sawyer's been so good with Garrett's Watch. He's expanded things a lot, and he's worked with all the other families and—" She clapped and Evelyn jumped slightly. "It's been hugely successful. Huge. It's been really successful. The house is really fancy."

Evelyn could only wonder what fancy was to the woman who had come to pick her up, driving barefoot.

"That's great."

"I think… I think you'll like it." Elsie sighed. "Of course, we don't have a great track record."

"What do you mean?"

"Oh, that's the thing. No woman ever stays at Garrett's Watch. Except my grandmother."

"Oh."

"I mean, all the wives leave. My grandmother was a mail-order bride, though. After my…my blood-related grandma left my grandpa ordered a new wife. Kind of like you."

Elsie kept talking after that, but Evelyn didn't pay much attention. She just let that sit. And marinate.

A mail-order bride. Was that what she was?

She had answered an ad. They had spoken on the phone. But essentially… She had gone out to the prairie. Well, she supposed this wasn't a prairie per se. She wasn't an expert on such things. But the mountains. The wilderness. The Wild West. And she was here to consider marriage. To a stranger.

"Here we are," Elsie said.

They turned down a gravel road with a large sign up over the top. There was a huge rack of elk antlers in the middle, and the words Four Corners Ranch across it.

To the left side were mountains, just in the short distance, while on the right was a broader expanse of field. The gravel road stretched on for what seemed like miles. There was a sign that said King's Crest, and then farther down there was another sign. Garrett's Watch.

They took a left turn, toward those big mountains, and the road went through a thick grove of trees. And then started to climb the mountain.

A feeling of dread started to climb Evelyn's throat as the road narrowed, and the side tapered off into a rather steep drop.

"No worries," Elsie said, waving her hand. "I learned how to drive on this road."

"Did Sawyer teach you?"

"Yeah, though Wolf definitely had a hand in it. Much to Sawyer's chagrin. Hunter helped, too."

"Who's Hunter?"

"Hunter McCloud. He's Sawyer's best friend. He's a pain in the ass. I dunno. Like having another brother."

"That's nice."

She was beginning to get a pretty set picture of Elsie's life, and why she was the way she was. She wondered if the girl had any female influences. Didn't remember her mother. Had been raised by men with names like *Wolf.*

"Why do the women leave?" she asked.

"I don't know," Elsie said. "I've certainly never wanted to."

Just then, the view in front of them opened up. And she saw a big log house. The driveway in front of it was flat, and it looked to be a single story, but she had seen the photograph of it online, and she knew what the front looked like. That it was built into the side of that rock face, looking out over the river. The pine trees surrounding the place were massive, like guardians for the household. The roof was shiny green metal, the house itself just stained wood.

"This is beautiful," she said.

And she meant it. It was beautiful because it was, of course. But it was also beautiful because it was so unlike the chrome and glass that she had left behind, and Elsie was so very different than anyone she had ever met in her life. She had successfully uprooted herself. And it was only now just beginning to sink in.

She had done something that people talk about. She had changed her life. And she would never have chosen it. Not if things hadn't been blown all to hell. But she…

She suddenly had a vision of her favorite cupcake ATM. One that she could walk to fairly easily from her apartment.

You have left the land of cupcake ATMs.

You've got bait and tackle and ice cold beer.

And it was the strangest thing in all the world, because the strange bubble of joy that she felt over having escaped was still there. It was just that… The reality of the situation was also suddenly right there. Butting up against that joy. She had run away to the middle of nowhere to meet up with a stranger who she might marry.

And there were no cupcake ATMs.

There wasn't a Nordstrom.

In fact, she hadn't seen a single place to buy shoes. And if the general store did in fact sell shoes, she was almost certain she didn't want them.

But the truck had stopped, and that meant it was time to get out.

She got out, and her shoes crunched on the gravel. She felt suddenly very tiny. Because the mountains loomed large behind her, and the house loomed large in front of her. And she was just Evelyn. Who had never been anywhere like this in her life, and who was… Not among friends. It had been easy to chatter with Elsie on the drive over, but she didn't know her.

Had she ever…had friends? She'd thought she had. To the degree where she'd started a business with those friends. Had included them in so many aspects of her life.

And kept a lot of things from them, too. Never shared about dancing and what leaving it meant. Never talked to them about her parents…

Yeah, well. Her not sharing every detail about her life was not equivalent to their brand of betrayal.

She swallowed hard. But for some reason, she wasn't scared. She was just nervous. Maybe she had no real basis for it, but she trusted Sawyer. She just did. Sight unseen.

The front door opened, and a man came out. He had on a black cowboy hat, and he was holding a baby. Those were the first two details she took in, but then there was… Well, there was the whole rest of him.

She could feel his eyes on her from some fifty feet away, could see the piercing blue color. His nose was straight and strong, as was his jaw. His lips remarkable, and she didn't think she had ever really found lips on a man all that re-markable. He had the sort of symmetrical good looks that might make a man almost too pretty, but he was saved from that by a scar that edged through the corner of his mouth, creating a thick white line that disrupted the symmetry there. He was tall. Well over six feet, and broad.

And his arms were…

Good Lord.

He was wearing a short-sleeved black T-shirt, where he cradled that tiny baby in the crook of his massive biceps and forearm. He could easily lift bales of hay and throw them around. Hell, he could probably easily lift the truck and throw it around.

He was beautiful. Objectively, absolutely beautiful.

But there was something more than that. Because as he walked toward her, she felt like he was stealing increments of her breath, emptying her lungs. She'd seen handsome men before. She'd been around celebrities who were touted as the sexiest men on the planet.

But she had never *felt* anything quite like this.

Because this wasn't just about how he looked on the outside, though it was sheer masculine perfection; it was about what he did to her insides. Like he had taken the blood in her veins and replaced it with fire. And she could say with absolute honesty she had never once in all of her days wanted to grab a stranger and fling herself at him, and push them both into the nearest closet, bedroom, whatever, and…

Well. Everything.

But she felt it, right then and there with him.

And there was something about the banked heat in his blue eyes that made her think he might feel exactly the same way.

And suddenly she was terrified of all the freedom. Giddy with it, which went right along with that joy/terror paradox from before.

She didn't know anyone here. She had come without anyone's permission or approval. She was just here. With this man. And there was nothing to stop them from… Anything.

Except he was holding a baby and his sister was standing right to her left. But otherwise.

She really *hoped* that he was Sawyer. Because if he was Wolf it was going to be awkward.

"Evelyn," he said. And goose bumps broke out over her arms. And she knew. Because he was the same man who had told her that she would be making him meat loaf whether she liked it or not.

And suddenly the reason it had felt distinctly sexual this time became clear.

"Yes," she said.

"Sawyer," he said. "Sawyer Garrett." And then he absurdly took a step forward and held his hand out. To shake it. And she was going to have to…touch him. Touch him and not melt into a puddle at his feet.

But she did. She stuck her hand out, and their skin met.

It was like an electrical current had charged her entire body.

Maybe this was the side effect of having slept with only one man in the past decade. And the knowledge that she was now free to do whatever she wanted, with whoever she wanted. She hadn't really been thinking in those terms.

Yes, they had brought sex up in the phone call, but she hadn't really gotten to the part where she could sleep with someone who wasn't Andrew.

Not that he cared that they were engaged. He'd been sleeping with someone who wasn't her for an undisclosed amount of time.

But Evelyn had been faithful. Evelyn had forsaken all others. Evelyn had waited for marriage until he was ready. Had put off her dreams of having children. All of that. For him.

Or maybe not. Maybe it had been for the life she'd fantasized about.

But either way, she hadn't been with another man in a long time.

So maybe her attraction, this insane intense attraction to Sawyer, was about that. Maybe it was kind of a rebellion. A revenge thing.

It didn't matter to her, though. Either way. It was just… She was drunk with the full realization of it, and it felt good.

His hands were so rough.

It shocked her.

Even more so, the fact that she wanted those hands on her body. Suddenly. Viscerally.

The corner of his lips tipped upward, an approximation of a smile.

Elsie had said that he wasn't emotional. She had a feeling she was seeing that in action right now.

But he wasn't cold.

She could never think that. Not when she could feel the heat.

"How was your trip?"

"It was fine," she said, lowering her hand and resisting the urge to rub it on her pants. "Fine. I mean… I didn't really expect the little plane."

He shrugged. "Only been on one once."

"You've only been on a plane once."

"Twice if you count the return trip," he said. And then he turned and started to walk toward the house. Elsie followed after him and Evelyn had to wonder if that was what he was used to. People just taking a cue off him. And him not having to offer any kind of explanation or invitation. She blinked, and then moved after him.

"I've got suitcases in the car."

"I'll get them," he said.

"Do you mind?"

And that was how she found herself holding June Bug for the first time. And her heart was lost. Sawyer might've made her want to strip all her clothes off and hop into bed, but this baby tapped into a sudden, immediate fierceness inside of her.

She was small and red with very dark hair and eyes. Very unlike Evelyn's own blond locks. But she was perfect. Absolutely perfect.

And right in that moment she realized… The whole truth of this situation. This little girl's mother had left her. She'd given birth to her, handed her to Sawyer and walked away.

And Evelyn didn't feel anger about it. She didn't feel judgment. She just felt… The immensity of the void that would be left behind by something like that. And the deep desire to fill it, along with the uncertainty that she might not be able to.

There was an enormity to this that she just hadn't realized, standing in her Manhattan apartment partly playing that she wasn't really doing what she was doing. That she wasn't really prepared to fly across the country and start an entirely new life. But she had done it. She had gone across the country and started a new life. And now she was standing there holding this child.

And surely it could not be *this* easy.

No. What she felt when he shook her hand was nothing like that movie she had watched. Because there was nothing half so sexy in those movies as what she wanted to do with him.

No, the colors were very smooth and desaturated in films like that. This felt very bright. Not simply a world of primary colors and simplicity. But something with a whole lot of complication. Colors in so many different shades that she couldn't name them all.

He returned a moment later with her bags.

And she felt buffeted from all sides by all the new things she was trying to take on board.

She heard the phrase *fish out of water*, but that implied a lack of something. A lack of the very thing you needed to breathe.

She didn't lack for anything right in this moment. She felt inundated. Barraged.

"She didn't cry," Sawyer said. "She doesn't particularly like anyone else but me usually."

Elsie crossed her arms and shrunk back. "She likes me well enough. It's just I don't really know what to do with her."

"When they're this tiny I don't think you have to do very much with them," she said, proud of herself as she shifted to holding her slightly differently. Feeling the transition easily. And she suddenly realized this was all a very big mistake.

Because what if she and Sawyer really didn't like each other? She already loved this child.

Staying a week? It would devastate her to leave.

She looked up at him. "She's beautiful."

And she couldn't keep the slight tremble out of her voice.

She could be this baby's mother.

And she suddenly wanted to weep, but she had an audience. And she didn't suppose that would go over hugely well with the man trying to evaluate her potential for being a wife and mother.

"Thanks," he said. And that was it. "Listen, I have to go finish up the day's chores. Not much. Just have to make sure everything is buttoned up. Wolf is bringing pizza from down in Elkton. So, we'll have some of that in a couple of hours."

She suddenly felt very tired, and very conscious of the fact that she was three hours ahead.

"That sounds good."

"Elsie is going to stay with you, show you the lay of

things. And… It might be a good chance for you to get to know… Free to get to know Bug."

And then he left. He just left. And she felt… She didn't even know what to feel.

"That's my brother," Elsie said.

"Right."

"She's cute, though, isn't she?"

Yeah, and her father was a stone cold fox, but she wasn't going to say that.

"Yes. She's… She's really beautiful."

And suddenly it all felt inadequate. The house was lovely, too, and she felt like she had deliberately taken no notice of anything in it because it was just all too much.

"You want a drink or anything? We got soda and beer."

"I'll have a soda. Thank you."

Elsie disappeared into the next room, and Evelyn turned and looked all around her, at the living room she was currently standing in. The windows across from her looked out over the water, and the couch faced that way. There wasn't a TV. She took a step toward where Elsie had just disappeared to, and saw that it was a kitchen. A big, expansive kitchen that was much more modern than she would have ever imagined a building like this could contain.

Everything in it was glossy granite, dark cabinets and chrome.

"Yeah, he paid someone to do the kitchen, the whole house, really, a few years ago. He said it wasn't really to his taste but everything in it is so nice that he doesn't care."

"I think it's beautiful."

Masculine, but beautiful. Sort of like the man himself.

She cradled the baby close, then walked over to a table that was in a windowed alcove, looking out over the water. She could see a dock down below, a rope swing.

"Is there a path that leads to the river?"

"Yeah," Elsie said. "And don't worry, Sawyer said that he's going to put a big fence up, so that Bug can't go toddling off the edge. This house wasn't exactly built with kids in mind. Of course, it was built initially when our dad had kids. It's just he never did anything with kids in mind."

Again, something else she said with levity, but that Evelyn couldn't imagine she actually found funny.

"Is there... A bathroom?"

"Oh, right," Elsie said, moving to collect the baby from her arms.

"Thank you."

"Down the hall," she said. "And there's one upstairs. I mean, there's a lot of stairs. But the closest one is down here."

She scurried down the hall, opened up the door and closed it behind her, leaning against it. And she was very seriously concerned she was going to burst into tears. The bathroom was very much like the kitchen. Nice, and surprisingly modern. But she didn't care about that. She just... She couldn't believe she was here, with a man who had lit her on fire with a handshake, and then walked out the door a few minutes later. Holding a baby that felt like her destiny. And she hadn't even told anyone where she was.

And she was grateful that Sawyer had gone off for another couple of hours, because she was going to need to cry for at least twenty minutes before she faced him again.

CHAPTER FOUR

HELL AND DAMN. *Hell and damn.*

"What's the matter with you?" Hunter asked.

"Nothing."

"Why are you out here, by the way? I said that I would handle buttoning everything up so that you could deal with the missus."

"She's not my missus," he said through clenched teeth.

"That's your plan, though."

Sometimes he liked having a friend like Hunter. A man he'd known all his life. They didn't have to speak a lot of words between them on account of the fact that they just sort of knew each other. They knew about the bullshit in each other's pasts, and their family issues. Knew the measure of each other.

And given that Sawyer would rather eat broken glass than talk about anything he might feel, it often suited him.

Right now, though, it was annoying as hell. He didn't want his friend to look at him and know a damn thing.

"Yeah," Sawyer grunted. "That is the plan."

"She here?"

"Yeah," he said.

She was here. And she was soft. The coat she'd been wearing looked like it cost a month's worth of rent in that city she came from, and she had a pair of black leggings and a sweatshirt on underneath. The combined picture just made her look…soft.

He had been able to get a fair assessment of her body. But it hadn't mattered. The minute those crystal blue eyes had collided with his he… Well, he was a man. And he was a physical man. He knew what the hell he liked when it came to women.

And for some reason, the minute he'd seen her, his body had decided that Evelyn Moore was what it liked.

Sure, he'd had a little bit of a stint of celibacy. Hadn't been with a woman since Missy had told him she was pregnant eight months ago. Hadn't seemed right.

But Evelyn did not look like the kind of woman that could…survive this. This place. The vastness of the landscape was liable to swallow her whole. She was the kind of woman who would expect…convenience and nice things and, well, softness.

Perversely, he was pretty sure that was why he wanted her.

All that softness…

He'd crush her.

Bottom line: it would be him, or it would be this place. But in the end there wasn't much difference. He was the land. He couldn't leave this place or separate from it any more than he could quit breathing.

But he knew from past experience this wasn't the place for that sort of woman.

And the kind of electricity he'd felt when he'd seen her…

It was a bad combination. A losing one.

"So, she's here," Hunter said, breaking into his thoughts. "She's here."

"What's the problem? Does she have a horn in the middle of her forehead or something?"

"No."

"Not attractive?"

He huffed out a chuckle, he couldn't help himself.

"Oh," Hunter said. "She's hot."

And yet again he wasn't liking how well his friend knew him.

"I just sort of figured if you sent away for a mail-order bride, you get somebody kind of maternal looking. And not someone that you want to…"

"Oh, come on now, Sawyer, are you getting shy on me?"

"I'm not shy. But this is an arrangement. And that means that I need to get my shit together. I can't say, *Hi, nice to meet you*, and then take her upstairs and have my way with her."

"Why not? Sounds ideal to me. If I was going to get married, that's the kind of arrangement I'd be after. I don't want to get married, mind you. But if I had a mind to, I'll tell you what, I'd be wanting some attraction."

"I don't. I'd like to feel… Something passable for her. But…not like this."

"You're a crazy asshole," Hunter said, shaking his head.

"I have a plan," Sawyer said. "I want a wife to help me with things. She's going to cook and organize and take care of Bug. And we're going to…have to figure out how to coexist."

"You want a ranch hand in a skirt," Hunter said, snorting.

Sawyer didn't see why his friend said it with that tone. "No," he said. "If I wanted one of your asses in a skirt, I'd ask for that. What I want is…a woman to be there for Bug. I want her to have a mother."

His own grandmother had been the most important influence on his life. She'd been stable, she'd been soft. She was the only reason he'd turned out halfway decent.

"Sure," Hunter said. "But you have to admit, it's a tidy arrangement for you, too. Cook, clean, sex on Friday night and your birthday and nothing otherwise disrupting."

He gritted his teeth. "You say that like it doesn't make perfect sense."

"Why not just hire a nanny?" Hunter asked.

"Having a nanny is not the same as having a mother, is it? The same as having your dad shack up with different women over the years isn't the same as having a mother. The same as...as the knowledge your mother left you never goes away. You get that, Hunter, I know you do."

Hunter shifted. "Yeah. All right. I can get that. But what makes you think she won't leave?"

"I don't know," Sawyer said. "What I was hoping for was... I wanted to be able to come to an agreement without any kind of feeling involved. That's why I didn't want her to be quite so pretty."

"I still don't see how this is a bad thing."

"Just wait till you see her."

She was the kind of woman that... Sawyer couldn't imagine her ever really being happy here on a ranch like this. It would be just like his mother. His mother had been too fancy for all this. She'd dreamed of something better.

She'd grown up in Pyrite Falls but she had always wanted to do more. Have more. See more. Then she got knocked up and had to marry Sawyer's dad.

She'd lasted all of four years before she'd gone off to Chicago. She'd written to him sometimes. She'd told him that he could fly out and come see her.

She'd said that a lot of times.

"Well, don't send her packing because you like her tits,"

Hunter said. "At least not until I see her. Maybe I'll like them, too, and figure a wife might be for me, after all."

"I will kick your ass."

Hunter laughed. "No worries. I have no interest in stomping all over your territory, Sawyer. I'm just proving a point. You don't actually want to send the lady away. Be rational."

Rational.

There was no rationality available to him right now. None at all. Not in the least. He had... He had no reasonable line of thinking at his disposal. Not at this current moment. He rode his horse out toward the stall.

Wolf would be back with pizza soon. They didn't often go to the trouble to get food, but he'd figured it would be a nice gesture given that she had flown all this way. Not to have her cook. And really, none of them should cook.

They got by, of course they did. But it wasn't the kind of opening that he wanted to present the woman that had come all this way to marry him. And he hadn't wanted to throw an apron at her and tell her to get busy.

"So how are things at McCloud's?" he asked.

Mostly because he could tell Hunter had a bee in his bonnet about something and Sawyer wanted to get himself out of the hot seat.

Hunter huffed. "Oh, you know. Same old. Gus is an antisocial asshole. Brody and Lachlan are burning their way through the buckle bunnies in Pyrite Falls. Tag shacked up with Nelly Foster."

"Nelly Foster? The schoolmarm's daughter?"

"The very same. I guess he's had a thing for her for... Ever. I don't know. They're happy, though. And that shocked the hell out of me."

"Yeah." Because if there was one thing he knew it was

that the McClouds and the Garretts had a pretty similar situation. They didn't seem fated to be happy. The McCloud matriarch had taken her leave several years ago, and their old man—always a mean drunk—had only gotten meaner.

Something big had gone down with him and Gus some years ago, but none of them ever talked about it.

Either way, the old man had gone, and he hadn't come back.

"Gus is wanting to start some kind of equine therapy branch… I don't know. He says he's going to bring it up at the next town hall."

The ranches had meetings, called town hall meetings—initially sort of as a joke, but it had stuck—every month to discuss the business, and any new initiatives. Always with the families, and their head ranch hands.

Four Corners was a community all on its own and when changes were made—like the move to use more land for crops, or a decision to plant more alfalfa—it concerned everyone. While each individual ranch kept a percentage of their own profits, some went into a shared pot that helped cover shortfalls for the collective.

It kept things running smoothly.

But that meant they were up in each other's grilles more often than not.

"Interesting," Sawyer said.

"He's got his head fixed on it, and you know how he is."

"Not half as soft and fluffy as the rest of us?"

Hunter chuckled. "Yeah. Look, my pet is the breeding business. And that's what I'm into. I'd love to have Elsie get involved with some of that."

He shrugged. "I mean, maybe *love* is overstating it, but she's interested, and I could use the help."

"I told you already, it's no problem. We can spare her."

He might have to hire someone else, but with Evelyn at the ranch…

Just her name stoked a fire in his gut.

He dismounted his horse and started to take the tack off.

"Hey, as much as I want to see your new lady, I'll give you an evening to yourselves. I'm gonna ride on home."

He turned his horse away from the barn and started to ride in the opposite direction, back toward McCloud's Landing.

Sawyer got his horse dressed down and put away, and then started to walk back to the house. He could've driven, but he hadn't, mostly because he was trying to draw things out. He gritted his teeth.

Maybe you've got more of your old man in you than you thought.

Hell, no. He wasn't second-guessing. He wasn't backing down.

Sawyer was a man who did the right thing.

And in the end, he had faith that this was the right thing. Whatever the initial impact of Evelyn Moore was.

She might not be the right thing.

No. He did have some serious questions about that, and they were going to need to outline some very specific tenets because… He could see her getting real sick of this real fast.

And he would not do that to Bug. The surge of protectiveness he felt almost disturbed him as much as the attraction he felt for Evelyn.

He was used to the protectiveness that he felt where Bug was concerned. But there was something sharp to this. Something with teeth. It was unexpected. He headed back up toward the house, just as Wolf was coming in the driveway.

"Just in time," his brother said, pulling his truck up to

the house and reaching to the passenger side and picking up a stack of pizzas.

Sawyer nodded.

Wolf took an appraising look at him.

"What?"

"*Hell and damn*, are you and Hunter psychic now?"

"Don't think so." He walked past Sawyer and headed toward the house. Sawyer shook his head and followed after him.

When he walked in, Elsie was there, but his eyes went straight to Evelyn. She was sitting on the couch, and she was cradling Bug close.

It was incredible, the way the baby had settled into her, the way that she settled into the baby. It wasn't really like anything he'd expected. He thought that it would work. Because he'd set his mind to it. On that score Hunter and Wolf were right.

But he hadn't expected… This instantaneous ease between her and the baby.

Between her and his *daughter*.

She looked up at him, and their eyes met, and he felt that same crack from earlier. She looked away quickly.

"You settled in all right?"

"She's been in the kitchen and the living room. And the bathroom," Elsie said.

Sawyer tensed. "You didn't show her to her room?"

"I don't know where you expect to keep her. She's going to be your wife. Isn't she sleeping in your room?"

Lord help him he was going to strangle Elsie.

"Not tonight," he said, his teeth clenched.

He looked back at Evelyn, who had turned the color of a beet root.

"Forgive my sister. She was quite possibly born in a barn."

"I *was* born in a barn," Elsie said. "That's a fact. Probably one of the reasons my mom ended up leaving, to be honest. She wasn't superimpressed that our dad hemmed and hawed about whether or not it was time to drive down to the hospital, and she ended up having me in the middle of the barn floor. And they had to send the Mercy Flights helicopter out."

Evelyn nodded, wordlessly, her eyes wide.

Yeah, this was going well.

"That's exciting," Evelyn said finally.

"It was a pretty exciting start," Elsie said. "Not that I remember it."

"All right, squirt," he said. "Go get forks and napkins and things."

Elsie scampered off, and Wolf continued on into the kitchen. Leaving them alone.

"Was she good?" he asked.

"She was… She was great. She's… She's wonderful."

"Sorry about my… My family. I… Sort of thought it would be easier to have them around, but now I'm questioning it."

"I like your sister," she said. "I… I should go get acquainted with Wolf, I guess."

"No one really gets acquainted with Wolf."

Does anyone get acquainted with you?

For some reason, he could feel that question as if she had spoken it out loud.

"I hope you like the house," he said.

"Just like the pictures," she said.

And he felt the other unspoken thing right there. They hadn't sent pictures of each other. They had talked on the phone, just last night.

"So…" He took a step toward her, and he swore she

shrank back. "Did you tell anybody that you went to Oregon to marry a stranger?"

"No, somehow I skipped telling my family that I talked to a cowboy on the phone and said that I would come be his homestead wife."

"I don't think the word *homestead* has ever once been used between the two of us."

"This is a homestead," she said.

"I guess it is," he responded.

"So, this is without a doubt the strangest thing I've ever done. How about you?"

"No," he said. "Well, I guess it depends on who you ask. Hunter and Wolf would tell you this is absolutely the strangest thing I've ever done, but then they're completely averse to marriage and commitment of any kind."

"And you're not?"

He considered his answer for a second.

"I was. But... There are some things that... There are things in life that happen, and you just realize everything's changed. And it doesn't matter who you were before, or what you thought about anything, or what you wanted. Things are changing, and you have to change with them. I have to make a change for her."

She nodded very slowly, and he felt gratified, because he knew that they did understand each other. At least in this.

"My entire life fell apart. I lost everything. I was supposed to marry Andrew next weekend. We've been planning that wedding for eighteen months. The venue that we reserved in the Hamptons is always booked solid. We got a cancellation. And that was eighteen months ago. It was going to be so beautiful. I had the prettiest wedding dress that you've ever seen."

He wondered if she was going to wear it to their wedding. Would they even have a real wedding?

This beautiful, pale creature that was sitting on his couch and looked like she belonged in a castle or something.

Not here on his ranch.

"I worked with my friends," she said quietly. "So, when they betrayed me, there went my business. My parents don't understand why I would call the wedding off. Not when all their friends have been invited and it's been announced in their social circles."

"Hang on," he said. "Your parents don't understand why you'd leave a man who cheated on you?"

"No. But then, I think that says a lot about the flexibility of marriage vows within their social circles. It's just all very cynical," she said. "And I guess I was never cynical enough about life. I thought my friends were my real friends. I thought Andrew loved me."

"Did you love him?"

He probably didn't have the right to ask that, but he felt like he should know.

She nodded slowly. "I was with him for ten years. All I ever wanted was to get married. I mean, and build my business. Which I did. But I wanted to get married and have a family. I thought that I could do all of it. I still think I could have. Andrew always wanted to wait until the business was doing a little bit better. He works in finance. And he has all kinds of opinions on… I'm sorry," she said, shaking her head. "You probably don't want to hear about all this."

"No," he said, standing there, folding his arms over his chest. "I do. I should."

"I just was saying… That I get it. I get that feeling. Like everything changed so now you have to. I really do."

"You might need to," he said. "It doesn't mean you're ready for it."

"No," she said, smiling slightly.

"I think you're going to miss the city," he said.

"How do you know?"

"Because," he said, "I'd miss the country."

"Right now... Right now all of that is too tied up in what I lost. In the life that I was imagining. I can't have that life. So I just thought... Rather than... I couldn't bear it." And suddenly there were tears in her eyes, and he really wished they would go away. He did not like emotions. Not at all.

"I cannot face living there and just going on like it didn't happen. Walking down those same streets. Going into work. Or starting a new company. Basically starting back where I was when I was twenty-four. No closer to anything that I wanted. No closer to... To success or... Being married. Having a family of my own. It made more sense to come here. It made more sense to come here and just get what I wanted. Because this is what I should have now. She is what I should... Maybe you didn't dream of having children, Sawyer, but I did."

He nodded slowly. "That all makes sense."

"Do you really think so? Are you just saying that so I'll stop talking and you can go have your pizza?"

"The second one."

She laughed. "All right. This could be interesting."

"What?"

"You know, normally when two people try to start having a relationship they spend a fair amount of time telling tales so that they can seem more attractive to the other person."

"That's what beer goggles are for."

"I see. How many relationships have you been in?"

"None."

"Somehow that doesn't surprise me. But... If... If we're going to do this. And we're going to make something based off of our desire to build a life, to commit to each other, and to do what's best for...for June, then..."

"Who told you that was her name?"

"Elsie."

He shook his head. "It's not..."

"Why June Bug?"

He gritted his teeth. "It doesn't matter. Anyway. Get back to your point."

"There's no reason for us to lie to each other. Ever. Because we're not trying to impress each other. It is what it is. What you see is what you get. So, I'll just tell you what I'm thinking."

"All right. I'll do the same." It was what he planned on doing, anyway. The thing was, romance and all of that... It wasn't really his thing. Never had been. And he'd never had to work hard to get a woman into bed. They were usually all over him before they left the bar—hell, he'd gotten laid in his truck more times than he could count. He liked it that way. He liked easy. Easy to put together, easy to take back apart. No scars left behind.

Except even his brand of casual sex had ultimately caught up with him. Had left scars.

Had left Bug.

Oh, well, that was why he was changing things. It was why he was doing this.

She stood, and he caught her scent. Something sweet and light. Vanilla and sugar. And he wanted to lean in, bury his face in her neck. Kiss that soft, elegant curve. Suddenly, he wanted it so bad, could see it so clearly in his mind, that it was nearly impossible to hold himself back.

But he did.

"Damnation, woman," he said.

Her eyes went to his, and dropped to his mouth. He had not meant to say that out loud.

"Let's go have pizza," she said.

"Right."

Have pizza, sit with his family. And then have a rational conversation about the way things were going to go forward.

And nothing more.

Because for now, there could be nothing more.

CHAPTER FIVE

EVELYN WOKE UP bright-eyed and ready to face the day. Things had been going pretty well. In fact, she was ready to call it a rousing success. Acclimating to country life hadn't been difficult at all. And she was figuring out caring for a child easily. Sawyer was handsome. And so far he had been easy to talk to.

She peeked in on Bug, who was still asleep, then went downstairs to begin breakfast. She set her phone on the counter, and then went hunting for eggs. There were only a couple left, which was too bad. But she knew that Sawyer had already eaten—he got up very early to be out on the ranch—so she only had to feed herself.

Her phone buzzed, and she looked down at the screen. Her mother.

She ignored it. She hadn't told anyone where she was going. She was off-grid. She was alone. Except for... Well, the entire Garrett family. But nonetheless, she was forging a new life. And she didn't need her old one intruding. Not now.

She started to cook the eggs in a pan on the stove, humming tunelessly to herself until June Bug started to cry. She wiped her hands on her pajama pants, and then went back upstairs, picking the baby up and slinging a burp rag over her shoulder. It was bottle time for sure. But she'd check the diaper first.

She was wet, so Evelyn changed her quickly before carrying her downstairs. But it took so long that by the time she made it back to the eggs they were browned. Horribly.

She huffed, and dump them into the trash. Then she stared at the frying pan. Getting egg off a frying pan was tricky on a good day. And this was a very bad scenario. A bad egg scenario.

But she left it for now, choosing instead to get to Bug's bottle, and then it was time for another diaper, and then the baby was fractious, and by the time she was finished doing things for her it was nearly eleven and Evelyn was starving. And she realized she hadn't even had a cup of coffee.

She hunted around, and couldn't find any. And then she decided that she needed to make a shopping list. She loved lists. Lists made the world go around. They were an integral part of an organized life. She opened up the cupboards, thankful that she had already done rearranging, and began to take inventory. She already had a fair idea of what was there because of the way that she had arranged things a couple of days ago. She opened up her phone and pulled up a few of her favorite recipes, making a list of ingredients she might need.

She listed a few items that were definite staples for her. Garam masala, tzatziki, bagels, oat milk…

She wrapped up the list, and then looked down at June Bug, who was now happily in her bouncy chair. "What do you say? Should we head into town? Maybe I can get myself a cup of coffee and we can go to the grocery store."

She had talked to Sawyer about which vehicle she could use—an extra car that sat out in front of the house. It did not have modern conveniences, but was new enough to have a car seat base system in it that Sawyer had showed her how to use a few days earlier.

She snapped June Bug's seat into the spot and got into the driver's seat. She did not drive habitually—there was no need living in Manhattan—but she knew how, and she had been intending on getting a car when she and Andrew moved out of the city. A person definitely needed a car living here. It was just…different.

She pulled out of the driveway and did her best to mentally retrace the drive she had taken to Four Corners with Elsie. The town was even tinier than she'd remembered. The buildings were made of vertical slats of wood, the roofs covered in moss. It took her a few minutes to fully accept that the place to buy groceries was the place that also had bait and tackle. And cold beer. She parked her car in front of the general store and simply stared for a minute. There had to be another town. But she couldn't remember exactly how far away it was. And didn't know if it would be the direction that she and Elsie had come, or if it would be the other way. And yes, she could map it, but she was just going to go with convenience.

There was an array of grocery carts in front of the store. None of them matched. She got out of the car and hefted Bug's seat out of it, then placed it down in the bottom of the shopping cart, and began to roll it forward, one wheel rattling.

The floor inside was… Well, it was Astroturf. The floor inside was Astroturf. The shelves seem to be in a strange order. PowerBait only one aisle away from cereal. The cereal was mostly brands she had never heard of.

But she managed to find coffee beans, so there was that. The back wall boasted an entire row of freezers, and there was a whole hell of a lot in the way of beer. When it came to the basics, she was sure she would be covered. But she slowly gave up hope of finding garam masala or

oat milk. She was also a little bit disappointed by the produce. She would've thought that living here there would
be something good.

She looked up and found the man standing behind the
counter was staring at her.

"Hello," she said.

"Howdy," he said. He pushed his thumbs through his
belt loops, and leaned back.

"Yes. Well. Is this all the produce you have?"

"Farmers market sets up out front once a week," he said.
"Sometimes I get leftovers. Otherwise, yes, this is it."

"What day of the week is that?"

"Thursdays," he said.

Well. It was Friday. So. Great.

"Okay. Well. Thank you."

"You new in town?"

"Yes," she said.

What a strange thing that he would know. But then, she
supposed quite apart from him recognizing her or not the
fact that she wasn't familiar with the inner workings of
the town or its lone grocery store was indicator enough.
It wasn't like there was a plethora of other places to shop.

"Is there a place I can get coffee?"

"You have coffee in your basket," he said.

"Yes," she said. "I mean, like… I would like a latte?"

"There's a cappuccino machine at the gas station."

She smiled. So, no, then.

No cupcake ATM. No actual coffee.

This was wretched.

"Right. Also, I need some work boots."

"We have those," he said.

He led her to the back of the store, where there was a

stack of brown, unisex-looking work boots in shoeboxes, stacked by size.

"Thank you," she said.

She sat down on a small bench—covered in Astroturf just like the floor—and began to try them on. But she had one boot on when Bug began to cry, and she had to stop and comfort the child. Unbuckling her from the car seat and holding her. That ended up taking a while. Because she had to fix her a bottle.

"Hey," he said. "Is that Sawyer Garrett's little one?"

She blinked. She was surprised the guy had been able to recognize a random baby.

"Yes. It is."

"Recognize the blanket. Because of the strawberries."

She looked down. The blanket did have particularly bright strawberries on it.

"Right."

"I heard a rumor that Sawyer was going to try to find a mom for the baby. Someone said he posted an ad on the internet. A news station came by."

"Oh. Well. He did."

"You're not from California, are you?"

The man looked like he was going to be offended by her answer. But she couldn't figure out if the answer was supposed to be yes or no.

"I am not," she said.

"Good," he said.

Well, that answered her question.

"I'm John."

"Evelyn. Nice to meet you."

"How are you finding the town?"

"All right. Is there a grocery store that's maybe a little bit of a drive away?"

He laughed. "Miss," he said. "You might as well have just told me my store's not good enough."

"Oh, no," she said, feeling really stupid. But everything felt so much smaller and personal here. And it's just... Groceries were not personal in New York. "It's just that I need some things. Like oat milk."

"Oat milk. Miss, I'm not trying to be rude. And I'm aware you're from the city. But as far as I know you can't milk an oat."

She blinked. "You don't... It's not... Never mind. I'm sorry."

"You mean you need a specialty store," he said.

She felt like she was in a specialty store. Not any normal grocery store, but she had a feeling that she couldn't say that without being even more offensive, so she was going to keep that to herself. "Yes," she said. "A specialty store."

"You could drive up to Mapleton."

"Okay. Thank you. I'll keep that in mind. But I'll probably just be back for the farmers market next week."

She finished trying on boots after June Bug quieted. Then she paid for all of her purchases and went out to the car. And when she lifted the car seat into the car, she saw that there was a small jar of hot sauce that had rolled beneath the lip of the car seat. And she hadn't paid for it. And with her muscles aching as she leaned into the car, getting very tired of hefting everything, she honestly considered leaving it there. But she couldn't do that. She was new to town, and all she needed was to gain a reputation as a hot sauce thief.

So she marched it and the baby back into the store, and went through the process of paying again. Then walked back out to the car, fitting the car seat in. And by the time she was finished she was sweaty.

She gave up on the idea of any coffee for the day, because by the time she got back to the ranch it was nearly two o'clock. And after that, everything went wrong. For some reason her yeast didn't work on her dinner rolls tonight—when she was typically unerring with them—and her bread came out flat. On top of that, she was using a roast recipe that required her to put the oven on broil for a few minutes toward the end, but she got interrupted by Bug crying, and ended up scorching the meat.

The whole house was filled with smoke, and by the time Sawyer got back she was half-reclined on the couch feeling defeated, and being well aware she looked that way, too.

"Is everything all right?"

"Great," she mumbled.

She got up and made her way into the kitchen, then she picked the roast up and dumped it into the trash. "I hope there's frozen food."

"There's frozen pizza," he said.

"Great. I'm going to go take a shower."

She grabbed one of the flat rolls, and bit into it angrily while she made her way up the stairs. She hoped he liked coming home to a mean, evil crone who hadn't even managed to get dinner ready for him.

But at least June Bug was sleeping.

She went into the bathroom and looked in the mirror. Maybe she wasn't good at this. Maybe she couldn't do it. It had all been great for two days, but two days was basically a weekend vacation. And now it was... Well, today had sucked. She was tired, her body hurt from carrying Bug, who had been incessantly fussy all day. The town felt nearly impossible. She didn't have the things that she needed.

She gripped the edge of the vanity and closed her eyes.

"Pull it together, Evelyn," she said to herself. "You can

order the things you need on the internet. And you'll be okay."

She laughed. She was honestly freaking out about oat milk and spices. Well, and the selection of work boots. And the fact that a man had known that she was new in town, just because she stood out. Just because she was there. It was just different.

And when she went to sleep, she felt hollow and hungry, and the silence felt oppressive. And she thought of what she would do if she was in the city. She would go out and walk. And the streets would be lit up like daytime. And people would be all around. But not here. Here she was alone. In this house. With a baby, and with Sawyer.

She felt guilty. She hadn't talked to him at all today. But then, he hadn't asked. Hadn't asked how the day went, hadn't asked... He hadn't come looking for her.

He's respecting your boundaries probably.

And she couldn't be pleased. So she figured she would just try and sleep it off.

THE NEXT MORNING Sawyer was determined to get to the bottom of Evelyn's sullenness the night before. He knew that they were still in a trial. He also knew that it wasn't the worst thing in the world if she decided that she wanted to leave. He was having his own doubts about the situation brought on by the... Well, hell. He was supposed to want to be with her because she was good for Bug. He wasn't supposed to want her around because he wanted to get his hands on her. But he could barely think about anything else. Not since he'd first laid eyes on her. He hadn't been with anybody since Missy had found out she was pregnant. So he was going on a year of celibacy. And while it would be easy enough to blame that for his attraction to Evelyn, he knew it wasn't that simple.

He knew it was her.

He made coffee, and breakfast, and he waited. At about seven thirty, he heard her footsteps on the stairs.

"Good morning," he said, knowing that his voice carried easily to where she was. He grabbed a mug and poured a cup of coffee. He had watched the way that she fixed it the other morning, and he was confident he could recreate it. When she walked into the room, he had it held out and at the ready.

"Good morning," she said, her voice sounding scratchy. She was holding Bug, and looking tired.

"Did you have a hard night?"

"No. She slept. I… I'm sorry. About yesterday. I…had not had a great day. I mean, it wasn't terrible. It was just I went to town, and I bought some groceries, but they didn't have all of the things I wanted, and I made kind of an ass of myself. Just… Cultural differences. Really."

"Cultural differences?"

"It's different here. And I didn't mean to insult John's store."

"Oh, he's fine," Sawyer said, waving his hand. "Unless you threw rotten fruit or something."

"I did not throw rotten fruit," she said. "Though, to be clear, I could have. Because the produce section was deeply suspect."

"Later you'll have to go by the garden."

"The garden?"

"Yeah. There's a big garden at Sullivan's Point and we all take food from it when we need it."

"Oh. Well, that's… That's great."

"Yeah. I'll… Give you directions."

She took a sip of her coffee. "This is perfect."

"Yeah. I watched how you did it."

She tilted her head to the side, a slight smile on her lips. "Oh. That's… That is actually incredibly thoughtful."

"I try." He brought some eggs and bacon to the table, and the two of them sat together, Bug content against Evelyn's chest.

"Would you like to go for a ride later?"

"A ride?"

"Horses," he said. "I ride with Bug all the time. So, I'll carry her, and you can just ride. We'll go on a trek to the lake."

"Oh, that sounds nice."

And she really did look a little bit brighter about that. And he wasn't sure exactly what his goal was. Because he should just be letting her figure this out. He just shouldn't be invested in any particular ending. This was a trial for both of them, and it was about doing the right thing. The best thing. Not about keeping her here just because he thought she was beautiful.

They finished breakfast, and he got Bug all set in her carrier, then they began to walk down the trail that led to the barn.

He noticed that Evelyn had on a pair of very sturdy-looking boots that didn't much go with the pair of very tight jeans and soft-looking sweater she was wearing. He tore his eyes away from how the jeans fit her ass.

"Where did you get the boots?"

"Oh, at the store. I figured that I would need… Something with a little bit more heft."

"Right."

He got the horses from the stall, selecting an older mount for Evelyn who he thought might be easy enough. He got them tacked up and ready to go in just a few minutes.

"So what you do is…"

Evelyn hefted herself up easily onto the back of the horse. "Horse camp," she said.

"Horse camp?"

"Yes."

Holding on to Bug tightly, he got himself up on his own mount, and then led the way down the road that would take them to Sullivan's Point, and farther down to the lake. It was open, with broad expanses of green fields on either side, and tall cypress trees that grew straight up toward the sky. "Wow," Evelyn said. "This is…"

And then her voice went unsteady, and he turned back to see that her horse was balking. He lifted his front legs up off the gravel road, and Evelyn let out a sharp sound.

"Hang on," he said, bringing his own horse to a stop. He was about to jump off so that he could grab her mount to steady him, when the horse reared back and unseated Evelyn completely. She landed hard on her ass on the ground.

He got off and went over to her quickly, his hand still on the Bug's back. "Are you okay?"

He reached his hand down, and she reached up, grabbing hold of him as he hoisted her to her feet. Her hands were soft. But there was gravel stuck to her palm, and he felt…unaccountably guilty about that.

But along with the guilt, there was heat.

Her eyes met his. And held.

Then she took a step back.

"There was a snake," she said, standing up slowly and rubbing her rear. "It freaked the horse out."

"I'm sorry," he said.

"It's fine."

She looked angry and determined.

And he hadn't expected that.

"This place might be out to get me." She huffed out a laugh. "No. That's dramatic. A burned roast and a bruised butt is hardly persecution."

Then she sighed and walked back over to the horse. Patting him on the neck.

"What exactly are you doing?"

"Getting back on, Sawyer."

And then she surprised him by putting her foot in the stirrup, lifting herself up and swinging her leg back over the horse. "Because that's what you do, right? You get back on." She blinked. "You get back on. You don't run away. You have to."

"Well," he said, suddenly feeling like they weren't talking about horses anymore. "You don't have to."

"Yeah, I guess you don't. But then... Then the fall gets the last say. Instead of you."

They didn't proceed until they were certain the horse had calmed. And then they went farther, down to the lake, and he had to admit, he was impressed with her fortitude.

"So, explain this to me," she said, surveying the lake.

"Technically we're at Sullivan's Point, and the lake belongs to them. But each of us has a segment of beach to call our own. Lots of celebrations happen here."

"Weddings?" She looked at him.

"I'm not sure there's ever been a wedding."

She nodded. "Right. Well. It's beautiful."

He looked at her. At her stubbornness, her strength and, yes, her beauty. "It sure is."

And if he knew one thing, it was that at this point... It wasn't just her beauty he admired.

EVELYN'S BUTT HURT. That was to be expected given the fall she had taken earlier. But she had gotten back on the horse, and she felt proud. She was also… Ruminating on the different things that were ricocheting around in her soul. Because whatever she had said about getting back on the horse… Her tendency was not to get back on the horse. And even yesterday she had been considering throwing in the towel because it had been… It had been awkward. Not terrible, but she'd been blocked by a few small, irritating things, and had found it difficult, and the idea of running again had seemed attractive.

She had to recognize her own track record of running. That she had come across the country, because it had seemed easier than facing the demons waiting for her at home.

Home.

That was all tangled and complicated.

Because she couldn't say that the apartment back in New York felt particularly like home. And certainly the people she had left behind couldn't be home.

Home wasn't here yet, either. And she was still avoiding phone calls from New York, from the people she had left behind, which she felt like was more… Avoidance. More of that…

It felt brave coming here. Starting over.

But there was an element of cowardice to it, as well.

And it wasn't the first time she'd done this. Some might call it throwing the baby out with the bathwater, she supposed.

But she wasn't going to linger on that too deeply right now; what she was going to do was take the baby currently in her care and go to the community garden. After their ride down to the lake Sawyer had given her directions to the garden, which were very easy to follow, since they had ridden down the same road earlier.

This time, she didn't ride a horse, though. She packed June Bug and a few baskets into the car, and drove herself over to Sullivan's Point.

When she got there, she was blown away by the little garden. Tall fences with climbing honeysuckle wound around them, and brilliant mountains were in the background. It was pastoral and amazing, and like every fantasy of living some country cottage life she had ever had. She got Bug out of the car, and walked over to the gate, which was extremely high. She wasn't quite sure why. She unlocked it and pushed it open. Sawyer had said that it was a shared space, and everyone on the ranch was allowed to take whatever they needed from it.

There were fruit trees, and rows of other fruits and vegetables, many that she didn't even recognize. Not without closer inspection. But when she did inspect more closely she found fat strawberries and raspberries. Cucumbers, zucchinis. Pumpkins. Tomatoes. So many tomatoes. And that was when she decided she was going to make a fresh, garden marinara sauce. There were even herbs.

She heard the sound of feminine voices, and turned to see two women coming her direction. Both wearing flowery dresses.

Evelyn's first instinct was to literally hide. To not have a human interaction that she wasn't prepared for.

But the gate pushed open, and there they were. One had strawberry blond hair, the other more of an auburn. And they were clearly related, their eyes the same color green, their smiles nearly matching.

One was very small, petite in all ways, while the other was taller, more willowy.

"Oh," the small one of them said. "Hello. I…"

"Evelyn," Evelyn said quickly. "I'm with... I'm... Saw-yer..."

The women exchanged glances. "Oh," the one with strawberry blond hair said. "Got it. You're the one. Obviously word travels quickly around the ranch."

"Right," Evelyn said. "I guess it would."

"I'm Quinn," said the small one. "This is my sister Rory."

"Nice to meet you," Evelyn said.

"We're the Sullivans," Quinn said. "Well. Not all of them. Our oldest sister is Fia, and then there is Rory after her. And Alaina is the youngest."

"Oh." All sisters.

"Are you... Are you staying?"

Something shifted in Evelyn's chest. "I don't know."

"Well," Quinn said. "You're going to have to come over and make jam with us sometimes. We do that. A lot of baking. A lot of jam making." They were both so friendly and cheerful, and Evelyn's first instinct was to turn away from it. And wasn't that the strangest thing. That she had jumped immediately into an engagement, but that she... Did not particularly want to jump into a friendship.

But if she had to really go over the betrayals that had occurred in her life, she was hurt by Andrew. And devastated by the fact that she was losing out on the life that she had planned for herself.

It was her friends that had decimated her trust.

And looking at these women now...

It just made her tired.

She didn't want to get to know new people. She didn't want to confide in them, or share anything about herself.

She just couldn't face it.

Of course, she couldn't be rude, either, because she was going to be seeing them again. And a lot probably. But that didn't mean that she had to spend time with them. That didn't mean that she had to...

And what happened to getting back on the horse?

She didn't want to ponder anything too deeply. She just wanted to get her produce and go.

Was she destined to have conversations every time she went searching for food?

"Thank you," she said. Because she couldn't say anything else.

"You're welcome." Quinn and Rory exchanged a glance. "We were surprised. When Sawyer became a father. Even more surprised that he's getting married. Except I guess we shouldn't really be. He's...traditional. In a good way."

And Evelyn found herself bristling. That these women knew things about Sawyer that she didn't. At this implied intimacy. How could she be getting jealous over anything with him already? It didn't make any sense. She didn't love him. She barely knew him.

She finished talking to the other women, gathered up all of her things and got back into the car with Bug.

And then her phone rang again. And she just still wasn't ready to answer it. She still wasn't ready to begin to untangle all the different things inside of her.

Didn't know how to reconcile running away with starting this new life. With finding ways to connect with people while feeling uncertain about ever having another friend. Or how to deal with the one she had left behind. Or if she even needed to. She did need to deal with her mother, she knew that. She just...hadn't felt ready.

When did a person get back on the horse? And when did one run?

She had done both things in the space of a week, and she wasn't sure yet which one was wise. Wasn't sure yet if what she was doing here was…reasonable. If she was going to stay.

But she had managed to get through being awkward in the grocery store, awkward in a garden and falling off a horse. And for all that there were difficult things about caring for a baby… She loved June Bug. Instantly. But with a measure of wariness, because she didn't know what was going to happen. Not yet.

You could still run. You can go somewhere where no one expects anything of you. You could start over again anytime.

But that didn't feel easy. Already.

It didn't feel… It didn't feel right. Or good. And now she just felt trapped. It was hard here but it was also too compelling to walk away from.

She was going to have to figure out how to exist in the struggle. To take a risk. To invest. Even when it was hard. And that seemed… Well, it was difficult. That was the thing.

At what point did you think becoming a wife and mother was going to be simple?

That stopped her right there. Because it was true. Marrying Andrew and having his children would never have been simple or easy. Life was going to be difficult sometimes, and she was going to find it hard. She knew better than that. Starting a business hadn't been easy. It was just that it hadn't been her… Her heart.

And this was all far too much like ballet, which had destroyed her and her sense of self.

Until she had the courage to break free of it. Leaving New York had felt the same.

Except… Except… Leaving things behind and not dealing with them at all… That wasn't really all that brave.

She wasn't sure she cared about being brave. But she did want to… She wanted to progress. She wanted to grow. Not just start over and rebuild. Again. Which would mean pushing through…this. Because one thing she was certain of… There was enough good here to keep trying. Even if she wasn't great at it right away. Even if it was difficult. Even if she sometimes felt silly. Even if she sometimes fell on her butt.

Because of June Bug.

But when she thought that, she saw Sawyer's face. But she pushed that out of her mind, and turned on the radio, and listened to country songs she'd never heard before all the way back to the house.

CHAPTER SIX

EVELYN'S PHONE RANG when it was still dark outside. She looked at the screen and saw that it was her mother…for the fifteenth time.

And she somehow felt certain she couldn't avoid this conversation any longer. The events of the past few days had been weighing on her. From the weird shopping trip, to ruined dinners, falling off the horse and feeling…afraid of friends.

She almost couldn't remember New York. It felt like a weird, hazy memory, but it was one that was deciding how happy she was letting herself be here.

And she had to face it.

She had to…get back on that horse.

"Where are you?"

"Honestly, Mother," Evelyn said, rolling onto her back and scrubbing at her eyes. "You wouldn't believe me if I told you."

"You go missing right before your wedding, and are out of contact with everyone for days, and that's all you have to say?"

Andrea Waldorf-Moore did not suffer fools. Whether or not they were actually fools or people she deemed to be fools by her own mysterious metric.

It was math she did quickly and with great prejudice,

and once her mother had made that determination there was no redeeming yourself.

"I'm in Oregon," Evelyn said, pushing her hair off her face and sitting up. It was still completely dark outside. Not even gray. She could see the stars.

She had gone to bed early last night. She'd had the idea that maybe she could get up and have breakfast with Sawyer.

Sawyer.

In all the uncertainty over the past few days…

There was him. Steady and strong and more handsome than any man had a right to be.

She had a running tally of all the times they'd accidentally touched. Burned into her memory. Burned into her skin.

When he'd picked her up from the ground after she'd fallen from the horse and looked into her eyes…

She blinked, her eyes still scratchy. "It's very early here," she said.

"Well, I didn't know you were on an entirely different coast. For God's sake. What are you doing there?"

"Nothing."

"Are you running away again?"

Her mother's words were like daggers beneath her skin. Because hadn't she been asking herself all these things over the past few days?

And she didn't have a good answer.

She'd needed a new start, but it had echoes of cowardice, and it was tough to ignore that.

Tough to ignore that she'd reverted to the same behavior she'd exhibited at sixteen.

She rolled over onto her stomach. This should be routine. It shouldn't hurt. Whatever she did wasn't quite good enough. There was no magical configuration she could fashion her life into. Well, there had been. And Evelyn had blown that. "Maybe I decided it was time to try something different."

"This is the problem with you, Evelyn. You have no follow-through. Why do you refuse to live up to your potential? You had finally made something of your life."

"Mom," Evelyn said. "If this is about me coming back home to marry Andrew... It isn't going to happen. I'm not going to marry a man that couldn't wait until a midlife crisis to cheat on me. Honestly. It's embarrassing. I'm still young enough to be the other woman."

"Just barely, darling."

Evelyn ground her teeth together. She and her mother didn't talk. And this was why.

"I might move," Evelyn said.

"You might move. To *Oregon*." She said the name sort of funny, with the *O* more like an *A* and the end like the word *gone*. Which was nothing like the way Sawyer said it. More like Oh-ra-gun, which she also thought sounded weird.

It was a weird word. But funny how she already thought it the way Sawyer said it.

"Yes," she confirmed.

"What's there, exactly?" It wasn't asked in a spirit of openness. It was the sort of question someone asked when they were looking for more pointed ways to poke holes in your decision.

And wasn't this part of why she'd been avoiding conversations with those she'd left behind?

Accountability. She had not wanted it.

But the past few days had brought a host of its own. Challenges and reality and failure, but also triumph.

This wasn't going to be perfect or easy. But she didn't

want perfect or easy things. She would have to struggle somewhere.

Why not here?

Why not with him?

She got out of bed and looked out the window. She could see a vast scattering of stars, and the impression of the moon over the water down below. "Cowboys, mostly," she said.

"Honestly, what are you doing? Are you having some kind of a mental breakdown?"

"I'm not having a mental breakdown. If anything I'm thinking clearer than I have for… For years."

"This is just like when you quit the academy."

This always came up. *Always.*

And Evelyn was always hurt by it. Always caught off guard. Like the wounds were fresh and the failure was recent.

"How is it… It is not like that. It isn't like that at all."

Of course, they'd never talked about the deeper reasons she'd left the ballet. She never had. Not with anyone. They'd known only that she'd been tired of it, and of course people just assumed she was tired of working that hard.

But it had been so much deeper than that.

She had never been good enough. She had never been *thin* enough. She had never been…much of anything. And no amount of disordered eating, practicing, causing herself injury had changed it. No matter how hard she'd tried to shrink into the perfect mold she hadn't been able to.

She had never been able to be what her mother had been at the prestigious NYC Ballet Academy.

She remembered standing outside the case in the hall that proclaimed the accomplishments of past alumni and seeing her mother, a former principal dancer for the New York City Ballet.

A dancer whose career had been cut short because of her pregnancy.

Her pregnancy with Evelyn.

And Evelyn had known she was supposed to be the fulfillment of that broken dream. But no matter how hard she'd tried she couldn't be. Loving dance hadn't been enough. Wanting to please her mother hadn't been enough.

She hadn't been enough.

She'd been on the path to killing herself trying to be enough. And only later, when she'd done more reading about disordered eating, really accepting her own tendencies and the fact she needed real help, had she realized just how badly she could have jeopardized her health.

Her fertility.

She'd worried about that for years after. That the quest for being thin she'd been on back in her dancing years had taken her true, deeper dream from her.

She'd gotten checked out when she was twenty or so, and the doctor had said everything was fine, but still. The realization that cutting and running, starting over when she had, had likely saved her in many ways, stuck with her.

And she'd found ways to thrive after burning all that down. Still managed to get accepted into a good college, and she'd worked toward a degree in business, met Hollyn and Kioni…and Andrew.

Decided to excel somewhere else. Prove she could be someone, after all.

But she could see now that any vague sense of approval she'd had from her mother had been purely based in those achievements. Primarily the achievement of Andrew, who was the son of a well-regarded New York politician and successful in the world of finance.

All these goals, all these symbols of success.

All these hoops to jump through and there was just never a point where it was enough.

"I met someone," Evelyn said.

"You *met someone*."

"Yes. I'm trying it out. So, I'm going to be here, in Oregon. Trying it out. I'll let you know how it goes."

"Evelyn Moore," she said. "We are on the hook for so much money for this wedding."

"I can afford to pay for all of it," Evelyn said. "Every last penny. Send me a bill. I don't care."

"So, you're going to have us face everyone alone? We have to explain your wedding's been called off. Are we going to have to speak to Andrew's parents?"

And of course this was all they could talk about. Money and embarrassment and what Evelyn had failed to do, and how much she cost her mother. But never the deeper things. Not ever.

Evelyn's patience snapped.

"Andrew can speak to his own parents. He can explain why he had to screw my best friend in the middle of the day in our shared office space. How about that? Why should that be *my* humiliation, Mother? Can you tell me that?"

"Evelyn," her mother said, her voice measured. "Men will do things. It doesn't mean you throw away the potential of an entire life."

"It does for me. I'm not throwing anything away. He's the one who threw it away. I would have married him happily. Loved him, been faithful to him."

"Did you talk with him?"

"There's nothing to say."

"When you're in a relationship with someone, you sit down and you have the hard conversations."

Of course, she and her mother had never really had any hard conversations. But it didn't mean she wasn't right.

But she was determined to behave differently now. She had stuck out those hard days, and she was committed to it. And she would…

She and Sawyer could have honesty. Real honesty like the kind she'd never had with anyone because their relationship wasn't founded on unspoken expectations. Her mother had given birth to her, so they were in each other's lives by default. She'd met Andrew just after college and they'd…

Well, they'd gotten their start the way everyone in a relationship did. You got to know each other slowly, and you became attached, and then when things went wrong it wasn't just as simple as walking away because you…sort of unwittingly got in too deep.

But she and Sawyer, they were choosing this. Cards on the table up front. It was about being sure that they were getting what they wanted, right from the beginning.

It was a different opportunity. A different type of honesty.

And she was…she was ready for it.

"Well, we might've been able to do that if I hadn't seen him… I'm sorry, I can't come back from that."

"This is what you do," her mother said. "You're a coward, Evelyn. You let everyone else clean up your messes for you. It's why you abandoned your spot at school."

"I'm done. Goodbye, Mother."

She hung the phone up, the weight of all of the unfinished…everything weighing heavily on her. She went to the bathroom, and then settled back into bed for a few minutes, until she was absolutely certain that she wasn't going to be getting back to sleep. She padded slowly down the stairs, feeling like an interloper, and hoping that she didn't wake anyone. But then she saw the light on in the kitchen. She heard movement.

She stopped in the doorway when she saw Wolf and Sawyer, already dressed with their jackets on, and cowboy hats on their head. Sawyer was wearing the baby in a pack on his front.

"You're still here," she said.

She'd hoped he would be.

"You're up awfully early," he said.

"Yeah, I... I wanted to catch you. Is there coffee?"

And he started to fix it, just how she liked it because he'd watched her. Because he'd remembered.

And a sense of home expanded in her chest.

The light in the kitchen looked overly yellow with no natural light from the outside mellowing it, and even beneath its harshness, his beauty was impossible to miss. His mouth was set into a grim line, that scar that she'd taken note of on the first day she'd arrived drawing her attention and making her want to ask questions. His eyes were the dark blue of denim. His face was rough with dark stubble. He clearly he hadn't shaved. It made her fingers itch to touch him.

Andrew had always kept his face clean-shaven, unless it was No Shave November, and then he had grown a horrible mustache along with the rest of the guys in his office.

She had hated it.

He'd claimed that it made him look like Tom Selleck. But since Tom Selleck didn't have facial hair that was thin and blond, she didn't see how that could be possible.

She hadn't said it, though, because she was nice. She

was a good fiancée. And she had not mocked him and his baby man facial hair. She wished dearly that she had now.

She looked at Sawyer's hands. They were battered and scarred, and she couldn't help but think of how rough they'd been when she touched them last night...

He was thrusting a cup of coffee at her, and she was simply staring. It took her a whole thirty seconds to realize.

"Oh," she said, taking the cup from him.

"I trust you slept well," he said.

The word felt loaded with friction.

"Yeah. Well. It's so... It's so quiet here."

"I expect it's very different to what you're used to."

"You could say that."

"Is New York City just like it is in the movies?" Wolf asked.

They were the first words he'd ever spoken directly to her.

"I don't know how to answer that. I mean, in some ways, sure. But there are a lot of things that movies don't show. Like how it smells on a hot summer day."

Sawyer laughed. "Like a bouquet of roses?"

"If there were trash in the roses, yes."

"I can imagine," Wolf said.

He looked different than Sawyer. He was also tall, but his hair was longer, and he had a beard. He was just a little bit darker, his eyes a deep shade of brown, rather than that denim blue.

"Where do you live, Wolf?" This was the first morning she'd managed to get up before they'd headed out, and she was surprised to find him here.

"Oh, I have a cabin just up the road apiece."

"What about Elsie?"

"Stone's throw away from mine. There's a whole lot of cabins and outbuildings nestled in the woods here."

"I see."

"Hey, I'm gonna go get started," Wolf said. "Why don't you do...whatever it is you need to do."

Wolf walked out of the kitchen, and a moment later she heard the front door close. And when he removed his presence it was like the room had filled up with a strange sort of tension. And the conversation with her mother faded to the back of her mind. Everything faded to the back of her mind.

Except Sawyer.

Sawyer, who remembered what kind of coffee she liked.

Sawyer, who had lifted her off the ground like she weighed nothing.

Damn, woman.

What would it be like to have a man like that...want her?

Had Andrew *really* wanted her?

That was the thing that was sitting there in the back of her mind. She dug through the disappointment, the anguish. All the crap that her mother was talking about... If she sifted through all of it, one of the biggest questions was... Why wasn't she enough for him? If he was having doubts about the marriage, that would've also been better. If his issue was commitment, or whatever, then she could have maybe understood it. But he had been intending to go through with the marriage. And that meant... That meant that he must be unsatisfied with her in some other way. And that was the thing that was nagging at her now.

Ten years they'd been together. How many times had he cheated?

And maybe on that front her mother was right. Maybe she should've stayed behind and asked some questions. But it was just all too painful. She hadn't wanted to do it.

Maybe the real problem was she didn't want to have deep conversations. She got mad at her mother for not having them, but there was so much she held back.

But it was hard. Because if she… If she cut herself open completely, exposed herself entirely and…and invited her fiancé, her mother, her friends, to tell her why these things had happened, then she would have to actually listen to the answers.

She didn't know if she could bear it.

Discovering that yet again and always, her best had fallen short.

Maybe that was the real reason starting over with strangers seemed easier.

She could remake herself with him. With no past history or mistakes.

Hide what she wanted to.

Share what she chose to.

"We haven't had a chance to talk much in the past few days," she said, ignoring her doubts. Ignoring the gnawing ache in her chest.

"There's been a lot to do. Plus the other night…well, you seemed pretty tuckered out," he said, his words like a caress. She looked up at him, and she suddenly felt the strangest impulse to put her hand on his face. To trace the line of that scar with her thumb.

She had never felt anything like this before. This instant, incredible draw toward another person. It was so… physical. So raw and real.

But maybe he didn't feel it. Maybe he didn't feel anything of the kind.

She had never considered herself…overly sexual. She liked sex, but it wasn't a major drive in her life. She and Andrew were both busy with work, and they'd been together for a long time, so when things between them had started to taper off she hadn't really questioned it.

But maybe there was something wrong. Maybe there was something wrong with her.

"What kinds of things did you want to talk about?" he asked.

She needed to pull her mind out from the bedroom and back on two important things. She just needed to. Because he wasn't thinking about that right now. And it was short-sighted.

Is it? You came out here to heal.

But she was thinking about marrying the guy. So, whether or not they were compatible in the bedroom was kind of an important question.

Thinking of him in that capacity—in the bedroom—made her palms sweaty and her hands shaky.

Her first time had been an act of rebellion. Part of her initial perhaps-I'll-just-self-destruct response to leaving the ballet academy. It hadn't felt good. It had just felt defiant. She hadn't been in a hurry for a repeat performance after.

After a few months of living down to every expectation her parents had she'd realized this was what her mother had expected. Cigarettes in her purse and bad grades. And that it allowed her to monologue about *all she'd sacrificed for Evelyn*, to throw it back in her face.

And she hadn't been happy, either. So she'd picked herself up and decided to try. But on her own terms.

Had put the lid back on her wildness, because it wasn't leading to happiness, either.

But even then it always felt like there were strings. The two men she'd dated in college before meeting Andrew had been handsome, high achievers. One from a wealthy family, the other there on a scholarship. And she was always consumed with…was she interesting enough or sexy enough? Was she doing what they wanted?

Andrew had stayed with her so at least her insecurities had been quieted by virtue of the fact he'd stayed in the relationship with her.

But he kept you separate, didn't he? Kept your lives separate. Your homes separate. Probably so he could have all the interesting sex he wanted on the side…

She might be wildly attracted to Sawyer in a way that was totally foreign to her, but it didn't mean she'd be anything special to him.

Or that it would actually be amazing when they slept together.

Her experience was that no matter how exciting the foreplay was, it didn't mean the event itself would be as good. That was when she got right in her head.

It brought her back to the academy.

Adjust your body. Are all your angles right? How is your form?

Just shy of brilliance.

Good, but not transformative.

"What exactly are you thinking? I mean, for this. For us," she said.

"I expect you should give it a couple weeks," he said. "Before you make a decision. Because once you make a decision… I can't have you going back on it."

"You said that already."

"I could hire a nanny, if I wanted a nanny. But I don't want that. I want her to have a mother."

"I understand that. I do." She took a breath. "You know I can't guarantee… I can't guarantee things between us. I don't think anyone can. But if I adopt her… If I become her mother, then that's going to be it. I swear to you, I'm never going to leave her."

And on that she was certain. That was what she needed to focus on. The baby.

Her throat got all scratchy, and her eyes got hot.

"My mother called me this morning," she said. She didn't really want to think about her mother right now, but she was. It was inescapable. When she was thinking about becoming a mother herself, how could she avoid it? And they had promised each other honesty.

As if you aren't holding some things back.

Well. Okay, so she was, but wasn't that the point of a new start? She got to decide what the people around her knew; she got to decide to be different. It wasn't lying, it was a choice.

"She doesn't approve of me being here," Evelyn said.

"She wants you to go back home and get married." It wasn't a question.

"Yes. That's exactly what she wants. I just… I've never been enough for her. I've never been anything but a disappointment. That's just… That's it."

"I see."

"I don't know if you do. I have always wanted a child of my own. Children of my own. I just want to love them. The way that they are. Because it shouldn't be that hard, right? To love your own children? To be proud of them? I just want that. I want to give them what I don't have. And I guess that… I guess that leads me to my next question."

"What's that?"

"Children."

"More children?"

"Yes. I want a big family, Sawyer. That is…a big reason that I responded to your ad. After investing ten years of my life in a relationship...having my engagement implode so close to the wedding, being thirty-four... I was crushed because I realized my dreams were just so much farther away than I wanted them to be. And sure, there are a lot of ways to achieve this, I know that. But if I wanted to have a husband, a traditional family...if I'd set about to do things the usual way it would be... I mean, probably at least three years before I was pregnant, and even then that's assuming I met someone very quickly. I want to have a baby. I want...children."

He paused, his expression hard. Unreadable. "I want you to listen to me, and I want you to listen really carefully. If you can't care for Bug the same way you would one of your own, if you can't think of her as one of your own—"

"No," she said. "That's not it. It's not." She closed her eyes, and thought back to the moment she'd seen June Bug's picture for the first time. "She is the most beautiful child I've ever seen. I felt...that night when I saw your ad, I felt connected to her in a way I can't explain. And whatever... Whatever happens between you and me, I..." Their eyes caught. And she remembered last night.

Hell and damnation.

He'd said that. When the two of them had been close.

Because he *did* feel it.

The way he was looking at her now. She took a step toward him, her heart hammering in her throat. And she saw his Adam's apple bob up and down as he swallowed hard.

She wanted to touch him. And she didn't understand how she could feel this way. While they were in the middle of a tricky discussion about parenthood. But it was just all tangled together, and one thing was certain: they were attracted to each other. It was undeniable. Impossible to ignore.

And it made her feel reckless.

Made her want to prove something.

"Sawyer…" She reached out, and her fingertips were hovering over his face when he grabbed her wrist and lowered it.

"No," he said.

"No what?"

"We need to talk."

"We… We *are* talking."

"Don't touch me," he said, his voice firm.

"Oh. Do you not—"

"If you touch me right now, Evelyn, I am going to end up putting this baby down, and dragging you upstairs and having my way with you. Do you understand me?"

His words set a pulse beating hard at the apex of her thighs.

"I think I do understand you."

"That's not going to happen. If I wanted to hook up, I would hook up. We need to decide the terms of our arrangement. And if you want to marry me, then sex will be part of it. But until then, nothing."

"Nothing?"

"No. Because we need to sort things out. And it needs to be logical. Do you understand me?"

"Why?" She felt dumb and slow, because she was completely addled by attraction at this point. Which was embarrassing, but it was just how it was. He seemed…intense, but he didn't seem addled. Which felt a little bit unfair.

"Because. Let me tell you a little something about my past. About my family. My father got my mother pregnant. And you know what the differences between me and my father right about now? I'm willing to do something to try to fix it. I didn't do things right. I was responsible, at least I thought I was, but condoms fail. And that's what happened. I was trying not to be my father, and here I am. But you know what my father did? He didn't learn from his mistakes. He kept getting women pregnant. Over and over. And then he'd bring them back here… He didn't marry them. He brought them back here, and he did a half-assed sort of commitment. Until they left. Until they left him, until they left their own children. I won't do that. Same as I wouldn't force Missy into a marriage or anything, or even try to talk her into one if she didn't want one, because I know how that ends. If you and I get married it's going to be because we want the same things. It's not to be because we lost control or anything like that."

"I understand," she said, her voice scratchy, except she didn't understand. She had been in a logical, staid relationship for ten years and…

Except she hadn't been. Not really. She must not have been, or he wouldn't have… He wouldn't have been cheating. And he had been.

"You need to get to know this place. Get to know Bug. And then tell me if you can make the kind of commitment I need."

"And what do I get to demand?"

"Nothing," he said.

She laughed. "How is that fair?"

"Honey, I'm the one that put the ad in, you answered it. I don't think you're in any position to make demands."

"Listen here, Sawyer Garrett," she said, "I have uprooted my entire life to come out here. So shouldn't I get something?"

"You get the house, you get Bug, you get me."

"Except I don't get you. You're not letting me sample you."

"Did you need to?"

"Thought it might be nice." And if her stomach was hollow with fear and disappointment, with the worry that she wouldn't be enough when he did sample her, well… She wasn't going to think too much about that.

"I'll tell you what. Why don't you come out and do some ranch work with me today?"

"I… You want me to work on the ranch?"

"You proved yourself to be a pretty capable rider the other day."

Because she'd gotten back on the horse.

"I guess I did."

"So, I want you to come ride the range with me."

"Why does that sound like a challenge?"

"I'll tell you why," he said. "It's because…even after all that, part of me doesn't think you're going to stay. I think you're going to get tired of not having your fancy coffee, and your nice boutique stores that sell…well, better boots than that." He indicated her work boots. "And you're going to get upset that you can't get takeout delivered to your house and… Whatever other thing that you like about living in the city. I think you're going to want to go home. You did good this week—you got back on the horse. But that was just this week. If you want to leave…that means there's no point in the two of us getting involved."

"I guess not." Something burned in her breast. Something angry. And maybe this was all to do with the conversation with her mother; she didn't know. The reflection on her former life. "Except I'm not going to leave. I made up my mind before I came out here. I want to start over, and I want to start over here. Now that I've met her, I'm not giving her back."

"We'll see."

"You don't know me. That's the problem. When I set my mind on something I make it happen."

You run away.

She pushed that aside.

This was different. She had all of her emotions tangled up in all those other things. And this wasn't the same.

She didn't love Sawyer.

And he didn't love her. It was a good thing.

A gift.

She wasn't going to desperately try and earn his approval the way she'd been trying to do with her parents. The way she'd been trying to do with her ballet. The way that she failed to do with Andrew. This new life was entirely about her. About capturing what she wanted, not about earning somebody else's approval.

She wasn't going to run. She'd decided that back when she'd fallen off the horse, even if she hadn't realized it.

And it was cemented today by the call with her mother.

This was her chance.

This was what she wanted. And sure, living on the ranch might take some adjustment, but she wasn't some… She wasn't going to run away because she couldn't get an espresso or a pair of designer shoes.

"Take me out to the ranch, then," she said, nodding. "I'm ready to ride again. I'm not afraid. And I'm not running."

"If you say so."

"I do. I've been thinking a lot about new starts, Sawyer, and you're right, I did think about leaving a few times this week. Because I've started from scratch before. I started from scratch here, and I'm only a week in…so why not… why not cut and run? Why fall off horses and be forced to live without oat milk? But I figured out the answer. This is the life I want to build. And you can't build anything if you don't tough out the setbacks."

"We'll see," he said, his face hard. "We'll see. If you're going to come out with me, you better go get something warm."

And she scampered off to do just that.

CHAPTER SEVEN

HE CALLED HIMSELF ten kinds of idiot as he stood out underneath the blanket of fading stars, waiting for Evelyn to come outside.

And come outside she did. Bundled in that same ridiculously expensive-looking coat, and the work boots she'd gotten at the general store. She was wearing a stocking cap with a big pink pom-pom on the top of it. She looked beautiful, and like a comical collision of worlds that called to him in ways he couldn't fully articulate.

"Come with me," he said, opening up the driver side of the truck.

"We're driving?"

"It's a bit of a ways down to the barn." He already had Bug buckled up in her car seat.

"You take her out with you every day?" Evelyn asked.

"Yep," he said.

He knew it wouldn't be practical after a time. But right now, it seemed to work. He went out with the diaper bag and bottles and she slept for a good portion of the time. Waking just to be fed or changed. Eventually, she would want to play. Eventually, she would be too wiggly to do things like this. And that was where Evelyn would come in.

And Evelyn would teach her all the things he couldn't. Like how to cook and whatever else this mysterious soft creature knew to do.

Like how to love.

He'd been honest with her back in the house. About what he wanted. About life here. But he hadn't told her...

Everything.

About himself. About his life. His family.

About the ways this place had broken him.

But there were some things she didn't need to know.

The past wasn't important. What was important was moving forward.

"To get back to the earlier conversation before we were derailed," she said, joining him in the cab of the truck. She closed the door, and he was assaulted by that scent again. All sweet and sugary. When she'd taken a step toward him that morning, he been in perilous danger of forgetting that he had the baby in a front pack.

He *nearly* grabbed her and crushed her to him. Kissed her until neither of them could breathe. But he was sticking by what he'd said.

Passion wasn't what this was about.

Attraction wasn't what it was about.

It really couldn't be about the two of them. Because that would be a recipe for failure.

They needed to get to know each other. Figure out how to bump along. They didn't need to be friends. He knew plenty of married couples who weren't friends.

But they needed to make sure they didn't have anything like passion.

Because that just...blew everything all to hell.

He could still remember the way his parents used to fight. The way they used to hurt each other.

And then the way his dad couldn't look at him after she left. The way his grandmother had been the one to show him unconditional love in a way that Sawyer had never learned to.

He had to try to figure out how to be like her.

"You want more kids," he said.

"Yes. It's what I've always wanted. A big house, loud and full of children and entirely different to the one I grew up in. I was an only child, Sawyer, and let me tell you…being the focus of your parents in that way is not… It can be really hard. To have your parents' dreams rest so squarely on your shoulders. It doesn't have to be right away. I will be happy, more than happy, to focus on June Bug for a while. I just want to know it's not off the table."

He couldn't reconcile that desire with what he knew about the life she'd had before. "All right, if you always wanted all that, then why don't you have it yet? Why were you living in the city? With a man, for ten years before marrying him?"

She sighed heavily. "I built a business with my friends. And it was really successful."

"That doesn't happen by accident," he said.

"No. You're not wrong. It wasn't an accident. It was something I worked really hard for. I wanted… I wanted to do that, too. I wanted to prove that I *could*. It was important to me, because I had to show that I was capable of it. But the family was next. I was getting ready to take a step back when Andrew and I got married. We waited on the marriage in large part because we were waiting for the business to get to a certain place. We had it set up so that everything was working primarily remotely, and we had reached a level of success that meant more delegating, that we were…faces of the company more than anything else so… So… Anyway."

"Sorry, it's not that I'm not… I don't know that I sound

all that modern. I know that women can have careers and families and things like that. It's just…" He wasn't quite sure what to say, which wasn't typical for him. If he wanted to speak, he did; if he didn't, he didn't. But in truth he hadn't given a whole lot of thought to women and careers because…

Well, he didn't know *anyone* like her. Gender had nothing to do with it. Now, the women who helped work Four Corners were strong as hell and he respected their ideas and contributions as much as any of the men.

But again, not something spoken or thought about. It just was. But at Four Corners, it was all hands on deck, always. Everyone did their part, and every part mattered.

But it felt grounded in where they were, who they were. She was an enigma. A woman who'd set out to build something that wasn't already there. She'd chosen it. And then she'd gone and chosen something totally different.

"I just really wanted to prove that I could," she said. "That I could have every success. All of it."

And that he did understand. Because there was an edge in her voice that suggested it wasn't just about her, or what she'd wanted, but about *showing* someone else. "Your mom?"

"She left her career to raise me. Career isn't even…the right word. She left her whole identity behind for me. She was a ballerina. The position she was in was so cutthroat, and she didn't have an easy pregnancy. And her position in the industry didn't wait for her. She could never get back to where she was but she was sure that I would have the same talent." She sighed. "It doesn't matter."

"You're a dancer?"

The slight pause said more than any combination of words could have. "I'm not anymore."

"Right. Well…" But his brain had shorted out, because now he was imagining her dancing. Except, if he were honest, his version of it probably wasn't the elegant sort of thing that she actually did. But he knew he'd like to see it.

"Anyway. This is just… It's what I always wanted. And I don't want to let go of something. At least not without knowing that's what I'm doing."

He cleared his throat. "It would be nice for Bug to have some siblings."

"So you're not opposed to it?"

He looked at her, long and hard. He wasn't opposed to making children with her, that was for damn sure.

"I never thought I'd have children," he said. "Not any. Because I didn't want… Any of that. My dad made it look like an endless trauma. But if you promise me…yeah. I already have a kid, I guess."

She frowned at him, her blue eyes narrowing. "You're happy about it, right?"

He didn't know what word he used to describe what he was. *Happy* didn't seem right. Being entrusted with this tiny life seemed way too heavy to be called anything like happy. All he knew was that the minute he'd first held her in his arms he'd known there was no question of ever giving her up. It had been just like that. There'd been no real decision-making about it.

"It's just who I am now," he said.

She nodded slowly. "I understand."

They drove on in silence out toward the barn, and when he got out of the car, he put Bug into the front pack. Then headed to the stable. Wolf had already been and gone, probably off to drive the cattle out of the north pasture with some of the ranch hands.

He planned to take Evelyn off grid, which under normal

circumstances might have created a temptation too sweet to resist. But the baby made a good buffer.

Anyway, he'd made up his mind.

When he made up his mind he didn't go back, no matter how tempting.

"Come this way," he said. She was gawking at the barn.

"This is huge," she said, gazing around the metal building.

"The operation is huge. We do primarily beef, and we have about one hundred and fifty employees helping us work the land. You have to go about five miles to get from our house over to the McClouds' house. It's eight miles down to the Sullivans' from there. We're about six miles off from the Kings'. Just across the way there."

"It's bigger than the town," she said. "I didn't fully realize. Not even when we went to the lake."

He nodded. "Yep. Bigger than the town."

"You've always been responsible for… So much. The livelihoods of so many people and… You could never walk away, could you? No matter how hard it gets."

Her words hit him in a strange fashion. "No. But I wouldn't want to, anyway."

"You wouldn't?"

He thought of his mother. Of all her requests to have him visit that had just been empty.

"No. Look, life gives you what it gives you. You can either take the gift, and take the shit as it comes, or… I don't know, I guess you don't. But you let people down. It's not in me to do that."

"I can tell," she said softly.

"Don't go turning me into a hero, Evelyn. I'm just me."

"Why don't you want me to make you a hero?"

"I'll disappoint you. And then you might want to leave."

The words were a lot more hollow than he'd meant them to be. "But you can't leave. Not if you make my daughter love you. Do you understand me? If you make my daughter *your* daughter. If you take care of her, you can never leave."

Not like he'd done. He hadn't been here when it had counted.

Not like his mother had done, when she'd left him without a backward look.

He remembered that day. Waking up. Four years old and calling for his mother. Calling and calling.

He could remember Wolf doing the same thing when he was about six. And he could remember his own, dead-eyed response that haunted him to this day.

It was a gift that Elsie couldn't remember her mom. At least Sawyer had always thought so.

"She's gone, don't be a baby. Quit crying. It's what they do. They leave."

"I swear to you," Evelyn said, cutting into the memory. "I'm not going to abandon her."

"Good. Like I said, we'll see if you're still here after two weeks."

"You're cynical, aren't you?"

"Why do you sound surprised by that?"

"I guess I figured a man who put an ad out there looking for a wife was maybe a little bit romantic."

He shook his head. "I'm not romantic. I'm not soft, and I'm not easy. I'll do my best to not be impossible to live with. But don't go turning me into anything I'm not. Honesty. That's what I promise you."

"I can work with that." But he could see that it really wasn't what she expected. Well, too damn bad. He was who he was.

"Let's get riding."

He got the horses out, and tacked them up quickly, leading the more docile of the two over to Evelyn. "He's a pretty easy mount. Soft mouth, responsive, but not jumpy."

"As opposed to the last one who had a fear of snakes?" she asked.

"Yeah, this one's just afraid of the dark, so it should be fine."

"Ha," she said.

She got herself up on the horse, no hesitation.

"So, you went to horse camp?" he asked, circling his horse around the back of hers.

"Yes," she said. "A couple of times. When I was on break from the academy."

"The academy," he repeated.

He didn't know what the hell that meant. Sounded fancy. Certainly fancier than anything he'd ever done.

"Yeah," she said. "The ballet academy I went to."

"You're going to have to explain that to me," he said, leading the way with his horse, and she seemed to take his cue without any hesitation.

"This is a western saddle?" she asked.

"Yes," he said.

He looked back and noticed that she was holding her reins in English style.

"One hand," he said, gesturing to the way he was holding them.

"I think I'll take one new thing at a time."

"Fair enough." He cleared his throat. "So, explain the academy to me."

They took a well-worn trail that would lead them up to one of the far pastures. The ride would take them along the river, and it was one of the prettier routes on the property—at least, in his opinion.

"It was a school, specifically designed around dance. Though we did all of our academic subjects there, too, plus comportment. All girls."

"Well," he said. "That's something."

"It was extremely focused. My mother went there. She was one of the youngest principal dancers ever in the New York City Ballet. She graduated early from the academy. And then she… Well, she got pregnant. With me. All she ever wanted was to get me in that school. They start accepting pupils at eleven. So that's when I started."

"Did you live there?"

She nodded. "It was a boarding school. The hall that we slept in was this old, beautiful house. It really was something. Really lovely. I loved it. Until I started hating it."

"Why did you hate it?"

She hesitated for a moment. "You seem like the kind of man who's used to getting exactly what he wants."

"How did you guess?" That was an oversimplification. It was what his brother would say, too. But, of course, there were a great many things that he hadn't gotten in his life that he wanted pretty desperately. It was just that he was good at making a new route. Something around the debris. That, he would say, was his actual skill.

"Well, I was used to getting what I wanted. I grew up in a privileged family. And I was good at things. I was extremely good at dance, very good in school. And then I went to this elite academy were everybody was special. Everyone was gifted. And it turned out I wasn't actually as gifted as the people that surrounded me. And I certainly wasn't more gifted than any of them. It was…disheartening, to say the least."

She paused. For a long time. He wondered about all the

things that should have filled that silence. The unspoken words.

"I sort of…imploded when I left. I couldn't be the best, so I decided…why try at anything? But that was when I discovered I wasn't ambitious just to please my mother and the thought of becoming a high school dropout and possible burnout didn't appeal to me at all. So I decided to find success on my own terms. I got my grades up, stopped flirting with boys and with illegal substances and I… I did well."

"And you started doing organization?"

"Well, Kioni, Hollyn and I were roommates at the same university and we were all a very particular sort of type A. And given my renewed desire to take some control over my life and my success…it began with our apartment. It turns out, I like putting things in bins, and organizing them by color, and many other people are interested in learning how to do it. Between the three of us, we took that experience and business classes and made something…big. Successful."

"These are the same friends who all knew…about the cheating fiancé or were cheating with him?"

"Yeah, the very same," she said. "And it's… I did that. I had a pinnacle of professional success, and I guess in a lot of ways, I reached the top. I walked away with a decent amount of money. And I was ready to move to the next phase of my goals, anyway. I want to be a mother. I want a big family. And I want… I want for my children to never feel like I did. That because I failed at something I wasn't…good enough."

"I figure trying to counteract your own parents' bad parenting isn't the worst starting point," he said. "At least I hope so."

She laughed.

They lapsed into silence again, the only sound the horses' hooves, the wind in the trees, the birds chirping.

"So, where did you go to school?"

"Here. On the ranch."

"Oh, right. Elsie mentioned that. That you all were taught on the ranch."

"In a one-room schoolhouse."

"You're joking. I didn't know anything like that still existed."

"It does. It was… I don't know. I didn't really ever have much use for that kind of…" He realized he was about to say *book learning*. And that he probably sounded like a bad country cliché. But it was how he felt.

For him, true knowledge was in the land.

He had wanted to learn everything about cattle. About the seasons. About when things grew and when they died. About when to let the ground put forth, and when to let it go fallow.

When to move his cattle to different pastures. When the grass was sweetest where, and how that impacted the taste of the meat.

Those were the kinds of things that mattered to him. They were the kinds of things that still mattered. Not that he didn't value his education. In the end, he was glad he'd read a few books. Glad he had a pretty solid understanding of math and science, because while he might not have appreciated it as a kid, he could see how those things helped him now. Especially running a business. But he certainly hadn't placed a lot of value on education at the time.

"It's all very Laura Ingalls," she commented.

"That's one of the books I read," he said.

She laughed. "Well, we have that in common, then."

And it struck him as strange that he had probably exchanged more words with this woman than he had with... Well, very many people besides the ones he routinely shared his life with. He and Hunter and Wolf could certainly shoot the breeze.

But she'd told him something about her past that hurt. And he couldn't remember the last time someone had shared something like that with him. If ever. He already knew the kinds of shit the people around him had been through. And he didn't talk to the women that he hooked up with.

"This is beautiful," she said. The words were hushed like she'd walked into a church, the reverence in her tone shocking. He looked behind himself, looked at her face, which was filled with wonder. Her blue eyes wide, her mouth dropped open. And he looked up, following the trajectory of her gaze. At the tall, proud pines that reached toward the crystal blue sky. At the river that ran alongside them, wide and fast flowing here, white where it moved over the rocks, the rushing sound a constant backing track to his whole life. And he took a breath. Of that fresh, damp air, laden with pine and the sort of damp wood smell that came with a fast-moving river. Unlike anything else, and sort of difficult to define.

And he felt like he was seeing it for the first time, filtered through that wonderment in her eyes, and it hit him somewhere deep and true.

Because this place was part of him. And he respected it, loved it. But some days, he didn't see it. Not really. In the way you didn't see your own nose, he supposed. Because it was just there. Because it was inevitable.

But there wasn't a blade of grass here that was inevitable to Evelyn Moore, and that was a miracle that he hadn't anticipated.

And something turned over inside of him when he realized it was the same for Bug. That everything was new for her, too. That the whole world was something she saw for the first time. That him riding out with her every day was making this place a part of her DNA, the same as it was his.

The same as she was his.

There was an enormity to the moment that he just wasn't used to. Because he had lived a life of quiet routine. For a long damned time. It was the way he liked it. Things for him had been pretty much the same for years. He got up, he did his work. Some nights he went out, but even that was full of routine. The same bar, full of the same people he already knew. He ordered the same beer, because he liked it, and why mess with a good thing?

Hadn't been answerable to anyone or anything, his only master the land that he worked, and the cattle that provided him with a livelihood. But this was altogether different. Wholly new and utterly singular. And it made it hard to catch his breath in the moment.

He was a man who didn't wonder much about the mysteries of the world. Because he knew all of the truth of his own world. Had accepted already the things you couldn't know—what the weather would do, if a calf would be born healthy. And he surrendered himself to the rhythms of the times and the seasons, the rising and falling of the sun.

He lived his life by those rhythms.

But he'd never had a child. He'd never had a wife. And he'd never ridden along a trail with a woman who was practically a stranger and listen to her talk about her life. It was unusual for him to feel like he didn't quite know what to do next. But he didn't quite know what to do next.

"So, what are we doing?"

"Well," he said, finding his feet again. Finding himself.

"Wolf's gone down to move the cows into the lower pasture. I figured we'd head out here and look for some stragglers. I know where they tend to go. Sometimes they resist being moved."

"Stragglers," she said. "Well, that sounds a little more exciting than what I was anticipating."

"Hopefully it won't be exciting, and it'll all just go easy. My aim is to not have an exciting day when I can help it."

Silence lapsed between them for a moment.

"So... Do you kill the cows?" she asked.

"Yeah," he said.

"It doesn't... It doesn't bother you?"

"No. Do you eat meat?"

"Well, yes," she said.

"Me, too. I have to say I sort of like knowing where my food comes from, beginning of the process to the end."

"But you take care of them."

"Yes. I take care of them. They take care of me. These animals are my livelihood. The meat, the leather. Everything. I respect them. I love them." And he realized it was true. Down to his soul. "Just like this land is part of me. It sustains me. I do my best to do right by it. When I die they'll bury me here. Then I can become grass and the cows can eat me, too. Circle of life."

"I think there's a cartoon about that," she said.

"Hey," he said. "I'm being serious. But yeah. We handle all of it. It's the most economical thing to do. Process what we can ourselves. Some of it we take down to the weigh station, and have it done there, because that's going to go out to the grocery stores. It needs to be evaluated a different way. Gotta be certified by the USDA. It's costly, and a lot of the smaller operations can't afford it. But I'm proud of the fact that we are able to keep up our quality and meet those standards. This is a family farm. Those are more and more rare. The ranch was dying under the care of our parents."

"Dying?"

"They all quit working together. Lost their sense of community. Gus McCloud, myself, Fia Sullivan and Landry King decided to change that. We got together, talked it all over and made a plan for a new system where we pooled money and resources, shared profits around. Pretty soon, everyone was on board."

"So are you all friends?"

"More or less," he said.

"What does that mean?"

"You don't work land together for generations without there being some…scandals, conflicts. Things happen."

"Like?"

"Well, there have been affairs. Though that's generations back now. But there was a Sullivan who ran off with a King some time ago—of course after they were married to other people. For the most part, there hasn't been intermarriage, though. None that's produced children. None of us are related. Which frankly I find to be pretty shocking, all things considered. Not like romantic partners aren't thick on the ground out here."

"That is something," she said.

"Yeah, I mean, we all more or less get along. Arizona King is prickly as a cactus to everyone, but it isn't personal. Fia Sullivan hates Landry King, and probably wouldn't cross the street to spit on him if he was on fire."

"Why?"

"I don't rightly know. Nelly Foster—whose mother was our teacher—used to hate Tag McCloud, but now they're engaged."

"Really?"

"Yes. So, I guess things change around here. But they definitely change slowly."

"Except Bug."

"Yeah," he said. "That was a big change. Pretty quick."

"Tell me about that," she said.

"What?" he asked.

"Her mother. You said she was a bar hookup."

The idea of talking to Evelyn about Missy didn't sit well with him. But he'd promised honesty, and she was asking.

"That was oversimplifying it. Missy and I... We had an arrangement. For a time. I'm not... I'm not one... Look, Hunter, Hunter McCloud, he's my best friend. He spreads it around. He likes to go out to the bars in the bigger towns and find a different woman whenever the mood strikes him. I just think that sounds like a lot of work. It's hard to meet someone who wants to have this kind of life. It's tough to *meet* someone when you live this kind of life. I have to be up before dawn, I have to go to bed pretty early. One night a week I go out..."

"It's just easier to have someone waiting for you that one night a week. Preplanned."

"Exactly. So Missy was my...preplanned engagement there for a while. I knew she didn't want to stay in Pyrite Falls. She really didn't. When she got pregnant with Bug she... She didn't want her."

"But you did."

"Yeah. Like I said, I'm not sure *happiness* is the right word. Or... Want. It's just... In that moment I knew things had to be different. That I had to be different. Missy and I had a bit of a deal. I agreed to help her get started somewhere else."

"Where did she end up going?"

"Chicago," he said, his humor about that still hitting that same, bitter place.

"Oh."

"Same place my mother went. I suggested it." Just thinking about Chicago made him feel bleak and washed out as the winter there.

"Why? You wanted to keep all the absentee parents there?"

He shrugged. "I guess so."

"You weren't in love with her."

He shook his head. He thought back to that moment when she showed up at his door, the mascara all streaked down her face, her hands shaking. And he'd felt *something*. He'd been concerned, that was for sure. But he hadn't felt... Well, much of anything. She'd told him she was pregnant and he hadn't felt emotion so much as a grim determination. That was when he'd offered marriage.

She'd said no.

They'd talked for hours that night. About what she wanted and wished for, about what she didn't want. And he'd realized, as she'd told him that she wanted to go through with the pregnancy but that she was thinking adoption, that he'd...

That he'd wanted to be a father to his child.

"Did you... Did you keep seeing her while she was pregnant?"

In this instance he figured "seeing" was a euphemism for "sleeping with."

"No," he said. "No. I... I took care of her. Paid all the expenses associated with it. I tried to do the right thing. After doing what was clearly kind of the wrong thing."

"I think it's better," she said. "That Missy made sure she didn't have regrets about her life. My mom had a lot

of regrets about hers. She *still* does. And it's really painful. To be the source of your own parent's disappointment.
You can't live out your dreams through a child. All it does
is hurt everyone involved."

There was something soothing about those words. An
affirmation he hadn't known he'd needed. It helped him
shake loose the rock of bitterness that was sitting in his
chest. That anger he felt on behalf of Bug that was so
deeply ingrained in him, even if he did know that letting
Missy go was the right thing to do.

"I just didn't want Bug to be hurt later. I'd rather she
didn't remember her. Maybe that's wrong."

"There's no… There's no clear right or wrong here. It
was a difficult situation, and you did the best you could.
Though most people don't consider putting an ad out for a
wife to be a viable solution."

"More people should try to do things the old-fashioned
way," he said. Aware, yet again, that there was a deep sort
of irony in his moral posturing when he had managed to get
someone pregnant that he wasn't married to. His grandfather would've tanned his hide for that. His grandfather had
been a steady figure in his life. So had his grandmother.
Losing them had been the real tragedy. Much more so than
his mother leaving. They'd gone peacefully close together.
And he'd been devastated.

He swallowed.

His grandmother especially, losing her had…calcified
something in him.

They rode up through the trees, the trail winding tight
around some big pines, and that was when he saw them.
Two little black juveniles, tripping around in the foliage.
And this was the curse of open range. They had fences to
a point, but not everywhere, and in general, the animals

roamed. But sometimes they had to move the herd to a new pasture. Usually staying in the general area they'd been deposited.

But these guys had missed the memo that today was a big move, and they were away from the rest of the cattle.

"There you go," he said. "We're going to have to drive them down with the rest of them."

"We?"

"Yeah," he said. "It'll be fine."

"But I don't know what to do."

"You know how to ride. Follow my lead." He rode up to the side of the beasts, flanking them.

"Follow me—we're going to loop around behind them, that ought to get them moving in the right direction."

"I did not know that I was going to be involved in ranch work," she said, coming up beside him.

"Yeah, what would you be doing if you were back home?"

"Organizing something. I told you, that's how I control the whole world. By putting things in bins, and putting those bins into smaller bins."

"Does that work with emotions?"

She laughed. "Yes, I find it does. Though that might be a displacement exercise, if I'm honest."

He maneuvered his horse around back of the animals, and she followed, just as he instructed. It was then the sleepy little steers seem to recognize that they were being shoved along. And they started to move out of the trees.

"There you go," he said.

He picked up the pace to a trot, and he could hear Evelyn keeping up with him in the rear. He held Bug tightly with one hand, bracing her as he smoothed the horse into a gallop, keeping up behind the animals.

The gait was smooth, and the baby wasn't overly jostled, he made sure of that. He was convinced that Bug liked it. Oftentimes it was the one thing that would settle her down. He didn't take her for drives—he took her out for rides.

They were in an open field now, headed down to the pasture where he knew the other cattle would be. And it didn't take long for him to see the other animals, and Wolf and about five of their employees out on horseback in the middle of them. The cows were moving on their own now, happily taking themselves to where the rest of their herd was. He stopped on the edges of them, breathing hard, and Evelyn came to a stop behind him.

"Found a couple stragglers," he said.

"Where all did you go?" Wolf asked.

"South timber. Along the river trail."

"She helped?" Wolf indicated Evelyn behind him.

"Yes," Evelyn said. "She did. See, I might actually be a real cowgirl before you know it."

Wolf laughed. And Sawyer shot him a warning glare. "Sure," Wolf said, composing himself. "A real cowgirl."

Sawyer stole a glance at her. She looked nothing like a cowgirl. Her jacket was far too fancy, for one. For another that knit cap was ridiculous. Her blond hair was loose and was now in a tangle around her shoulders. Elsie would have put her hair in a ponytail or a braid to keep it out of her way.

Not that you told her you'd be running cattle down.

In fairness, no, he hadn't. But still.

He realized right then that he didn't want or need her to be a cowgirl, though. He was fascinated enough by who she was, and that was a hell of a thing. She was different. It had been a long time since he'd met anyone substantially different from himself. Hell, had he ever? There were small-town locals, different than him because they weren't entrenched in ranch life. And then there were ranchers, like him. Levi Granger, who had a piece of land adjacent to them, and was a mean, unfriendly cuss. But, of course, Sawyer would still have a beer with him.

But that wasn't different. She was singular in this place. This wild, rugged space. And he wanted to reach out and touch her as much as he wanted to turn away from her.

Both impulses were equally strong.

"You did good," he said instead, aware his voice was gruff. Aware he sounded more like his father than he would have ever liked.

She wrinkled her nose. "Thank you."

"It was a compliment," he said.

He felt defensive. Mostly because he didn't know exactly how to talk to this kind of woman.

Did he really know how to talk to women? Suddenly, all of the interactions in his life seemed unbearably simple. He hadn't been trying to figure out how to know somebody. And he'd been certain that this would be easy. Because it was supposed to be void of emotion, and uncomplicated by nature as a result. But this... This whole situation where he had to care. Where he had to care about whether or not he said the right thing or came across in the right way... Well, that was uncharted territory.

Honesty.

Just stick with honesty.

"Oh, I take it as a compliment," she said. "You just sounded very surprised."

"No offense," he said. "But you're... You know."

"I'm what?"

"A city girl."

Her lips tugged into a reluctant smile. "I suppose I am." The air felt thick between them, which was strange, because the air was just normal. All around them the way that it always was. And his brother was watching them.

"Well, I'll take you back to the house," he said. "Maybe give you a chance to…get acclimated to the place."

"You can leave Bug with me," she said.

It was the first time she had called the baby something other than June.

"Yeah, all right," he said.

He looked over at his brother and nodded. "I'll be back."

And then he and Evelyn set off toward home. And there was something companionable riding beside her. And thinking of that place as home. A place they might share together.

Maybe this was going to work out better than he'd imagined, after all.

CHAPTER EIGHT

"I'LL BE BACK at sundown."

He had driven her and Bug back up to the house, and now she was standing in the doorway, holding the baby, feeling intoxicated by the smell of him. By the dark stubble on his face. By the urge to run her fingers along the edge of his square jaw. She wanted to tell him to stay. Wanted to grab hold of the collar of his jacket and cling to him. But fortunately, having her hands full of baby prevented her from doing that.

He had said no. *No sex until marriage.*

It made her want to *laugh.*

Sure, she had come out for a simple sweet movie, in theory, but she hadn't anticipated the attraction that burned between them. And it wasn't like he was making that declaration because he was an old-fashioned gentleman or anything like that. It was just that he wanted to make sure their connection was…something other than the physical. And she sort of understood that. Understood that he was coming from a place of his own damage.

But she…

Well, she was not feeling very confident in herself and it was…

It wasn't great.

The gift of Andrew cheating on her was something that

kept on giving. Heartbreak at first. Betrayal. The anger of disrupted plans.

And a sense that maybe she wasn't enough for him. He'd needed to get sex from another woman.

Maybe she wasn't appealing enough. And she *hated* that.

She'd had therapy to get to a place where she was okay with her body.

Because when puberty had hit her, it had hit hard. She'd gone from effortlessly conforming to the lines and shapes required for ballet to having hips and breasts and a layer of padding on her stomach that hadn't been there before.

And all around her were these other girls who seemed slim by accident. No matter how many pieces of pizza they ate or how many handfuls of candy they took out of a bowl during a slumber party.

Work harder. You aren't working hard enough.

That's what the dance instructors had said. If Evelyn were putting in the effort the other girls were, she would be thinner.

You're getting a little round, dear.

Her mother, upon Evelyn's visits home, had always expressed concerns.

That shape won't make the right lines.

Control was Evelyn's friend and always had been. Control made her steps perfect. Made her movements graceful.

Control.

So she'd controlled her portions. Smaller and smaller. Organization of food. And she'd begun to get smaller, too.

And then her period had stopped and she'd passed out during a rehearsal and had lost her role, anyway. And what was the point of it?

Then she didn't *"have the stamina."*

That had been the last straw. She'd been breaking her

body to try and rise to the top and she still couldn't manage it.

That was when she'd left.

Feeling ugly and misshapen and weak.

It was one reason she had hurriedly cast her virginity off in high school.

Somebody had wanted her body for *something*. Just as it was. Something she could do. And it had seemed like a great way to deal with the shame and deep sense of inadequacy that she clung to from her time in dance.

And now all those feelings were rearing their ugly heads, and she wanted... She just *wanted*.

But he had to go out and work and she was going to stay here. And instead of grabbing him she rubbed the back of the baby's downy head. "All right. I'll see you then."

And as soon as he left, she determined that she was going to make some meat loaf.

There was a little crib for Bug that she had observed was meant to move between the living room and the kitchen, and she put the baby down in it, after placing it in the kitchen, and began to hunt around for what she would need to accomplish the meat loaf. She was right in assuming that there was beef.

There was an entire freezer full of it.

She spent ages perusing recipes on the internet and studying them to make sure all the moves she would make today would be perfect.

No mistakes, no burned dinners.

She knew where everything was, and she had already started the process of putting things together in way that had a better flow for her, but there was still more to do. She had bought the most recent groceries—or scavenged them from the garden—so she knew where all the food was.

She chopped onions and herbs, prepared bread dough and set it to rise.

It took her four hours, but she finally got the meat loaf into the oven. And the kitchen was pristine.

She wanted to order some products, bins and other organizational tools, to get everything into a place that she would like it, but the problem was that the things she would like to use would have to come from her old company. Which she had gotten rid of her stake in, and which she didn't particularly want to support.

She went and started looking at the items online of a competing brand. They weren't what she would choose. Because they weren't what she had helped design.

This was a whole situation where she was cutting off her nose to spite her face.

But, oh, well. She had taken her nose out to Oregon. She had removed herself from the situation. She was just going to have to make do with a few things that were different than the way they would've been in her old life.

And she had to admit that her meat loaf smelled pretty good. But she had taken great pains to make sure it had an amount of seasoning in it that would turn it into something other than a mushy brick of meat. She'd found a recipe online that had sounded persuasive, and if Sawyer liked it…

The idea made her stomach turn over.

She took a deep breath, and set about peeling potatoes. There would be mashed potatoes either way. And whether or not she liked the meat loaf, there would at least be some simple carbohydrates to get her through. She had no problem eating an entire bowl of mashed potatoes all on her own.

Of course, she hadn't asked him if Elsie and Wolf would

be joining them. But they did live in their own houses. And really, there should be enough food either way.

She started to pace. June Bug woke up and needed some attention, and that provided her with the distraction. But then the baby went back to sleep, and twilight began to fall, and Sawyer still wasn't home.

She stood at the kitchen window, looking down at the river below, at the way the moon skipped over the rippling water. And then she heard the front door close. Only one set of footsteps, which hopefully meant it was just Sawyer. Her stomach twisted.

She turned around, gripping one of the dining chairs, looking at the dinner that she had spread out on the table. Green salad, mashed potatoes, rolls and meat loaf.

And then there he was, standing in the doorway, wearing the same thing he had on earlier—of course—his black cowboy hat, black T-shirt and snug jeans. And she felt like she was having an out of body experience. Those broad shoulders and chest, his narrow waist, muscular thighs... She took a moment to pause and appreciate his hands. Battered and masculine, so very large. His forearms, corded with muscle, a large scratch on the left one, running from his elbow down across to his wrist.

"What happened?" she asked.

"Huh? What?"

"Your arm," she said.

"Oh," he said, dismissive. "Nicked on some barbed wire. Not a big deal."

"It looks nasty to me," she said.

"Yeah, I should probably clean it up." He paused at the table. "Meat loaf," he said.

"Yes," she said.

"Where's Bug?"

"Just in her crib."

He nodded. He disappeared for a minute, and she heard him speaking in soft, low tones, quiet and soothing enough that she knew he wouldn't wake the baby up. She heard his footsteps off down the hall, and she had a feeling he was headed off to clean out that scratch. She finished setting the table, and opened up the fridge, regarding the contents. She took a beer out of the fridge and opened that for him.

And when he returned, she held it out. "Drink?"

"Thank you," he said, regarding her with a strange light in his eye.

"You're welcome. Did you find anymore...stragglers?" There, she could make conversation with this cowboy she was planning to marry. She could.

"No, the rest of it all went pretty smooth. Why exactly did you make meat loaf?"

She attempted to smile very innocently. "I'm on good behavior," she said.

"Well, good to know."

"I believe you also said to me that I would make you meat loaf whether I liked it or not."

"So you decided to make sure you were in control."

"Maybe."

She caught herself biting her lower lip, and she realized that she was flirting shamelessly with him, which was kind of funny, because she couldn't remember the last time she'd ever flirted with anybody. It made butterflies take flight in her stomach, made her feel... It made her feel young. Like there was possibility all around her. Like she really was in a different space. Not just geographically, but emotionally.

"Sit down," she said.

He did, at the head of the table. She hesitated for a moment, but then took her seat to his right. She watched as he filled his plate up with food, and kept on watching as he took his first bite. He closed his eyes, a low, masculine sound of pleasure vibrating through him. And she felt an answering echo of it inside of her. His T-shirt stretched tight over his chest as he leaned back in his chair, and she felt something else flutter, lower inside of her.

Desire.

She really did want him like she'd never wanted anyone else before. She wanted to sweep the rolls and mashed potatoes to the side and launch herself over the table into his arms. And that she would take him over a good yeast roll really did say something.

What would it be like to be married to him? To have access to him anytime she wanted?

Alternatively, what if he wasn't that into her? He'd said that he was attracted to her, but...

She kept on watching him while he ate.

"This is amazing," he said, looking up at her.

"So did I pass this particular bride test?"

"None of it is a test," he said. "It's just about making sure that...nothing implodes. Or that you're not desperate to get back home."

It was laughable. Getting back to New York was the last thing she wanted. She just wasn't interested, not at all.

Struggling here was better than the life she knew there. She was confident, at least in that, at this point.

Not because she hated it or anything like that. It would always be part of her. It was her home. At least, it had been, for a very long time, and that wasn't just a race because she had a bad experience, or because she was...running away. It was just that she felt like she had exhausted the possibilities that were available to her there. And she hadn't even begun to scratch the surface of the ones that existed here.

Today she had…herded cattle. Which was something she could honestly say she never would've thought she'd do. Or wanted to do. But she'd done it. And there was something… There was something incredibly healing about that. That she'd done something she had never thought she could do. And then she'd made meat loaf. She felt… Entirely removed from the life that she had been living before. And the fact that she had the capacity to be this different, to do these things… It made her feel…powerful.

But one thing that was really beginning to concern her, the one thing she didn't think she could stand, was marrying him without the assurance that he was as into her she was him.

Physically.

She didn't know the man, so it wasn't like she had an emotional attachment to him. Though she had enjoyed talking with him earlier today. It had been harder than that, talking to Andrew on a good day by the time the relationship ended.

You haven't seen Sawyer on a bad day. You were with Andrew for ten years. And it wasn't always hard or bad.

All right. Fair point.

But she didn't have to know him to know that she wanted to jump him.

"Are you going to eat?" he asked, his eyes appraising her.

"Yes," she said, taking a large scoop of mashed potatoes from the bowl.

"You have to have some meat loaf."

"I do not," she said.

"You need protein."

"I like carbs," she said.

And the ability to put carbs on her plate without feeling guilt was one of the great triumphs of her life. With therapy, she had managed to separate her weight from her virtue, and her value, and that had been a difficult thing to do.

At this point her main goal in life was that she not have to buy new clothes simply because her old ones didn't fit. And she felt like that was pretty reasonable. She actually didn't usually think about it.

But finding out her decade-long relationship wasn't actually secure, and being on the verge of sleeping with someone new, plus recounting her time at the academy earlier today…

Even though she hadn't talked about her issues with disordered eating, it had forced her to think of it.

"Have some of the meat loaf."

She finally gave in, and when she took a bite, she had to admit that it was all right. It still wasn't going on the list of her favorite foods, but she had managed to make something that was edible to her. A good thing, all things considered.

"I'll be able to make it sometimes," she said. "I can stomach it. Which is good. Because you know compromise is important in a mar…" She let that trail off.

"Well, I certainly wouldn't starve."

She looked at him, and she suddenly felt flushed. Honestly, his *waiting till marriage* mandate seemed like a waste. They were two grown adult people sharing a house together alone—save for a sleeping baby—and there were some very interesting things they could probably find to do with each other.

Insecurity pricked at the back of her throat, making it feel tight. She had never slept with a man she didn't know before. She had slept with men she wasn't *in love* with, sure, but in the last ten years she had only been with a man she knew, and very well. And she wasn't exactly feeling superconfident in her charms. The idea of being with him…

It was exciting. Almost by virtue of the fact that they were strangers.

They finished up dinner in relative silence, and when they were done, he cleared the table, and started to do the dishes. She let him. Sitting and watching his broad back as he did so. He didn't complain, didn't say anything about the fact that he'd been out riding all day or anything like that. Maybe that wouldn't last. Maybe eventually he would expect her to take more on board. He opened up one of the cabinets.

"This is different," he said.

"Right. Sorry. I spent some time organizing. So, there are zones."

"I can figure it out," he said. "Looks good."

Something in her just...ignited. She wanted him. And it was beyond anything. Beyond sense or reason, or even why she was here. Which was why she suddenly realized something. Something deep and very important.

She was going to seduce Sawyer Garrett. Before marriage.

It was only after dinner last night that he realized he hadn't mentioned to her that the town hall meeting was coming up. That it was, in fact, today. He'd been planning on his contribution being beer, anyway, but if he'd talked to Evelyn earlier, perhaps it could have been something better. Dinner the night before had been amazing. More than amazing. Of course, it hadn't been food that he was hungry for, not in the end. Sure, it was amazing meat loaf, but mostly he'd been thinking about getting her naked and laying her across the table and having her for dessert. He hadn't, though, because he stood by his convictions. About what he thought was best for them. And for this arrangement.

And he found he wasn't neutral on the subject of it working out. He'd been worried, those first few days, but…but she'd gotten back on the horse. She was great with Bug. The house looked amazing, the food was delicious…

And you want her.

No. He wasn't going to make it about that.

Of course, he was coming back to the house early because given that it was late spring, and getting warm outside, they had decided to have the town hall in the middle of the day, down at Sullivan's Point, and he had to come back to get the beer.

And there was Evelyn, sitting on the couch, holding Bug. She was looking down at her, and talking to her, her face lit up in a wide smile. She looked up when she saw him, and her expression changed. And then the color in her cheeks mounted, and he felt an answering heat in his own veins. "I wasn't expecting you," she said. "Did you need lunch?"

"No," he said. "Thanks. I… Actually, I forgot to tell you that there's a town hall meeting today."

"Oh," she said.

"It's not a big deal. I just… I needed to come back and get the beer."

"Where is it?"

"We have them at Sullivan's Point. They have a huge barn we keep set up for meetings, a big front lawn where we all eat, a firepit. It's great."

"I… Can I go? Or is that too weird for you."

He had a feeling the news he'd ordered himself a bride had whipped through the other families like wildfire already. Elsie would have gleefully told Alaina, who would've told her sisters Quinn, Rory and Fia in turn. And of course Hunter knew, which meant the rest of the McClouds knew.

It was possible it hadn't trickled up to the Kings yet. But not likely.

"Word spreads faster around here than a wildfire. And that's pretty fast. So, I think if we can be certain about one thing it's that everybody already knows you're here. It's like when I found out about Bug. I barely knew before everybody around here did. No privacy when you live on top of each other like this. You get used to it."

"Well, I would like to see the rest of the spread. If it doesn't bother you."

"Not at all. That's the point. Of all this."

She bit her lip. She'd done that last night. He was pretty sure she was being deliberately provocative. And he was also pretty sure he didn't mind. He did, however, wish that he was the one biting that lip. There was an edge to the attraction he felt for her, and he found it pretty welcome honestly. The intensity. Because it called to the something inside of him that he... Generally didn't indulge.

And you can't do it with her. Not now.

She stood from the couch, holding Bug out away from her, and then kissed the baby's face. And that did something to him. Something strange. The easy affection that she had with his daughter was... Well, it was exactly what he wanted.

"You're good with her," he said.

"I don't really have any experience with babies," she said. "Being that I was an only child. I didn't have any siblings to play with, and I don't have any nieces or nephews. But... I did always know that I wanted this."

"How?"

"I don't know. Maybe because my mother was so hard on me. I just wanted a chance to... To show that it could be different. To have it be different in my life. A different sort of mother-daughter relationship. Parent-child."

"See, for the same reasons, I decided just the opposite. That I wouldn't have kids."

"But you were certain. When you found out she was coming."

"Yeah, because then it was inevitable. And then it's not hypothetical, it's just… Are you going to be the same kind of person that your parents were, your parents that you… That you hated… Are you going to be better? Different?"

Hated.

He didn't think he'd ever said that out loud before. That he hated either of his parents.

But he did.

Because his father had never been able to man-up and be what his children needed. Because Sawyer had found it in himself to be there. To take a stand.

Because his mother had left him when he'd been a little kid who'd done nothing but depend on her. Because even after that, he'd… He'd been willing to sacrifice everything to chase a relationship with her when she didn't care at all.

"Would you mind if I went and changed?"

"Not at all."

She handed him the baby, then disappeared, and he did his best to not try to mentally catalog what articles of clothing she was taking off while she was gone. When she reappeared, she was wearing a pair of blue jeans and a black T-shirt. And somehow she still looked soft, fancy and expensive, even in something that simple.

She had a sweater draped over her arm, her blond hair falling in loose waves around her shoulders. She didn't have any makeup on. She was bright and fresh-faced, and yet again, all he wanted to do was lay her across the nearest surface.

Good thing they had somewhere to be.

He bundled Bug up, and they got into the truck, neither of them saying much of anything beyond bland pleasantries as he pulled out onto the road that cut through the ranch. It would take at least fifteen minutes to get to Sullivan's Point. Longer to get down to the lake that was at the corner of the property, which he would have to show her sometime soon. But probably not today.

Evelyn rolled the window down, and a warm breeze blew into the truck. She stuck her hand out the window, and he had to remind himself that even though he was driving on ranch roads, he needed to pay attention. Because otherwise… He was going to get distracted. He might cause an accident.

He took another peek at her. She was smiling, her face tilted up toward the sun.

"It's beautiful," she said.

And he had to agree. Though he didn't think they were thinking about the same thing.

They turned onto the side road, which was shaded by a line of locust trees, and bordered by green fields. Sullivan's Point was softer than Garrett's Watch. Not quite so rocky. The white farmhouse was backed by a field, with majestic mountains behind that. A huge weeping willow bent and swayed in the front yard. There was a clothesline strung between the tree and the front porch, and a passel of chickens ran free-range all around.

He looked at Evelyn. She was watching the proceedings with a wary expression on her face.

"What?"

"Oh, nothing," she said. "I came here to use the garden and I met Rory and Quinn. They were very nice."

"Yeah, they are."

She looked at him, a strange glint in her eye. "Are they pretty friendly with you?"

Jealousy.

She was jealous.

Well, damn. "I have never slept with one of the Sullivan sisters, thank you very much."

She sputtered. "I didn't ask."

"But you're jealous."

She wrinkled her nose. "I don't trust people right now, okay?" She sighed. "I don't… I don't know how. And I was in a relationship for a long time and he slept with someone else and I… I don't feel very attractive right now."

All he could do was stare at her. "You don't…you don't feel attractive?"

"No. Because what's going to stop a man who's with me from getting bored and finding another woman? Andrew had to sleep with another woman, presumably because I… am not…good in bed or the right shape or something."

The. Right. Shape.

Everything about her shape looked just right to him. He was obsessed with it.

"Evelyn," he said, his voice rough, his hands tight on the steering wheel. "You're beautiful. And some asshole with commitment issues hell-bent on running away from his promises shouldn't make you feel like there's something wrong with your body. I've spent the past week thinking a lot about your body. It's perfect."

Her cheeks turned bright red. "Oh. *Oh.*"

"I don't have any interest in sleeping with anyone else."

"But you don't want to sleep with me yet?"

"I want to do this right, that's all."

But it was tough. It was damned tough.

"You have a lot of opinions about what's right," she said softly.

"Yeah, if only because I've seen a lot of shit go wrong."

The Sullivan sisters were going in and out of the house, placing bowls on a series of tables—none of them matching—set up end to end across the grass. There were at least fifty chairs lining them, also not matching. Some folding, some looking like they had come from the antique store, or out of the old farmhouse itself.

He parked the truck and got Bug out of her car seat, thankful to be out in the open air rather than closed in tight with Evelyn and his slowly fraying self-control.

The other ranchers were starting to arrive, along with different laborers. Elsie and Wolf were already there, Elsie chatting away with Alaina Sullivan, Wolf sitting in a chair drinking a beer. The McClouds arrived shortly thereafter, Hunter taking a seat near Wolf, and his brothers also sitting down at that end of the table. Unsurprisingly, the Kings showed up last, and almost the minute Landry's boots hit the dirt, Fia Sullivan stalked back into the farmhouse and didn't reappear.

Evelyn hung back for a moment. Just a moment. And then the smile on her face became determined and she stepped forward, introducing herself to everyone, and when Fia finally did reappear, it was with a giant bowl of salad and a determined grin that looked a lot cheerier than was natural.

"Hi," Evelyn said, stepping forward, "you must be Fia."

"And you must be Evelyn," she said. "Word travels quickly through our family."

"I already met your sisters," Evelyn said. "They seem lovely."

"They have their moments," she said. "How are you surviving the Garrett clan?"

"More than surviving. I'm really enjoying getting my tour of the different properties. This is beautiful."

Evelyn was unfailingly polite, and easy with…everybody. Denver, Justice and Landry King didn't seem to intimidate her. Neither did Daughtry King, who arrived last with the Kings'—for lack of a better word—ward, Penelope, in tow. And even more surprising, Arizona King didn't seem to bother her. Arizona, who was about as friendly as a basket of snakes on a good day, didn't seem to put her off too much. Or at all.

They assembled around the table, and Gus McCloud stood, offering to bring up the first order of business. "I'm thinking of expanding what we do at McCloud's Landing."

And from there, he went on to pitch the idea that Hunter had already told Sawyer about. Everyone seemed receptive, but Gus offered to send out paperwork outlining the potential expenses, profit, loss and everything else. There were a few other updates, requests for different improvements that would require shared funds to be used, and all were voted on unanimously.

And when that was all finished, Brody McCloud stood, and lifted his red Solo cup. "All right," he said. "Now it's time to get this meeting started."

CHAPTER NINE

EVELYN WAS BUZZING with all the activity happening around her. There was lively conversation, good food and now a bonfire. When Sawyer had mentioned a town hall meeting, she had pictured something remarkably different to what had actually occurred. Instead, this was a mostly social gathering, as far as she could tell, likely a reward for all the hard work they put in. And a chance for them all to see each other.

It was impossible not to get caught up in the energy of it all.

Or maybe she was just still on a high from what Sawyer had said to her in the car.

From the heat in his gaze.

He *wanted her.*

And as much as she hated that she'd needed that boost, she had. It had made it easier to interact with the other women, and she was... Well, she was glad that she had, because they were really interesting women.

Fia had told her more about the garden, and how everything they were eating came from Four Corners. The hamburgers and steaks coming from Garrett and King cattle, the salads had veggies from their collective gardens, cheese from the dairy cows at the ranch.

They talked about the baking they did and the way they made jam, and gave the history of the Sullivan farmhouse.

It was such an amazing community. She had never re-ally seen anything like it. She noticed that even in a large group of people Wolf was fairly silent and taciturn.

Sawyer was… Sawyer. Measured, polite. The perfect gentleman, really. But…guarded. Even when he smiled it was never too wide. Even when he laughed, it was never for too long.

Elsie on the other hand didn't have the restraint her brothers did. She was lively and vivacious, talking with her hands, she and Alaina seemingly discussing different trail rides they would like to go on.

"Endurance rides," Elsie clarified when Evelyn asked. "At least fifty miles."

"That seems…intense," Evelyn said.

Alaina agreed. "It is. But it's fun. You get to test your-self against the elements. Plus, it's just… All that time on the back of a horse. I couldn't ask for anything better."

Horse girls.

And all the while the chatter went on, her attention kept straying back to Sawyer. And she felt resolute in the thought she'd had last night over meat loaf. She was going to seduce him. The only question was how.

"Hi," came the sound of a new voice.

"Oh, hi," Evelyn said, turning and finding a woman with light brown hair standing there looking at her. She was… It was the strangest thing. She was objectively quite plain, but there was a radiance to her countenance that made her striking. Her features were strong, and they took hold of you—it only took a moment.

"I'm Nelly Foster," she said. "I'm with the McClouds. I mean, I'm engaged to Tag McCloud."

She'd heard of this mysterious Nelly. Right from Sawyer, just yesterday. He'd said she was with Tag like it was big news, so she imagined here it must have been.

"Oh," she said, not sure if she was supposed to pretend that she didn't know who she was, or if it was customary to have heard about a person through gossip. Well, everyone here was acting like they had already heard about her.

"Sawyer told me about you," she said, deciding that was the appropriate cultural norm.

"Oh?"

"Yes," she said, hoping she hadn't miscalculated.

She was feeling ready to try out this *making friends* thing and she didn't want to mess it up before she even got started.

"Well, Sawyer mentioned... He mentioned you when he was kind of explaining the relationships of everybody around here. And the schooling situation. If I remember correctly, your mother was the teacher?"

Nelly laughed. "Which means he undoubtedly told you that I was a mousy librarian?"

"No." She shook her head. "He didn't."

"Sorry," Nelly said. "I didn't mean for that to sound as ferocious as it likely did. I mean, in fairness, I kind of am a mousy librarian. At least, I always have been. But... I mean, I am still. Just...with him now."

She regarded the other woman, who looked entirely comfortable with herself, and the situation. And Evelyn didn't know what it would take to make her feel that way.

She'd had her trust betrayed by people she'd known for so long. Time didn't equal trustworthiness.

She had to make a decision. To be suspicious of everyone around her, of Sawyer, of all the women on the ranch...

Or to be new.

That was the point of being here, wasn't it?

She was going to choose to be new.

"You've probably heard, then, that I'm Sawyer's mail-order bride?"

Nelly laughed. "I did," she said. "But I wasn't going to say it."

"I don't mind."

"It looks like it's about time for dessert. Should we go get it?"

The women all stood up and headed toward the farmhouse, with the exception of Elsie and Alaina. Evelyn decided to go with them. Sawyer was holding Bug, and making conversation with the McClouds, and he didn't seem like he needed any kind of intervention.

The women started to pull cakes and pies out of their various places, and funnel them out of the house.

"This is like a bakery," she said.

"A lot of it is contributed by the different families who work here," Fia said. "I can't take all the credit."

"Or she would!" Quinn shouted.

"I brought Snickers cake," Nelly said. "I might be a little bit bland, but my taste in desserts is not."

"Clearly you're not all that bland, if you landed one of those men," Evelyn said.

The fact of the matter was, *every* man that she had seen on this ranch was solid gold hot. Certified by the USDA, she imagined.

She was proud of herself for remembering that terminology.

Nelly laughed. "Well, fair enough."

"We don't need one of them to validate us," Fia said stiffly.

"She has issues," Rory said.

Yes, Evelyn had noticed that, especially combined with Sawyer's comment. About Landry King.

She had to wonder if they were exes, but nobody had said that, and it seemed as if it was something that people around here would've been specific about it. Loudly and gleefully.

They seem to delight in the details of each other's lives.

"I don't need to be defined by Tag," Nelly said. "But I don't mind him as an accessory. Or anything else."

"Suit yourself," Fia said, wafting out the front door.

"Pay her no mind," she said. "She's especially salty about Landry today."

"Why?" Evelyn asked.

"That's the thing," Nelly said. "We don't know."

"You don't know?" She had the feeling that was odd, considering how close they all seemed.

"We don't know," she repeated. "And you may have noticed, but we are all pretty much in each other's business all the time around here."

"I did notice."

"Let's get all the s'more fixings out," Nelly said.

"S'mores?" Evelyn asked.

"Yes. You're familiar, aren't you?"

"Of course. I just haven't had them since I was a kid."

"Oh, we make an effort to have them every time there's a bonfire," Quinn said.

There was no pretense at it being a meeting once the sweets hit the table. Once the marshmallows were being roasted. There were kids running all over the place, laughing and having fun, and the adults seemed to be enjoying themselves just as much. And it didn't take long for an informal band to join up and start playing music.

It wasn't like anything Evelyn had ever seen before. It was just pure, unfettered... Celebration. For no real rea-

son other than that this place around them was so beautiful, and they had all these resources at their disposal. For
no real reason other than that they lived. And so they were
enjoying it. Not because they'd earned any sort of reward,
or because they were performing their relevance to the
world. This was about reveling in the fruits of their labor,
and it was infectiously joyful to be a part of.

It was Elsie who handed her a stick with a marshmallow on it. And she stuck it in the middle of the fire, only
to feel a large, masculine hand come down over her wrist.

"No, no, no," he said, drawing it back.

She looked up, but she had already known that it was
Sawyer who was touching her. Because she could feel it in
not very dignified places.

"You don't put it right in the flame," he said.

"I have never roasted a marshmallow before," she
sniffed.

"Well, that's not how you do it," he said. He sat right
next to her, his hard thigh pressing against hers. He wasn't
holding Bug anymore, and she looked around, but couldn't
tell what was going on in all the movement, and all of her
brainpower was being taken up by... By him. "What you
do," he said, his voice low and intimate as he grabbed hold
of her hands and guided them down low into the firepit,
"is put them over the embers. Otherwise, you're going to
catch on fire."

"And I don't want to do that?" she asked.

"No. And if you do, you don't go waving it around or
you're going to fling a burning marshmallow onto somebody's face."

"You sound like someone who's seen that," she said.

He chuckled. "No. I haven't. That's just some country
wisdom for you. It's free."

He didn't move, and she didn't want him to. Instead, she let everything he'd said roll over her, that bit of *country wisdom*. You didn't want to stick it directly in the flame. It would just catch fire.

And right now, holding it over the ember, she could see the marshmallow getting gold and brown, expanding as it sat there over the heat. Maybe that was a metaphor for the two of them. They couldn't go jumping directly into the flame or...

She looked up, and their gazes caught and held. She could feel tension stretched between them, and she didn't want to do anything but stare right at him.

"Watch out," he said, jerking the stick back away from the fire. Her marshmallow was smoking. Again, a metaphor. Because she felt like she might be also.

"Saved it," he said.

"I was distracted."

His gaze dropped her mouth, and she was suddenly very conscious of the fact that they were surrounded by people, and yet it felt like they might be the only two on earth.

He moved away first.

"Here," he said, reaching over and grabbing a graham cracker, then putting a row of chocolate squares on the bottom piece. He positioned it at the base of the marshmallow, then grabbed another piece of graham cracker, sandwiching it over the top of the marshmallow and pulling it off the stick, leaving behind a perfect s'more. He handed it to her. She took a bite, and the marshmallow stretched, leaving sticky goo on her cheek.

Not very dignified, but she could see that he wasn't put off by it at all. He watched her eat it.

"Am I really all that interesting?" she asked.

"Just your mouth," he said.

And she blushed. She actually blushed, like she was fourteen and not thirty-four.

She just didn't know how to do this. This flirting thing. This seduction thing. And all things considered, she didn't actually think that chowing down on a s'more was overly seductive. Though he seemed interested regardless.

She finished eating, and the music started to pick up tempo. A giggling Elsie and Alaina hopped up and started to dance, and Elsie took hold of her hand, drawing her over to where they were. Her hands were sticky, but it didn't seem to matter. And the three of them sort of started to shake their hips and move in incredibly bad rhythm.

It didn't take long for some of the Sullivan sisters to join in, then Nelly Foster and a man that Evelyn presumed was Tag McCloud started to dance together.

And she just felt *light*.

Like she'd risen up high from those ashes, after all.

She looked across the bonfire and saw the Kings, sitting there drinking beer, unmoved by the music, and Wolf holding a similar posture. The McClouds, on the other hand, came right out and started to dance, Hunter taking his turn with just about everybody, rebuffed, though, by Elsie. He was strong, and he held Evelyn effortlessly, spinning her. He was good-looking, too, though he didn't ignite the same feelings that Sawyer did. And at the end of her last spin, she found herself colliding with her potential-fiancé's solid chest.

"Cutting in," he said, shooting Hunter a dangerous glare.

And then she found herself in his arms, and she wasn't thinking about his strength in an abstract sense, or whether or not he was a good dancer. She wasn't even sure if her feet were still moving, if they were moving at all. Or if it was just her head that was spinning. She could remember the first time she'd met Andrew. She'd thought that he was handsome.

She thought that he was charming and pleasant, but she had never felt like the world faded away when he held her in his arms. She had wanted to impress him. She had felt a little bit tongue-tied, a little bit awkward, and had worried endlessly that she might not have any sort of appeal where he was concerned. But it hadn't been this. It had never been this. Everywhere his hands made contact she burned.

And she wanted to shed her clothes, shed her skin, become something else entirely. Because she felt like she couldn't be... She couldn't be herself and contain any of this. Not the Evelyn that she had ever been. The one who was so consumed with what other people thought of her, with showing them. She couldn't be that person. Not and withstand this, and she didn't know what any of that meant. Didn't know...anything.

But out here in the middle of all this that was different, in the middle of all this that was singular, she felt like maybe it was possible. To be the kind of woman who could withstand this. To be the kind of woman who could harness it, who could take the lead.

Because hadn't she come out here for something entirely different? Hadn't she come out here to make a new life for herself? Hadn't she come out here for this?

She hadn't realized at the time, but this was the bottom line of it. She wasn't all that she could be. She was trapped. She was trapped in that endless cycle, in that limited perspective of what a dream even could be. And there was so much more world out there. So many more kinds of people, and so many more options to be. And she didn't know any of them.

She had achieved. There was no question about that.

She had been on the brink of marriage, she had been in love. She had reached the height of a career. Making it beyond everything that she had ever thought was possible. TV shows and celebrities, and so many things she had actually never even dreamed of. And yet it hadn't fixed her life. It hadn't transformed her into anything that felt completed. But maybe that was just life. Maybe life was a series of finding new capacities inside of yourself and seeing all that you could be. Maybe there was no finish line. Maybe there was only learning more. Learning to be more, learning to… To want more. On your own terms, even, because hadn't she wanted all those other things based on the terms of what those around her valued?

It wasn't that she didn't care about them. She hadn't been living solely for other people, and she wasn't going to rewrite her reality to make it half so simple. To lie to herself and say that she had only been doing what other people had expected of her, because that wasn't true.

She had burned down that world that she had been in for her mother's sake, and even that wasn't quite so straightforward.

She had loved to dance.

She had simply faltered beneath the weight of the expectations. Her inability to succeed on the level that had been expected of her. She had loved to dance. She had loved her apartment in Manhattan. She had loved that view. She had loved the people that were in her life, but that hadn't insulated her from betrayal.

And here she was in this life, completely and utterly different, and she was loving it, too.

It created more questions than it did answers, and she didn't quite know what the end result of it would be. Except that she enjoyed being in his arms. And she enjoyed having her body beneath his hands. And it made her want to push the bonds of what she'd been before, to see just quite how different she could be.

Change.

And she realized that so much of life was resisting change. That if you had to change, you took into account all of your strengths, and all the things you already had been, and shifted. Rather than metamorphosing.

But this... This was a potential rebirth.

Maybe she was romanticizing an attraction in a way that she shouldn't. And she was reading way too much into a campfire, and s'mores. But right now, the possibilities felt limitless in a way they never had. Right now, she felt like she was rewriting her story in a way she had imagined possible. Throwing out the guidelines of what was, and creating an entirely new being.

It was something she was never going to be able to explain to the people she'd once known. It was something she could hardly explain to herself.

But she wondered if Sawyer might understand.

For some reason, she wondered if he might understand.

She put her hand on his chest, and then slowly slid it up behind his neck, and before she could think about what her next move was, she found herself starting to lean in, and then she found herself being set backward.

"Thanks for the dance," he said. "I should go check on Bug."

"Oh, where is she...?"

"One of the ranch hands' wives is holding her. I should make sure she's not... I should make sure she's not fussy."

And he left her standing there, left her feeling cold and somehow more alone than she had before he'd taken her into his arms.

It wasn't a rejection. A public rejection, even though it felt like one.

No, it wasn't that.

He had to go see to Bug. That was all.

She blinked hard, and tried not to take any of that on board.

But she went and sat down by the fire, and she found herself joined by Nelly, who put another marshmallow roasting stick in her hand.

"Are you okay?"

"Fine," she said."

"Except you're not," Nelly said.

"No," she said. "Really not. I... I don't know why. I just don't quite know what to do with him."

"You're attracted to him."

"Oh, yes," she said, sticking the marshmallow into the embers when she wanted to defiantly stick it into the flame. But if she left it to smolder, then it would melt. Slowly but steadily. Hadn't he showed her that?

"What's the problem?"

"He wants to wait," she said, flicking Nelly a glance. "Until marriage."

"Oh, Sawyer," she said. "I don't know him that well, not as an adult. But believe me when I tell you, I think his childhood did a number on him."

"Well, whose didn't?" she asked, glaring at her marshmallow.

"Good point. But you know men. They're just a little harder."

"Not exactly marshmallows," she said. "They require a little more heat."

And then she followed her defiance and stuck the marshmallow straight into the flame and let it go up in a blaze.

She drew it back and then blew it out. With one half of a breath. There, she hadn't flicked it, she hadn't burned anyone. And so maybe the marshmallow was a bit crispy. But it was done. So both methods worked. She ignored the fact that it was fully charred on the outside. And built her own clumsy s'more without any of the finesse that Sawyer had demonstrated. But she took a bite of it, and it was good. And she hadn't had to wait.

"I'm going to seduce him," Evelyn said to her new friend, who she felt certain would understand, based on their acquaintance of a collective forty minutes.

"Oh, I'm always in favor of seduction."

"I just have to figure out how."

"I don't think men are that difficult," Nelly said. "I seduced Tag while wearing ankle socks."

"That is a rousing recommendation for the chemistry between the two of you."

"I think it might just be a rousing testament to the simplicity of men."

"My experience is that men can be tricky," Evelyn said.

"Well, I haven't got any experience other than Tag," she said.

That successfully shocked Evelyn. "Really? Tag is your only... That's... That's very sweet."

But she was thankful for all the experience that she had, because she was going to have to call upon it to deal with stubborn, hardheaded Sawyer. She just knew. Because he was a man who wasn't going to give up his power easily, and she needed him to do it. And so, she needed a strategy. A game plan. It was very important. Very, very important.

It was a very good thing that she had brought all the lingerie—unused—that she had intended to wear on her honeymoon. Because… Well, she'd figured that if she was going to get married…

Oh, yes, it was a very good thing she had come prepared. She was going to wage sensual war against Sawyer Garrett. She was going to push them both right into the flames. He wasn't going to know what hit him.

And the very best part of that thought was that she felt… Excited. Not afraid, not ashamed, just purely, wholly, ready.

CHAPTER TEN

THE TRICKIEST THING had been deciding what to do with Bug. Nelly had spent the day with her, while Evelyn baked her coconut cake, and made eclairs, while she had prepared her lasagna and set her bread out to rise.

She had thought maybe she could ask Elsie to help care for Bug, but then had decided she didn't really want to telegraph her intentions to Sawyer's sister.

It was all too fragile.

She had the raciest set of underwear she'd ever owned ready to go in the bedroom. She was going to take a shower and make sure that she was smooth everywhere and smelling amazing before she put it on. She was going to start with food, and then get into sex, and she was going to make sure that it was a night to remember.

For both of them.

Desire flared between her thighs.

In the end, she'd decided to ask Nelly for help. Since Nelly was her partner in crime for this particular pursuit.

Nelly, who absolutely understood just how it was when you were in lust with a man and desperately in need of getting your hands on him.

She'd heard more about Nelly and Tag's origin story last night. Apparently, one drunken night on Nelly's twenty-first birthday, Tag had offered to take her virginity as a gift, if ever she needed him to. She had waited nine years to make good on it, but had then gone up to see him with the intent of just getting it over and done with so that she could move on and find someone else. But in the end, the two of them had ended up falling in love with each other. It had turned out that Tag had actually had feelings for Nelly for years, her plain spinster status notwithstanding.

It had really warmed Evelyn to hear their love story. Even more, it had warmed her to get to know Nelly. To feel like she might not just make a family here, but also… friends.

Nelly and Tag were opposites, at least to anyone on the outside looking in. But it was obvious that where it counted most, they weren't. Where it really counted, they were like each other. She thought their story was beautiful, and she really loved hearing it, but she didn't need all those feelings to enter into her situation with Sawyer.

This was about reclaiming herself.

Her confidence, and knowing that whatever happened, one thing she really couldn't cope with was feeling like she was in a marriage with someone who didn't desire her. It was on the list with making sure that he wanted to have more children, quite honestly. There were just some things that she couldn't fathom never having.

You were willing to not have it with Andrew.

It was true. She had been willing to deal with the level of passion that they had. But the fact of the matter was, it had seemed suitable to her. She hadn't realized there was any kind of problem. Not until she had found out he had been pursuing passion with another woman. And then it had all become abundantly clear.

But that was the problem. The same thing with all of her realizations at the campfire last night. She had hindsight, and she had it in spades. But it was so much harder to see all of this when you were in the middle of it. And that, she supposed, was the real gift of being prepared to marry a man that she didn't really know. They had nothing but clarity. The kind of clarity that you normally only ever had in the rearview mirror. They weren't steeped in hopes and lies and blind spots because they simply wanted to make something work. They were putting together something that they would both find enjoyable to live with, and for her, testing his resolve where she was concerned was essential.

At least, that's what she was telling herself. That it wasn't just because she was weak and infatuated.

And that she wasn't lying to him or pushing him for the sake of it.

Because he had wanted honesty, and she supposed that it was technically not all that honest to have been told by a man that he wanted to wait for marriage, and then gone ahead and decided to seduce him, anyway.

She probably had two hours before he came home, and she wanted to spend at least an hour of that getting ready, and she was going to have to put the lasagna in the oven just before then. She was timing it all out in her head while planning what to do with all her restless energy for the next fallow hour.

She decided to take a walk. Find flowers for the table. She knew that there was a substantial amount of wildflowers out on the property, because she'd seen them when she had gone riding with Sawyer the other day. She was wearing a floral skirt and a white T-shirt, which was just warm enough for the spring sun that was shining somewhat pale in the light blue sky. But it would be a quick walk, so it would be just fine.

She started up the trail that she and Sawyer had taken the horses on, the one that went along the river, just beneath the trees. The sunlight filtered through the pine canopy, shadows and slivers of light playing over her skin as she walked. She closed her eyes, taking in the fresh air. Marveling at the difference of this. Walking in isolation. Where she didn't have to worry about strangers accosting her, but...

It occurred to her that she didn't actually know what wildlife she might have to worry about. That unsettling thought wrapped itself around her like a blanket, and then she couldn't quite shrug it off. It compromised her peace, but she did keep on walking, because she had been out over the ranch quite a bit over the last week, and she hadn't seen any animals other than cows. Still. It was a little bit disconcerting.

She paused at the edge of the river, and looked down. There was a cluster of purple flowers with vertical petals unfurling at the top, and crisp dark points that looked like freshly sharpened pencils pointing toward the ground. She had never seen a wildflower like that before, and she went over to the edge of the bank, intent on reaching out and grabbing them. But her foot hit a slick patch of mud that had simply looked like sand but was actually something briny and slick, and she found herself tumbling back. She pitched herself forward, which helped to regain a little bit of control, and practically windmilled her arms one over the other as she tried to keep from collapsing. But instead, she found herself falling straight into the river.

The water was freezing. And much deeper than it looked right there. She was instantly submerged, and she kicked her way to the surface, the wind practically knocked out of her chest by just how frigid it was.

She screeched an obscenity, and kicked her way back toward the shore, her fingers and shoes finding the rocks that lined the bank slick. She launched herself up out of the water like a particularly angry cat, now lying flat on the muddy bank. She felt like a drowned rat, and she imagined she looked even worse. She was heaving, gasping for breath, trying to deal with herself, when she heard him.

"What in the ever-loving hell?"

She opened her eyes and looked up, and saw Sawyer, upside down and racing toward the bank.

"Woman," he said, "what the hell did you do?"

"I fell into the water," she said, sitting up. But then, he was right there, kneeling beside her, and she felt utterly horrified. She was muddy, she was wet. She could only assume she looked like a drowned rat, when she had just intended to get fully dressed up and look amazing for him.

Absolutely amazing.

The outfit that she had picked out was all slinky, finely webbed lace that he would have been able to see her body through, in scandalous detail.

And now here she was in a muddy T-shirt, and a flowery skirt that was plastered to her thighs. She felt ridiculous.

She coughed and sat up, very aware of the fact that her hair was matted and clumpy. She sighed heavily and then he had his hands on her face. "How did you fall into the water?"

Her eyes met his, all that blue. And she felt like she was falling again. Felt she was going to sing beneath the surface of the attraction between them. That would pull her under. That she would be completely lost in it. Lost in him.

"I… I was trying to get some flowers and I…" She shivered. She shivered, not because she was cold. She shivered because he was so close. Because he was just right there. Because he was so…him. So warm and intoxicating and male. And he moved closer to her. She shivered again. He wrapped his arms around her, and he was so warm and…

"I'm going to get you wet," she said.

"I don't care," he said, gruff.

"Bug is with Nelly," she said, the words coming out clumsy, halted.

"That's good," he said. He brushed his thumb over her lip, and she felt a water droplet slide down her chin. She was so cold and he was so... He was so warm. And she wanted to taste him. More than she wanted anything. And this wasn't the smooth seduction that she had planned. She looked ridiculous, not beautiful. She wasn't wearing her sexy underwear; she hadn't just had her shower and shaved her legs. She wasn't prepared for this at all. She wasn't prepared for him. But suddenly, she found she couldn't resist him. It was so funny that she had set out to seduce him, because in the end she felt utterly and completely seduced. And she didn't want to fight it. In fact, she realized that when she angled her head toward him there was no fighting it at all.

Break free.

Be the Evelyn you didn't know you could be.

And she stretched up, and she touched her mouth to his.

And it was like fire. From the instant their mouths met, it consumed them. She had never had a kiss like this. She had never felt anything like this. To say that she had felt desire before in the face of this was... Well, it was laughable. She had just been marveling at Nelly, and the fact that she had only been with one man, and felt thankful for her own experience, but there was no experience here. There was nothing. Nothing but this... This thing. This explosive, magical thing. It was heat and fire all at once. Need layered on top of need, along with a deep satisfaction that she was finally doing it.

Finally kissing him.

Him.

She felt the slick heat of his tongue against the seam of her mouth and she parted her lips, admitting him. She was trembling. That space between her thighs hot and needy, aching with the desire to be filled by him.

Immediately.

There was no finesse, no pretense, no uncertainty. It was all heat. All fire and flame and all-consuming desire. She wiggled from her position up on the ground, and she was unbearably conscious of the fact that her clothing was wet and sticking to her body, which only highlighted the fact that it felt thin, insubstantial against his questing hands, which was good, because even this thin fabric was far too much between them.

His hand skimmed over her curves, large and uncompromising, coming around the front of her body to cup her breasts, his thumbs teasing her nipples. She gasped, letting her head fall back, letting him kiss her throat, down across her collarbone. Then his hands moved down farther, to the hem of her shirt, and he pushed up beneath them, his rough palms making contact with the tender skin of her stomach.

"Bug is with Nelly?" he asked, sounding drugged.

"Yes," she said.

And he didn't question her. Not again. He just kissed her. Kissed her while his hands roamed over her curves. Kissed her like he was dying.

She shivered, even against his big warm body, and he picked her up, gathering her against him, and started to carry her into the trees.

"Where are we—"

"You'll see," he said, his words harsh, his throat sounding tight, his voice thick.

There was a narrow trail, one they couldn't have taken

the horses on, and it wound its way through the trees, up into a secluded spot, completely shrouded by foliage. And there was a cabin there. Tiny, somewhat run-down looking.

"What is this?"

"This is the original cabin," he said. "The original one room that Abraham Garrett built when he settled Garrett's Watch."

He pushed the door open to reveal an interior that was surprisingly dry, warm and well-kept. It looked recently swept, with a bed in the corner that had a quilt spread over it. It was a small bed.

And when she had thought of having him, it was on the large bed in the main house. That bed was big enough for all kinds of acrobatics. For her to crawl across the mattress and tempt him with the shape of her figure, which she already knew that he liked.

In a big room where she could stand back and show him how her body looked in that underwear. Where she could maybe even engage in a striptease. She had some insecurities, but one thing she knew was how to move. With grace and fluidity. She might not have been able to make the lines that ballerinas' bodies were honed for, but she knew how to make the right lines to tempt a man. That, she did know.

None of that was set up here. And she was still wearing white cotton disappointments beneath her clothes. But it didn't matter. Because all she wanted was to be with him. To be naked. To be pressed up against his body. All she wanted was to be connected to him. Consumed by him. She wanted him inside of her. And that was as far ahead as she was thinking...

He set her down on the floor, and she kicked off her squishy, sodden shoes, and he looked at her, banked heat in those blue eyes. An electric flame.

Then he rocked back on his heels, grabbed hold of his T-shirt and stripped it up over his head.

Her mouth went dry.

Her powers of thought evaporated, any word she might've wanted to speak completely dissolving in her mind.

She had never seen a body like his. Not in person.

His muscles were rugged, honed on the range, not in the gym, and it was obvious. He didn't have that beefcake quality you saw on men who took mirror selfies and posted them proudly on the internet talking about the virtues of not skipping leg day. He had an ease with himself, that much was clear, but it was different than the urge to show off.

A man like Sawyer didn't need to show off. All he had to do was show up.

The dark chest hair that covered his well-defined muscles there made her palms itch with the desire to touch it. His finely cut abs made her mouth water. And suddenly, she didn't know why she was just standing there. When she could be tasting him. She practically launched herself across the room, pressing her hands to his muscles and leaning forward, licking him. He groaned, grabbing the back of her hair and tilting her face upward, consuming her mouth in a kiss. This was wild. It was raw, it was unlike anything she'd ever experienced before.

Honesty.

That word rang in her head, echoed like a bell.

Honesty.

There was no need to lie. No need to lie about how much they wanted each other, no need to hide it. There was no need to play a game. There was no need to engage in a well-choreographed seduction. Not when there was this between them. This deep, weeping need that came from inside of them. This thing, this passion, that was so far beyond them. Minimizing it, waiting, that was the lie. Because it was right here, ready to boil over, ready to consume them both at any moment.

And it was… It was intoxicating. It was the most real thing she had ever experienced in all of her life.

Need. Desire. Void of any kind of self-consciousness, void of any care about what she looked like. She didn't care. Maybe she looked like a ravenous beast, pressing kisses to that glorious body, maybe she seemed unlady-like, maybe she seemed ungraceful. But it didn't matter. She was a woman who wanted him. And that was the truth, so it didn't matter how anything seemed. All that mattered was what was.

She moved her hands to his belt buckle, but he fended them off, stripping her wet T-shirt up over her head, his lips curving into a wicked smile. And that was when she saw something else.

Because she had seen Sawyer as a steady man, a man who knew his mind, who knew what he wanted, who was deeply attractive because of that. But she hadn't seen this.

The wildness. That untamed quality. He was not a man who could simply be seduced. Whatever control she thought she had… It wasn't there. Because he was taking charge here. And she wanted to let him.

He reached around and unhooked her bra with prac-ticed ease, that wicked smile sending sparks shooting off in her stomach.

Control didn't seem so important, not now.

And suddenly, it was like everything flipped.

She knew what it was to live in the city and possess a certain amount of arrogance over her sophistication. All the things she knew, all the opportunities that had been opened to her. And she had come here, to this man, who had only been on one plane trip, while she had done a fair amount of world travel herself. This man who had never been to live theater, who hadn't had the cultural experiences that she had. This man who had lived on this ranch for his entire life, who hadn't met celebrities or anything of the kind. It was easy for her to think that with him she might have the upper hand. But she didn't.

He knew things.

He knew the earth. And what made things grow. He knew how to sustain life here on the ranch. And he knew things about her body that she couldn't begin to articulate. He was a man who built things with his hands, who knew about the essentials of life. She didn't know more than him.

She knew different.

And together, all the things they knew spanned a lot. And it felt miraculous. Them coming together like this. The two of them who maybe should never have even met, and never would have if it weren't for him posting that article, if it weren't for her going on that rabbit trail of clicking links.

It was a miracle, them together.

Two people who shouldn't be. And yet who… Who were connected in some way that defied explanation. Because what else could this be? This was more than attraction. This was chemistry on a whole other level. This was need that she had never experienced before, that she had never known existed.

She was tempted to call it fate.

Except, right then, it didn't matter what she called it, because there was no more rational thought when he took her in his arms, those big hands splayed across her back, and lowered his head, nuzzling her breast before pulling one nipple into his mouth. He made a rough, deep sound of satisfaction, and she shivered, not with cold.

"You're so beautiful," he said. "And I have wanted…"

But he didn't finish his sentence; instead, he transferred his attentions to her other breast, sliding the flat of his tongue over one tightened nub before taking it deep into his mouth, as well, sucking her hard. An answering pull ignited between her legs, a pulse of desire that made her cry out.

Oh, how she wanted *him*.

Oh, how she wanted *this*.

She felt suspended on a tightrope, between pleasure and pain, as he pushed his hand down beneath the waistband of her skirt, beneath the waistband of her underwear, cupping her bare butt cheek and squeezing tight.

He stood back, pushing the rest of her clothes from her body, examining her with a hunger that she had never seen in another man's eyes before.

He looked like he was going to eat her whole. And she was going to lie back and let him.

"That man who made you feel like… Who made you feel like you weren't enough, not beautiful enough or sexy enough… He should be shot," he said.

The conviction in his voice left no room for argument.

"You're perfection. Every curve. Every line." And then, as if to demonstrate his point, he walked forward, his muscles shifting with the movement. And she could see the bulge behind the denim of his jeans, evidence of how much he wanted her. And her fingers itched to undo that belt, to see him in all of his glory. But then he grabbed hold of her hips and dropped to his knees, pressing a kiss to the softest part of her stomach, before kissing one side, and then another. Before settling his mouth right between her legs and licking her. She gasped, arching forward, grabbing hold of his shoulders as he licked his way deep between her legs.

"Oh," she said, the words catching in her throat.

And then she was pushing her fingers through his hair, clinging to him as he licked and sucked, as he pushed her closer and closer to a need, a release, that was so far beyond her experience she was almost afraid of it.

She considered herself a woman of average experience. A woman who was comfortable with sex, with pleasure, who had been reasonably comfortable with her body before the hiccup with Andrew's infidelity.

But Sawyer had stripped everything away. Everything she had ever known. Her control, her comfort, her plans, and he had left her with blinding need. The tension inside her body went so far, so hard, that she was afraid of what would happen when she shattered. Because it felt impossible.

She couldn't even breathe past it.

And then he pushed two fingers deep inside of her, his tongue swirling around that sensitive bundle of nerves there, and she broke. She forgot to resist. There was no resistance. It was nothing more than a simple undoing. A breaking of everything she was. A shattering that left her in crystalline shards on the floor of that cabin.

He was holding her up, and she became aware of it when he lifted her up off the ground and she folded into his arms, when he deposited her boneless on the bed. And then he stood back, undoing that belt buckle finally.

She was panting, spent, uncertain that she would ever be able to come again, when he slowly undid the button on his jeans, lowered that zipper, kicked off his boots and took off his jeans and underwear and pushed them to the side, leaving him naked for her appraisal.

He was so big. And she had been told repeatedly in her life that size didn't matter. That women couldn't feel anything past a certain point internally, anyway. That bigger was simply bigger, and she could see now that it was because those men couldn't hold a candle to Sawyer Garrett.

And he was beautiful.

The most glorious naked body she had ever seen in her life. Every indent, every muscle, a testament to his hard work. And that glorious, masculine part of him, so thick and hard for her... Well, no one could tell her that size didn't matter, not now. Because she had experienced exponential pleasure beyond the telling of it just by looking at him. She would've said that she didn't give a particular care about the look of that part of a man's body. But she would have to revise that thought. Because she wanted to write sonnets about him. Wanted to make a sculpture in his honor.

That was how glorious he was.

Every man on earth paled in comparison. Certainly, every man she'd ever seen naked. She couldn't imagine anyone could hold a candle to him.

And she imagined that she had said as much with her eyes, which was why his smile became one of supreme masculine satisfaction, why he began to move toward her with the languid grace of a predator, coming down over her on the bed and kissing her deep and hard and long.

She reached down between them, curving her fingers around his hardened length. She squeezed him, her own internal muscles clenching tightly in anticipation.

She had been certain that there was no way she was going to climax again. She'd never been multiorgasmic, but certainly not after something like that. That had been a seismic event. She'd been certain that she would need days to recover from that.

But she was ready. Ready again. Ready for him. She wanted to feel all that hard masculinity inside of her. She wanted him, right there. She met his gaze, sliding her tongue over her lips, and then she kissed him, her hands still around his manhood. And when they parted, he was breathing hard. And she whispered against his mouth. "I need you inside me."

He growled, pinning her to the mattress, and she suddenly found both of her wrists gripped by one large hand, held tight over her head and pushed into the mattress. "You're a bad girl, aren't you?"

"Not usually," she said.

"What did I tell you? About how we had to wait."

"I can't wait," she said, panting. "Please."

He situated himself between her thighs, took himself in hand and pressed the thick head of his cock to the entrance of her body, teasing her there for a moment before sliding the head up through her slick folds and teasing that bundle of nerves again. She started to gasp, pant, unable to take the sensual tease. He did that until it was built up to a fire inside of her. Until she was whimpering, practically weeping, begging for him to claim her.

"Please," she gasped. "Please. Please."

He gripped her chin, holding her face steady, bringing his face down close to hers. "Please what?"

"Take me," she gasped.

"You want me in you?"

"Yes," she said.

"How much?"

"I can't breathe," she said. "I need you. I need you inside me, Sawyer."

And on a groan, he thrust hard inside her, filling her. She gasped. He was so big that the sensation was shocking, deeply pleasurable, as he made her feel like she was stretched to the breaking point. And then he rolled his hips forward, the movement a slow glide of torturous pleasure. He moved his hands down her back, her hips, reached around and cupped her ass, lifted it up off the mattress and started to thrust hard inside of her, taking total control of the movements. And all she could do was surrender. Surrender to the sensual assault.

This glorious overwhelmingness of her senses. He thrust into her hard and growled, grinding his hips against hers, and she went right over that edge again.

She hadn't been expecting it. Hadn't even felt it building. But she shattered. Again. And again. And he whispered things against her mouth, dirty promises and sweet compliments, tumbling from his lips with ease.

And then she felt him start to come undone.

She could feel it, because she had done it herself now three times. Fracture. And then shatter. He groaned, his blunt fingertips digging hard into her hips as he spilled himself inside of her. As he gave himself up to this thing between them completely.

He rested his face in the crook of her neck, breathing hard. And he held her there like that. Suspended between reality and fantasy. But then, the whole episode had been. It had the kind of sweet glory that you expected from a dream, but it had been slick and raw and physical, far beyond what a dream could accomplish.

She burned with it still.

They were both breathing hard, and he pulled away from her.

"Shit," he said.

"Surely it's not *that* bad," she said, pushing herself into a sitting position, suddenly feeling... Small. Embarrassed. And triumphant at the same time.

He wasn't happy, that much was obvious. But he also hadn't been able to control himself. Even when she had been... Well, decidedly not at her physical best. She had somehow managed to seduce a man having just accidentally fallen into a river, while half-coated with mud. There had to be some kind of triumph in that.

But he was angry. And she didn't like that.

"It's just not... We have to get married," he said. "We need to get married and sort all this out."

"I was planning on staying," she said.

"I didn't use a condom."

His words washed over her. And she felt just a little bit angry. Because maybe this was just how it was for him. He already had a baby from being careless with sex. So maybe it wasn't her, after all.

"Well," she said. "That's just par for the course with you, isn't it?"

That sounded so petty and hurt and small, but that's what she was.

"I always use a condom," he said. "I don't know what happened with Missy. But I used a condom the night Bug was conceived. I didn't forget. I never forget."

"I feel like there is tenuous evidence of that, Sawyer," she said.

"I am always in control," he said. "I don't...lose it, and pick women up off riverbanks and drag them into the nearest cabin to screw their brains out. Whatever you might think."

She shouldn't be appeased by that. She was, if only small-ly.

"Well, good to know that you did it today. And that it makes you angry."

"I told you, I wanted to make this decision based on… what was best."

"How is this not best?" she asked. "We're attracted to each other."

"Because my parents had this kind of relationship. This… They fought all the time. Then they were locked in their rooms screwing the other half of the time. It's not what I want for Bug. It's not what I want for her life."

"Then let's not do that. Let's not be that. Wanting to have sex with each other doesn't make us… It doesn't make us unreasonable. It doesn't make us robots that are enslaved to our baser urges. Or two people who can no longer think rationally."

"In my experience, it damn well does." He sighed. "Promise me," he said. "Promise me."

"I promise, Sawyer." She sat up and put her hand on his cheek. "I was never going to be able to leave her. Not ever. Not after I held her. Not even the first time. I'm not your mother. I'm not somebody that… I've been a lot of different places, I've lived different lives. I've been a dancer. I've been a professional organizer who has experienced a fair amount of success. I've been engaged. I lived in the city. And I've exhausted the magic that exists for me there. I might not always know exactly what I want. But I'm a woman who knows what I don't want. I don't want to live on other people's terms anymore. And I want to be here. I want to see what this place has in store for me. That is what I want. I'm confident in that. As confident as I could ever be in anything. I don't have questions about what could be if I go out into the broader world. But if I were to leave here, if I were to leave her, and this, I would be left with nothing but questions."

"Well, what are you doing Saturday?" he asked.

"Funny story," she said. "I was supposed to get married that day, anyway."

"Then let's do it."

"All right," she said, feeling her stomach hollow out.

"Marry me," he said.

This was what she wanted. This place. This man. This marriage.

She knew it.

It was a relief to know it.

"Yes, Sawyer. I will marry you."

He didn't kiss her. Instead, he got up off the bed and started to collect her clothes, which were still soaking wet. He examined them critically.

"Don't put these back on." Instead, he moved his boots over to her, got down on his knees and took his dry socks out and pulled them up over her feet. Then he put her feet in his boots, which were far too big. Took his T-shirt off the floor and put it over her head, helping ease her arms through it. Then he took the quilt off the bed and wrapped her in it. He got up, completely naked, bent over and took his jeans off the ground and pulled them on. He had no shoes. No shirt. Then he collected her wet clothes and bundled them into his arms. "Let's walk back to the house."

She felt small and taken care of. And it was just the strangest thing, because compared to the other proposal she had received... This wasn't all that romantic. He didn't look overjoyed. He didn't look excited. He seemed grim and resigned, rather. But the gestures he had taken in the aftermath were something else entirely. Something sweet and full of care that demonstrated his feelings in a way it was clear he couldn't with his voice, or his words or facial expression.

They went outside and he wrapped his arm around her, walked her back to the house. His feet were bare. He'd given her his boots.

She couldn't get over it.

And they thankfully didn't encounter anybody along the way. The quilt was wrapped around her enough that no one would be able to see anything of her body, but even so, it made her feel a little bit jumpy. She huddled against him, and when he opened the door to the house, she padded upstairs and took one look at the red bra and panties laid across the bed and laughed. But she put them on, because hopefully they would have a repeat performance of what had happened in the cabin in his room tonight. She put on a soft, simple sweater dress, because she was still feeling slightly chilled from her unceremonious swim in the river.

She came back downstairs to discover Sawyer standing there, sadly fully dressed.

"Shoes and shirt are optional in my kitchen," she said.

"You made cake," he commented.

"I did," she said. "And there's a lasagna that I really need to get in the oven, but now it's going to take forever for dinner to cook. I'm sorry about that. So why don't I heat up the oven and we can have cake first?"

"Bug's with Nelly," he said. "And you made this."

She took her risen loaf of bread down and put it in the second oven.

"Yes, that's the size of it."

"Why?"

"Oh," she said. "Because I was planning on seducing you."

"Really?" He looked at her with narrowed eyes.

"Yes. And no, my spill into the river wasn't actually part of the plan."

"What *was*?"

"Can you see out those windows?"

"No," he said. "It's one way."

"Good." She bent over and put the lasagna pan in the oven, then turned to face him, gripped the hem of her sweater dress and wrenched it over her head. Leaving herself standing there in high heels and red underwear.

His jaw went slack. And she was incredibly gratified.

"This," she said. "This was the plan."

"Well. *Fuck.*"

"Do you like them?"

"I don't actually have words for them."

"You turned out to be a little easier than I anticipated," she said.

"I forgot that I'm supposed to be mad at you about the sex."

"I think it was something about being measured and reasonable. And you are afraid of me leaving."

"Not for me," he said gruffly. "It's because of Bug."

"I get it. I do."

She set a timer, because Lord knew she was about to forget exactly what she was doing, then crossed the room and sat down right on his lap. He moved his hand right to her ass. Looking at her body with frank male appreciation.

"I needed to seduce you."

"Why?"

"Because," she said, the words choking themselves off, "I found out that my fiancé of ten years was cheating on me. Which means there was something I wasn't satisfying in him. And it scared me to think about marrying a man that I wanted more than he wanted me."

"You don't want me more than I want you," he said. "It's not possible."

"I'm really appreciative of that. And of you sharing that with me. But I... Oh, I really couldn't face being alone in this feeling. I can't describe to you how stupid I felt. Walking in on the two of them. Knowing that he was... That he was with her while he was with me. I felt...disgusting. And unwanted and unclean. I saw him having sex with her."

"I will never do that to you," he said, his blue eyes deep and sincere on hers. And she trusted him. She didn't know why or how, but she trusted this man she had only just met even after the betrayal of her fiancé.

"I actually believe you. That surprises me more than anything else. I have to say."

"Look, I'm... I'm not easy. You've been here for just under a week, and I have been on pretty damn good behavior. I'm stubborn, hardheaded. I know what I want, and I know who I am. I'm a lot of difficult things, but one thing I'm not is a liar. I'm not a liar, and I'm not a cheat. I never would be. You have my word on that."

She nodded. "I trust you," she said. "I don't actually know why. I just know that I do."

"Good. Trust me on that. Because this?" He moved his hand down her body, smoothed it over her curves. "This is as honest as it gets."

"Can I put my dress back on or do I need to eat in my underwear?"

"Oh, I was going to suggest we go upstairs until the timer goes off."

"We only have about twenty minutes."

His lips curved into a wicked smile. "I can work with that."

CHAPTER ELEVEN

HE'D LOST HIS head the night they'd first had sex. He couldn't deny that. The next day, he had his head on a little straighter. But it didn't really matter, because the day after that, they were getting married.

"You're what?" Hunter and Wolf asked at the same time.

"Getting hitched on Saturday. Got the marriage license sorted out yesterday. So, it's all good."

"You're just getting married. What happened to the two-week thing?"

"Have you seen her?" he asked Wolf.

"I thought…that was a bad thing."

"I'm only human," he said. "I don't have it in me to be that restrained. Apparently."

But it didn't matter what his brother or Hunter thought, or Elsie, for that matter, who expressed a healthy amount of skepticism while making sure he knew how much she liked Evelyn, and that it wasn't that, it was just that… Wasn't he worried about her being a city girl and all of that?

Hell, yeah, he was. None of his actual concerns had eased. But he wanted her. Wanted her enough that he was willing to make some rash decisions and see where it went.

He'd decided they'd get married down at Sullivan Lake. It was a nice spot. And he figured whoever had a mind would show up.

It didn't need to be a big deal.

But he wanted to give her something other than a court-house wedding, because she'd said that the wedding she was meant to have Saturday was going to be something all kinds of fancy. And he hoped that she didn't wear that wedding dress that she was supposed to wear for that other man. He didn't like to think about that man. About him touching her. About him having her the way that Sawyer had.

He was a territorial ass apparently. But he'd never been engaged before. Evelyn was going to be his wife.

His.

And that meant something a hell of a lot different than any of the hookups that he had had before.

He didn't know why. Just that it was.

Maybe because she was going to live with him. In his house. Share his life. It just was different, there was no getting around it.

Saturday was a beautiful day, thankfully, so the outdoor wedding thing was going to work out just fine. He decided to wear black jeans and a black T-shirt.

He figured that was about as fancy as he needed to be.

Evelyn had ordered Bug a dress online. She'd mentioned that, without making any mention of what she herself might be wearing. He thought it was sweet. That she'd thought of Bug.

She always had. From the first moment she arrived. And it gave him a sense of confidence that whatever happened between the two of them… She would be there for Bug. And that was what mattered more than anything. It wasn't about them.

He went down the stairs, ready to head out the door and get the truck prepared to drive them over to the lake, but when he arrived at the entry of the house, he could see out the window that there was a car in the driveway. Nonde-script midsize sedan, white.

He frowned, and jerked the door open. A man got out, tall and lean, blond. Not taller than Sawyer, but not a shrimp, either.

"Where's Evelyn?" The guy looked confused.

Well, join the club. "Who the hell are you?"

"I might ask you the same question," the guy said.

"No," Sawyer said. "You might not. Since this is my house. And I'm not the one that showed up at *your* front door."

"Her phone says she's here."

"Her phone?"

"We're on the same plan. I can track her."

"Well, hell," Sawyer said.

Because then it all became clear. This was Andrew. Because what other man would be on Evelyn's same phone plan? That was an oversight.

But then, if he could track her phone, presumably she could track his...

This man was bold. He had cheated on a fiancée, who could track his whereabouts. He had a lot of follow-up questions for this douchebag.

"She and I are supposed to be getting married today," Andrew said.

"Well, I have bad news for you," Sawyer said. "Because she and *I* are getting married today."

"Who the hell are you?" he repeated.

"Sawyer Garrett."

He knew the guy didn't know who he was. But he was Sawyer Garrett. Boss of Garrett's Watch. And this dick was on his turf. He had no damn right to swan up to his place and ask who he was.

In Pyrite Falls, Oregon, he ought to know who the hell Sawyer Garrett was.

Everyone else did. It was time for this motherfucker to learn.

"She doesn't know you," Andrew said. "She can't be marrying you."

"She knows me pretty well," Sawyer said.

He thought back to that night they'd spent together. And because Bug had been gone, they had spent all night on each other. It had been a damn revelation. He was a man, and he'd always liked sex.

But with her it felt like something else entirely. It was transcendental, and he didn't give a whole lot of credit to that kind of crap.

But with her... Well, with her...

And he felt a little bit guilty even hinting at the kind of intimacy they'd shared with this guy. Because he didn't deserve to know about it. Because nobody did. It wasn't something to be bragged about, or bargained with. It was between the two of them. A raw and fragile thing.

But he was pissing him off. So... Again, Sawyer was only a man.

"Can you explain to me what the hell is going on here?" Andrew asked.

"Again, you're the one that showed up at my house. You're the one that's here uninvited. You don't get to roll up here and start demanding explanations, do you get that? This is my house, and as far as I'm concerned, she's my fiancée."

"She didn't exactly break up with me."

"I think that when she caught you having sex with her friend she had every right to leave and not give you any kind of explanation."

"Yeah, she would think that," he said. "But that's just like her. Evelyn doesn't like to have any kind of fuss. It makes her edgy."

He was doing it, too. Trying to flex on his intimacy with Evelyn. Granted, she'd been with the guy for a long time. Ten years, she'd said. So, he had to admit that it wasn't as if he didn't have a certain kind of claim to it. But Sawyer wasn't going to allow it.

"She's done with you," Sawyer said.

"Go get her." Like Sawyer was a damn servant.

"I don't take orders from city boys. Particularly not city boys that show up at my place acting like they own it. Let me tell you something, son, you don't own this place. You sure as hell don't own me. You don't tell me what to do. You might be used to you saying jump and having people ask you how high, but I'm not one of them."

"Evelyn," Andrew said, raising his voice, and Sawyer had half a mind to punch him, lay him out flat right on the ground.

But then the door opened, and Evelyn appeared, wrapped in a silky robe, and it made desire kick right through Sawyer. He looked at Andrew's face, and saw that she had the same effect on him.

Rage rolled through his veins.

"Evelyn," Andrew said. "We need to talk."

"Do you want me to kick his ass?"

Evelyn looked at Sawyer, then she looked at Andrew. "I need to talk to him."

EVELYN DIDN'T WANT to talk to Andrew. But the fact that he was standing there in the driveway of Garrett's Watch, that he'd flown all the way here from New York… She had to.

She realized it suddenly. It was supposed to be their wedding day.

But now it was supposed to be her wedding day to Sawyer, and it had always been meant to be. She felt that in her bones. She didn't question it. She knew that this was what she was meant to be doing. She knew it. And that meant that she needed to deal with Andrew, and there was no risk to it.

Looking at him didn't hurt.

How had it only been... It hadn't even been a full two weeks, and yet he seemed like a distant piece of her old life that had nothing to do with who she was now, or where she was standing now. And yet, the fact remained that she had left their situation unresolved, and she couldn't do it now.

"Let's go inside," she said.

She opened the door, and let him into the living room. She felt underdressed, which was absurd, because Andrew had seen her naked hundreds of times. But they weren't together, not anymore. So it seemed wrong somehow. And she realized, with a strange out of body clarity, that they hadn't had real intimacy for a long time. Maybe ever. And perhaps that was why... Perhaps that was why she had felt so self-conscious when they'd made love.

But you don't even know Sawyer...

Okay, maybe that didn't make sense. But she felt a disconnect between the two of them that was so sharp she couldn't ignore it. And it wasn't just because of one betrayal. It wasn't that simple.

"What are you doing here?"

"I've been wondering where the hell you were."

"You found me." Obviously.

"I tracked your phone. I remembered that I could do that." Something about the way he said that rang hollow. An obvious lie.

Had he been lying that badly the whole time? She really hadn't been paying attention, if so.

"You just now thought to do that?"

"I figured you would come home. I was giving you a chance to make a reasonable decision. I was giving you space."

"I'm sorry," she said, "I'm unreasonable? I'm unreasonable. Me. How exactly did you want me to handle your betrayal?"

"We had problems, Evelyn."

His words slammed into her. Not simply the surface unfairness of them, though that was certainly present in her response. It was the truth in them actually. That they'd had problems. And that she had ignored them. That she had ignored every check inside of her regarding their relationship, to the point where she hadn't even registered them. She had just...let them go.

She had been so invested in nabbing that success. In finally being in the space in her life where she could have the marriage. The children. To top off all of her personal professional successes. That was where she had been. She had been so...wedded to that. Absolutely and completely.

And so when weeks had gone by without them having a meaningful conversation, or even a real conversation at all, she let it go.

When their sex life had sort of faded into something perfunctory, something that mostly happened on special occasions, or after dates, she had let it go. When he had started to get passive-aggressive, and registering his unhappiness with the way that she did things without ever actually making it a conversation, she had let it go.

They had been together for so long that she had found ways to try and tell herself it had to do with them being

MAISEY YATES   195

comfortable with each other. With them being steady. But those things were only true if there was intimacy.

Intimacy. That word again.

She had believed they'd had it, but she wasn't entirely sure she knew what it meant.

He had been lying to her. And it hadn't been…that smooth.

But she hadn't wanted to ask questions. She'd avoided hard conversations. She had let it all be like this.

"When did you start sleeping with Hollyn?"

"I don't see what that has to do with anything," he said.

"It has…" She closed her eyes to try and get a grip on herself. "Please tell me. Honestly, you don't have any right to come here being angry at me."

"I thought we were getting married."

"Did you really?"

"Well, you never spoke to me. Only your parents did."

"I'm sorry, did you find that humiliating? Because walking in and actually seeing you having sex with the person that I have called my closest friend for all this time…"

"The sex was just a symptom of our bigger issues," he said.

"Okay, but that's a lot like saying you got hit with an anvil, but maybe you died of the cold you already had."

"So you're saying if I hadn't cheated, then you would've stayed?"

Yes. She would have. Because she had learned to ignore all the small things, so only something big was ever going to shake her out of that malaise. It was a disconcerting realization. Stunning actually. And she found she really didn't like it.

"Yes," she said. "And I never would've realized we had problems that were so deep. But you didn't tell me that you were unhappy. And what I can't figure out, Andrew, is why you still wanted to marry me today. I mean, before I caught you. Did you think that you were going to marry me and keep on sleeping with her?"

"I don't know," he said, and for the first time he looked like he was at a loss.

For the first time he was acting a lot less like the villain in one of those movies she liked so much. The pompous, sniveling ex come in from the city, only to blame the heroine for his bad behavior.

For the first time, he looked *ashamed*.

And she felt…conflicted. There was no excuse for what he'd done. But she was looking at the issues she'd brought to this relationship with uncomfortable clarity.

"I don't know what I was going to do. I fell into that with her, and it made me feel good about myself. You think you know everything, Evelyn, and you just… You had a way of looking through me. You were obsessed with planning the wedding. With your dress, with all the details. You loved your mother having to eat crow. Especially as the business started to take off. You had your face in your planner more often than you had it present in a conversation with us."

"And you insisted that we continue to live separately. You were sneaking around behind my back."

"Yes," he said. "Yes, I was. I… My dad cheated on my mom," he said.

His words shocked her. Because his father was such a well-respected man, and his mother along with him. And they'd been married for nearly forty years. She would never have thought…

"It made home life hell," he said. "And I never… I never thought there was any justification for that. I never thought there was any reason for a man to cheat. I despised it. And

I did it to you. I think part of it was… Not wanting to deal with it. I didn't want to call it what it was. So I compartmentalized it. I did what I was doing with her and then interacted with you like nothing was going on. I kept everything separate. So, I did figure we would just get married."

"What did *she* think? Did she think that you were going to leave me at the altar or something?"

"We didn't talk about it. Honestly. Whatever she imagined was going to happen… That's not… I don't know. I didn't have a relationship with her."

"Did she come on to you?"

"Does it matter?"

"Yes," she said. "It does. Because I'm trying to make a new life for myself, and I'm realizing that part of my problem is I didn't deal with the old one. Because here you are. And I don't really feel sorry for you that my parents had to tell you that we weren't having the wedding. My reaction to you and Hollyn together should've been your first clue. But… I should've talked to you. And no matter what happened… I didn't talk to you. Because I didn't want to have this conversation. So let's…have the conversation. Tell me. Tell me what you were feeling and why, and…you can tell me what I did wrong."

She had been protecting herself in all her relationships. Keeping back a certain amount of herself, making sure not to invite conversations she didn't want.

"Yes, she came on to me, but… I put myself in the position. I knew there was…interest from her and I made sure the opportunity was there. I feel bad," he said. "I feel really upset that I sabotaged our life together. I'm really angry that you… What did you even do? You came out here and… hooked up with some redneck?" He shook his head. "And I know I don't have the right to feel upset about that. Because I did sleep with someone else. But it *kills* me that you did."

"Yes," she said. "I did sleep with him." And she was petty enough to get some pleasure out of the fact that it bothered him. "But if you were hoping to come here and find a reconciliation, I have bad news for you. I'm marrying Sawyer. Everything fell apart for me when I caught you with her. Everything. I couldn't… I couldn't stand it. I couldn't stand to be in the city. I couldn't stand to be in a place where I thought… This is the problem. I wanted so badly for us to be okay that I ignored the reality in front of me. I didn't want to see us crumble. But I can see now, very clearly, that I was more in love with the life I wanted us to have together than I was with you."

"What?"

"I just wanted…a husband. And children. And I was willing to keep a surface idea of peace in order to achieve that. I didn't want to rock the boat, I didn't want to—"

"You want all that so bad you came out here and…is that what this is? With…him?"

"I answered an ad. But it's what we both want. You and I, we had a relationship, and I was using that to get me where I wanted to be, but Sawyer and I both…we've been up front about what we want. It's not unspoken. He needs a wife and a mother for his daughter and I want to be that wife and mother."

Andrew pinched the bridge of his nose. "You're not making any sense."

"I know," she said, looking at the man that she had been with for ten years.

It was so much time. So many kisses. So many promises. So many dreams that had included sharing a life with him.

And now… It was just different.

She couldn't see that life now. Her visions of her future had been firmly replaced with Sawyer. With Four Corners. And she realized that wasn't going to make sense to most people. That she was so firmly and utterly sure of what she wanted without having spent even a fraction of the time here, with Sawyer, that she had with Andrew. But it didn't matter what other people thought. It didn't matter what they believed. What mattered was her. The changes in her. The revelations that marked this new part of her life. This new chapter.

"Please come home with me," Andrew said. "We don't have to get married right now."

"Well, we couldn't," she said, laughing. "The resort is booked out months in advance."

"And where are you getting married here?"

She smiled. "I don't know. I don't actually care."

"Do you love him?" he asked, frowning.

"I've only known him for two weeks."

"Did you love me?" he asked, more pointed. And it would be easy to be reactionary. It would be easy to yell at him and ask him what right he had to ask that question. But instead, she just looked at him.

"You were a habit," she said. It sounded cruel, and she didn't mean it that way. "Like brushing my teeth. I knew that I would wake up in the morning and I would do that, and you would probably be there. Because we would've spent the night together. Companionably, mostly. You were the person that I texted when something good would happen, or when something bad would happen. But let's be honest with ourselves, with each other, do you think that it would've been any different if you were texting Hollyn? Or if I were texting someone else? Were we just looking for a place for our words to go? How long has it been since it mattered that it was you? Since it mattered that it was me?"

He looked dumbfounded. Maybe she didn't make any sense. She felt like she did, though. "I don't know what the hell that's even supposed to mean."

"We were just…bumping along. We were just each other's partners, so that we wouldn't be alone. Don't you see that? And don't you want more than that?"

"I don't…"

"Do you love Hollyn?"

He looked at her, with a flat expression on his face. "Her family isn't right."

"Are you serious? You would sleep with her, and there's something wrong with her family? What? Because she's from Louisiana, and they don't have money, and you can't imagine her white trash relatives showing up at your wedding?" Weird how she still wanted to defend Hollyn even though she had betrayed her royally. The fact remained that she did. She wasn't going to argue with herself. "How dare you?" she asked.

"Hey," he said. "You know how it is. Families like yours, families like mine, they have expectations. Does your family know that you came out here to this dust bowl?"

"The dust bowl is in Oklahoma, but nonetheless, they know that I met someone. They don't know that I'm getting married."

"I still don't understand. You want a baby so much you were willing to just grab the first guy who came along with one? Like he's the prop you needed for your dream? Doesn't matter who the husband is as long as you get one?"

"Yeah," she said, feeling guilty when the word left her lips because Sawyer was more than that.

All right, she hadn't given him the brutally honest whole

story of her life, but she hadn't told that to anyone. And it wasn't about that, anyway. They had expectations they'd clearly laid out and they were both willing to do what they needed in order to meet them.

That made it different.

The foundation of the relationship was this common goal. So maybe he was a…convenience. But so was she, and she knew it.

But she thought of the way he kissed her, thought of the way that his hands moved over her body.

He mattered.

Intimacy.

That would take time to grow. But she was going to have to decide what she wanted that to look like. What she decided she wanted them to look like. She was going to have to decide what kind of marriage she wanted, because the fact was she was marrying the man. She was promising to be with him forever. And it was an intense sort of connection, and intense sort of promise, because there was a child involved. A child that she wasn't biologically related to, and if she didn't hurry up and adopt Bug… Well, she wasn't going to have any claim to her at all.

This marriage, the adoption, all of it was so important. It was a real, bone-deep commitment that she was making, and… If she was going to commit herself to a life it had to be different and better than the one that she'd been willing to engage in with Andrew.

The one that had fallen apart like a Jenga tower that day.

Their house had to be solid, built on the rock just like the house at Garrett's Watch. It had to be.

"Andrew, I did love you," she said. "And I don't know when I fell out of love with you. It wasn't when I caught you with Hollyn. I thought that it was. But you're right. There were problems. Potholes in the road, and we just kept on driving. We didn't stop to examine what was wrong. We didn't talk to each other. Not beyond the pleasantries. We didn't take care of our relationship. Because we were both so confident that we were the right kind of person for each other we didn't notice that everything was going wrong."

"So that's it?"

"Yes," she said, standing firmly and facing the unpleasant thing. Not running away. "Yes. That's it."

It was a strange thing, to say those words to a man she had such a long-standing relationship with, and know that she meant it. That she was closing the door. And she felt sadder right then than she had when she'd discovered him cheating, because at least then she had a sense of defiance.

She could see the good things about him now. And there had been good things. She could also see…a lot of bad things she'd willfully ignored. Not the bad of cheating, but that he was a snob. That he was chained to the expectations of his parents, and she hadn't dug deep into it, because the reverse would mean him digging deep into her.

But she had fallen for him, for real, back then. She hadn't let herself think about when they'd met, the first date they'd gone on when they'd driven to Vermont and gone apple picking and gone on a hayride.

When she told him she didn't kiss on the first date, but at the end she'd kissed him, anyway, because she'd thought he was so cute.

About all the times he'd walked her home at night from work, to make sure she got there safely. Holding her hand.

About the way he'd given her his jacket when she was cold, and sometimes she didn't bring one on purpose so that he would.

But thinking about those things now… The way that

they were hazy, the way those feelings felt, so far in the rearview mirror, so different to what she wanted now. So different to what she needed... It was melancholy, sure, but it also left things very clear.

Because then she could think of the good, and also the truth of him and his flaws, not just the thing that had broken them up...

She didn't want him as her husband.

She didn't him as the father of her children.

Sawyer *wasn't* a prop. Because she wanted him as both of those things. Him.

She started to walk toward the door. Then she pulled it open, and gestured. "Unless you want to go to the wedding, I have to get ready."

"You are actually going to marry this man you don't even know?"

"I don't know how to explain it," she said. "Except...I might not be in love with him now, but he's the man I want to fall in love with."

"What the hell does that mean?"

"I don't know. I don't know how to explain it, like I said. Not even to myself. But you're right, I haven't known him very long." And she'd only had one blistering night of sexual pleasure with him. "But I want him. I want this place to be my future. I want him to be the man by my side. And I'm really, really sure of that."

"Right. You think you know that... But you had ten years with me, and now suddenly you don't want to be with me. So maybe you don't know your own mind as well as you think."

"No. It took that experience to realize that I could be that certain about someone this quickly. Because I didn't feel desperate to marry you. I felt my biological clock ticking and that was about it. I want to marry him. I want to be with him. I want to build a life with him."

"What kind of life can you even have out here?"

"I don't know," she said. "But I'm really desperate to find out. And it's not to show anyone, it's not to rub anyone's nose in my success, because no one in my family would recognize this as success. Hollyn wouldn't. Kioni wouldn't. You don't, I get that. But this is just about me. I need a new space to call my own. I need to make a life that makes me happy. Not one that just looks like something other people might want."

"Well, when you come back to New York, my number will be the same."

"Mine won't be. Because I'm getting off your plan. I don't want you to track my phone again."

"Keep your number, Evelyn, they'll transfer it. Don't be dramatic." He stopped in front of the door. "I really loved you."

She thought back to the girl she'd been when she met him, because she had been a girl. Twenty-four and out of college and embarking on her professional journey with her friends. Excited to live in New York, excited to meet a guy like him who was serious about success in the same way that she was, and didn't behave like a frat boy the way a lot of other men in their demographic did. That girl had really loved him with the whole capacity of what she was capable of. But the woman that Evelyn had become really didn't. Cheating aside, she just didn't.

He shook his head. "What am I supposed to tell everybody?"

"Tell them I lost my mind. Tell them you cheated. Tell Hollyn you want to marry her. Honestly, Andrew, if you want to be with her, man-up and make a life that looks like what you want. But mostly, what you do, what you want, isn't up to me."

"I don't know what I want," he said. His eyes were hollow, and she almost felt sorry for him.

"I *do* know what I want. And your lack of knowing your own self can't be my problem."

And when he left, she realized she had never told him that she used to love him. But it didn't matter, because she couldn't explain herself to him, anyway. There was no explaining what she felt right now. There was no explaining herself to anyone. Especially not when she couldn't even untangle all of it for herself.

She went back upstairs, and grabbed the white, silk slip dress that she had decided to wear today. It fell down midcalf, a little longer in the back than in the front; the top was a V-neck that showed off a whole lot of cleavage, but Sawyer really liked her cleavage. A little red lipstick and a pearl necklace were all she had to complete the effect. And she realized that she didn't have a ring for him. She didn't know if he had one for her.

She took a breath, plucked up her courage, then went downstairs to get married.

CHAPTER TWELVE

IT WAS ELSIE who had ended up offering to bring Evelyn over for the wedding. He had seen Andrew leave in a huff, so he had known that she was still intent on having a wedding, even though the prick had showed up.

Unbelievable.

Elsie had declared that it was bad luck for him to see Evelyn, and he didn't want to tell her that he'd already seen her, and her robe, and prior to that in much less, so it wasn't like he was going to be surprised. But he obeyed his sister, and went down to the lake with Bug and Wolf.

He looked down at Bug, who was wearing the frilliest little pink dress he'd ever seen, and she was far too little to understand. She looked around with her dark blue eyes, that generic new-baby color that he knew would change. Her fists were rocking back and forth, her mouth slack. She put her fists in her mouth, and he knew that she was about to get testy with him. So he took a bottle out of the diaper bag.

"Only you can't spend too long on it," he said. "Because I'm getting married."

She didn't react to it. She just happily snuffled at her bottle. Not for the first time he wondered if she would be better off with someone else. The very idea made his heart twist. But it was his deepest fear. That somehow by staying he wasn't doing her any more favors than Missy had done by leaving.

But he was giving her Evelyn.

And Evelyn was wonderful with her.

Evelyn would know how to do all the things for Bug that she needed. She would know how to talk to her about her feelings. She would be there to bandage her skinned knees when she fell. She would know how to talk to her about puberty and boys and all the things that made Sawyer want to go out and get in a fight even now.

His grandmother had done that for him. Had set him down and told him the facts of life. Had told him if he ever mistreated a woman she'd skin him like a bobcat.

It made him smile even now.

Marrying Evelyn was the best thing he could do for Bug. And it would give her a life here on the ranch. This ranch that was her legacy. All right, as a dad, he might be a pretty shady legacy, but Garrett's Watch was a good one. That was for damn sure. He couldn't deny her that.

His chest felt like it was burning, and he did his best to take a breath and pushed that aside. His old man had been such a blank wall. Not doing much of anything for his kids beyond making sure they were fed. He'd never known any tenderness in his life if it weren't for…

He missed his gram more than just about anything right then. She would've worn a blue dress with a string of pearls. Her Sunday best. It was what she always wore. And red lipstick. Because that was fancy. It made him smile just to think of it.

"She was the best lady," he whispered, looking down at Bug. "I hope you got some of her spirit."

"She's here," Wolf said, interrupting his thoughts.

He looked up, and saw Elsie's car just as she stopped. There was a handful of Four Corners people assembled for the wedding. The McClouds, the Kings and the Sullivans, naturally. Because they always showed up for each other's shit, whether they really wanted to or not. It was just part of being bonded together the way that they were.

Several of the ranch hands had showed up, as well, along with Nate, from Becky's, and of course Pastor Dave, from the First Baptist Church down the way. He'd had to get a pastor, obviously.

She got out of the car, and his heart stalled out. He was standing by the lake, his back to the water, and there was a grassy walk that led up to the sandy shore. Her dress was blowing in the breeze, along with her blond curls. A flower was woven into her hair by some kind of feminine magic he could never have guessed at, and she had a string of pearls around her neck. Her lips a beautiful ruby red.

He had his grandmother's pearls, in a box in his room, along with the other keepsakes that he never looked at because they made him feel things that he didn't want to feel. He had never mentioned them to her. Hell, he never mentioned how much they meant to him to anyone. Wolf barely remembered their grandparents. Not in the same way that he did. Elsie even less. He was the one who'd had the longest relationship with them. He had been sixteen when his grandma died. Elsie had only been six.

He didn't even think he'd ever told anybody he had those pearls. Those keepsakes. But he did. They were damned important to him. So damned important.

And while those weren't the pearls, they were enough to make him think of them. Enough to make him feel like Gram was there, watching. Like maybe she even approved.

And then all thoughts of his grandmother burned away completely, because the closer she got, the more overwhelmed he was by her beauty. She was just the most incredible creature he'd ever seen. The dress clung to her curves, her breasts plump and tempting, as glorious as he remembered them. And two days was too long without his hands on them. She was marrying him. Not that prick that had come from New York City. She was marrying him. This soft, improbable creature that shouldn't want to be here. That didn't fit on his ranch, or in his life. But here she was.

"Do you want me to hold Bug?" Wolf asked.

"No," he said.

Because he had to remember that this was about her. This was about doing right by his daughter. Not indulging his libido. But damn, it felt indulged.

She walked toward him with a scraggly wildflower bouquet in her hands, her eyes downcast, a little smile on her lips, and his heart did things he didn't know it could do. He adjusted his hold on Bug, and handed the bottle to Wolf. The baby was sleeping now, a trail of milk running down her cheek. She gave a little sigh, contented. She looked milk drunk, and right about then everything felt a little bit too real. Felt a little bit too much. He'd avoided this his entire life.

Babies. Marriage.

And here he was, in the middle of his soft, beautiful child, and the soft, beautiful woman who was going to marry him.

He wanted…something. Something to do with all the restless energy inside of him. Like for a bear to come crashing through the trees so he could wrestle it. That would make him feel better. It would do something to satisfy the intensity inside of him. Because God knew there was nowhere else for it to go.

She came to stand in front of them, and the pastor took his position. Everybody was just standing. There were no chairs set up or anything. Just a circle of people standing around. Those same faces that he'd seen all of his life. On this ranch that he'd always lived on. With the person who was very new to the earth, and a stranger who was very new to this place. Bug, stuck here by virtue of birth, the same as the rest of them here, he supposed. And Evelyn. Who was here by choice. In spite of the fact that it was entirely different to where she'd come from. Different to the place she'd known all of her life. She had uprooted herself to be here with him, and somehow… It escaped him, until just now, just what a humbling thing that was.

He felt brought low by it.

Her fiancé had flown across the country to come after her, and she had chosen to stay. She had chosen this place. She had chosen them.

She had asked him what he was offering her, and he'd said… He was the one who put out the ad so he didn't have to make an offer. And suddenly that felt like shit.

He had warned the pastor they didn't have rings. But that had been a dumbass thing to do. He was going to have to get her a ring.

Something that was worthy of her. It wasn't like he didn't have the money. Hell, he barely spent any apart from what he bought for Bug. Everything went back into the ranch, except what he needed for necessities. A whole bunch of money just sat there in a bank account.

"Glad you came," he said when she reached him.

"Yeah," she said, offering him a small smile. "So am I."

His breath caught, and he turned to the pastor.

"All right," Dave said. "Let's get to it, then. Take each other's hands."

They did.

"Sawyer, do you take this woman to be your lawfully

wedded wife? In sickness and in health, riches and rags, for better or worse, till death do you part?"

"I do," he said, surprised how easily the words came out.

"Do you, Evelyn, take him, in sickness and in health, richer or poorer, better or worse, till death separates you?"

"I do," she said.

"Then what God has joined together no man can put asunder. By the power invested in me by the state of Oregon, and by God Almighty, I pronounce you husband and wife."

And that was that. The shortest damned wedding ceremony on record.

"You can kiss each other," he said.

He hadn't expected it to be quite so casual. He had been naturally suspicious of the pastor in flip-flops since he had shown up to town, and honestly, he felt justified in that suspicion.

But the ceremony had been efficient, and he had not forgotten that rings wouldn't be part of it. So he supposed he couldn't complain.

Still holding Bug in one arm, he wrapped his hand around the back of Evelyn's head, and pressed a kiss to her mouth. He felt her tremble beneath that kiss, and what he wanted to do was hand the baby off now, pull her up against him and indulge himself.

But he decided that wasn't maybe the best thing to do with an audience.

When it was over, there were mild cheers from those in attendance, and he noticed that they had already dropped the tailgates on the trucks and gotten out coolers.

"Just like these degenerates," he muttered. "Any excuse for a party."

"Well," Dave said. "I'm going to have to go. The official stance on beer is not so much."

"Well, God and I will work it out later," Sawyer said, accepting a beer from Wolf.

Elsie handed one to Evelyn, and he...suddenly felt kind of embarrassed. Because what the hell kind of wedding had she just walked herself into? He suddenly had a thought, and he stepped to the side, still holding Bug, and put in a call down at the bar. "Do you have the number for the Silver Falls resort?"

He got it from the bartender, then dialed it on his phone, making sure there were rooms available before he committed to anything.

"Hey," he said to Wolf. "Do you think you and Elsie could cover me with Bug for a couple nights?"

"Sure," Wolf said. "If you like."

"Yeah. I... I think I need to take my wife on a honeymoon."

"Well, that is one of the first sensible things I've ever heard you say. If you're going to get married, you better work on keeping her happy. At least for the first few days."

"Yeah, I'm working on it."

She seemed happy enough, laughing with the Sullivans and drinking her beer. But that man who'd come by earlier... He planned something fancy for the two of them. He bet their honeymoon was supposed to be in Barbados or some shit. Probably not at a mountain resort that was not a whole lot different than where they lived. But... It was something. Yes. It was something.

CHAPTER THIRTEEN

EVELYN FELT LIKE she was experiencing a head rush. She had married him. They had really done it. It had been brief, and impersonal. But there had been something… Also deeply personal about the whole experience. The fact that he had been holding Bug in the dress that she had chosen for her. That she had been part of the ceremony, a reminder of why they had decided to do this. And then he'd handed her a beer.

A beer.

And she was having what seemed to be a tailgate wedding ceremony, and it just seemed about right.

She wasn't unhappy about it. Her old life had literally come chasing after her, and she'd had a chance to turn away from this. Away from him. But she hadn't wanted to. But she wanted… She wanted to promise him more things that had come up during the ceremony. She wanted to talk to him.

Really. Deeply.

About what she felt, what she wanted. All that they could be.

And maybe share things about herself, and how she'd come to be here, and what she was realizing now about the way she avoided hard conversations. About how she'd nearly self-destructed after she'd failed at being perfect in dance.

And she wanted him. Most of all.

Her hands were sweaty. She wondered what tonight would hold.

And she just knew that no matter how unsteady she felt, no matter how surreal this felt, it still felt like the right thing. She took a breath, taking another sip of beer.

"Hey," Elsie said, grinning broadly. "Wolf and I are watching Bug tonight," she said. "Sawyer is taking you somewhere fancy."

She blinked. "He is?"

"Yes," Elsie said, her smile increasing.

"Did you just blow my surprise?" Sawyer asked. "Get out of here, you pest," he said, giving Elsie a light punch on the shoulder. She looked unrepentant, and scampered off toward the Sullivans.

Sawyer turned to Hunter. "Go deal with her," he said.

"No thanks," Hunter said. "I don't want to get on the wrong end of Elsie. I might end up with her teeth embedded in my flesh."

"No less than you deserve," Sawyer said.

"Arguable," Hunter retorted.

But he went off toward Elsie, anyway, and she looked like an irritated cat when he entered into her sphere.

"I just wanted him to go harass her," he said. "Because God knows she annoys me."

"Did you really have something special in mind?" she asked.

"It's nothing. I mean, it's not actually fancy. You have to understand... Remember Elsie was actually born in a barn."

She laughed. "I'm just... Thank you. For doing something. For doing anything. That's really nice."

"The bar is so incredibly low."

"It's actually not," she said.

He shook his head. "So, thanks for marrying me instead of that asshole."

"I could've married him," she said. "He was angling for me to go back with him. But I didn't want to."

"Why?"

"Maybe we can save the discussion for tonight."

She wanted a long talk. With just the two of them. She didn't want to be interrupted. And she didn't want to share him.

She wasn't jealous of the women at Four Corners, or anyone else. But they had all known Sawyer longer than she had. She wanted something special. Something that was theirs.

They finished drinking beer with the family, then they drove back to the house together after both of them gave Bug a kiss goodbye. It was weird not to have her. They had that one night together without her, but still, she was so used to caring for her, to getting up with her at night, to the day in day out of having a baby… It had already started to feel so natural. So much a part of who she was.

And she felt a little bit giddy with the freedom of not having her. The way that new parents often talked about feeling.

She packed her lingerie. All of it, because she didn't know exactly what she'd be in the mood to wear. And then she met him downstairs with her bag slung over her shoulder. Her heart was thundering hard. That kiss at the wedding had only reminded her of the intensity of their connection. Even with an audience she had felt completely and totally under his spell. Like they were the only two people who mattered.

That was an interesting thing about being confronted with Andrew. He suffered so badly by comparison to Sawyer. And it wasn't just looks, though she would lay bets that pretty much anybody would pick Sawyer as the better-looking man, but it had to do with that chemistry. Something that time was never going to be a factor in. Because she had never felt that for Andrew. Or indeed for anyone. She had never even known the capacity for such desire existed inside of her.

But that was the thing to watch with Sawyer, she had a feeling.

Because it would be easy to be blinded by that passion. Not in the way that he was afraid of it. That it would make them be awful. She and Andrew's relationship had gotten swallowed up by routine. By what the other represented. It had gotten turned into a token. A box that was checked on the list of achievements that they had both wanted. She was the kind of woman that he needed to marry. He would make the perfect husband. They had been compatible. And those things had taken place of an actual deep, intimate relationship.

While she had a feeling with Sawyer…hot, frequent sex could take the place of conversation any night of the week. And while she wasn't wholly opposed to that, it was just they needed to build something else on top of it.

Because that was what she craved. If she and Sawyer didn't know each other, she didn't know how she was ever going to know herself.

The man was a mountain. Remote and hard and…she wanted to climb him. But more than that, he was hard to figure out. She knew there was more to him, deeper parts than he was willing to let on.

And she wanted to know him. All of him.

They got into the truck, and when the door closed, she felt like all the air had been sucked out of the cab. And she figured… Why be cautious. She launched herself across the space and into his arms.

And she kissed him. Right there in the driveway.

He grabbed hold of her, hard, angling his head and taking the kiss deep. Her heart was thundering wildly. Her whole body on high alert. But she managed to pull herself away, settle herself in her seat.

"A preview," she said.

"Lord have mercy," he said, turning the car and pulling out of the driveway, and out onto the two-lane highway. She hadn't been on this road since she had first come to Four Corners. Which she now thought was a little bit funny. But she hadn't been tempted at all to explore the town yet. Such as it was.

"Where is this place we're going?"

"About forty miles up the highway," he said. "It's supposed to be really…fancy?"

She laughed. "Fancy, huh? That doesn't sound like you. Have you ever been?"

"No. It's got a spa, though."

"Do you know what happens at spas?" she teased.

"No."

"Are you going to get a massage?" she asked.

He shifted. "Only if you're giving it."

"You're not already harboring fantasies of another woman rubbing lotion over your body?"

"Honey," he said. "I forgot other women existed."

Her breath caught. "Well, that is a refreshing change."

"Oh, compared to that absolute tool that you were engaged to before?"

"Yes. Compared to that absolute tool."

"What exactly did he say to you?" Sawyer asked. "How did he try to justify himself?"

"Surprisingly, he did a little bit less justifying than I imagined he would. I mean, it wasn't like he didn't try. But… He… He was right. We were having problems. And I was happy to try to not notice them. I let them slide. Because he represented something that I wanted. And what he did was so wrong. But I think that I… I think he wasn't happy. Really. And he did the wrong thing. You don't cheat on somebody just because you're not feeling blissfully happy in your relationship. This is not what you do. But I wasn't perfect. I stopped fighting with my mother, or explaining myself to her, years ago but I still…want to prove myself to her. Except it's funny, with you, out here, I just don't care about that. Not anymore."

"Easy to do, I guess, when the people are a few thousand miles away."

His words caught something in her chest. "Maybe. Being confronted with him did make it really clear that I'm just not dealing with the things back home. I wasn't dealing with them when I was there. I suspected things between us weren't good and I just didn't want to know. I didn't want to talk about it because I didn't want to have hard conversations. I just… I hate failing, Sawyer, and I thought that I had dealt with that. Because when I left ballet I self-destructed. If you can't be perfect, why try at all? But I rebounded from that. I thought. But I was just still avoiding ever having to face imperfections in my plans. Still burning things down and running away when things got…hard."

"Hey," he said. "I'm not exactly a bastion of emotional health and stability. I wouldn't take any criticism from me."

"I want… I want to be happy."

"Hell, who doesn't?"

Except she privately wondered if he had ever really given much thought to it.

"Are you *happy*?" she asked. "Or are you content?"

"Isn't it all the same?"

"I don't think so. I want joy."

"When I look at Bug," he said. "I... I don't know. I feel something... It makes me feel grounded. And it also makes me feel like I'm stronger. And weaker all at once. Like I'd tear open the earth if that's what it took to protect her. Like I'd scale the highest mountain. I don't know if that's joy. But it's purpose. I've got a lot of purpose. And I'm pretty good with that."

"I like that. A lot of people spend their whole lives looking for purpose. Questioning it. There's something nice about being certain that you found it. Doesn't there need to be more than that? You work the land all your life, and then what? At the end of the day you... What do you have?"

He cleared his throat. "Something real to pass on to my children."

"But you weren't going to have children."

He shrugged. "I guess it doesn't matter when you belong to something as big as Four Corners. It's a legacy we built that goes on to all the families' future generations, to everyone who works the land. And Wolf and Elsie will probably have kids. I always thought so, anyway."

"You sure about that?" she asked.

"Pretty sure." He sighed. "I mean, Wolf maybe not but..."

"Elsie was quite literally born in a barn."

"Still. Someday... Someday she'll find some man and settle down." He sounded not superhappy about the idea, though. Such an older brother.

"Where? She knows all the men on the ranch. She's known them all of her life. She hasn't shown any interest in them so far."

"They need to grow up, is all. The ones in her age group. Plenty of the ranch hands' kids that we grew up with work there now. It's just they're in their early twenties. Men in their early twenties suck."

She laughed. "No argument from me. Though it has to be said, men in their early thirties haven't done much for me recently, either. Present company excluded."

"Appreciated," he said.

"No problem."

"The land is enough for me. Bug is enough for me. Knowing that I've given her what she needs to have the kind of life she deserves."

She made a musing noise. "It's just… I don't know. Maybe that's the difference between the kind of work I did and ranching. I'll tell you… I really enjoyed helping people organize their lives. But there was a point… Where that wasn't the point. There was a point where just being good at my job wasn't really the point. Because the problem was I got really consumed with being everything my mother said she couldn't be because of me. Because of her broken dreams. I wanted to fix them at first." She let out a slow breath. "Sawyer, I've never told anyone why I left the academy. Why I quit dancing."

There was silence for a moment. "Do you want to tell me?"

That question, that simple question, made her heart lift. "Yes. I do. I… I started dance there when I was eleven. And by the time I was thirteen, puberty hit and, well." She gestured to her curves.

He looked out of the corner of his eye. "You're…hot?"

She laughed. "I have boobs. Big ones. And hips. And I am not built like a lithe ballerina. And I really, really needed to be." She sighed. "Dancers tend to be a certain body type. Ballet is traditional, and it's based on lines and shapes and you have to make those shapes. Curves like mine…disrupt that."

"Did they say that to you?"

She nodded. "Yeah." She breathed out, long and hard. "I was never going to get a principal position looking like I did. There was no push for inclusion then, no body positivity movements. I couldn't just…follow an account on social media that showed me different kinds of beauty. There was one kind of beauty that was acceptable, and one kind of shape you could be in dance. I had to be that."

"What happened?"

"I quit eating."

The truck slowed. "You…quit eating."

"Yes. I mean, I did eat. I counted jelly beans. I liked to eat in even numbers. Control. I just wanted to take control because when hormones and puberty hit and changed my body I felt out of control. And it worked. I got thinner. But I wasn't strong anymore. My period, which had only barely started, stopped. And then I was dancing in rehearsal and I fainted. Another girl replaced me and ultimately got my part and I realized… I was never going to be good enough. I could kill myself with my eating disorder and die not good enough."

"Evelyn, I don't know what to say. You're…perfect to me. I can't… I want to personally destroy everyone that made you feel like you weren't."

She put her hand on his leg. She didn't know what to say because this was so deeply personal to her. Because she hadn't told anyone ever just how bad it was.

But she'd wanted him to know.

She needed him to know.

It was the only thing she knew to do that was different.

The only thing that felt like more. She'd hidden this part of herself for so long. Always hiding pieces of herself. Always protecting herself.

She didn't want to do that anymore.

"Honestly, I would've married him if he hadn't cheated on me. I wouldn't have realized that it wasn't the kind of marriage I wanted. I just wanted a marriage."

He cleared his throat. "And what kind of marriage is it that you want?"

"Well, we're a lot closer, I can tell you that." She breathed out, long and slow.

He hadn't run from her. He wasn't even judging her.

"How close are we?"

She put her hand on his thigh, and let her fingers start walking up toward his package.

"I am driving," he said. "And I am not about to crash the car."

He still wanted her.

"Well, this is a good start," she said. Feeling guilty because she had just been telling herself she couldn't let things get all muddled by sex. The problem was she wanted to feel a little muddled.

Couldn't she tonight? Couldn't she just pursue this on their wedding night? It seemed fair.

She'd just told him some things that were very exposing. And his attraction to her made her feel good.

"Honesty," she said. "What you've already promised me."

He's the kind of man I want to love. Those words stuck in her throat. Along with anything else she might've said.

She didn't really know what to say next.

Instead, she focused on the scenery, which was incredibly beautiful.

The trees that lined the road were broad and mature, and the leafy green plants that covered the ground created the surreal fairy forest that drew her in. She had never considered herself much of a nature girl.

She liked to *do* things.

She liked to be able to get out and walk in a busy city when her head was cluttered up with thoughts. When she didn't know what to do, and when she was upset. She liked to put on her headphones, put the sound of music over the top of the noise. And give herself a beat to stomp to.

Out here there was so much silence.

Layers of it.

So different from silence in the city, which always felt ominous. Turning onto a street to be greeted by total quiet was not a good thing.

But here, it was serene. A quiet that settled over her and down into her bones.

The pace was slower, the minutes rolling by, rather than ticking with insistence. And the nights were filled with their own music. Thick with it. With the sound of the crickets, and the rushing water. Sometimes she swore she could hear the twinkle of all those stars.

And who knew there were so many?

Millions of them scattered across that velvet sky like crushed diamonds. She had never thought that she could be happy in a place like this. Instead, she was discovering new levels of happiness. New kinds of beauty. New things that excited her. She was somewhat pleased by the fact that it felt easy to ride along in silence with him. Neither of them having the baby was a convenient distraction. Which she knew they often both fell back on to keep their hands busy. And it wasn't a strange sort of silence, or one where they were ignoring each other. She was very aware of him.

She always was. She wouldn't entirely call it comfortable, however. Because being this close to him while not actively consuming him could never be anything like comfortable.

There was a beautiful, ornate wooden sign that said Silver Falls Resort, and Sawyer took a right turn up that road. It was paved, with lights strategically placed to shine upon clusters of native plants that had clearly been planted there to be thicker and more prominent than they might have grown normally.

"You sure you've never taken a woman here before?" she asked, unsure why she was being a jealous pill, considering the man had just married her and all.

"No," he said.

"Just checking."

"I really haven't been here before. I've just seen the brochures."

"Oh," she said. "Well, that is nice."

"So, hopefully it's nice," he said. "Not some kind of tourist trap."

"Well, even that it would make kind of a funny story."

"To tell to...?"

"Everybody back at the ranch."

"You have people you talk to there?" he asked, teasing, but only a little.

"Are you worried that I'm regretting my choice?"

"I mean, tell me what man in my position wouldn't?"

He was stoic. As always. But there was an underlying truth to his words that made her chest feel a little bit tight.

"I had a chance to back out," she said. "I didn't take it. If I trust you to not be a serial killer, all things considered, I think you need to trust that I'm not just going to abandon you."

"I know," he said.

"Do you?"

"I do," he said, his voice rough.

But the conversation ended, because they pulled up to the front of the resort. He put the car in Park and got out, opening the door for her. She got out of the truck, and he grabbed both bags, hefting them effortlessly and walking them inside the place. The lobby was charming, with a river rock floor, and a large, bronze statue of a salmon that she wouldn't have said would be to her taste, but that was quite charming in context, dominating the center space.

"Sorry," he said. "I guess it's kind of rustic."

"I was just thinking how much I liked it," she said.

He walked up to the counter and took care of check-in while she wandered around, examining the surroundings. He returned a moment later with an actual key.

"I haven't seen a place that didn't have a card for entry in...a very long time."

"Nostalgic," he said.

She laughed. But she was feeling jittery. Like a teenager or just like a woman who was really, really in lust with her husband.

Her husband. All right, she had left a little bit about him wanting to wait until marriage. And they hadn't waited. Obviously, but the idea of having sex with her husband... It thrilled her. Caught something deep inside of her and held her in thrall.

"They said they would park the truck," he said.

"Oh, how nice," she said.

Mundane conversation to be having while visions of him naked danced through her head.

But then, that was her life with him so far. All these quiet moments with an underlayment of the extraordinary. Always so intense. No matter what they were doing. Whether it was discussing meat loaf or that the valet at the hotel was doing his job.

Their room was all the way at the end of the hall, and he pushed the key inside and turned the lock, opening it. And it was…magical. There were massive windows that looked out over mossy rocks, waterfalls that had been built up around the windows and pine trees and mountains beyond. It was completely secluded. Nothing back there but nature. That fairy forest feeling flooding back.

The room itself was huge, with a large bed laden with pillows. She wandered over to the bathroom, where the door was open. She saw that there was a very large tub.

Then she looked over toward the windows, and noticed that one of them was actually a sliding glass door. And beyond that was a hot tub. All secluded. And suddenly, she very much liked the idea of getting in there with him.

"It's something," he said.

She looked at his face, trying to get a read on what he actually thought of the place. He didn't travel, he'd said as much. So had he been to a place like this before? If he hadn't brought a woman here, then maybe he'd brought one somewhere else that was similar. But… He was just such a no-frills kind of guy. Did a place like this even mean anything to him? All humans liked to be comfortable, she supposed.

And why was she thinking these things rather than asking him?

"You come to places like this often?"

He huffed a laugh. "Never."

"Well, do you like it?"

"I said it was nice," he said.

"Right. Do you like… Do you like hot tubs?"

His head whipped over toward her. "Are you asking me if I want you to be hot and wet next to me?"

"I wasn't. But I guess you could interpret it that way."

"The answer is a resounding *hell, yes*, at least, to my interpretation of it."

And she could see that romance with him was going to be a little bit hard-edged. But hadn't he said that? That he wasn't a romantic.

And your heart wants him to be.

He's the man I want to fall in love with.

She gritted her teeth. She didn't need any guff from herself. She couldn't imagine anything more annoying.

Luckily she had packed a bikini, for just such an occasion. She had a feeling, at least she hoped, that it wouldn't stay on very long.

She banished all of her emotional misgivings and focused on the physical. And again, she wasn't going to let it overshadow the emotional. She understood that there were things that they needed to deal with. She did. But… Well, it was their wedding night. And she wanted him. She wanted him desperately. The connection that they had was not like anything else she'd ever experienced, and was it wrong to want to have a taste of it?

Uncomplicated.

Especially on the day that she had vowed to spend her entire life with him. In sickness and in health and all of that. It seemed fair.

She moved toward him, and wrapped her arms around his neck, kissing him. Then she smiled, and turned away, grabbing her day bag and heading into the bathroom to get changed. She found the bikini, which now seemed unbearably scant, all things considered. But she was excited.

Excited to be with him. Excited to… Well, to consummate their marriage.

And now who was sounding old-fashioned? Honestly. She was just so…

He was her husband.

He was her husband.

That hit a spot in her chest that she hadn't expected it to. Meant something, mattered in a way that she hadn't expected it to. She had thought that because they were strangers… Because they were doing it for reasons other than love that it wouldn't feel so momentous to have said those vows to him. Not by a river. It certainly wasn't a country club. Not a beautiful resort that was reserved months in advance.

A smile touched her lips. No. It was a lake that you could only get married at if you were part of the Four Corners family. It was more exclusive than anything. And the exclusivity of it didn't matter. The fanciness, the lack of it. None of it meant anything. Not in the face of how momentous a thing it had been to pledge her life to him.

Her finger shook as she tried to tie the strings on the bikini. Then she took a breath, and walked out of the bathroom.

His eyes burned.

"I didn't bring a bathing suit," he said.

Heat made her scalp prickle.

"Well, then I guess you better hope that back deck is private. Or I'm going to be using the hot tub by myself."

And he did exactly what she hoped he would do, he stripped his shirt off, a wicked grin on his face.

And it seemed like it would be an easy thing, the simplest thing, to block out the heaviness of the moment. That momentousness. That it would be not such a big deal, after all, to push the emotions to the side. They would have to deal with them later. Of course they would. They would have to do something to build that... That intimacy that she was so concerned about. The intimacy that she had lacked with Andrew. But right now, right now they could just focus on their connection.

The deep, intense sexual attraction between the two of them.

And he was beautiful. That was what she wanted to think about. That was what she wanted to focus on. His body. The way that he appealed to her. The way that he called to her. In a way that only he could. His shoulders were broad, his chest beautifully defined. His abs... She could compose sonnets about his abs, but it would be a waste of time.

She would rather be kissing them. Licking them. Running her fingers over them. And with a wicked glance, she beckoned him to come out onto the deck with her.

He followed, and she slipped into the scalding hot water as he stood there in the entryway, casting a fairly unconcerned glance out at the trees beyond. Where they were assured of a certain level of privacy. Then he put his hands on his belt buckle and started to undo it. Put his hands to work on the closure of his jeans, lowering the zipper slowly. Her breath caught in her throat. Her entire body poised on the edge of a knife.

And he did it. Stripped naked right there outside. He was hard already. Ready for her. And not ashamed of it in the least.

And it made her heart squeeze tight. That this beautiful man wanted her the way that he did. Her mouth was dry.

He got down into the hot tub with her, and crossed the space, pulling her into his arms and kissing her. Her heart started to beat painfully hard. She was dizzy.

She put her hand on his chest and pushed away lightly, moving to the other side of the water.

His grin went predatory, and everything inside of her responded to that.

Shuddered, and went limp. She wanted him to catch her. Oh, she wanted him to catch her.

He put his hands on her hips and fitted her over his lap, the hardest part of him pressing against the part of her that was most in need of him. She swallowed hard. She put her hand on his jawline, beneath his chin, and dropped a kiss on his mouth. He moved his hands around her back, slipped his fingertips beneath the strings.

"I've never had a wife before," he said, his voice gruff. "I don't mind it."

And as far as he was concerned that was poetry. She was well aware of that. And she felt it. More than any beautifully worded card or romantic speech from any other man. Not that there was any other man. Not in her memory. It was only him. Only Sawyer.

And suddenly, the words that he'd spoken twisted inside of her. Reverberated. Echoed. Wife.

And there were so many things she didn't know about this man. Who wasn't just a man she was attracted to. Not anymore. He was her husband. Her husband.

"Why do you call her Bug?"

She hadn't known that she was going to ask the question. Not until it had fallen out of her lips.

And then suddenly he turned to granite. This man who had been so hot and ready only moments before.

"Why do you want to talk?"

"I just thought…" And then he was kissing her. Hard. His hand went around to the back of her head, crushing her face to his. And she knew. She just knew that this was him trying to distract her. She didn't know why. She just knew that it was. That he didn't want to answer that question. Desperately. Really. He didn't want to talk to her about what he called the baby Bug. He didn't want to talk at all.

And she should resist that. She should tell him no.

She should make him talk.

But he was there. And he was Sawyer.

And he was her husband.

And this was what he seemed to need.

And maybe, right now, that was intimacy.

SAWYER'S HEART WAS beating hard. Her taste flooded him. And she was all around him. Slick and wet in his arms. He loved it when she was wet. She had been cold and wet when she'd fallen into the river, and now her skin was hot. That bikini was driving him crazy and he wanted to get it off her. And her question…

It had hit hard up against a brick wall inside of him. A place that he couldn't go. Not now. No, not now. He couldn't do this with her. He just couldn't do it. But this… This heat. This he could do. This was good. It was perfect.

He started to undo the bikini, bare her breasts for himself. They were perfect. Ripe and glorious, and they filled his hands. He squeezed her, looked up at her face, saw the pleasure clouding her eyes. She didn't want to talk. Not when they could do this. He knew it. She wanted him just as much as he wanted her. She'd tried to seduce him. Because she wanted to make sure that he wanted her just as much as she wanted him. It was laughable. He wanted her so much he couldn't breathe past it.

He couldn't do this shit. He couldn't do the *getting to know you, let's talk about our feelings* stuff.

But he could do this.

And he would show her.

That he wanted her just as much as she could ever want him. Just as much as anybody ever could. That he was desperate for her.

All right, he wasn't ever going to be able to be the most poetic husband. And maybe this was never going to be the kind of fancy that she wanted, though she had done a good job of pretending that she was impressed by it.

Maybe her standards had just lowered enough from having spent the last couple of weeks in Pyrite Falls.

He could only hope.

He wasn't going to be able to give her a life that was fancier than the one she'd left behind. Wasn't going to be able to give her more status. He was never going to be that guy Andrew. Was never going to show up in a fancy, long coat that kind of matched the one that she already wore. Wasn't going to have those glasses that he thought looked kind of ridiculous but other people seemed to think were sophisticated. Wasn't going to be polished and smooth.

But he was going to be true to her.

And he was going to make her body feel things that she had never thought possible.

He would keep her satisfied. He would. He'd keep her mindless with this. He would give them both this wonderful, intense pleasure until neither of them could breathe past it. Until it didn't matter what the hell else there was.

And maybe that flew in the face of not making it about them. Right now, he didn't the hell care. No. He just didn't. He couldn't.

Right now, the only thing was this. The only thing was them.

And he'd been trying to make it not that. He'd been trying to remind himself that this was for Bug. That this was to give her the kind of family that she needed. And it was.

But as for the two of them, if he had to keep her there by fucking her senseless every day, well, then he'd damn well do it.

Maybe that was the thing. Maybe he shouldn't fight the passion. Maybe he should work with it. Maybe it would be the thing that kept her there. Maybe it would be the thing that set him apart from Andrew the asshole.

Yeah. Well, he would damn well take it.

They didn't need anything but this. But promises and desire. That was enough. It would be enough.

He lowered his head, taking one sweet nipple into his mouth and sucking it hard. She gasped, letting her head fall back. Then he stood up out of the hot tub, lifting her with her legs wrapped around him, the hard press of his cock right where she wanted it. He knew it. Because he could see it. In her pleasure-clouded eyes. Could sense it in the response of her body. He knew her. Better than he knew himself. At least in this.

Maybe that didn't make any sense. But they hadn't made any sense from the moment they first made contact with each other. When her voice had practically given him a hard-on while she talked about how she didn't like meat loaf.

He took them both out of the hot tub, and carried them back into the hotel room. He deposited her on the bed, none too gently, and stripped the bikini bottoms away from her. Pushing her back up the bed and parting her legs as he did, clutching her thighs and lowering his head between them. And he consumed her. Got lost in it. In the taste of her, and how slick and wet she was for him. In the sounds that she made. And good God, did she make sounds. Didn't hold anything back. She dug her fingernails into his skin, pulled his hair, begged him. Said desperate, filthy things that left him feeling like he might die if he didn't have her. But he didn't let himself.

He just kept on pleasuring her.

With his lips, with his tongue, his fingers.

He pushed them inside of her, because he remembered how well she liked that the last time he'd done it, and she broke apart. But he didn't stop. He didn't stop until she came again, and again. Didn't stop until she was gasping and begging, crying out his name like a prayer. Or a curse. He couldn't be certain.

And he didn't rightly care.

He kissed her inner thigh, kissed her all the way down her legs, then moved back up her body, holding her chin steady as he kissed her. Then he held himself steady and pressed the head of his arousal to the entrance of her body. Then he flexed his hips forward and thrust home. He clenched his teeth together, fought to keep himself from coming right away. She was just so hot and tight.

So perfect.

Damn anyone who'd made her think otherwise.

She opened her eyes and looked up at him, licking those kiss-swollen lips, and he felt something crack apart in his chest. He clenched his teeth and did his best not to let himself come apart. He gripped the covers as tight as he could, bucking his hips forward. Then he reached around underneath her ass and pulled her up against him, each thrust violent. Each one trying to block out the feelings in his soul by trying to keep the ones in his dick as focused as possible. He wanted it to be about their bodies. He wanted it to be about this desire. He didn't want it to be about anything else.

But then his mind went blank of everything. Everything but her. Everything but this moment.

Everything but Evelyn.

His wife.

I've never had a wife before. I don't mind it.

That was an understatement. This was everything. *She* was everything.

"Evelyn," he said, his voice hoarse.

And it pushed her right over the edge. Her internal muscles clenched tight around him, and he lost it. Completely. Thrusting while inside of her until his climax grabbed his throat like a wild beast. Tore a growl out of him that echoed in the room. And when it was done, he could barely catch his breath. All he could do was lie beside her, breathing hard.

She rolled over to her side, pushing his hair off his forehead. Her blue gaze speculative. "It's hard for you, isn't it?"

"What," he said, huffing out a laugh. "If you mean my dick…"

"Well," she said, "that is hard. That isn't what I meant. I mean feelings."

He laughed, and it felt like it cut him. "Are they easy for anybody?"

"No."

He felt stripped raw, and he didn't like it. Like his skin was extra sensitive. And he should've just answered her damn question before he thrust inside of her, because now things felt even more confused. Now things felt really difficult. And before they just felt like an inconvenience.

"Well, then why do you say that about me like it's… Like it's anything."

"Never mind. Thank you. For this." She rolled over and

traced shapes over his chest with her fingertips. "This is really beautiful."

"You're beautiful," he said, lifting her fingertips to his lips and kissing them.

There was something like hope in her eyes just then and it about killed him to see it. Because it felt misplaced. Because he didn't feel worthy of it. Not in any real way. Because she deserved... Well, she deserved the whole world.

And he wasn't even sure he could give her a single star.

"Do you just take care of everybody?" she asked.

Her question seized something up in his chest. "I don't know. How well I take care of anybody probably differs depending on who you ask. Whether or not they're mad at me at a given time."

"It seems to me that you've done a great job caring for Wolf and Elsie."

"Wolf would kick my ass if he heard you say that I took care of him. Really... I haven't always looked out for Wolf. He's... He's been through some things, and it's nothing I can fix."

"What?"

He felt guilty talking about his brother's past. It wasn't his business, and Sawyer made an art of staying out of what wasn't his concern. Wolf never talked about it. Wolf never talked about anything.

His brother was proud, and he was hard. He made Sawyer look soft, and that said a lot.

But the way Evelyn asked made him want to share.

"He was in love once."

"Wolf was?"

"Yes." He lifted a shoulder. "It was a long time ago. He was...sixteen, seventeen. Somewhere around there. They were young."

"What happened?"

"She drowned."

"Oh," she said. "Poor Wolf…"

"Like I said. It's not something that he talks about. But he… He feels it. It changed him."

"Well, you couldn't stop that."

"I know. That's the thing. There's a whole lot of shit you just can't stop."

It was the kind of thing that terrified him when it came to Bug. That there was so much he was not going to be able to spare her from. Protect her from. There was just… There was just a lot of shit out there in the world.

"But you were there for him. And he knew it. That has to count for something."

"This is about as here for somebody as I get," he said. "I'm not sure that… I don't know."

"And Elsie? How young was she when her mother left?"

"I don't know. She was…six." He knew. He knew exactly how old his siblings had been when their mothers had abandoned them. He didn't know why he was pretending that he didn't. He didn't know why he was pretending it didn't matter when it did. He didn't know the why of a whole lot of things.

"How old were you?"

"Four," he said. "Doesn't matter."

"It does, though. You said you'd been on a plane once."

He jerked away from her. "Look, there's no point talking about any of this. Not right now."

She looked like she was going to argue, but then she didn't. Instead, she sat up, put her hand on his chest, leaned in and kissed him. "You're right. Tonight it's just you and me. Did you want to get a massage?"

"I have never let a stranger put their oily hands on me, and I am not about to start."

"I was led to believe that you let quite a few strangers put their hands on you."

"That's different. And I always buy them a drink first."

She gave him a saucy smile. "I don't see how it's different. Or at the very least I don't understand how you're playing off that it's somehow less salacious than a professional massage."

"Just *no* on the strangers touching me."

"I have an idea," she said.

She went into the bathroom, and returned with a bottle of lotion.

"Lie down," she said.

He lifted a brow. "You gotta give me a few minutes, Evelyn. I can't perform on command." But he had a feeling with her he could. He had a feeling he could get it up right now if she wanted him to.

"Get your mind out of the gutter," she said.

But then she was naked and sitting on his back, and there was nothing not dirty about where his mind was right now. Because the press of her skin on his made him want to turn right over onto his back and thrust inside her again. Watch her ride him.

He winced at the cold when she squirted lotion onto his back. But then she put her hands right on him and started to slide them over his muscles.

"Why don't you just let me make you feel good?"

"I would accept a blow job," he said.

"And I'm happy to give you one," she said. "But I would bet that you've had a few of those in your life."

"Guilty," he said.

"So what I'd really like is to give you something that no woman ever has."

"Well, you already married me."

"True." He let himself settle into the rhythm of her hands moving over his skin, her fingers digging into his work-worn muscles. And he had to grudgingly admit, even if only through wordless groans, that it felt pretty damn good.

"You have a wife now," she said. "So I'm going to take care of you sometimes. I'm going to massage your muscles, and make you meat loaf."

If these were their real vows, he'd take it.

"Also blow jobs," he said, feeling groggy now.

"I promise," she said.

Then he did flip over, and she squeaked, landing on top of him, her breasts crushed to his chest. He pushed her hair off her face and kissed her. He was in a damn good mood. He couldn't remember the last time he'd felt this good.

"I think this is going to work," he said.

"Feels like it's working to me," she said, wiggling her hips against his.

"I hate to overtax you," he said.

"Overtax me," she said. "I'm begging you."

He kissed her, and things started to heat up between them again quickly. And they never did see much of the rest of the resort. They saw that bedroom. They saw the hot tub a couple more times. Tested the seclusion of the balcony right along with it. They also tested out the tub, the shower and the carpet, come to that.

They ate meals in bed, played a few rounds of Go Fish, which Evelyn had said she found so charming and old-fashioned that, in her words: she could hardly deal.

"Hey," he said, one night as they lay on the floor with the blanket from the couch thrown over them. "I appreciate that you told me. About…about the eating stuff. Is there anything you need now to…support you?"

She shook her head, her heart expanding. "I got a lot of really good therapy. I never talked to anyone in my real life about it, but I did talk to professionals. I think the good news is the root cause of the actual disorder was very situational. I feel…insecure about all of it still. Like admitting I had that problem makes me weak."

He kissed her then.

His heart hurt. He didn't know quite what to say. But he knew the truth. So he figured he'd speak that.

"You aren't weak."

And when it was time to get back home, he felt pretty regretful. He could've stayed away with her for a lot longer. And that was sort of a strange feeling. To not miss Four Corners. Not even a little bit.

But he did want to see Bug. So it was time to get back. He couldn't leave her with Elsie and Wolf indefinitely.

"Don't say anything," he said when they got back in the truck, headed back to the ranch.

"About Wolf?"

It surprised him slightly that she didn't miss a beat when he'd said that with no context.

"Yeah," he said. "He doesn't like to talk about it."

"No. Of course not." Silence stretched between them. "So Wolf has been in love," she said. "But you haven't been."

He shook his head. "Never seemed worth it to me. And what he went through didn't exactly sell it."

"No. I imagine not."

When they arrived back home, Wolf and Elsie were at the main house. And he immediately took Bug from Elsie's arms.

"Some greeting," Elsie said.

"Good to see you," he said to his sister.

Wolf grunted.

"You need to learn some manners," he said to his younger brother.

"Me? You ought to learn some, too."

"What do I need manners for? I've already got a wife."

Yeah. This was going to work.

CHAPTER FOURTEEN

SAWYER'S WORDS REVERBERATED in her head. *What do I need manners for? I've already got a wife.*

He was being funny. And she knew that. It was just it… He was feeling settled now. And that was good. She wanted him to feel secure. She didn't want him to think that she was going to leave him at any moment. Because she wasn't. The couple days away with him had been… Well, if she hadn't felt bonded to him already, if it hadn't been increased by the marriage vows, that two days they'd spent all over each other in the hotel had done it.

The physical intimacy between them was unmatched. And it was more than just sex. There was a way that he anticipated her needs. A way that she was able to follow the cues of his body, figure out just how to touch him to make him lose his mind.

There was all of that. But when it came to conversation… There was a wall up. There were no-go areas that were so clearly marked. And she didn't know how to… She didn't know how to get past that. And she knew that she needed to, if she wanted to make something real. Something deep.

And now that she had noticed just how hard and thick the walls around him were, she couldn't unsee them. And it wasn't just her. Even Bug… He cared for her. It was obvious. He was so fiercely protective. But he wasn't… He wasn't soft. He held her like a man ready to fight an entire army to keep her safe. But he didn't speak softly to her. He didn't go all tender ever. And maybe that was just him. Maybe it was who he was. Maybe he was never going to be the kind of man who softened over much. Maybe he was always going to be more action and less emotion. And maybe there was nothing wrong with that.

Except she felt like there was more in him. She felt like her connection with him was deeper than that. Crying out to get to the bottom of him. Understanding everything about him. She wanted… She wanted everything he had to give. And that was it. She just suspected he had more to give. That they could be more. That they could be everything.

More than just passionate nights spent tangled in the sheets, tangled around each other. That was great. And it was wonderful. Singular. It had never been like that for her with any other man. But she didn't just want a piece of intimacy. She wanted all of it. Every last bit. And those words stuck with her, because as far as she was concerned it spoke to the fact that he felt like it was finished between them. Like they'd made all the progress they needed to. Because of course he was happy as long as he was getting massages and blow jobs.

And it wasn't that she was unhappy. It was just that she had realized some things about relationships. And maybe she wanted too much too quickly. That was entirely possible. Maybe she was being unrealistic. Maybe she was being unfair. They were having a family dinner tonight. Which was different, she was given to understand, than the big meetings with everyone. Because it was just the Garretts, and usually Hunter McCloud.

"So Hunter is your brother's best friend?" she asked Elsie as she got the rolls out of the oven and put them on the table.

"Yes," Elsie said, reaching immediately for a roll.

Evelyn reached out and slapped her sister-in-law's hand. "Not for you," she said. "Not yet."

"I'm hungry," Elsie said. "I didn't realize that I was being sent to help you in the kitchen to actually help. That's sexist. I might be a woman but I don't know the first thing about this."

"Don't you want to learn?"

Elsie frowned, "Have you asked Wolf if he wants to learn?"

"No," Evelyn said. "Fair point. I guess there's no reason that you should particularly want to learn to cook."

"No," she said. "I'm supremely happy when you fix dinner for all of us. It's a treat. But I also don't mind having nachos at my house. That I can handle. I'm good at nachos."

"Well, that's just fine. Because I don't mind cooking for you."

"Did you have a big job in New York?" Elsie asked.

"Yes," Evelyn said. "We had..." And she realized that Elsie wouldn't understand. About social media followers and celebrities or any of that.

"Yes," she repeated. "And I really liked it. But it just didn't mean anything anymore when I found out that my friends weren't the kind of friends I wanted."

"Not *real* friends," Elsie said.

"I don't know. I think they would consider themselves real friends. Even with the glaring errors and betrayals that occurred at the end. And you know, I think... I don't know. Maybe if I had stayed I would've been able to keep working there. At first I didn't think so. But..." Except she realized that if she had stayed, she would've forgiven Andrew. If she had stayed, she would've left the business behind, anyway. Because her biggest dream was this. Having a family.

Not the kind of family that she'd had growing up. Not the kind of love and affection she got from her mother, which was always tinged with judgment. Not the vague disinterest of her father. She had thought that it boiled down to a husband and children, but it was more than that. She realized that now. She realized that while sitting in the kitchen with Elsie, who really did feel like a little sister. She liked cooking for them. She wanted to reach Wolf, who was so distant, and force him to be her brother. And she even wanted to take care of Hunter, because Sawyer saw him as another member of the family. It was more than just Sawyer and Bug. It really was.

And she never could have had it with Andrew, but she hadn't known enough to realize it at the time. Exactly what it was she was craving. Exactly why she had come out here. Because she had recognized that the soul-deep longing inside of her was not going to be fulfilled there.

Only a few minutes later, the men all came in from working outdoors. Sawyer was holding Bug in a pack on his chest, and he and Hunter were talking. Sawyer laughed. Evelyn felt a stab of envy at her husband's friend. He knew him. He had known him since he was a child, so even if he never wanted to talk about his feelings or his pain, Hunter just knew. "It smells great."

That compliment came from Hunter.

Hunter had an easy manner about him. And she remembered what Sawyer had said about him. That Hunter was just fine hooking up with strangers. It didn't really surprise her that he had an easy time attracting women. He was beautiful. Dark hair and eyes, dark stubble around the square jaw. His smile was the kind that made you feel happy, even if you weren't. She imagined that was actually probably the basis for his friendship with Sawyer. Because

Sawyer was like granite. And he wasn't effusive in any way. And she wondered if Hunter's ease gave him something. She hoped that it did. He was such a closed-off… Difficult creature.

And he was rapidly becoming a man she didn't just want to fall in love with. But a man she was pretty sure she was already in love with.

That realization made her frown over her gravy.

"It can't be all bad," Hunter said, crossing the kitchen and taking the bowl from her, setting it on the table. Sawyer had sat down in his chest pack, and positioned Bug in his arms, and he shot his friend an irritated glare. "Can you not openly flirt with my wife," he said.

"Somebody needs to do it," Hunter said.

"Knock it off, Hunter," Elsie said, punching him on the shoulder. "You're being a dick."

He turned and grabbed hold of Elsie's arm, and if Evelyn was not mistaken, she saw a little color rise in her sister-in-law's cheeks, and she did not think it was just irritation.

"Don't," she said, jerking away from him.

"Come on now, Elsie. You know you're my favorite girl."

"Hard pass."

Sawyer, for his part, seemed oblivious to the interaction. Or maybe he wasn't. It was legitimately impossible to tell. The biggest range of emotion he showed was during sex.

Elsie and Hunter continued to bicker all while sitting down to dinner, which was wonderful, if Evelyn said so herself. Truly, she'd excelled herself, and she was not above giving herself a little pat on the back. Even if it was quiet.

With the people around them, and with the flurry of activity along with it, she would've expected that the tension between them would feel a little bit more manageable. It didn't. It was tight and heavy all at once, making her feel like she was tied to him by an invisible string. She could feel his eyes on her, even while they ate.

"These rolls are amazing," she said.

And she realized that, in the end, she had said so herself.

"Hell, yeah," Hunter said. "Did you make them?"

"I did," she said.

"They're good," Elsie agreed, and Wolf offered a grunt.

She looked over at Sawyer, who nodded slowly. And it was that slow, taciturn nod that she felt. All the way down.

It was Hunter and Elsie who easily filled the silence, Wolf and Sawyer twins in relative silence. Not that they weren't speaking; it was just that they weren't men to fill up that silence with their own words. They were happy to sit in it.

She marveled at that a little bit. Because she had noticed the silence all around her since she moved here. And she had also noticed that it was her tendency to avoid silence. Now that she couldn't... Well, it was interesting. Yes, Bug often cried. She was fractious and noisy on occasion, but it was still different to the noise that she could fill her entire being with in the city. The kind of noise that chased away thoughts.

The baby crying wasn't a good distraction. Instead, it brought out all sorts of emotions in her. Protective instincts.

She wondered how long it would take before she felt secure enough to think of herself as June Bug's mother. It wasn't that she didn't love her. Or that she didn't feel a bond to her. It was just that... She felt uncertain here with him, and she didn't quite know why. Like she could still barely believe that this was her life. That things had actually changed. That this was for real.

And she knew that he was the one who was concerned

about her leaving. She was resolved. But even with the marriage vows, even with the intensity of the connection between them, she felt… She didn't feel all that secure here. She just didn't.

And it was easy to look at him and think that he was the reason why she didn't feel secure. Or as close to him as she wanted to.

And it was true, she was working on changing. On giving more of herself. And it was also true that it seemed like something they should do in trade-offs. That it was something they should take turns on. He should give a little, she should give some back in equal measure. And on and on it would go, until their skills were balanced, and they had met in the middle and that magical place of emotional intimacy she had been fantasizing about of late.

But she was beginning to recognize that it wasn't going to work that way. That it couldn't. That she might have to grind her scale all the way into the ground before she could get him to lay a piece on his side. Before she could get him to offer her something.

It made her heart thunder hard. Because it wasn't going to be about cooking meals, or simply taking care of June Bug. If she wanted to forge a relationship with him on her terms, based on who they were to one another… Well, then the sharing was going to have to be deep, be from her. From her heart and her soul.

But she was going to have to dig deep. She had exposed parts of herself to Sawyer that felt vulnerable and fragile and she had to keep…living like that.

And she was going to have to do it willingly. And she was going to have to figure out what the answer even was. That was the problem. There wasn't a clear path to vulnerability because people spend their entire lives finding ways to cover up their insecurities. To hide the places that were easily wounded. Tender. You protect them even from yourself.

Without knowing it. Without meaning to. It was just what you did. Like a reflex. Like when somebody threw a ball at you when you weren't ready and you squeezed your eyes shut and threw your hands up.

A reflex.

But she had to find a way to get past it. She had to find a way to not just make her surroundings different, but to make herself different in them. Because if she couldn't do that... If she couldn't do that, then what hope did she have? Of anything?

"There's dessert, too," she said, realizing all of a sudden that she'd been sitting there quietly while Elsie and Hunter bickered about something to do with land management.

"Thank you," Elsie said brightly, all too willing to find an excuse to disengage with her current rival.

"Can I help with anything?" Hunter asked.

She could sense Sawyer's irritation. "I've got it," he said.

He stood, wordlessly helping to clear away the plates, then getting out some small plates for the cake. She put her hand on his shoulder. "Thank you."

He nodded, and that was the only acknowledgment he gave to the gesture, but she felt it profoundly.

She wondered what vulnerability would even look like to him. On him.

Part of her rejected it. He was so strong. He wasn't like anyone she had ever known. He was stoic in the extreme. But she found a sort of comfort in that. Like standing next to a mountain she knew wouldn't crumble.

She didn't want to put any cracks in him.

But she wanted to feel close to him, too, and that was the problem. A mountain was always going to feel remote.

And so, she didn't know the answers to interacting with her husband. Except that it was going to require that she give more. That she give more deeply. More genuinely. In a way that she never had.

They ate dessert, all having a round of ill-advised coffee with the rich chocolate cake, and then bidding a cheerful farewell to Hunter and Elsie.

She had moved into his bedroom. At least, mostly. She was finding it a slow process to bring all of her things over. And she felt like that spoke of the half in, half out situation.

"I should get all my things moved into the bedroom," she said.

"Yeah," he said. "Sure. Unless you want the space or…"

"No," she said. "I really don't need the space. What I would like is to just… To make it clear. That we are together."

"We are together," he said, leaning in and kissing her lips. The gesture was reassuring. The words affirming. But she was still left with a strange nagging at the center of her soul.

"You never told me," she said. "No, let me start over again. You deliberately avoided telling me before. Where does her name come from?"

She wondered if he would rebuff her again. Change the subject again.

"My grandmother."

"Oh," she said.

"She was called June. June Garrett."

The words were flat and simple, but she could sense a wealth of feeling there. Behind brick walls built so high she didn't know how she'd ever scale them. There was so much he didn't say. So much.

"Is she the one who... Was she the mail-order bride?"

He grunted, nodding as he did, which she was sure was in affirmation.

"But what about Bug..."

"I don't... I don't especially care to talk about it. To talk about her."

"Why?"

"The pearl necklace you wore at the wedding," he said. "She had one just like it."

"Oh," she said, well aware he hadn't answered the question, but also aware that whatever he was doing was leading somewhere. And she wanted to let him lead.

"Yeah, I... Come here. I'll show you."

She wiped up one last wet spot on the counter, and then followed him out of the kitchen, walking behind him up the stairs and back toward the master bedroom. He opened up the closet, the one that contained just a few of her things, and reached up, taking a box down from the top. Inside that box was a flat, pale blue velvet one. He opened it. There was an antique pearl necklace inside, the most beautiful she'd ever seen, nestled in pale satin.

"This is beautiful," she said, touching it. "Mine wasn't anything like this. It wasn't even real. Very nice costume jewelry."

"These are real," he said. "I want you to have it."

"Sawyer... You don't need to give me your grandmother's necklace."

"I want to. I haven't had a chance to go get you a ring, and don't think I haven't thought of it. I have. In my line of work... Most of the men don't wear wedding rings. So... I haven't thought much about rings ever. But it did occur to me on the day of the wedding that I should've gotten you something. And I appreciated the necklace, because it reminded me of her. I think if she'd been living, she would've given you those to wear."

"That's really lovely," she said. "I... I don't even know what to say. Thank you. Thank you for giving me this." Because she realized that whether he knew he'd betrayed it or not, June was clearly a piece of him in a very profound way. That he called the baby June Bug because of her. That he had saved this necklace. And that he was now giving it to her...

She felt like truly this was a piece of Sawyer Garrett that she held in her hands. And it didn't matter that it was worth a lot of money, though it very clearly was; that wasn't the point. Sawyer was a careful man. He didn't say things he didn't mean. He didn't hold on to things he didn't need. That meant he needed this necklace. And it had been stowed away and kept safe all this time because of how much he needed it. It was more than sentimental. It was part of the fabric of who he was, and she was absolutely certain of that.

"Can you tell me about her?"

"Not much to say, really. Though I think the story of how she met my grandfather's a pretty good one. His first wife left. Common enough now, but quite a scandal then. He had three children, it was the 1950s, and he wasn't equipped for raising three boys. So... He decided he needed to find a wife. But he couldn't go messing around trying to date women about town. He thought it was too messy. Plus, especially back then, there were not half as many women as there were men. Particularly not eligible. So, he put an ad in a paper in Boston. Asking for a wife who wanted to come out to Oregon. To the frontier. June responded."

"What was her life like in Boston?"

"She was bored. That's what she used to tell me." A smile touched his lips, and she felt it deep in her soul. There was a look in his eye that she'd never seen before. He was reaching back and sharing something that came from deep inside of him. "It was a lot of society...gatherings. I don't know, really. She was from a rich family. She married a rich man. But he was... He was cruel. And when it became clear that June couldn't have children... Well, his violence increased. She left him, but she was afraid. Afraid for her life. And when she saw my grandfather's ad, she thought... Might as well take her chances. He bought her a plane ticket, and she flew out to Oregon. They were married immediately. Basically sight unseen. And she told him on their wedding night that because everybody knew who she was in Boston she hadn't wanted to chance killing her husband no matter how cruel he was, but that she rought herself to a place where she would be comfortable killing a mean man if it came to it. So if he did anything unkind to her, she would make him pay for it."

She studied his face, hard as granite and not betraying anything he might feel. "She sounds like quite a woman."

"She was. But my grandfather wasn't a cruel man. He was good one. She was... About the greatest gift our family ever got. She was a mother to my father and my uncles. She was a grandmother to me."

"What happened to your other uncles?"

"Well, unfortunately, the brothers never did get along, and the way that things run here... If you don't get along, it's not going to work. My uncle Ted moved out to Copper Ridge. Started a ranch there. Got married. Figured probably that he'd escaped some of that Four Corners curse. But you know... His wife left him, too."

"She did?"

"Yep. And then he died. I have cousins over there, but I don't know them all that well. Same as the family that went out to Lone Rock. Eastern Oregon. A few hours away. Don't really know them."

"That's sad. Especially considering the way this ranch was set up. It feels like it was set up to keep the families together."

"Yeah. I know that it was. But if there's one problem the Garrett family has it's… Well, we're a bunch of hardheaded mules, and there's not a lot of room for compromise."

"I can see that," she said.

"What's that supposed to mean?"

"Exactly what I said. You and Wolf get along okay, though."

"Probably because some days we can go eight hours without speaking more than five words to each other."

She laughed. "Oh, is that the ticket?"

"Seems to work just fine."

"You're a good guy, Sawyer Garrett."

"Try," he said.

And she knew he wasn't just being wry or funny. He meant it. He tried to be good. It meant something to him. It mattered. And she had a feeling it was because of his grandmother. Who had said she wouldn't hesitate to take out a mean man.

"I think she would be proud of you."

He shifted. "That's what I hope. Every day."

And she knew then that the conversation was done. And she took the necklace and walked into the master bathroom, putting it right on the side of the sink where she kept her makeup. Then she quietly exited the bedroom and took an armload of clothes still on the hanger out of the closet, bringing them back into the bedroom.

"Are you going to do that now?"

He was sprawled out on the bed, still wearing jeans and the T-shirt he had on all day.

"I was thinking about it."

"I was thinking about having a shower," he said.

What she knew from experience was an invitation to the provocative. Since they'd gotten married she hadn't had a shower to herself.

"Go ahead," she said. "I'm going to finish moving my things in."

"I have a better idea. I'll help you. And then we can take a shower."

"I'd hate for you to be up too late."

"You're worth it," he said.

And she decided that she would go ahead and call tonight a win.

CHAPTER FIFTEEN

SAWYER WAS BEAT after a day of trying to round up some particularly naughty cows. Plus dealing with a hole some of them had busted into one of the few fences on the spread.

Honestly, sometimes cows were just assholes.

He was looking forward to dinner. Which was something he'd gotten used to quickly. But he was going to come back home and there would be a warm meal waiting for him.

Part of him was feeling a little bit scathing of himself. That he'd gotten used to it so quickly. That he gotten so soft with it. He just settled right into having a wife. But there was a voice in the back of his head that seemed intent on reminding him that it may not be as permanent as he would like it to be. There was no real way of knowing. Only she knew. Only she could possibly know if she'd stay.

She seemed happy. She had moved all the things into the bedroom, which she had seemed to think was an essential task last night. He hadn't been that much help. He'd been mostly interested in all the fancy clothes she brought in. And how much he wanted to see her in all of it. When the weather heated up... It would be good to see her in some of those little sundresses she had. The underwear drawer she'd compiled was obviously the most interesting. That couldn't be denied.

But when he walked in, he did not smell dinner, and his wife was standing there, clutching a large basket in front of her body. She was wearing a white dress that made all those other things not seem quite so important. It was thin and filmy, and he wanted to get his hands on it. Wanted to get his hands on her.

But she had that look on her face that she had when she was engaged in a scheme. It was funny, that he knew her well enough to recognize that. He also knew her well enough to know that he had to let the scheme play out. Mostly because, in the end, the scheme ended up being interesting for him. At least, that was how it had been every time so far. And he was a man who was smart enough to learn from past experience. Positive reinforcement, negative reinforcement, he responded to either one.

"Bug is down until at least nine," she said. "And I decided we should have a picnic for dinner."

"Really?"

"Her baby monitor reaches all the way down to the river. I figured we can go down there."

"Specifically," he said.

"Yes," she said. And she just grinned at him, and offered no further details.

"You're up to something," he said when they opened the front door to the house and headed down the path that went to the riverbank.

"Yes," she said, giving him and impish grin. "I am."

"Now," he said, "I find that mildly exciting."

"You probably should."

"Good."

"It's amazing here," she said, looking up at the trees. He followed the elegant line of her neck, admired her profile, the gentle sweep of her blond eyelashes and the slight bump in her nose that gently sloped down before a tip that turned up slightly. She was beautiful. In a deeply specific sort of way. Evelyn wasn't the sort of woman you could ever confuse with another. She was absolutely, 100 percent Evelyn.

"I'm pretty fond of it," he said, his chest getting tight.

"It's just… In the city… I realized that I used the noise. I told you about how…badly damaged I was when I left the academy. And when I left, I left. I left every piece of that me behind. It was the only way I could think to heal."

She sighed deeply. "I never wanted to think about dance ever again. I never wanted to do it again. It… The crushing…weight of being between my mother's expectations and the expectations of the people at the school. The pain of having my body start to develop and just kind of get away from me, and turn into this thing that was so incompatible with what I wanted to do. With who I wanted to be. I felt like I was fighting a war with myself every single day. And the people around me were standing right beside me only too happy to hand me a sword so that I could attack myself. There was nobody leading the charge to say that I was good enough the way I was. Nobody standing by to tell me that I was enough. That's just not how it was then. It isn't how it is oftentimes when you're in these kinds of closed circles where everything is so competitive that people can demand a level of perfection that is honestly just… They can demand a kind of perfection that is extraordinarily narrow. Because so many people want to be there. And there are girls whose bodies will bend that way. Whose development will support those demands. I just wasn't one of them."

She blinked hard, and continued. "And I was angry. I was angry at myself, mostly, because for the longest time I couldn't figure out why I couldn't be that. Because so many people just could. And why could I not pull it together? Why couldn't I make myself into something acceptable? Why couldn't I be that special creature that they were looking for? And it was so quiet there, and I hated it. I hated how narrow it was, and how focused. And how I couldn't escape it. Because we ate and slept and breathed ballet there. Because it was all classical music and conversations about routines. Because I just wanted something to distract me. And so… It all boiled over. It all boiled over and I just told everyone what I thought of them. I told them all to go to hell. And after that I just ran. I went back to the city, and I wouldn't stay home. And I would sneak out at night. I would walk the streets, I would take the subway to Times Square of all places, and I think that's so funny now, because I hate Times Square. But the lights were so bright, and it was always busy. And I could just… Let it all wash away. And that was what I wanted. And I chose a life that kept that pace. Even though I stopped trying to rebel against everything, because I realized I wasn't going to be able to make a life as an angry rebel, because I realized that succeeding was going to be the biggest rebellion of all, and that it mattered a lot more. I never thought that I would like the quiet. I never thought that I would want to sit with myself. With my thoughts."

His chest felt full to bursting. She'd told him about the physical effects the eating disorder had had on her body, but this was the deep emotional pain of the whole thing. Of what she'd lost. The dreams that had been taken from her.

And he cared. But hell if he knew how.

"You can drown your thoughts out pretty good," he said. "Even in silence. As long as you keep busy enough." He spoke from experience. It was that of a man who was good at sitting in the broad expanse of nature and listening to the earth rather than himself. It was an art form. And he perfected it.

"Maybe it's a matter of perspective," she said. "Maybe it doesn't seem half so quiet to you as it does to me."

"No," he said. "Everything makes a sound. Everything's trying to tell you something."

"I like that. I like that about this place. I like that about you. I think you know things that I'm just trying to learn about. And I appreciate it."

"Look, I don't know anything about ballet. Not a single damn thing. Except there's a Christmas one. And that is one thing my grandma mentioned about Boston that she liked. She would go see *The Nutcracker*. I know that. She watched it sometimes on VHS. She said it wasn't the same. I thought it was boring, and I never watched more than thirty seconds of it. So everything I'm about to say, recognize that it comes from being pretty damned ignorant. But isn't the point of that sort of stuff to… To bring people joy? Isn't that the point of all that shit that we don't need to survive? It's like whittling a stick into a particular kind of shape. You don't need to do it, but you do it because there's something about it that calls you. So… What the hell is the point of an art that tortures the people trying to share it?"

"Some people would argue that perfection demands a little bit of torture."

"Who's to say what's perfect? Like you said, you spent years looking for noise on the city streets, and to you then that was perfect. Now this is perfect. What's perfect changes. And it means different things to different people. Just because somebody decided a long time ago that something looked perfect a certain way doesn't make it true. And it doesn't make it permanent."

"You don't say a lot of words," she said. "But I like pretty much all the ones you do say."

"Well, I figure the less I say, the more I up my odds of that remaining true."

"What was it like growing up here?" They came to the clearing by the river, and settled in by the trees.

"It was good. I mean… Kind of a little kid's paradise. Not a whole lot of rules, not a whole lot of fences."

"You don't talk about your dad."

"I don't have much to say about him."

"You mentioned hating your parents."

Well, hell. He had. But it was complicated So damned complicated. She was sharing with him, telling him about her pain, and managing to find a way to be what she needed was beyond him, and the last thing he needed to do was go digging into his own shit.

"Look," he said. "I don't have a lot of memories that center around my dad. He was busy. He was busy with the ranch, and I get that. It's a tough life, it's tough work, and it doesn't care that you have a passel of kids and no wife to take care of them."

"But you didn't want to do that to your kids."

"No," he said. "Because… Look, there is no call to be worked up about it, not now. I can't control it. I can't fix it. And I turned out just fine. Wolf and Elsie did, too. We managed. We survived. Why pitch a damn fit about it? But I knew I wanted to be different. I knew I wanted her to do more than survive her childhood."

"How old were you when June died?"

He didn't want to talk about that. More than anything he just didn't want to talk about June's death. His own failure. "Sixteen."

"I'm sorry. She must've really… She practically raised you, didn't she?"

Her words scraped raw, close to the bone. "She did.

And I'm grateful for it. I'm grateful for the discipline that Grandpa gave me, and for the care that she gave me, because it helped me pass some on to Wolf and Elsie. Because I had to do it. There wasn't anyone else."

"They're so lucky they had you. Wolf and Elsie."

"Yeah. Well. You don't talk about your dad," he said.

"Oh," she said, laughing. "I expect my dad suffers from a very similar thing to yours. He… He just didn't do much of anything. I don't know that he… He married my mother because he got her pregnant. It was a bit of a scandal. It was… He was older, and he was married. My mother was seventeen. They covered all that up, and they got married. He already had children… I never really understood why he left his first wife and married my mother, and I don't think it's because he loved her. I think actually he was just hoping to not get arrested. And that was the only way her parents would agree to just go along with everything. If she had all the protection. He was distant. He'd already raised his children. I was never all that interesting to him."

"So you have half siblings?"

"I don't really know them, either. I guess that's the thing. I don't really know him. I don't know his other children. I don't… I spent a lot of time in boarding schools, at summer camps. I don't know that I can necessarily say I know either of the people who had a hand in creating me very well. So when you say your dad was distant, I get it. I understand. And I understand knowing that it needs to be different. For so long I've had a driving need to have children to prove that I could be better. But now that I have Bug to take care of, it's not about that."

"It's not?" he asked, his throat getting tight.

"No. That's actually been…the strongest and biggest miracle about being here. I'm just not living for anyone else anymore. For what they did or didn't do for me, for what they might think. I'm living for my own happiness. My own joy and fulfillment, and I get so much of that from taking care of her."

"What about your business? I mean, I get that you left it because of what your friend did."

"Yes. And maybe someday I'm going to want to figure out how to get back into some kind of business in some capacity or another. But I don't feel a burning urge to do that right now. And you can rest assured that if the moment comes, I'm going to tell you. And we'll talk about it. But I'm just enjoying living in this moment. In these moments. Where it's not about proving anything or solving anything. It's just about being."

"I'm glad."

He felt a strange short of shift in his chest. In his soul.

"Do you talk to anyone, Sawyer?"

He grunted. "We just talked about how I don't talk."

"Am I the first person, though? That you really shared any of this with?"

"Yes." He hesitated before saying the next words. Because they sounded odd, even in his own head. "You're the first stranger I've ever really gotten to know."

"Really?" She laughed. "What does that mean?"

"I grew up here. I felt like I grew up knowing all these people. That's what it was like here. A huge, built-in extended family. So yeah, there were deficits. But we could go to the Sullivans if we needed anything, and Mary Sullivan cooked birthday cakes for us after Grandma died. There was always somebody. Always somebody to make sure nothing got entirely missed. Or is it something truly important didn't get left undone? The people at Four Corners aren't perfect, but they're here for each other. But yeah, we were never strangers. Our families were born knowing each other. And as for the broader town, it essentially stays unchanged. And while new people have moved in, it's not like I've made great friends with anybody off this ranch. I've known Hunter McCloud my entire life. He's just as much of a brother to me as Wolf, when it comes down to it. And there's Gus and Brody and Lachlan…"

"And you don't really get to know the women you've hooked up with."

"Not anywhere past the biblical sense, no."

"Well, I'll take it. Being the person that you talk to. However many words you use."

"Thanks."

She opened up the basket, and took a blanket out from it, spreading it down on the ground. Then she started to unpack the basket, and he'd assumed that it was going to be a cold dinner, but it had just been well sealed, keeping all the heat in. There was roast chicken and green beans, and more of those rolls she had made for them last night. And what he didn't know how to say was that it wasn't just that he'd never gotten to know anyone, or that he didn't talk to anyone. It was that no one had tried to take care of him like this in a long time. And when he thought about having a wife, it hadn't been for that reason.

In his head, it had been so cut and dried. Get married, have food made for him, have his daughter taken care of, have sex on tap, more or less. And yeah, he guessed he had those things with Evelyn, but he'd underestimated what it would feel like to have all those things. Because it wasn't just dinner she put so much work into it. The amount of work she put into it demonstrated how much she cared. The way that she took care of June Bug wasn't just like being a nanny. It wasn't. And then there was the way she made love to him. Not perfunctory, not as if it was a chore. She made love to him like it was her great joy. Like she'd die if she didn't have him, and no woman on earth had ever responded to him quite so enthusiastically as Evelyn, and she was his.

His wife.

Yeah, he hadn't understood what it would mean exactly to have someone in his life in this capacity, because he never had before. Because he'd never even dreamed about it.

Dreaming is dangerous...

He had never believed in that sort of thing, anyway. At least, not once he grew up. Not once he started to know better. He believed in what he could see. And what he could touch. And precious little else mattered.

It couldn't matter.

But Evelyn was here now, and he could touch her.

He reached out and dragged his thumb over her cheekbone.

She smiled. "Am I allowed to ask what you're thinking about?"

"Chicken," he said.

And she knew he was lying, he could tell. But she didn't say anything. She let him get away with it. And he let her make him a plate of food, and hand him a beer. And he watched her eat, watched the way the wind whipped through her blond hair, the fading twilight casting her in a lovely glow.

She was like an angel. And he just wasn't that kind of man. To go around thinking those kinds of things. But there was something about her. And he never felt anything like it. That seemed too pale a saying. He hadn't known a thing like it existed on God's green earth, and he considered himself an expert at all the things that came from that earth.

All the things that were natural to humans, that was what he thought he knew about.

So it might not be the ballet or fancy things like one might find in a city. All the things that men had made for themselves. Idols fashioned out of money and iron. But the things that were real.

That was what he had decided he knew all about.

That the only real mysteries of the universe that mattered were the ones that belonged to it, not the ones that humanity had brought to it. But this was one. A new one. And it made him wonder about all the other things he didn't know.

And Sawyer Garrett didn't like to not know.

They sat in silence. And it was companionable. The kind of silence he liked. Where you could settle in with the person beside you, confident that you were walking the same path. That was the comfortable feeling he had whenever he worked the range with Hunter, with Wolf. Even with Elsie. This was different. It was more than being on the same path. Working toward a common goal. It was sitting and knowing that their hearts were beating for the same reason.

Bug, he supposed. Maybe that was where that came from.

"I actually… I had a reason for wanting to come down here."

"I figured you did. Given that you are one hundred percent obvious when you have a scheme."

"I'm obvious to you?" She looked delighted by that.

"Yes, Evelyn, you are obvious to me. And I find that to be a damned delight."

She laughed, the sound ringing over the surface of the river. "Well, I live to be an endless delight to you, Sawyer."

And somehow he felt that she meant it.

She stood then, her dress billowing around her legs. It

was almost see-through, it was so diaphanous. He didn't even know where that word had come from. It lived somewhere in the dark recesses of his brain. All the reading and schooling he had to do that he thought was stupid at the time. But he hadn't realized that it had been for this.

In service of this moment.

So that he had the vocabulary to sum up Evelyn Garrett.

Evelyn Garrett.

His wife.

She stepped away from him, and toward the edge of the water. And then she stepped in, shrieking. "It is freezing," she said.

"Well, yeah, you didn't know that? You've fallen in before."

"I forgot," she said. "Anyway, that was like a sudden baptism. It was over very quickly. It knocked the wind out of me, but I didn't have the time to...overthink it."

Then she straightened her shoulders, and moved her arms into a curved position in front of her. She turned her head to the side, her neck craned at a particular, elegant angle. He had noticed that each of her movements seemed perfectly placed before. He had noticed that she moved with a kind of grace that seemed uncommon. But he had not understood why, not fully, until this moment. Her movements were a dance.

Because Evelyn was a dancer. Evelyn was a dancer who had put it all away. Who had rejected it in anger.

No matter that she had tried to crush that part of herself up and shrink it down.

And he'd said to her, only a few minutes ago, that this was one of those things, like whittling a stick, that wasn't essential to the world. But he could see that it was part of every line in her body—every line that she had been told was wrong. How could he say it wasn't essential?

What the hell did he know?

And then she began to move, up on her toes, her arms graceful and elegant as they swept across her body, over her head, as she bent at the waist and lifted one leg bent from the water, flicking it outward and casting water droplets off her skin, diamonds flung out into the twilight sky. She spun, and her toes dragged the top of the water, creating a wave around her. She bent, drawing her arms down beneath the surface and when she came back up she spread more sparkle all around. He was lost in her magic. In her movements.

He had never sat and watched a ballet. But he would sit and watch this one for the rest of his life. She was showing him something. Giving him a part of herself.

And it was perfection.

It didn't matter what anyone else had to say. It didn't matter all the things she had been told. She had risen up from all that, and she could still create this. Just for him.

This woman who—in his opinion—should be dancing in front of a sold-out auditorium filled with people.

Dammit but she was beautiful.

And it echoed in his heart like truth, all that beauty, all that grace. It echoed in his heart like its own beat. Part of him. In him. Through him.

And when she was done, she stood and bowed slowly, like a queen. And he stood, wading out into the water where she was, not caring that his boots were soaked, that his jeans were wet. He grabbed hold of her, and he met her there, in that magical space she'd created, and he kissed her. He didn't believe in magic. He didn't believe in fairy tales. There wasn't a damn thing on earth that had ever given him a reason to. Except for her.

Except for her.

And somehow, out there in the river with her, kissing her soft, incredible lips, he felt like maybe some of her magic had reached inside of him. Touched these cold places inside his chest that had gone frozen years ago.

He lifted her up from the water, taking heavy steps through the current, taking them both back to land. She was mostly dry, only the bottom of her dress wet, and she had the presence of mind not to wear shoes. Much smarter than he was. He found the closure on the back of her dress and undid it, let it fall down below her breasts, revealing the filmy white bra she wore beneath.

"Won't someone see?" she asked, and her timidity in this moment in the face of her previous bravery just made his heart squeeze.

"Not here. It's secluded from all the other houses. And unless someone else has a mind to come down to the river to have a tryst, I doubt they're going to be out and about at this hour."

"A tryst?" She smiled. There was an impish gleam in her eye.

"Well, I don't know what you call it. Maybe it's something different when it's your wife."

He kissed her. Kissed her like he was savoring her. He had done desperate. He had tried to use sex to put distance between them. He didn't want that. Not now. What he wanted now… What he needed now… It was something else entirely. He needed to show her that he recognized the gift that she had just given him.

"Have you danced?" he asked, against her lips. "Have you ever danced since then?"

Tears shone in her eyes, in the moonlight. "No," she said.

And he kissed her again. Deeper, harder. Because he'd known that. Somehow, he'd known that. This was somehow different. Different than all the other times. Because something was different in him. Like she had... Changed him fundamentally. Maybe by showing him there were things he didn't know. By making him wonder about all these things he never had.

Maybe just because she danced for him. And no one else in all this time. Because that meant that Andrew had never seen her dance, that poor bastard. He had no idea what he'd had. But Sawyer knew. Sawyer knew full well, and he loved it.

He pushed the dress down her body the rest of the way, left her in that white underwear she was wearing that did things to him... Indecent things.

He stepped away from her, divesting himself of his clothes, and then he lay down on the blanket, settling her over his body. He stripped off that bra, left her breasts bare.

"I want to watch you dance naked someday," he said. "I want to see all those lines you were told were so wrong. Because I gotta tell you... You're perfect." He craned his head upward, kissed the lower curve of one breast. "Absolutely perfect. I've never seen a damn thing like it. And there's nothing, not anything in my whole life, that I could've told you would make me sit through a ballet. But I could watch you dance for the rest of my life."

He meant it. That was what shocked him the most. Along with the look on her face. Like she'd been given a gift. And a tear slid down her cheek. All he wanted to do was wipe it away. All he wanted to do was make it so she never cried again.

It was like that feeling he'd had for Bug. But different,

too. But that feeling he wanted to fight something. Tear the world to pieces if it dared threaten her. He wanted to hunt down every single person that had ever made her feel like less than she was and destroy them. Unequivocally. That was what he wanted. And in that moment he felt like he could. With his own bare hands. He felt like he could tear the world apart and build a whole new one. Just for them.

He felt powerful and weak all at once. Gazing up at her beautiful body.

He grabbed the band at the leg of her panties and swept the center aside, exposed her, pushed his fingers through her pale curls and started to pleasure her. She began to rock her hips over his. So tantalizingly close to where he wanted her.

He wanted her to lead the dance. At least, when he was ready to let her. He would take her right to the edge first. Right there.

He pinched that sensitive spot between his fingers, and she let out a sharp gasp.

This was a dance he knew. This was one he was good at. Except it felt like something entirely new with her. Like he might not actually know the steps. And that was when he realized that the steps were irrelevant. Because it wasn't about generally being good in bed. It was about being good for her. Being everything for her. Everything she needed or could ever need.

And he felt unequal to it. That was the bottom line. Because he'd never been everything anyone needed. And he normally didn't waste time worrying about all that. Not anymore.

But this changed things. She changed things.

He put his focus back on her body. On what he could see. On what he could touch.

How was it that she made him more connected to his body, but made him more connected to those things he tried to deny, as well. Those things he couldn't hold on to. Those things he couldn't see.

Those things that were of the earth, but somewhere more heavenly, that he didn't like to ponder all that deeply.

He didn't know how it was possible. Didn't know how she was possible.

But he put all his attention on her. Kissing her stomach, stroking her between her thighs. Telling her how beautiful she was. And then he positioned her over his arousal, lowering her slowly onto him, sinking into her inch by torturous inch. And it was a moment where the physical met with the spiritual. Perfectly. Not at odds. His heart was beating with her. All that she was flowed through his veins. And he felt her. Felt himself. Grounded to the earth. And up in the stars at the same time. She tossed her head back, planting her hands on his chest, sounds of pleasure issuing from her lips as she moved her hips in a sinuous rhythm. Then she began to move, setting a pace that drove them both wild.

Until he couldn't take it anymore.

He reversed their positions, taking control. Taking the lead, because he couldn't handle the aching, slow sweetness of what she was giving them. He was rough. And he was basic. Crude, even, with his deep, hard thrusts, but it was who he was. And this was how he met this graceful, sensual creature. This was what he had to give her. And she was still here. Crying out her pleasure. Clinging to him like she didn't ever want to let him go. And if that wasn't the very definition of a damned miracle he didn't know what was.

She dug her fingernails into his skin. Called out his name. Her internal muscles pulsing around his cock. And then he lost himself.

But it wasn't like just coming. It was like a door inside of himself opened up, and everything that he'd held back poured out.

He lowered his head, pressing his face to the curve of her neck as he growled out his release.

And then when it was over, he gathered her close to his body and lay beneath the stars. He could see the baby monitor in the basket, still glowing green, indicating that it was in range. And Bug hadn't made a sound.

"She used to call me that," he said.

"What?"

Damn that open door. His chest felt flooded with things. With memories. And he hadn't meant to say that. It was just that he'd been thinking of Bug.

"Who used to call you what?"

He rolled over onto his back, resting it against the ground. "My grandmother used to call me Bug."

CHAPTER SIXTEEN

EVELYN FELT POSITIVELY UNDONE. By what had happened between herself and Sawyer, the dancing, and then that... She was overwhelmed. She hadn't even had enough time to process that she'd actually done it. That she had allowed herself to form those movements. Her muscles burned, because she hadn't done it in so long. But she felt...lit up. Set on fire from the inside out. And it was perfect.

But she hadn't expected this.

She had hoped. She had hoped that if she had torn open her old scars and bled all of these things out that he would do the same. But she had never been holding that as a ransom. She had never thought that it would actually occur.

"And so she's June Bug. Because of your grandmother."

He nodded. "I never knew why she called me that. Just that she did. It was the only thing in my life that ever felt like..."

He didn't finish. But she understood. It was the only affection, the only real, open affection, he had ever experienced. And it was what he knew to pass on to his daughter. All he understood.

"It must've devastated you to lose her."

Because she understood that what he'd lost when he lost his grandmother was the most real parental figure he'd ever had.

"I... My grandpa died two years earlier. He had... It was

unexpected. He had a heart attack. Out in the field one day.
And he'd always been strong as an ox, but he'd never gotten
his cholesterol checked or anything like that. He thought
doctors were quacks, and that was pretty much his feeling on it. I get a physical every year, for what it's worth.
But… He never did. And he had a ticking time bomb in his
chest. One day it went off. That was it. That was that. She
was devastated. My dad never shed a tear. And June just…
She cried and cried. I held her because my dad wouldn't.
Because at fourteen I knew that I had to be the man that
he wouldn't be.

"For his own mother." He cleared his throat. "I just… I
knew that I needed to make some choices about who I was
going to be. But there…"

"What?"

"Two years after grandpa died, I went to Chicago to see
my mother. That's the one time I got on a plane. I… I went
to Chicago, to chase down a relationship with someone who
honestly didn't care about me. And before I could get back
June died. I didn't get to say goodbye."

It wasn't a flowery story. It wasn't a long story. There
were no details. No embellishments about feelings. But
she didn't need them. She could feel them. She could feel
them in every word that he had spoken. He had left this
ranch one time. He had gone one time to see the woman
who had abandoned him, and the one who had been there
for him all along had died.

And she knew… She knew full well that for him… For
him that was unacceptable. It was devastation. It was something that undermined his sense of who he was. He hadn't
gotten to say goodbye. He'd come back and she'd simply
been gone. She'd been gone.

"And did anyone hold you when you cried?"

He looked at her. "I was sixteen. I didn't cry."

And again, he'd said more with those few words than most people could say with a whole monologue.

He hadn't had the luxury of crying. Because there would've been no one there to hold him. He was the one who had done that. He was the one who had taken care. He was the one who had given his grandmother space to grieve. But who would do it for him? Nobody. His mother was gone, his father simply didn't care, his siblings had been young. He had been so badly, badly neglected and left behind.

"It wasn't your fault."

"It feels like it," he said. "It damn well feels like it. It feels like… It feels like my leaving broke something. And you know, the worst part is when I got back, and she was just gone, I couldn't accept it. I kept thinking… I kept thinking any minute she'd just come walking through the door. And I thought… I thought I dealt with all that shit. Because I already lost my mother. She chose to leave. Just up and did. I thought I…"

"You didn't think that you would have feelings?"

"No."

"Sorry. I think the bad news about life is that you catch feelings, and kind of just keep on having them."

"Yeah. I figured that out."

"Oh, Sawyer," she said, touching his face.

He really thought that he could reason it out. That he could solve his pain with logic. That he could accept his mother leaving, and put his grandmother's death in the same space. And at the same time, part of him blamed himself, and she knew it. He wanted logic and martyrdom all rolled into one, and he wanted to feel bad, then punish himself for it.

Because he wanted so desperately to be a good man, and he'd had so few examples of it in his life. Of anybody trying to be great for him.

"Did you have a good visit with your mother at least?"

The look that he gave her could have turned a lesser woman to stone. "I never went back."

And the door on that was closed. She'd had one little window into his soul, and then he closed it off. But she would carry it. Close to her heart. Close to her chest.

Bug. His grandmother had called him that.

It was something she knew about him now. It was something that made her understand him better.

She had given a whole lot, and he had given what felt like a little in return, except that she knew for him it had been…exposing. Searing.

"You're a very complicated man, aren't you?"

He looked at her. "No. I'm simple. I just want basic things…"

"That's bullshit. Do you believe that? Do you really believe that? You want to protect yourself, but you want to give Bug everything. You are deeply sentimental, and you love the people that you love so much."

He shifted. Uncomfortable. And she realized that word did something to him. Made him feel something he didn't like. Because she could sense his full withdrawal. Completely away from her. The total shift in his demeanor.

"I know you don't like feelings," she said.

"It's not that," he said. "It's not that simple. I just… Look, I don't know how to be functional. I don't know how to be a father. Nobody showed me how to do it. All I know is that mine was bad at it. My grandpa was a good guy. He had a good moral compass. He did a decent job. But it's not 1950, and I can't be the kind of dad that he was around then. Because that's what he was. That's what my grandparents were. And maybe... Maybe it's not that I need you to be the softness for Bug. Maybe it's that I need you to show me how to do it. Because I don't know how."

"I think you do. I think you just... You're afraid of it, is all."

"I'm not fucking afraid."

"It's okay if you are. Sawyer, I don't... I don't know what I'm doing here sometimes. Except I know it feels right. And it doesn't matter that it seems crazy or that most other people could never understand it, because I know that it feels right. Even when I don't get what drove me here. Even when I don't get what spurred me to make this decision, I know. I know it was right. But I'm afraid. All the time. I've been afraid that you might ask me to leave."

He looked at her like she had grown a second head. "I wouldn't ask you to leave. I asked you to come."

"I know. But there's something about this that feels fragile. And maybe it's just that it's... That it's different. It's different to anything I've ever experienced."

"Really? Even with Andrew?"

She laughed. Hysterically. "How... How could you even think that you... That he... I can't even compare the two of you. I can't remotely compare the relationships. I want more from you than I ever even thought to want from him."

He looked at her like he might ask what that meant. And she sort of hoped he wouldn't. Because she didn't know how to define it. She was hungry for Sawyer. For pieces of him that he had never shared with anyone else. Just for the depths of his damn soul. And it sounded crazy, and she didn't know how to ask for it, let alone what it would be like to have it. She didn't know how to tell him what she wanted, so how was he supposed to give it to her? She recognized the futility in her feelings. So she really, really hoped that he wouldn't press.

He didn't.

She would be brave enough, maybe someday, to have the conversation.

She just didn't feel brave enough right now.

"This is new territory for me," he said. "Like you said."

"I know," she said. She sat up. "I guess we'd better get dressed."

"Yeah."

They did. And it was just a strange sort of anticlimax, after the intensity of their coming together. It had been like that on their little honeymoon, too. These moments of such intensity. Such honesty. Moments where she felt like she was making progress with him, and then…not.

Maybe the problem is you don't actually know what you want.

Or at least you won't admit it.

Yeah, that could very well be the problem. But she didn't know what to do with it now. So they collected all of their things, and went back to the house. Went upstairs to their bedroom.

She got into the shower, and he joined her, kissing her neck and running his hands over her curves. Starting something with her again. She liked that. But they were unable to finish because then Bug started to cry, and they shut the water off, towel dried and Sawyer put on a pair of pants so that he could grab the baby. By the time Evelyn was dressed and out of the bathroom, he was lying in the bed, holding her against his chest, soothing her. She was so sweet, crunched up against his chest like that. Snuggled into him.

And suddenly the last little bit of defense in her heart broke.

That was her baby. Hers. And it was so easy for her feelings about Bug to get tangled up in her feelings with Sawyer. And finally enough, it was a revelation about her name that finished that for her.

It was all linked. She was part of this man, this... difficult, wonderful, singular man who was changing her in ways that she hadn't known she could change.

He called her Bug. Because it was how he understood love. *Love.*

She wanted, in that moment, so desperately to give voice to the groaning in her soul.

To say out loud that this was her family.

Family in a way that she had never experienced before. But there was just a little piece of herself that held back.

A little piece of herself that was afraid.

Family for her had always been such a loaded thing. Her father so distant. Her mother always wanting things from her. For her to meet benchmarkers. For her to perform. Be better. Be good enough. And nothing was ever good enough.

But she didn't feel that here. She didn't feel that with him. She didn't feel that with them.

But she decided to push all that aside. The fear that crowded her chest, and join him on the bed. She cuddled up next to him, and put her hand on Bug's back. "Was she hungry?"

"I think she still is. But I picked her up and she got a little oversatisfied with herself. I think she likes it when she can say jump and I'll say how high."

She laughed. "Oh, Sawyer. You are in so much trouble."

"I am?"

"What about when she wants a pony? Or a new dress to go to prom?"

"She's going to go to the school here. There is no prom."

"What about when she wants to date one of those ragtag boys out there on the ranch?"

Sawyer went stiff. "No. Because I know how those boys are. I grew up with their dads."

She laughed. "I think you're going to be a big pushover."

"I'm strict," he said. "I'm sure I am."

"No. I think she's got you wrapped around her finger."

He looked up at her, and for a moment, she saw sheer, unmitigated terror in his eyes.

The poor man really was living his worst nightmare. She could see that. He had a tiny, helpless thing in his care that he couldn't help but love.

There was that word again. And it took her a while to fully realize... He had never said the words. He didn't ever say that he loved Bug. She knew that he did. It was evident in absolutely everything about him. But he didn't say it. Not to the baby, not about her. In fact, he never said it about anything. It was like it didn't exist in his vocabulary.

It wasn't that it wasn't in him. It was absolutely in him. He was a man who loved with action. Deeply and from his soul, she had seen it. But the words weren't there. He had changed the entire course of his life for the baby now held in his arms. That he loved her was evident. In all that he did. In all that he was.

He had told her about the trauma that Wolf had suffered. And he had talked all around what she was sure was his own. The way he had lost his grandmother. The visit with his mother.

There were things that he couldn't share. And she understood that.

Understood that words weren't part of the essentials of

his life. But she wondered… She wondered if he needed to learn. She wondered if he needed to figure out how.

But right now, she wasn't going to push it. Right now, she was simply going to rest.

With her family.

CHAPTER SEVENTEEN

"THE MCCLOUDS ARE going out skeet shooting," Wolf said, late in the afternoon when he and Elsie were all settled on horseback and surveying the fence line they had just repaired.

"Sounds fun," Sawyer said.

"You say that like it's a root canal," Elsie said.

Maybe he did. But he didn't mean to. It was just that he was kind of looking forward to getting back to Evelyn tonight. Which was likely why he should go out and go skeet shooting. It hadn't escaped his notice that his entire life had shifted into something almost unrecognizable lately. He worked, sometimes with Bug, sometimes without her, but mostly he wanted to get back to Evelyn. He couldn't help it. She was what he thought about. All day while he rode that range. He needed to get himself back in the saddle, so to speak. Things were getting muddled with her. In a way that he didn't really want. Yeah, he wanted her to be happy. He wasn't averse to the emotion himself, it was just that... It was reminding him too much of another time, and he didn't care for it.

"It does sound fun," Sawyer said. "Forgive me for not squealing with joy. Should I have jumped up and down? Would that have made you happy, Elsie?"

"No. Seeing you jump up and down would not make me happy. Not in the least."

"Then be careful what you go asking for."

"The Sullivans are getting together to do jam tonight," she said. "Fia got a whole mess of strawberries from the garden."

"Tough choice. Exploding clay pigeons or slaving over a hot pot?" Wolf said. "I just don't know what I would do."

"Stop it, Wolf," she said. "I know you're a dick, you don't need to perform it all the time to try and remind us."

Sawyer actually did feel bad for Elsie. Because the problem was, this was the place his sister was internally caught in. She had formed an attachment to doing things with the guys. Her life had necessitated it. And he could see that it meant she was always caught in the middle. He wanted to come up with a way to make sure Bug would never feel like that.

Never feel caught between two worlds. Maybe it was his own fault. But he had never known the Sullivan girls all that well. And while he loved that Elsie had a friendship with Alaina, he had never done a great job of figuring out how to integrate them better into their lives. Maybe he should have learned how to make jam. Maybe that was his failure. Maybe he hadn't brought enough of those homey things into Elsie's life.

"I'll go shooting," Elsie said. "But only because I recently behaved like a lady by helping Evelyn in the kitchen."

"You know, you could shoot for a while, and then go do jam, or the other way around. You know where it will be."

"No," Elsie said. "It's fine. I'll just go up and shoot. I don't mind."

"I just need to make sure that Evelyn's fine with Bug. I don't want to bring her up there. Then her protection would be kind of big."

"She would look cute, though," Elsie said.

"That is true," Sawyer said. The image of Bug with giant yellow ear protection on was cute. He was pretty determined not to turn into that person who was overly impressed with everything about the life they had created. But he *was* pretty overly impressed with the life that he created. She was beautiful. And adorable. And he had never been much of a sucker for adorable. But here he was.

He rode out to the house, cleared everything with Evelyn, dropped Bug off and headed back up the mountain, where Wolf, Elsie and Hunter, along with Brody, were already setting up the target thrower for skeet shooting.

"You got let out on good behavior," Brody said. "Good to see you, Sawyer."

"It's a marriage," Sawyer said. "Not a prison." Deliberately missing Brody's intended humor.

He knew he was being taciturn. But that was just part of who he was. So Brody could deal.

"All the same to me," Brody said.

"I hear that," Hunter replied. "But Evelyn's a damn good woman. You should be so lucky, honestly, Brody."

"I'll endeavor to keep avoiding it."

"No kidding," Elsie said. "I have no desire to be tied down."

They all looked at his sister.

"What? You can't handle it when I say it? The last thing I want is some man cluttering up my house and telling me what to do. I don't need muddy boots in my doorway. I don't need all that ego taking up my already precious space. I don't need to be asking for permission to go out. Plus, I don't like doing laundry as it is. The last thing I want to do is double it."

"Elsie, my wife does your laundry."

"Maybe I need a wife," Elsie said.

"Whatever floats your boat."

"I don't mean… I didn't mean that," Elsie said. "I just mean, it cuts both ways. Men can be just as much of a millstone as women. So don't go posturing with all your nonsense."

"Oh, I didn't say men couldn't be," Brody said. "It's marriage. Not the gender."

"That's right," Hunter said. "To have to be answerable to one person for the rest your life is a recipe for unhappiness."

"Sure as hell. I hate all my brothers, because I live with them, or near enough to it."

"Damn straight," Hunter said.

"Familiarity breeds contempt," Brody continued.

"That seems… Seems mean," Elsie said.

"We're mean," Brody said.

"Absolutely horrible," Hunter responded.

"Women can only tolerate us for a short amount of time. And that's the real thing. It's not that we don't like women. It's just that you can't like anybody when the relationship is past its sell-by date. I have a great relationship with every woman I hook up with. Because it only lasts as long as I can be charming."

Sawyer was getting sick of Brody and Hunter's two-man show. He looked at Wolf, who clearly agreed.

"To be honest," Wolf said, his voice rough. "I think that's bullshit." He shouldered his shotgun. "Pull."

Brody pulled the lever on the target thrower and released the clay pigeon into the air, and Wolf shot it, sending pieces of bright orange clay all over the place. "I was in love. If I could've spent every day of the rest of my life with her I would've done it. Through all these petty annoyances that you're griping about. Maybe they're wrong. Maybe it's not better to have loved and lost than never loved at all. Maybe it's better to be an ignorant asshole who's never left the shallow end of the pool, and doesn't have any idea what he's missing."

"Hell," Hunter said. "None of this has anything to do with you. Or what you lost. Breanna was a really nice girl…"

"I know," Wolf said. "I am well aware of what a nice girl she was, thank you."

God bless his brother, who didn't speak all that often, and certainly didn't drag out his own pain any more often than he needed to. But he had pretty successfully shut Brody and Hunter up.

"You like being married," Elsie said. "Don't you, Sawyer?"

"I chose to get married. So obviously I had decided there was some merit to it."

"That's Sawyer," Hunter said. "He gets every damn thing he sets out to get."

"Yeah," Sawyer said. "Except I ended up with a whole hell of a lot more than I set out to get. Considering I was going to avoid becoming a husband and father."

"Still." Hunter snorted. "You've done a decent job with it. I'll give you that."

"It's true," Wolf said. "I could never have done what you did. I'd be a miserable father."

He didn't think so. Wolf was… Well, Wolf was tough, but the thing about him was he loved hard and fierce. That was the real issue. Not that he had never been able to love, but that when he had, it had been so deep he'd just never been able to find it in him to do it again.

Sawyer often wondered about his father. Because he seemed to fall in love easily. Easily and often and never mourn the one he lost for all that long. Cavalierly having children he didn't connect to all that deeply. And their mothers... Their mothers having cut ties with them as quickly as... As quickly and easily as anything.

He wondered where that loyalty in Wolf came from. As for Sawyer... He had always worried he was more like his parents.

Sure, he decided to do the right thing. But there were parallels in some of the things that happened in the past that he didn't really care to examine.

"No," Sawyer said. "You'd do fine with it. Because you're not someone who leaves."

"Yeah," Wolf said. "Lucky for me. My feelings are as stubborn as I am."

"Pull."

Wolf shot the next clay disc. "Still, think I'd be a shitty dad."

"Look, if Sawyer can do it," Hunter said, laughing, "anybody can."

"Knock it off," Elsie said. "Honestly, don't you know when to quit. You don't need to rip my brother over the fact that he's a decent human being, and a good father. And the fact that you think you do says a lot about your own fragile situation."

"Easy there, Elsie. Maybe you should be off jarring jam with the ladies," Hunter said.

"Maybe you should be off fucking yourself," Elsie returned.

"Hey, now," Sawyer said. "I don't need you to defend me from this loser. Remember, I've known him all my life."

But there was something about the conversation that wasn't sitting easily with him. And it was just... It was silly, because it had to do with the sameness of it. The reminder that actually he was the same damned person that he'd always been. And he was surrounded by people who had known him his whole life, so it wasn't like he could run from it. It wasn't that what they said was particularly getting to him. But that it was reminding him that he was... He was Sawyer Garrett. He was the same man that he'd always been. He was his father's son.

Even worse, he was his mother's son.

And there was something about what Brody had said. About how the key to his relationships was that he didn't stay in them any longer than he could be pleasant.

What did Evelyn really see in him? In this? She had explained to him, pretty exhaustively, that she liked the silence here. That there was something about being in the country that appealed to her. He knew that she loved Bug. But... He wasn't that shiny-faced Andrew guy. And he never could be. She had asked what he could give to her, and that stuck with him.

There were things he could give. But he just didn't know... If they were the right things. He really didn't. He didn't know how to compete with her former life, and he didn't know what he was going to do if there was ever a point where she realized this new life couldn't make her happy for longer than... A few months, a few years. He had gotten so used to having her... He had gotten so used to having her he didn't know what his life might look like if he didn't have her.

"Hey," Elsie said. "Shoot. They're just being them."

"I don't need to be consoled, Elsie, thank you."

"I didn't say you did," Elsie said, getting prickly.

"Sorry," he said. She was trying to be nice to him, and he needed to figure out how to... He needed to figure out how to say the right things, how to not just be... How to not just be him. Because, yeah, taciturn was fine with

Hunter and Brody, especially when they were being tools. But maybe he needed to figure out how to be different so that he could be different with Evelyn. So that he could be different for Bug. So that he could make sure he didn't… fall short in the way he had done with Elsie.

"I'm glad you're my brother, and not either of them."

"We can hear you," Hunter said.

"Oh, no. How sad for your ego."

It was Elsie's turn to shoulder the shotgun. "Pull," she said.

And she hit the clay pigeon, as unerring as Wolf had. And he knew she would've done just as good of a job with the jam.

So maybe… Maybe he had done okay with her, after all.

And maybe he didn't need to worry quite so much about everything else.

CHAPTER EIGHTEEN

EVELYN STRAPPED BUG to her chest and drove her car over to the Sullivans' farmhouse so that she could take her place in tonight's jam-making extravaganza. Assembled in the farmhouse were Nelly, Fia, Quinn, Rory and Alaina. The girls were wearing various assortments of adorable aprons, and the Sullivan sisters had their hair—which ranged from strawberry blond to a deep auburn—piled up on their heads as they bustled around the kitchen like frilly hands.

Alaina was the least hen-ish, her horse girl energy bringing more of a centeredness to her movements. Fia had a wooden spoon in her pocket and legitimately reminded Evelyn of a classic drawing of a housewife. Nelly was more serene. As she always was. She hadn't really gotten to know Quinn or Rory yet, but from what she'd observed Quinn was the chattier of the two, with Rory often drifting off into some sort of daydream.

"What kind of jam is your favorite?" Alaina asked.

"I don't know," Evelyn said. "Jam is something I haven't made. I'm very good with bread. But I have always bought my jam at the farmers market."

"Are there farmers markets in New York?" Rory asked. "I feel like I've read about them."

"Oh, yes," she said. "Lots of them. Even in Manhattan. And it's also fun to drive out to places like Vermont and go up to farm stores and things. I enjoy it."

"All the states are so tiny over there," Fia said. "It's easy to get between them."

"True. Plus you can take trains. I gather it's not as simple to do here."

"No," Quinn said. "It's a lot fewer and farther between with the trains. I mean, there is one, over in Klamath Falls—you can take it down to California."

"Still, not quite as convenient."

"No," she said. "And anyway, the ranch mostly has everything we need, so we spend a lot of time here."

"Plus," Fia said, "it's a lot of work. So by necessity we have to spend a lot of time here."

"Do you actually... Do you do all the same work that the McClouds and the Kings and the Garretts do?" The biggest difference between those families and this one was that there were men. The Sullivans were all girls.

"Oh, some of it," Alaina said. "But we have horses. Which is different than the Garretts and the Kings. Mostly, we have ranch foremen. We handle a lot of the management. But any of us can fix the fence."

"Or shoot if need be." That came from Fia.

"Shoe a horse, engage in a little light blacksmithing," Rory said. "Though I'd rather read about it than do it."

"Muck a stall, foal a mare." That came from Quinn.

"So you *all* know how to do all of that?" Evelyn asked, deeply impressed.

"It's the hazard of growing up on a ranch."

Nelly craned her neck. "I managed to learn to do none of that."

"Your mom was the teacher," Fia said. "It's a little bit different. But we don't really do it anymore. We lease out the ranch and take an income off that, and we're putting our resources into getting our produce operation off the ground." Fia got animated when she launched into that topic. "We just always had to make do. But my mother always said that women can do any job a man can do, and what we can't do, we can delegate with more efficiency. Because we are willing to delegate."

"She sounds smart," Evelyn said.

"She is," Fia said.

"So where did your parents go?"

"Well, after our parents got divorced," Quinn said, looking distressed about it even now, "my dad left. Took his new girlfriend and went to California." Evelyn couldn't tell if the girlfriend, or going to California, was the bigger sin. "Left Mom and all the girls here on the ranch. But my mom had had enough of ranch life. She was here because of him. We don't know any other kind of life. But she does. We told her we'd take a chunk of money from Sullivan's Point to pay for her new life. So, she went to Hawaii. And she is happy there."

"Very happy," Rory said, her tone slightly detached.

"And we'll be even happier if we ever have time to visit," Fia said. "But she says she loves the weather."

"That's really… I mean, that's really great that you guys recognize that she needed something different."

Fia shrugged. "I don't think any of us could survive somewhere else even if we wanted to. We're Sullivans. This is our land. Our family land, and it's important we all stay together and work it how we can."

"You'll all stay here?"

"Yeah," Quinn said. "We're moving toward making the gardens our big business. We're planning on opening a farm store. Right now we sell in John's and we sell at a roadside stand, but we're getting bigger than that. I want to make it a destination." She grinned. "Like I said. Women figure out how to get the job done."

Evelyn liked these women. These women that were so very determined in what they did.

"Well, if you ever need help with expansion, I have started a business before."

"You have?"

"Yes," she said, and she proceeded to tell them about the organization business. After much interest, she ended up taking out some pictures of houses that she'd done on her phone, and showing them the way that she would re-work their pantry.

"This is genius," Alaina said.

"I didn't ever think I could get excited about cleaning," Rory said. "But this makes a case for it."

"It would add a lot of efficiency to what you do. It would make things a whole lot easier."

"Well, if you want to help with that, we can pay you."

"I would be happy to help. And you don't need to pay me. Because I am sure that we can actually work out some trades, and if I ever do have a mind to seriously get into business, it would probably be helpful for me to have you as my spokeswomen. I understand that people around here might not necessarily be into this as a point of it being trendy. But it could be useful. Big spreads like this with so many things. What I could do with organizing the work-flow…"

"Don't be silly," Fia said. "We're obviously going to pay you. And… If you could help with things like the barn, tack, all that kind of stuff, it would be perfect."

"I… I would love to."

And she hadn't realized that she had been…missing this. Missing the chance to help people in this way. To actually do work. And that she found a way to do it while taking care of Bug, while being here… It just confirmed what she was already feeling. That this was the place she was supposed to be. That it was wonderful and perfect.

"I think you're really on to something," Fia said. "There's just so much stuff involved in this kind of life. Having a little bit of help figuring out exactly what to do with it… I think we could all use that."

And just like that, she felt like a useful piece of the team, and she hadn't realized how much she'd been wanting that. To feel not just a part of the Garrett family, but a part of Four Corners, which was becoming such a beloved place to her.

She had come out here looking for a husband. And mostly looking for a reset, given the state of her life. She had found so much more than she'd anticipated. She had found friends.

"Maybe I'll organize while the second batch of jam is going."

"You don't have to ask twice," Fia said.

And that was how she found herself sitting on the floor surrounded by things, happily sorting through them, with her baby in her arms and her friends all around her, laughing and talking.

And for the first time in a very long while, Evelyn felt light.

SHE HAD BEEN putting this off. She had been putting it off because she didn't want to deal with it. But it was time. She really couldn't avoid it any longer.

She needed to FaceTime her mother. It had been a few days since her triumphant jam making and organization at the Sullivan place, and she was feeling even more entrenched in life than she had that night she had finally accepted that Sawyer and Bug were her family for real. And now it was time… Now it was time to actually commit. To actually tell her parents what she'd done, though she was sure that Andrew had come screaming back to them with some version of the truth, and to draw her line in the sand with them.

To have the hard conversation.

It only took one ring for her mother to pick up.

"Is Dad there?" she asked.

"No," her mom said. "He's golfing. Why did you call my phone if you wanted to talk to him?"

"Well, I want to talk to both of you," Evelyn said.

"Sorry."

"It's fine," she said. "I'll talk to you first. I just wanted…" She lifted Bug up high so that phone camera could see her. She was sitting on her and Sawyer's bed, Sawyer still out working. "I wanted to introduce you to your grandchild."

"Evelyn," her mother said. "You weren't pregnant. I know you weren't."

"No. I wasn't. But… I told you I met someone. That was only half-true. I read about a rancher online who was looking for a mail-order bride. Because he had a daughter. And I answered his ad."

"Are you crazy?"

"I've already done this with myself, and with Andrew. I made a decision that a lot of people wouldn't. I made a decision I never thought I would. But I'm settled. I'm very happy. And I want you to know about June." She figured she should not call her Bug in the presence of her mother. She wanted to hope that her mother would understand the situation. "Because regardless of the relationship that we had growing up, you are her grandmother. You and Dad are the only grandparents she has a chance of ever knowing. All I ever wanted from you was acceptance. All I ever wanted from you was for you to be proud of me. And I did absolutely everything that I could to make that happen. I wasn't the ballerina that you were, and I get that. I get that it really disappointed you. So I tried to be really successful in business. I tried to find a husband that you would approve of. I tried to make your sacrifice worth it. But in the end, I just had to find myself. And I had to figure out how to live for me. And that's what I've done. That's what I've done here. I get that you don't understand. And that you probably won't. So the only thing I can ask you is this… Do you want to keep having any sort of relationship with me, do you want to be a grandmother? Because I need to know that before we can move forward. I need to know that you'll be good to June. That you'll accept Sawyer as a son-in-law. If you'll just come visit us sometimes. Or call us or something… I can work with that. But if you're going to be combative, if you're going to be scathing, if you're going to be disapproving of the decisions that I've already made, then I just can't have you… I can't do to June what you did to me."

Her mother looked stricken. And much like her conversation with Andrew, it forced her into an uncomfortable emotional space. Where her personal antagonist wasn't a maniacal, cackling villain. But a person. Entrenched in her own point of view.

It was…a thought that pulled her up short. Because personal growth was great, but she wasn't an island. There were people she loved, and part of understanding herself was going to include understanding them. And she was going to have to pause.

If she was going to have to speak the hard truths, she had to listen to the hard responses, too.

On some level she'd always known that. It was why she'd avoided those truths like she had. Because it could be a monologue, but that would only be self-satisfactory.

It had to be a conversation for healing to occur.

"Evelyn... I love you. I only ever wanted what was best for you. I only ever wanted what I thought would make you the happiest. I was never happier than when I danced ballet. I wasn't ready to be finished. But I did choose to have you. I did choose to marry your father to try and give you the best life possible."

"No, I'm sorry. I do understand that."

"I know that I... I'm judgmental. I understand the last phone call we had wasn't pleasant."

"That's an understatement," Evelyn said.

"I don't know where the last thirty-five years of my life went," her mom said. "I... I threw them away. I never fully accepted the life that I was in. And all I could do was romanticize the one that I left. Because there is nothing quite like possibility rather than certainty to make you romanticize what you could've had. And I've been sitting here asking myself what in the hell would've made me happy. You marrying Andrew? You being close to me? I don't know the answer to that, Evelyn. You may not believe this, but I tried to do the right thing. I tried to direct you in the way that I wished my mother would have. I wish that someone would've told me how important decisions were, and how big consequences could be, and how talent needed to be cherished. So that's what I tried to do with you, and I ended up making you feel pressured. Until you ran all the way across the country because of me. Until you couldn't even talk to me about the decisions you were making, about what you were doing."

"I'm sorry," Evelyn said. And she felt… Genuinely sorry. Genuinely sad. Because her mother didn't mean to hurt her the way that she had. Because she didn't mean to cause her scarring and trauma. Because there were other people who had factored into it and who had made her feel that way, along with her own personality, which was geared around wanting to please.

Because her mother wasn't the single villain in the piece. Because suddenly she could see her mother as a lost teenage girl, letting go of her dreams. A woman who had settled for a life, rather than intentionally going out and making one.

"I didn't know you felt that way," Evelyn said. "I didn't know you felt lost. You always seem so certain to me. So certain of what would make me happy."

"Because I thought if you had something that was yours… Something that didn't belong to your husband… I thought that would make you keep hold of who you were. I thought it would keep you from becoming like me. All I have is your father's status. And all I had was your success. And I don't actually ever want you to be in that position. And I would've pushed you straight there, without meaning to."

"Mom, I…"

"Do you have any idea how scared I was when you quit dance? Because I thought you were going to be better than me. I thought you were going to pursue it more seriously. And then you left, and you were smoking, and I know you were fooling around with all those boys… I just saw you becoming like me. Except maybe even with the worst sort of boy who couldn't even give you money and comfort."

"No, I was being irresponsible then. I was. I was being

rebellious, and I was acting out because I was angry. Now I have her," she said, looking down at the baby. "And I understand…how big it feels to take care of a child like this. How impossible. I don't know if I'm going to do the right thing all the time with her. I was certain that I would. Just… I was certain that doing the opposite of what you did was going to be the key. Because I was really angry at you. But you tried to do the opposite of what your parents did, didn't you?"

"I did," she said, looking away. "But look where it got me."

"I just don't think the answer is in anger," Evelyn said. "I think the answer is love. And that's the conclusion I keep coming to no matter how long I sit with this. I know you might not understand the decision I made. But Sawyer is the best man I have ever, ever known. He's solid and he's…" He was the man she loved.

He was no longer just the man she wanted to be in love with. She loved him. She loved him with everything that she was.

"I love him so much. And I know I haven't known him that long. But he… He gave up everything that he believed about himself, not just physical things, but all his fears, to decide to be a single dad to his daughter. And then he decided to deal with another fear and find himself a wife. Talk about a man that's just doing the best he can with what he's been given. He amazes me. He really does. He's the kind of good that I didn't think was real."

"I told you, I sat with myself and I asked… What would make me happy? And what I've realized is that I need you to be happy," her mother said. "Or what was the point of anything I supposedly sacrificed? Just shaping you into me, that's not enough. I want you to be happy. Whatever that looks like."

"And you'll come visit?"

"If I have to come by myself I will."

"Well, I hope that Dad will come. Like I said, Bug could really use grandparents."

"Bug?"

"Oh, it's her pet name. It's what Sawyer calls her. It's what his grandmother called him." She cleared her throat. "You know, Sawyer's grandmother was the most important woman in his life. There's just always more time, Mom. To make whatever life you want."

They talked for a while longer before getting off the phone. Evelyn felt…hopeful. One great conversation didn't heal all the years of distance and hurt, but it was a beginning.

A very important one.

But the thing that stuck with her now, that resonated in her, rang through her, was her realization about Sawyer.

She loved him. She was in love with him.

And when she had answered his ad, she had never really… That had never actually been the biggest priority for her. Love.

In fact, it had been the farthest thing from her mind. She had thought she would start over. She had thought that it would be a way for her to claim something for herself, but she had never… She had never imagined that it would be the place for her to fall into the deepest love she had ever even imagined.

She hadn't realized how much it would change her.

It was so strange to think that she had been a particular sort of person for the first thirty-four years of her life, and now she felt... Not entirely unlike herself but not the same, either.

But she had been seeds before. Maybe that was the thing. And it had taken this time for her to grow.

And here at Four Corners she had grown. She had grown strong and she had grown tall.

And love... Love was the bloom, which had just fully taken shape.

And love, she realized, was the beauty that would always be worth fighting for. No matter how difficult the fight was.

CHAPTER NINETEEN

"I THINK IT's time we got the paperwork together for Bug's adoption."

It was maybe kind of an abrupt greeting, and the way that Evelyn stopped at the stove, midstir on whatever she was cooking, and looked back at him, confirmed it.

"You think so?"

"Yeah," he said. "I think… As far as I know, stepparent adoption is easy. Especially in cases like ours. Missy forfeited her parental rights when she left, so as of now, Bug only has one legal guardian. And it's me. She's young enough that there aren't extra interviews or approvals that need to happen. And basically what we need to do is schedule an initial hearing."

"That seems easy."

"Yeah," he said. "I printed off some forms."

"Hang on just a second." She took her spoon out of the pot and tapped it on the side, then she took the pot off the heat. She walked over to the dining table and sat down, and he sat down next to her, put some forms out in front of her and she perused them thoughtfully. "And you feel good about this?" she asked.

"Yes," he said. "This is what I want. You're not having second thoughts, are you?" The idea made his stomach go tight.

"No," she said. "I'm not having second thoughts at all.

I'm thrilled. But... No, I just wanted to make sure that you're all right. I know how much she means to you. I love her, but I don't want you to feel like you rushed into anything out of desperation."

"It sounds to me like you're backtracking."

"I'm not backtracking," she said. "I promise you. So it's actually really hard for me to say that. Because I don't want you to take her from me. I don't want you to rethink what we have. But I can't always tell what you feel, Sawyer. Actually, I can never tell how you feel. I can tell when you're aroused, and that's just because your body doesn't lie. As for the rest of you, the rest of your feelings, I don't always know. You're very difficult to read."

"I say it how it is."

"With literally no more frills than necessary. And sometimes... Sometimes women need some frills, Sawyer. Sometimes we need more reassurance than just a couple of words." She looked at him expectantly. "Or at least I do."

"Well, I want you to do this. I literally married you, Evelyn. I can't make it much more clear. I don't expect my grandmother ever formally adopted my dad and his brothers. I just don't think that's how they did things back then. But she was every bit their mother. And I believe in that connection. I believe it's stronger than genetics. Blood doesn't mean a damn thing. It's all who sticks around. All who chooses to be part of your life. And you already decided to be that for her."

"Yes," she said. "I know. Don't read anything into this. I just... Like I said, I just wanted to be sure."

"I'm sure," he said. "I'm as sure as anybody could be."

"Okay," she said. "If there's one thing I know for sure,

it's that there's no point questioning you once you've made up your mind."

"You're not the first person to say that to me," he said.

"No, I imagine I'm not. All right," she said. "Let's see the paperwork."

She grabbed a pen out of a little bin that he didn't remember being there, then filling in her personal information. They'd already done this together when they did their marriage license. He'd seen her full name. Her birthday. Her Social Security number. All those very secret things that made a person who they were. In the system at least. He couldn't say that he had a whole lot of thoughts about the system one way or the other.

"I… I expect you might be wanting a name change."

"Oh," she said. "You were thinking you would change her name?"

"I put June Bug on the birth certificate. I doubt she'll be thankful for that later in life."

"Well, what do you want to call her?"

"I figured I wouldn't get too attached to anything, because whoever I married was going to want to have a say in it. She's your daughter, too, after all."

She sat for a moment, totally silent. "I think we should keep June. It was your grandmother's name, after all."

"It's a bit of an old lady name," he said.

"That doesn't matter. It's her name. And she will give it a new identity. A new life. But she'll carry her great-grandmother with her. All the time. Also, your grandmother wasn't born an old woman, you know. It was at one time a little girl's name."

"Yeah," he said.

"Sawyer, I can't read your mind. Do you want her to be named June or not?"

"I don't expect it matters."

"Because you'll just call her Bug?"

"Well, not at her prom or anything, but…"

"Sure, Sawyer," she said. "You told me once that you were a man who made decisions. And that was what set you apart from your father. I believe you. I know that's true. What I don't understand is why you can't just tell me what name you want to give the baby. I don't think you called her June Bug by accident. I think you did it because those names are important to you. And I can certainly see the merit in taking Bug off her birth certificate and just leaving it as something you call her. But I think that June matters to you. And if you want to keep it, then you need to say so. Don't make it about my feelings. Or what you think they might be. Make it about yours."

"It's just…sentimental, I guess," he said. "And there's no call for me making big decisions based on sentimentality."

"That is why people make most of their decisions, Sawyer. We choose to stay with people because of sentimentality. We choose to keep certain items because of sentimentality. We make the same recipes over and over again that we might not even like to eat all that much because of sentimentality. So my honest suggestion would be that if you want to name your daughter out of sentimentality, you do it. But I feel very strongly that you're actually selling it short. That you're not actually being honest about how important this is to you."

"Seems to me that you're the one that thinks it's important," he said. "So you might as well do it."

"Stop it," she said. "It's like talking to a brick wall some-times."

"It may surprise you to learn you're not the first person ever say that to me," he said.

"Not at all. Honestly, Sawyer, why is it so hard to just say that you want this."

"I do. Fine. I'd like that to be her name. But it's hard to use it, because then it reminds me. And I don't really know quite what to do about that. I want to give her this in my grandmother's memory. Because she deserves it. Because she came out here, and she dedicated her life to a scrubby pack of boys, who then turned into shitty fathers, and she did her best with her grandkids, too. And her grandkids… Look," he said. "I don't know the answer to this. I don't know how to… I don't know how to do this."

He felt resistance inside of him. Something pushing the words back down his throat. Tightening around his chest. He didn't have words for this. The people in his life already knew his struggles. They already knew his story. She didn't. He had to find ways to explain himself. Why he did things the way that he did, why he felt what he did. Which people were important to him, and he didn't the hell know how to do that. He just didn't. And it felt impossible. On top of everything else it just felt impossible. To put into words what June had been. To put into words what it felt like knowing…

"I get sad when I look at her. Along with the happiness. I'm sad that June will never see this. Her namesake. I'm sad that she won't get to see me…be a better version of myself than I ever was while she was alive. I don't know…what to do with all of those things. Because they make me feel like I have ground-up broken glass in my chest. And there's no space for that kind of carry-on in my life, Evelyn. None. There was no one here to listen to me bitch. When my mom left, my dad said pick up and carry on. And when Wolf's mom left I told him the same thing. Pick up and carry on. There's no use crying."

"But you didn't tell your grandma to pick up and carry on when your grandfather died. You understood that. You understood that there has to be space for grieving."

"There's not when you're a rancher. There's no space for it. There's no time. We got cattle to tend to, the land keeps moving in its rhythms, and death is part of that rhythm. And you don't stop and get all wound up about it. There's no point."

There was something in the way she moved that made him want to draw away. But he didn't. He let her touch him. His shoulder. "Maybe all that stuff inside of you is just unshed tears, Sawyer, did you ever think of that? Maybe you're still so sad because you've never given yourself the time to feel it."

"No, I'm sad because she's not here. And nothing will bring her back. She was the single most important person in my life. That's just the truth. I never loved anybody as much as I loved her."

"Except for June Bug," Evelyn said softly. She put her hand on his, and his first instinct was to draw away. So he did. She looked hurt by that, but he didn't need her to comfort him like he was a child.

"My word, you're infuriating," she said, getting up from the table and going over to her pot again, putting it back on the burner.

"What are you making?"

"Pot roast. But I think I've decided that dinner is for

emotionally conversant adults, and you don't make the cut. Hunter might be able to stay."

"Great. Hunter. Don't be fooled by his facade. He's pretty fucked up. Just because he doesn't show it. Just because he hides it well behind a smile doesn't mean he's all right."

"Are you jealous? Are you afraid that I might like him better than you?"

He growled, getting out of his chair. "Do you?"

"Well," she said. "At last. Some emotion. I was beginning to think you didn't have any."

That frustrated the hell out of him. That she would say that. That she thought that. Because that was the damned problem. He was full to the brim of all this... All this shit he didn't want to feel. And it was why he couldn't talk about anything. It was why he couldn't explain...any of this.

"You don't know what you're talking about."

"Because you won't tell me anything."

"What the hell is it you want to know?" he asked. "You want to make sure that I have a heart? Is that it? All right. Let's do this, then. Let's just have it out. You can just... You can just get all of it. In one... In one story.

"I went to visit my mom in Chicago. It was a big-ass deal. My dad was mad about it. June scraped together a bunch of her money to buy me a ticket to go. I wasn't half as grateful as I should've been. I was an entitled dick because I was sixteen years old. And all I could think was I was finally going to see my mom. My mom, who left me. But she was who was important, because of course. Because of course the woman who had abandoned me when I was a child was going to be more important than the woman who had stuck around and bandaged my scrapes and raised me. I was in such a rush when she dropped me off at the airport, I said, 'Don't bother to park. Just let me go in.' She wanted to make sure I was going to get off all right because I'd never flown before. But I didn't... I didn't want to slow down and I didn't want anybody to have to treat me like I didn't know what I was doing."

"Sawyer, that's just being a teenager. We're all obnoxious when we're teenagers."

"I got out of the car, and she said, 'I love you.' I shut the car door and I went into the airport. I didn't say it back. I didn't really mean to not say it, but I... But I just didn't. I was in a hurry. I didn't even think about it again. I got on the plane, I flew to Chicago. When I got to the airport my mother didn't pick me up. So... I tried to figure out where she was, but I couldn't get ahold of her. She changed her number. Something. Or it was just disconnected because she didn't pay her bill. I asked about getting a flight home, and the fare exchange was going to cost five hundred dollars. And I didn't have five hundred dollars."

"What did you do?"

"I didn't want to call my dad. I didn't want to tell him that she didn't show up. I didn't want to... Grandma had given me a hundred and fifty dollars. One hundred and fifty dollars to spend on the trip. So I took it and I got a cab at the airport. Wandered around for a while in the snow. Got something to eat. Then I found a homeless shelter. That's what I did for five days."

"Sawyer," she said. "You didn't... You didn't call anyone to come get you?"

"No. I couldn't add to that expense. At the time the ranch wasn't doing all that good. Under my father's management there were a lot of problems. And it would've had to come out of the bigger pot. And that just didn't seem fair. Not when all the other families weren't part of the problem. And I was the one that wanted to go. I was the one that wanted to do it. My dad didn't want me to."

"What was it like? Staying in the homeless shelter?"

"They asked a lot of questions. But I looked older, so nobody really pushed it too hard. I just said I was passing through and I was on some hard times."

"That must've been…"

"I didn't need any of the food. I left every day and got myself something. I had that cash. It was just a roof over my head that I couldn't afford. But I didn't need to take any more charity than I had to."

"Sawyer. That wasn't being a freeloader. You were a boy who was abandoned in a city you'd never been in."

Even now, he could remember the feeling. That total sense of disconnect. Of being in that strange place with all those great tall gray buildings. Going down and walking along the river with his hands in his pockets and his head low. And then finding a place to walk around the lake. Frozen, the wind blowing off it chilling him to the bone. But it had been like the ocean, and it had made him think that maybe he could sail away home.

Counting down the days until his plane left.

He'd wandered into a park one day, and seen a big metal bean. Huge and right in the center of it. And he wondered why the hell so many useless things existed in cities.

Sculptures of beans, big frozen lakes and mothers who didn't want their children.

"Finally, it was…the day of my flight. I went to the airport early, bought myself a cheeseburger at the McDonald's in the airport. I had to make it home. And when I got there, it wasn't June in the car at the airport to pick me up. It was Hunter."

"Your dad didn't come?"

He shook his head. "No. Hunter came to get me. And he told me that… He told me that June was dead. And it was like… It was like the whole week didn't even happen. It was like none of it mattered anymore. And the only thing I could remember was that I got out of that car and I didn't tell her that I loved her. She said it to me, and I didn't say it back. And then she had a brain aneurysm and she died. I spent a week alone in a city that I didn't give a shit about, just wanting to see a woman who didn't give a shit about me. While the woman who loved me most died. I feel like I've spent every week after that alone. And I could've had five more days with her. Five more. But I was gone, chasing after something that didn't even matter. I couldn't even slow down to tell her that I loved her. So there you go. And there you have it. There's why it's not so simple to say her name. There's why it hurts to think about her. Because I let her down, I'd—"

"I am so sorry," Evelyn said. "I'm so sorry that happened to you, Sawyer, but that isn't your fault. You didn't fail her. You didn't fail anyone. That was just incredibly sad. And I am very, very sorry that it happened. I am so sorry that you lost someone you love so much, and that it was compounded by the fact that you had just had the worst week of your life."

"I survived it," he said.

But when he thought about it, he thought about the way he had felt isolated. Like he was on an alien planet. The way he had felt uncertain and unsteady in the world, which was the first time that it had ever happened to him. He had gone from a place that he knew like the back of his hand to a place where he knew no one, and had no idea of the way that it worked. He'd never been around so many people. He'd never felt cold like that before. He'd never seen buildings that tall. And he had just... He'd found a way to shut off.

Because it had been too much. It had been too intense. So he just sort of figured out a way to push it down. To put one foot in front of the other. To do what needed doing. He needed a place to stay. Because he didn't have enough money for lodging.

He had enough for food, so he didn't need anything like that. He had brought a decent enough coat, even though that Midwestern wind had been a bit of a shock to him. He had his hat. So mostly, he spent his days walking with his head down, sightseeing, he supposed, but he didn't exactly give a shit about any of the sights.

He had learned something on that trip. He had learned how to take his feelings and turn them into fuel for action. He could do it, and if he did that, he wouldn't have to feel. And eventually, he could handle everything around them.

When he'd found out about June, he was already numb. And so he'd just push that down, too. Push that down along with everything else. And now Evelyn wanted to know. Evelyn wanted to know when she didn't know how hard all this was. When she didn't know... She just didn't.

"It's not okay," he said. "And I have to live with it. But I'm really good at living with it. I'm going to be here for Bug. I'm here for you. But I can't... I can't do this thing where... I just share everything that pops in my head, where I tell you everything that I'm feeling, because I just don't... I don't feel like that."

"That's a choice," she said.

"Yeah. It is a choice. And I made it for a reason. I'm not about to change who I am. I am exactly as advertised, Evelyn. I never promised you that I would be anything other than this. In fact, I said, absolutely directly, that I'm not romantic. That I am what I am."

"Yeah, I know," Evelyn said. "I know you did. I know you did and you meant that. And I said it was all right, because I didn't know what I wanted from you."

She turned around to the oven, and pulled out the roast pan.

"I'm going to let you eat," she said. "Only because withholding food from you seems like a mean thing to do, since all of this centers around the fact that you're emotionally constipated."

"Thanks."

"I feel sorry for you," she said. "I really do. So, so sorry, and I really feel sad for myself sometimes about the things that happened to me, but you won, Sawyer. Because that... That kills me. That that happened to you."

"I don't need your pity," he said, everything in him recoiling from it.

"Maybe you don't need my pity. But you have it. Because that is just awful. How could she do that to you? You were a sixteen-year-old boy. A sixteen-year-old boy who flew across the country for the first time to see his mother, and she didn't come pick you up. She wasn't there for you. And that is not your fault. It is hers. The people in your life that should have loved you failed you. And that has nothing to do with you."

"One person didn't," he said. "I failed her."

"You know what, maybe you hurt her feelings," she said. "Maybe, with all her wisdom, she didn't let it bother her.

Maybe she just knew, with all the wisdom that she had
from all of her years, that this stupid kid was just a teenage
boy. And she knew that when she saw you again you would
say it. And she knew that you felt it, whether you said it or
not. But either way she didn't quit loving you. She never
stopped. And she didn't die not loving you."

"Stop," he said. "I don't have anything to say to this. I
don't have anything to say about it. It's not... It's done."

"But it's not done. Because the things that hurt us echo
inside of us until we grab hold of them and figure out how
to make it stop. It doesn't just stop. The way that things
happened with dance. I was so hurt by that. I was so hurt
by what I couldn't be. I was so... But I got rid of that echo.
When I danced for you. I got rid of it when I stopped holding it hostage. Because that's what I was doing. I withheld
dance for myself because I couldn't be perfect at it. Because
I couldn't please my mother with it in a very specific way.
But I can please myself with it, so why not do it sometimes.
And now it doesn't have to hurt me. Now it can be something that I have. Something that I love. Again.

"And I... I talked to my mom. I talked to her and I told
her. I told her how much she hurt me. And you know what,
she was sorry. And I'm not saying that your mother would
be. Because nothing that my mom did was on the same
level as what yours did to you. But I had to do something
to make all that stop. I couldn't just wait. You can't just wait
it out. You have to actually...recognize it. And you have to
do something with it."

"Why?"

"Because it is keeping you away from me. And right
now you can hold Bug, and comfort her whenever there's
a problem, but later it won't be like that. She'll become a

little girl who talks and has her own opinions, and a teen-ager who will need you to listen to her and share with you. I know that what you want more than anything is to spare her any of the scarring that this world gave to you and to me. But we are going to pass it on, Sawyer, unless we look at it deeply.

"When I talked to my mom… She mentioned to me that she tried to be just the opposite of her parents. That what she tried to do was push me because her parents didn't. To demand perfection, because she thought that it would… Keep me disciplined. But it just buried me. And I don't think that's the answer. I think the answer is…honesty. I think it's stopping and looking at yourself and looking at the things that life has done to you and trying to ask your-self why you make the decisions you do. Why you want your children to do these certain things. I wanted to have children because I wanted to prove to my mother that I would be better at being a mother than she was. How's that for continuing a cycle. I was just going to pour all of my own issues right on top of Bug, and I wasn't going to do it on purpose. I wanted to be a good mother. I wanted to be a supportive mother. But I can't make her life about me. About my issues. That's just asking for generational pain. That's just me passing it on. And we have this chance. We have this chance to be something new for her. We have a chance to be something new for each other. And I think we have to take it. I think we have to, because if we don't, then what are we going to become?"

"I'm already what I was going to become."

"We're the same age," Evelyn said. "And over the last weeks, I have grown into something completely different. I found something here that I didn't even know I wanted.

And that's why I'm pushing you. Because I'm not just your mail-order bride. I am your wife. And I am committed to this life with you. I am committed to making it the best life it can be."

"I'm hungry," he said. "Can this pause until after dinner?"

He was more than hungry. He was... He felt tired in a way he couldn't quite articulate. Weary down on a soul-deep level.

"Let's eat," she said. She cleared the paperwork and put food down in front of him. And he felt uncomfortable. Because she was still doing all this for him, and he could feel that he was falling short. Falling short of what she wanted from him.

"What is it you want?" he said, well aware that he had just been the one to put the conversation on hold, and then hadn't honored it. "Because you're saying all this to me, you're asking for more from me, and you're great, Evelyn. You've done a whole ton of shit for me. You cook me dinner, you know I find you attractive as hell... I don't know what else you want. You're just telling me you want more. Is it just that you want to know my pain? Because I don't really see the point of that."

"Did you not see the point of me sharing mine?"

"I didn't say that. I never said that."

"No," she said, closing her eyes. "I know you never said that. I know you didn't. It's just... If you don't see any point to you sharing it, then it must... Don't you see that it means the same? It's how you got to know me."

"But why? That's what I don't get. This works well enough."

"I don't want well enough." She let out a long breath. "I didn't really want to tell you this over roast and potatoes.

But I love you. And that's what I want. I love you, and what I want is for you to love me."

WELL, SHE'D SAID IT. And she knew that he wasn't going to be thrilled to hear it. She knew that it wasn't going to mean a whole hell of a lot to him.

Her chest felt bruised. Everything that he'd said to her about his mother... About that week in Chicago. It was the worst thing she had ever heard. Her poor, proud husband. That he had been abandoned like that. Neglected. That he had been... What hurt her the most was knowing how devastated he must've been, and realizing that he hadn't shown it all. That he had gone through all of these things. Every last one of them, without showing his hurt. Without showing the devastation he must've felt. That destroyed her. And she knew that it was the key to him. To why he reacted to things the way that he did, rather than why he didn't react at all.

"I don't know what to do with that," he said.

"I don't know, maybe you'll fall in love with me, too?" It hurt to ask that.

"That was not part of the bargain. This wasn't... It wasn't part of it," he said, tossing his fork down on the table.

"Oh, is it a bad thing to have your wife love you?"

"It's just not what this was supposed to be. I told you. It needed to be a thing apart from passion. That had nothing to do with the two of us."

"Too bad," she said. "Because it has been about the two of us since the moment we first talked on the phone and you got me hot and bothered talking about meat loaf. Because somehow I knew. Somehow I knew when I looked at that article that you were the man for me. I came out here for this easy, Christmas-movie, feel-good sort of romance. And it doesn't always feel good, Sawyer. It's hard. What I want from you is something I know you don't want to give, what I feel for you is something I know you don't want me to feel. But it's too late for me to go back and feel any different. It's too late for this to be any different than it is. I... I fell in love with you. Not in an easy, smiling, wandering through the streets of a small town kind of medley with cheerful music playing in the background. I fell in love with you while I pulled back all the layers inside of myself and got down to asking the question of why exactly I have done everything I've done in my life the way that I have up till now. Why I was never actually in love with anyone for the first thirty-four years of my life. Why you are actually the first person I was able to fall for. I wasn't ready until you. And nobody else was you.

"And I want so badly, so desperately, for this to be the best marriage that it can be, for our life together to be the best life that it can be. And I am willing to do whatever I have to do to make it that way. And if I have to... If I have to crawl across broken glass to get there, then I will. I don't want to be the person standing here confessing that I'm in love. I don't want to be the person taking the risk. But I will. I will for you. I will for us."

"This was never supposed to be—"

"It doesn't matter," she said. "I came here to be a mother. I came here to show my mother that she was wrong about me. I came here so that everyone would have to marvel at the fact that I had done this wild thing. I came here as a rebellion. But I am staying here because you are everything that I want. I am staying here because of us."

"What if I can't give you what you want?"

"I married you," she said. And suddenly, everything inside of her cracked open, and she saw herself. An alternate version of herself, the Evelyn she had been before she had begun to love this man. She could see her burning everything down and walking away. Because that was what she had done in the past. Because that was how she had gotten herself out of the academy. Because it was how she had handled the situation with her friends, with Andrew. With her mother.

But that was not the Evelyn she was now. This Evelyn wouldn't walk away. She was going to stand, and she was going to fight. For what she believed in, what she believed could be between them. For everything that she believed they could be. She was going to fight.

But she realized if she didn't walk away it might mean standing in the flames.

Because while she might not burn it down, they might both catch fire, anyway.

And she would stand, and she would burn with it. With him.

"I am going to be here. I have made a commitment to you. I have made a commitment to our daughter. And I am not backing down from it just because it might be difficult. I am not your mother, Sawyer. I am your wife. And I made a promise to you. That for better or for worse we would stick this out. So I'm just going to be here. Being an inconvenient pain in your ass, proving to you that love is real. That love is stronger than that terrible moment when you won't say it back. Because it doesn't break just because you didn't say it. It doesn't. It doesn't go away. Not for me, and I swear it didn't for June. Whatever you think you did, whatever you think you didn't do… I swear to you it wasn't enough to put a dent in that love. It wasn't enough to stop it. Not with her, not with me. I want to hear it. And I'm sure that she did, too. And I know that June will. Your daughter will want to hear it from you. She will need it. Your daughter needs you to find that inside of yourself. I'll live if you don't. But she… She needs it. So you need to figure this out. And I will be here. You are not wandering the streets of Chicago alone coping with an emotion way too big to handle. I am not letting you be in isolation with this. It is about us. About you and me. About me saying that you need to do better. About me saying that you need to find a way to be a better man."

"I am already the best man that I can be," he said, standing up and planting his hands on the table. "This is as good as it gets. But I'm here. Isn't that enough?"

"Was it enough for your dad to just be here?"

"It's different. He didn't take care of anybody. He didn't—"

"What scares you the most, Sawyer? That you might be your dad, or that you might be your mom? Are you actually just sitting here burning with the guilt that you left *once*? And that when you did things fell apart?"

"Just stay away from things you don't get, Evelyn."

"I don't get them because you won't tell me. Which means I have to guess."

He started to walk away from the table, and she went with him. He went up the stairs, down the hall to their room, and she went with him.

He sat on the edge of the bed, staring into Bug's crib.

"I didn't invite you to come in here."

"Too damn bad. It's my bedroom."

"Dammit," he said.

"Tell me what's wrong."

"I don't have the words for it," he said. "Has it ever occurred to you that you just want me to be a man that I can't be?"

"No," she said. "Because that's bullshit. Because it's selling yourself short. You could choose to fall short of my expectations, if you want."

And suddenly, he launched himself off the bed, grabbed hold of her and wrapped his arms around her. And he kissed her. And there was a wildness to this kiss. It was different than every other time they'd come together, where it was driven by lust and attraction. He was broken. Shattered. She could feel it. He didn't have words. So he was giving her this. He walked her out of the bedroom, where Bug was sleeping so peacefully, down the hall to the bedroom that used to be hers. And he stripped her clothes off with each step. And she let him. Decided to give herself to him in this way, too, even though everything hurt. Even though it was painful. Because for whatever reason, he needed this. Because this was the vocabulary that existed between them, and so if it brought him closer to finding the words, then she wanted him to have it. By the time she hit the mattress, she was naked. And he was soon after. And she rose up on her knees, bending over in front of him, taking his arousal into her mouth. He groaned, pulling her head away. "No."

"Shut up," she said, pushing him back and taking him into her mouth again. She loved doing this for him.

She loved giving him pleasure. Loved pushing him to the brink and watching him as he began to shake. She loved giving to him, because she knew that it actually made him feel things. Because she knew that it gave her the power.

In so many ways, she could see how this seemed like a submissive act. But it wasn't. Not between them. Not now.

Because he needed her, and he couldn't get a handle on his feelings. Because she knew he would love nothing more than to take charge and make it about her pleasure. Give himself some control in this situation.

But she wouldn't allow it. He was shaking, his trembling hands gripping her hair tight, steadying themselves, tugging hard. And she knew that the anger that tinged his every movement was just emotion. Whether he was angriest at her or the feelings, she didn't know, but it didn't particularly matter. She would be a safe place for it. For all this. Because she was ready. She was ready for those floodgates to open, and for him to come roaring out from behind his defenses. Whatever he was afraid of, she was prepared. Whatever he was holding back, she was ready.

"Evelyn," he growled.

And then she licked him, from the base to the tip, rose back up and kissed his mouth. "I love you," she said. And she found herself pushed down to the mattress as he thrust inside of her, his big body looming over her. And she knew that he wanted to hear it again. Knew he was practically ready to beg. Because as much as he hated it, it was just what he needed. Because as much as he wanted to deny it, he was desperate to be loved.

He was so desperate to be loved.

"I love you, Sawyer," she said, and he growled, thrusting deep inside of her body, giving himself over to the deep, never-ending desire between them. "I love you," she said until it became a punctuation mark for every thrust. For every groan of need that passed between them. Until it was like water, flowing over them both. Until it was common.

And precious all at once. Because it had to be. It had to be both. Because she would bet that this man had heard it so few times in his life since his grandmother had died. Had he even heard it once? Because it was his worst memory, his most cherished memory. Because he needed to believe that it was real.

"I love you," she whispered into his ear, and he started to shake uncontrollably, coming apart over her, his orgasm endless, so intense she thought he might come apart at the seams. All those granite seams.

And his release pushed her into her own. Because the pleasure that echoed in him found its way into her. Because he was part of her. Because they were meant to be. And it didn't matter if that made any kind of sense, it didn't matter if it shouldn't be real. It simply was. Because how else could her life have fallen apart at the most perfect time? How else could she have become ashes right when she needed to? So that she could find her way to being a phoenix. Just in time to be new in this life that was made for her.

"I love you," she said, and she started to cry, with him still buried deep inside of her body. "I love you so much, Sawyer."

CHAPTER TWENTY

HE ROLLED AWAY from her, pressing his fists to his eyes. "I can't do this," he said. "I cannot fucking do it."

"You have to," she said. "Because you married me. Because I am your daughter's mother. Because I am your wife. And so you have to do it, even though it's hard. We have to do this. We have to find our way to it." He rolled off the edge of the bed and stood, like he was going to leave. "I'm going to follow you. And I am not going to walk away. You have spent the last eighteen years of your life hiding whenever you have an emotion. Shoving it deep down so that not even you have to look at it. But you're going to do this. And you're going to do it with me. We will overturn every rock inside of you and examine every scorpion we find under it."

"Well, you learned that from living here."

"I damn well did," she said, sniffing. "You break my heart. Because I have never known a better man than you, and I have never known a man who was so closed off to absolutely everything."

"What the hell am I supposed to do?" he said. "What the hell... How else am I supposed to be? Can you tell me that? I just... I don't know what to do. I have a baby, and I never wanted one. And for the first time in my life, I just... I am at a loss, Evelyn. I don't know how to be a husband. And I didn't mean... I didn't mean to drag you into all that

I don't know. But I needed help with her. And I thought that I could just fling a wife at it like a Band-Aid or something. But I didn't think about the fact that you would be a person. And that I would... That I would feel things for you." He turned a circle in the room, pressing his hands to his forehead, and she could see that he was at the end of his tether. That there were emotions flooding him that he did not know what to do with. "What do you do when you just feel like... Like you can't be everything to the people around you, or even anything. Because I did my best with Wolf and Elsie, and I think I fucked them up, too. Because my dad just didn't give a shit. And because my mom just... Are we cursed? Are we? Is there something wrong with me? Why the hell did she ask me to go to Chicago if she was never going to show up? Did she just want to torture me? Did she like it?"

There were so many questions, and suddenly, he looked like a boy. He looked like a boy who needed his mother, his mother who had never been there. And she realized that he had had so many things taken from him... And whatever happened, whatever she did, she would not take one more thing from him.

"You're enough for me," she said. "Do you have any idea how much you changed my life? I know that everything before now has been so hard. I know that you never expected to be in this place. I know that you were just planning on protecting yourself to the end of forever, and I don't blame you. Because nobody gave you any reason to want children. Nobody ever gave you any reason to want marriage. But you're just too damned good to not do your best. And I love that about you.

"Maybe your dad wasn't made to be a dad. Maybe your mom wasn't made for this place. Maybe Missy wasn't made for you. But you were made for me. I know it. I have never felt anything so deeply. Or so true. Because I became the person that I always wanted to be, the person I never realized I could be. Because this is the first life I have ever lived that was just enough. On its own. It has nothing to do with what my mother thinks of it, what my friends think. I don't care if anyone's impressed. I am. And there is such a deep joy in that. And I know the difference. I know the difference between a life lived for other people and a life lived for yourself. And I wish that I could… I wish I could turn my chest open and show you. Show you how different it is inside of me than before I met you. Before I met Bug."

"I don't think I'm any kind of good enough to go changing your life over."

"But you did. You did change my life. And I don't know that it matters if you can see it or not. Can't you trust me? Can you believe me?"

"Everybody leaves me," he said.

"I'm not going to leave you."

"You probably should," he said.

"Stop it. Because now you're just being a martyr."

"Fair enough, right? After everything. I don't have any evidence of this working out. I don't… The only thing that I have ever done with any kind of success is figure out how to just…push anything I wanted away. Just put what I felt second. That's the only thing I have ever figured out how to do to survive. And I'm good at that. It lets me take care of things here. It let me take care of Wolf and Elsie when they needed me. Let's figure out how to be there for Bug without…"

"Are you mad at Missy?"

"Hell, yeah," he said. "I'm serious. I'm furious. I hate her. I hate her and… I'm so damn grateful I'm not bound to her for the rest of my life. I am… I'm not better than my dad. I'm not. And I'm not better than my mom. And that is what… That's the worst part."

"That you're just a human being?"

"I thought I could figure out how to be better. But I got someone pregnant that I didn't even love. That I didn't even care about at all. Another woman who would've stayed for a while, maybe if it were a different time. That's the thing. Thirty-five years ago? She might not realize she could've had a choice. She might've just… Gone along with it. Because she would've thought that maybe having babies was what she was supposed to do. Because it was what everyone said women should want. So maybe she would've stayed for a while. And I wouldn't have wanted to marry her because… I would've known. The fit was wrong. It was just wrong. And maybe I would've sensed that she didn't want to stay. And maybe I would've just been… The same old cycle. Maybe that's it. Maybe none of us are destined to be any better."

"Do you really believe that? Because I think if you did, you wouldn't be trying so hard. And you are trying really hard."

"What if my best isn't good enough? What if I'm not good enough?"

"You're good enough. Believe me. What you are is afraid."

"Being afraid is the mechanism that keeps you safe."

"What reward is there for being safe?"

The minutes rolled on. And it felt like they said the same words in new combinations. Her voice was half-gone. It was gone half past three and her soul just felt dry. Her eyes were gritty.

This night just felt endless, and this was the prize. For not walking away. For not running.

She nearly laughed.

But she was too tender.

She had him, though. She was here, in this room, with him. And that was the decision she'd made. To be with him. Through this. In this.

"I love you," she said, the words raw now.

He looked at her, his eyes hollow and desolate.

"I can't say it," he said. "I can't say it."

She got up off the bed, and pressed herself to his back, wrapping her arms around him and holding him. "I can say it. I can say it for both of us. I love you. I really love you, Sawyer." And when he took a breath she felt that it wasn't steady. She felt a catch. She felt that emotion inside of him release.

She couldn't see his face. She knew that he didn't want her to. But she held him. She held them through it. Then they walked down the hall together, and went to bed. And she lay there, feeling like her lungs were burning. Her throat was sore from talking. Her heart hurt from all the truths that they'd shared. From the fact that it wasn't just solved. From the fact that neither of them had magically changed on the turn of a dime. And she lay there with him. Unsure about what was going to come next. Except for the fact that she was going to stay. And so was he. Maybe someday she would be confident enough that he felt love, even if he couldn't say it. Maybe. But she put her hand on his chest, over his heart, and she fell asleep, and even while she dreamed, it was flowers and loving him.

SAWYER DIDN'T SLEEP. His heart was bloody. His entire body destroyed with the effort to keep on breathing. He hated this. He hated this reckoning that had come for him. The endless roll of emotions, one after the other. The grief over June. The hollow anger that he felt over that week in Chicago. The fear that came with it. The devastation. The way that he felt so small.

And he just hated all of this. He didn't want to have these feelings, but he was having them. He didn't want to be... He didn't want to be pushed like this. What he wanted was for Evelyn to fall in line. For Evelyn to just give him what he wanted. Hadn't he told her it wasn't fair for her to ask things of him when she was the one who had answered his ad?

He breathed out heavily, sitting up. And he turned to look at her. She was there. She was still there. In spite of everything. In spite of all the things he'd said.

He stood up, and walked down the hall, heading back to the room were Bug was. And he looked down at the baby. This baby that he hadn't wanted. Did that make him bad to admit that? That when Missy had first told him she was having the baby, he had felt like it was his very worst nightmare? He hadn't wanted any of this.

Because he hadn't wanted to be brought to this moment. He turned around and went back into the bedroom where Evelyn slept, and he looked at her. And he just stood there. Until her words began to echo inside of him. Until they started to drown out all the other voices in him. If he was his father. If he was good enough. And the worst thing of all, the yawning, aching silence where his "I love you, too" should have gone back to June. He had never said it. Not once.

Not to Elsie. Not to Wolf. Not to June Bug.

Because it was like he still owed them to her.

Isn't your whole life enough?

The fact of the matter was, he lived for her. Everything

good that he did was because of what his gram had done for him.

And suddenly he realized, clear as day, that his entire life, his entire heart, his very reason for breathing, was a resounding "I love you." That woman that had meant so much to him. He also realized that... He had thought that maybe punishment would keep him in line. That maybe holding everything back would be the key, to never giving in to the weaknesses that his parents had passed down to him. But that was where she was right. That was where he had the choice. To make the most defining thing in him the weaknesses, the shortcomings, of his parents. Or the love that June had given to him.

And he realized that he had let it freeze in his chest. Along with everything else. And what was the point? What was the damn point if he didn't pass it along?

It made his knees buckle. He stumbled over to the window and went down, putting his face in his hands. And as the sun began to rise, casting a rosy glow on everything around them, his shoulders began to shake, and everything inside him broke. And for the first time in his memory, he cried. For his mother leaving. For June's death. For his regret at having not been there. For the joy and terror inherent in Bug's very existence. June's very existence.

His June. His little piece of his grandmother here on earth with him. And he didn't have to call her Bug. He could still, because it was cute. But he didn't need that distance in his tribute. He could just say it now, plain and easy.

And he was so grateful for Evelyn's love.

For that most of all. Because it was the thing he deserved the least, and the thing that he needed most. Because it was the key that had finally fit into the lock, that had finally opened everything up inside of him.

And suddenly, he felt soft hands on his bare shoulders. Felt her face press between his shoulder blades. And her cheeks were wet, too.

And she just held him.

And finally. From the depths of everything he was. He said, "I love you."

EPILOGUE

IT GOT EASIER to say. But it never meant any less. After that night he first said it to Evelyn, he went and picked baby June up, and said it again. Then he had taken Evelyn to bed and said it a hundred times more.

When he got her the biggest ring he'd ever seen, not because he thought she needed it to be impressed, but because he wanted the whole world to notice it, and know she was his, he'd said it again.

He'd said it easily the first time he had become an uncle, bursting with pride over the new life that had come into the family—however unexpected it was.

He had said it a little bit less easily, but no less genuinely in the end, when he'd had to welcome a new brother-in-law into the fold. Conceding that Elsie was in fact an adult, no matter his misgivings about her choices... He had to accept it.

And the guy was a good friend, anyway. So what could he do.

It was Evelyn who'd said it to him the first time he got on a plane again. And she kissed his hand as they were about to take off, knowing that there were a lot of bad memories inherent in this kind of thing for him.

It was surprisingly easy for him to be in New York. It didn't really remind him of that trip to Chicago. But then, nothing did. He'd imagined that he could even go there, and wander those same streets, walk the same path, and it wouldn't feel the same. Because Evelyn would be with him. And so would June.

He met Evelyn's parents, and they were honestly thrilled to be grandparents to June. They made plans to come and see Evelyn and Sawyer before they even left the city.

And after Evelyn went out to lunch with her friends— her former friends, former business partners—and came back gritty and sad, he held her and said it over and over again.

And a few weeks after that, when they'd arrived home, and he found out he was going to be a father again…

He didn't waste a moment at all. He told her then. And then he got on his horse and rode out into the middle of the field, and he looked up at the sky, with the mountains all around. And he closed his eyes and breathed in the wind. "I love you, too."

They might be eighteen years late, but he knew those words went up on wings. And that they went exactly where they needed to go.

When he walked back in the door, Evelyn was there with June sitting on her lap, her face so bright and lovely it lit up everything inside of him.

"You know, back a few months ago, I didn't know all that much. But I knew I needed a wife. I needed you, Evelyn Garrett."

She stood up, keeping June on her hip as she closed the space between them and kissed him on the mouth. "Just as much as I needed you." She smiled. "You know, the day that I caught Andrew cheating on me, I thought my life had fallen apart. But it turns out, that was the first step to it coming together."

And he figured it was a good time to say those magic words again. Because it always was. "I love you."

And then he did better than saying it. He showed her.

* * * * *

ONCE UPON A COWBOY

Especially dedicated to a tale as old as time.
Fairy tales will always be magic to me.

CHAPTER ONE

IT WASN'T EXACTLY an enchanted castle. But then, Belle wasn't silly enough to expect an actual enchanted castle. It had been a nice story to tell herself on the long car ride that had carried her from Seattle, Washington, up into the hills of Pyrite Falls, Oregon. But it had only been that. A story.

Still, based on the letters that had passed back and forth between herself and her new employer, a picture had begun to form in her mind. Of the wounded beast up in his castle, cursed because of a betrayal—by an evil fairy—hardened and frozen by the years… And in desperate need of help.

She had been devastated when the bookshop closed. But there just hadn't been enough steam to keep it going. She had tried, but after her grandmother's death, and the medical bills that had piled up and everything else…it just hadn't been feasible.

Fairytale Books had closed. But Belle's love for books remained. It was why, when she had packed up her car to start this journey, to start her new life, she had taken a bare minimum of outfits, and of many other things. But she had filled the car full of books. Most of the books that had been left in the store. Children's books.

For the kids.

She was so excited to meet the kids.

She put the car in Park and turned the motor off, looking at the cabin in front of her.

It loomed a bit. But that was okay. She was ready. More than ready. She got out of the car, and took a deep breath, gathering her overnight bag, which also had toys in it, and charged toward the door.

"I have confidence in me," she said. The mantra would get her through. It had gotten her this far. That and weaving fairy tales.

"Intruder!"

She looked up, just in time to see a water balloon being hurled from the rooftop, and not in time to dodge said water balloon.

And then came another one. And another.

"Oh," she shouted, and tried to get out of the way, but a small boy appeared from behind a large pot, which did not have a plant in it, and just seemed to be there for the sole purpose of concealing him, large slingshot raised. And another water balloon fired from that.

"Whatever you're selling, lady, we don't want it."

"And if you're from the government, that goes double," came the little voice from up above.

"I am neither from the government nor am I selling anything," she said. And she refused to react to the water. Because they wanted her to. Because this had been an ambush and the boys—John and Joe, she didn't know which was which—were trying to get to her. She had been warned. That they had fierce tempers and even fiercer ways of displaying them.

"While I appreciate the opportunity to shower—I have had a long journey, and this has been quite refreshing—I would like to call a cease-fire."

"You don't have any ammunition, lady," the boy behind the pot said. "You're not in any position to be calling a cease-fire."

"But I do have toys in my bag. And if you soak them through, they may be ruined."

"I bet we don't want your toys."

"Maybe not," she said. "But what about Imogene?"

She had thought that might soften them. And it did.

The little bandicoots scampered off. Both of them wearing only overalls with no shirts on underneath. Well. She had known that it would be an adventure. And she had signed up for it. Specifically. She took another step toward the door and started to knock when it jerked open. And she was greeted—this time not by a child—but by a very grumpy looking man. She had to look up to see that he was grumpy. Because he was just so tall. And…broad. He had a cowboy hat tipped down low on his head, a brutal scar running from his forehead down over his eye through his lip. It was a miracle he still had both eyes judging by that scar. But he did. And they were…they were beautiful. Blue like the sky, and in stark contrast to everything else about him.

The man himself was monstrous. Bordered on being a beast. But his eyes…

"If you're selling something, we don't want it. And if you're from the government…"

"You also don't want it. I am actually clear on that stance. But I am Belle Langford. We've exchanged emails."

He snorted. "We fucking have not."

"Oh," she said. "I beg your pardon." She was not used to such salty language. Her grandmother didn't allow it, and it wasn't common to hear in her little bookshop. She did sometimes read it in books, and in certain contexts it made her face very warm. "I thought that you were Adam Winchester."

"I am. But you sure as hell haven't exchanged emails with me. I don't have a computer."

"I… You have children. John and Joe and Imogene."

"What the hell is this?"

"I thought that I was coming to take a position as nanny. And housekeeper…"

"Son of a bitch."

And suddenly, a bright pink Cadillac convertible came rolling up the driveway with smoke trailing behind it grandly. "Oh no."

A voice came from the vehicle. The car stopped suddenly, and an elderly woman got out, round and wearing all pink, just like her car. "I'm late. I'm sorry. I didn't mean to send you up here completely unaware."

And Belle had no idea which one of them the woman was talking to.

"Fucking hell, Debbie. What did you do?"

"What a nice way to greet your mother-in-law," she said.

They looked at each other for a long moment. "I'm worried about you."

"I know you are. But that doesn't give you call to go meddling in my business. What the hell are you playing at?"

"I'm not playing at anything, Adam. You need help. You are up to your eyeballs."

"You've been just a fine help…"

"We are at each other's throats all the time. And I am the kids' grandmother, and I don't want to be in a fight with you. I like to take them for outings. I like to take them on vacations. I like to be Grandma. I can't be primary caregiver, especially when their dad's snarling at me all the time."

"So you did what?"

"I hired you a nanny."

"I don't need your money, Debbie."

"I didn't say that you did. But this is my gift to you.

You need a housekeeper, and you need a nanny. And here she is."

"I really don't need your guilt babysitter."

The woman—Debbie—walked across the driveway, closing the distance between herself and Adam. "You listen to me, Adam Winchester—you have a hard head, and you always have. I thought you would be good for Laney, and I stand by it. You would've been good for her, if she could have been good for you. I don't approve of what she did. I don't approve of her running off, I don't approve of her abandoning these kids, I don't approve of her abandoning you. But I lost her the same as you did—she doesn't speak to me anymore either. And yes, I do feel some guilt about it. Because I'm her mother. So obviously something that I did…"

"It isn't your fault, Debbie. It's not."

"I appreciate it. But I'm not looking to be absolved. All I want is to make sure that my grandchildren have a better life than this."

"They're fine," Adam said.

Belle was beginning to feel like an unnecessary accessory to the entire thing.

"Wait a minute," she said. "Are you telling me that I emailed with you, Debbie. And I never emailed with him—Adam."

"That is the size of it."

"He doesn't have a computer," Debbie said. "I do. I've been on Facebook for fifteen years."

"I'm sure she's really impressed by that, Deb."

"Don't pay attention to him. He'll be grateful for your presence once you get going…"

"I don't want a stranger in my house."

"You have an extra room," she said, fiercely.

"Look, I don't want to be where I'm not wanted," Belle said, a little bit of panic starting to rise up in her chest. She really did try to believe in the goodness of the universe, in spite of the fact that her life had been pretty difficult up until this point. She had been raised by her grandmother, and she knew what it was like to be abandoned by...well, not just her mother, but her father, too. She had thought that she would have something in common with these kids. And that she could make a difference. She had wanted that. It had given her a sense of peace and happiness after having lost the bookstore. "But I did get rid of my apartment, and I functionally don't have a place to stay, because I was certain that I was coming here to work, and it would be very difficult for me to go back."

"You would put the poor girl out on the street?"

"I didn't ask the poor girl to come here," he said.

"Give it a month," Debbie said.

A month. She had been expecting a lot more job security than that. But then, she supposed that...she should know better than to count on something like that. Of course she should. She should know better because anything can happen at any time, and nobody was guaranteed anything. A month would be...at least enough of a chance to figure out a plan of action if it didn't work out.

"I told you already I don't want..."

"You don't want a stranger living in your house. Well, Adam, the problem is that you work from sunup to sundown. You're exhausted and so are the kids, all the time. They're unsupervised half the time, and I know you mean well, but it's too much time spent alone."

Two small faces appeared from behind the house. The boys were back, clearly fascinated by what was happening.

And for the first time, Adam seemed to actually look

at her. Really look her up and down and take in the sight of what had happened to her. Water balloon residue and all. "Yeah, okay," he said. "She can have a month. But she won't last. Three days with these varmints will send her running for the hills."

"I'm sure that they aren't…varmints," she said.

"And I'm sure they are. They're my kids, after all and I say you won't last for them. You're welcome to give it a try, Miss…"

"I did say."

"I didn't catch it."

"Langford. Belle Langford."

"Ms. Langford. You are welcome to try to make my house a home, and to make my…varmints into kids. But I have a feeling you're going to find that it's an uphill battle."

"And what about you?" she asked, feeling more than a little bit irritated by the whole situation. "Should I try to make a man out of the beast?"

And then his face did something quite horrifying. He grinned. But it wasn't an easy grin, not a happy grin. No. Somehow, it was more frightening than any sneer could've been.

"Oh, I don't change, Ms. Langford. I'm as immovable as a brick wall. Implacable as stone. As damned stubborn as these here mountains that surround this place. That isn't poetry—it's a direct quote. Just some of the few things that have been said about me. So yeah. Do your best with the kids. Do your best with the house. You don't need to worry about me."

And then, just like that, he went back in the house, leaving Belle standing there in the driveway with Debbie, and the two little hellions.

"I am sorry about that," Debbie said. "Only, I started

to get in touch with you as myself, but it seemed awfully ridiculous. Explaining to you what happened with Adam and with…with my daughter. And it just seemed easier to write it from his point of view. Well, the point of view he doesn't know he has. Which is that he wants what's best for the kids. I know he does. He's drowning. And that he won't admit. He won't admit it. He just…he doesn't have it in him. But the kids are half-feral."

"Hey," one of the boys said, coming out from behind the house. "We're not feral, Grandma."

"No," she said. "I said you were half-feral, John. I didn't say you were all feral."

"I don't even know what that means." The other boy came back from around the side of the house, maybe a half an inch shorter than the other. And she would have to try to remember that this one was Joe. He must be.

"It means wild," she said.

"Is that why Mom left?"

And it was Belle's turn to speak. She couldn't help it.

"Absolutely not," she said. "Adults do things sometimes because of their own problems. But kids are not the cause of those problems. Adults have a lot of years to have things in their mind play tricks on them. To have the things that scare them get bigger and scarier."

"Like the monster under the bed," John said.

"Yes," Belle said. "Like a monster under the bed. They aren't real, you know, those monsters. But they can feel very real. And you can start to treat that imaginary monster like a pet. Giving it food and water, and letting it get bigger and bigger in your mind. Even though it isn't actually there. But you can take it with you into adulthood, that fear."

"How do you stop that from happening?"

"Things are scariest when they're in the dark. When

you don't see them. If you drag it out, and let everybody know, this is the thing that hurts me, this is the thing that scares me, you can start to deal with it. And that keeps it from getting too big."

"Huh," John said. "That's a weird story." And then like that they disappeared.

"Well…" she said.

"That went beautifully," Debbie said. "I'm sorry about my son-in-law. He's gruff. He always has been. But it's only gotten worse… Well, since. You understand. I'm trying to help. Sometimes I think he finds me meddlesome. I guess he isn't wrong. I am meddling a bit. But it's only because I love those kids. And I love him. I know it doesn't seem like it right now, but there are things about him that are lovable."

"Well," she said. "I will focus on the kids. Even he said I could do that."

"I just hope that he… That he finds his manners enough to show you around. Here's my phone number," she said, handing her an actual slip of paper with the phone number on it. "If you need anything, you just let me know, darling. And I will be happy to come and help you. I'll be your fairy godmother."

"Well. Thanks."

Except then her fairy godmother got back in her pink convertible and drove away, leaving Belle standing there.

"Joe," she said. "John. Come on out."

The boys did. She was still wet, and becoming very aware of it. "I want you boys to help me bring my things into the house. I'm wet now, and that's because of you."

"No," Joe said, running away. John seemed a little less certain as to whether or not he could openly defy an adult.

"John, if you help me, I'm going to make a cake. And you will get to have the first slice of that cake."

"A cake…"

"Yes. A cake."

"We only get cake for birthdays. And even then, it's just the gross kind from the grocery store."

"Mine won't be gross. And it won't be from a grocery store. I will even make the frosting from scratch."

"All right. I'll help you. Joe doesn't get a piece, does he?"

"That will remain to be seen."

"What about Imogene? She didn't get a chance to help with things."

"Isn't she only three?"

"Yes."

"Well. Then I will just let her have one for being three."

"That's good. She's the best little sister in the world. She's so cute." John looked genuinely pleased to be speaking about his sister.

"You can tell me all about her while you help me with my things."

And without waiting for Adam to reappear, she lifted her bag up, and she charged through the front door.

CHAPTER TWO

A NANNY. A HOUSEKEEPER. His mother-in-law had lost her mind.

But then, was she even his mother-in-law anymore? There was no law holding him to her. His divorce was finalized, thank you very much. Along with the full custody of his kids, since his ex-wife had decided she wanted nothing to do with them.

He sighed and shook his head. It wasn't that simple. And he knew it. He couldn't hate her, no matter how much he wanted to. She had a prescription pill addiction, and PTSD from her time in the military... He couldn't really blame her for what was going on. But she couldn't take care of the kids. Her boyfriend was dangerous to be around... None of it was good. All that was a recipe for total abandonment. And Debbie could make wide eyes and blame herself all the hell much she wanted. But it wasn't even that simple.

He'd like to blame himself, and he couldn't. The simple truth was, they weren't meant to be. They'd tried it; it hadn't worked.

They'd reconnected about five years after they'd met in basic. She'd wanted kids, and he figured why not. It had seemed like a reasonable enough idea. Make a family, work the ranch, but he hadn't realized how bad things were. And the postpartum depression after Imogene was born—you should never have a baby to try and fix what was already broken—had only exacerbated things.

But hell. It had been a flawed experiment from the start. Two wholly screwed-up people trying to make something out of what they had left and… It hadn't worked out.

He thought the kids were doing all right. They got to run around the ranch and do whatever they wanted to. That was how he'd spent his childhood up here. He hadn't minded it at all. Of course, then he'd gone and joined the army and made his mother cry, his dad's words. And his injury had just about given his dad a damned heart attack. Which had then become an actual heart attack. His mom had killed herself caretaking him. And his dad had gone soon after. He'd had a good childhood here, good parents. He thought he was giving his kids the same, but Debbie had taken issue with it. God forbid.

Because the woman was like a dog with a bone when she set her mind to something and there wasn't anything Adam could do about it. And he didn't have it in him to alienate her. The kids had lost enough. They didn't need their dad feuding with their one living grandparent.

He stormed out of his bedroom and back into the living room, to see John and Joe scrabbling into the house. Joe's arms were blessedly free of any burden, while John was hefting a large box of books. And right behind the boys came that woman.

She was small. With straight brown hair that hung limp at her shoulders, long bangs that covered her eyebrows. Her nose was pointed and upturned and gave him the impression of a very small mouse, not at all helped by the large, round, gold-rimmed glasses that covered very big brown eyes.

She was wearing the kind of sweater he had only ever seen on grandmothers, in a very mustard yellow, open over a floral dress that went down past her knees.

"What's your name again?" he asked.

"Belle."

"Okay." And he just stared at her, because he had no idea what he was supposed to do with this stranger who was expected to take up residence at his house.

"Debbie said that there was a room for me?"

She said it gently, like she was talking to a child, or somebody who badly needed some form of guidance.

Okay. Well. He supposed he did need guidance.

"Yeah. Down the hall. I guess you can take your stuff there."

"Thank you."

She nodded her head, and her glasses slipped down the bridge of her nose, and she hastily push them back up. Then she quickly walked down the hallway, her brown boots clumping on the floor.

For God's sake. What had Debbie gotten him into?

"Debbie said that one of my responsibilities would be dinner. And I have promised the children cake." She reappeared. "Do you have groceries?"

"Yeah. We've got some."

He wasn't going to admit that mostly he had a freezer full of frozen lasagna and frozen garlic bread. The kids would eat that every night. And he didn't much care to fight with them about healthy eating. Hell, he'd been a piggy kid, and he'd grown up just fine. He could lift whatever he needed to, work a full day; he'd certainly passed physical fitness tests in the military, even after he'd taken shrapnel to the face. Not eating his green beans when he was twelve hadn't hurt him. The same as coffee all day and booze all night didn't seem to hurt him now.

Maybe he was just made of sterner stuff than some people. His kids sure were.

"Is there a store?"

ONCE UPON A COWBOY

"Yeah. There's a grocery store down the way with some basics. And a farm stand down at Four Corners Ranch. It's this massive spread run by some of the area's founding families."

"A farm stand! How lovely. Maybe I'll go down that way and see what I can find."

"You didn't even look to see what I had."

She looked around, sniffed delicately and pushed her glasses up again. "No offense. I don't think I need to."

Then she turned and walked out, and he felt...scathingly insulted by a woman who could just as easily pass for a rodent.

She came back in with another box. "You can keep standing there or you can make yourself useful."

"I am not an accessory to this crime. I don't know a damned thing about you, and you're supposed to be taking care of my kids. I would have you out on your ass except Debbie would never do anything to hurt the kids, so I'm sure that you're not a secret criminal of any kind."

"Oh, no. She did my background check. Which I am loath to inform you is extremely boring. I have no skeletons in my closet, absolutely nothing interesting at all in my past. Really, I am incredibly dull. I'm happy to tell you anything you want to know. I'm used to talking to people. All kinds of people. I've run a bookstore since I was in high school. My grandmother needed help with it, and I stepped in. It became my whole world. She died, it had to close and I didn't have anything left. So here I am."

Neat. A life story in thirty seconds or less. At least she was economical.

"How old are you?"

"Twenty-four."

Fuck.

"You're a babysitter."

"I am not a babysitter. I assure you. I took care of my grandmother in the last years of her life. Really, I was a full-time caregiver and bookstore owner for the last five years. I like to take care of people. I like making their lives easier. It's something that I can do... And when I saw the posting that Debbie had put up about the job, it resonated with me. She said that the house was very sad."

"*Sad?* My boys can do whatever they want. What kid doesn't want to run wild outside?"

"And your daughter?"

"Well. She's a little small to do whatever she wants. The boys get to do kindergarten and first grade down at the one-room schoolhouse on Four Corners. Imogene mostly spends the day with me."

"I like that she gets to spend the day with you. But, wouldn't it be good if she had some options? She could stay home and play."

"Yeah," he said.

But he had gotten pretty accustomed to not letting his little girl out of his sight.

"My wife left when Imogene was six months old. I'm the only parent she's ever really known. And she's basically been glued to me ever since."

"You've been doing this by yourself for two and a half years?"

She looked filled with sympathy, and he hated it. He didn't need sympathy. He didn't want it.

"I decided to do this. To be a father. Have kids. I may not have planned on doing it by myself, but I wanted the kids. It didn't work out for her. That's okay. Just try to take care of herself."

"That's a pretty giving attitude of you."

"Seeing combat of any kind..." He gritted his teeth. "My wife and I were in the military together. Years ago. Long before we got together. The thing is, that experience affects people differently. She didn't make it through unscathed. I consider her a casualty of war. It's not up to me to say she could handle things differently. Do I wish she hadn't been a victim of it? One of the walking wounded, with injuries you can't see? Yeah. Do I hate her? No. I can't do that. When everything in her mind is working right she loves the kids. But she's made a lot of choices that are pretty hard for her to come back from."

"Wow." Those brown eyes grew extra soft, and he didn't know what to do with that. He didn't understand...softness. His parents had been great. But his mom had been a no-nonsense farm woman, his dad a pretty hard-out rancher. His wife had been a steely kind of woman. Physically fit and relentless. He liked her a whole lot before the drugs had gotten hold of her. Hell, he still liked his memories of her. He liked that the kids had her spirit. Because he would never let who she was be tarnished by what had happened.

He would always honor her intent.

But yeah, as for softness? No. He wasn't used to it. Couldn't say he liked it.

"I don't need your sympathy."

"Sorry," she said. "It's just I feel it. A lot of it."

"Holy shit, woman, let's go get the rest of your stuff."

He helped her grab the boxes—there were so many boxes of books. Was there even anything else?

"I only have one suitcase of clothes. And a box of shoes. Shoes take up a lot of room. That's just a practicality. I saved the rest of the room for books. Because I had so many children's books."

He had never been a big reader. But then, he had never

much sat around engaging in idle time. And there was something…strange about this. All these books, and any one of them his kids could pick up and read. He felt like Belle had opened the door just now. One that he hadn't known he wanted open for his kids.

It was the first time he had had to stand there and look at something he never would've thought of. That he never would've provided. An option he would've taken off the table for them without even realizing it. The first time he had to face that his own closed perspective might limit where the kids got to go.

Tenderness.

All right. Maybe he felt some of that for his kids. But he was pretty hard, and life with him was hard. He was just doing things the way his parents had done it.

Maybe having this soft little…thing would show them something different. And maybe that wasn't a bad thing.

"Well look. I've got some work to do. Imogene is napping, and I'm happy to leave her down for it, or get her up and bring her with me. It's up to you. But she doesn't know you and she might freak out."

"She's three? I think I can handle her. I used to do story time down at the bookstore."

"Well, you can walk down to the farm stand from here. Just down the driveway and straight down the road. The opposite way you came. Can't miss it."

"How do you know it's the opposite way I came?"

He shrugged. "Because you would've seen it. One of the Sullivan sisters should be at it. They're all redheads. So you'll notice. You can take Imogene down in the wagon."

"The wagon?"

"The boys can show you."

"What about the boys?"

"You can leave them. I'm on the property."

She grimaced, and he could tell that she judged him.

"That's how my parents did it," he said.

"Well. I don't mean to… I guess that's just modern… My own… They're not my children."

"Do whatever the hell you want, lady. I've got horses to go put away."

And on that note, he walked out of the house and headed out toward the barn. He wasn't going to worry about her. He wasn't going to worry about the kids. Was that not the point of all this?

Thirty days. If by the end of it he couldn't live without her…well, all the better.

CHAPTER THREE

SHE DECIDED TO take all the kids down to the farm stand.

"Who are you?" one of the boys said, bringing up the rear.

"I'm Belle," she said.

"That doesn't mean anything to me," he shot back.

Belle sighed.

She had a cranky, sleepy-eyed three-year-old in the wagon. Her blond hair was frizzed out around her head, her eyebrows knitted resolutely together. The little girl had been extremely unenthused by Belle's presence, but Belle wasn't deterred. Adam needed help. That much was clear. After she left, she had looked through his cupboards. They were barren. He had a lot of beer, a lot of frozen food and very little else. And she was going to make sure that she made a difference. She made an impact. Of course, Imogene had not stopped asking for her daddy after she had woken up. Which made Belle feel better, actually. Because at least it demonstrated that Adam's kids loved him. He was gruff—there was no getting around that—but he definitely seemed to love his children. And they loved him back. He wasn't a beast.

She shivered. She wondered how he had gotten the scar. In the military, she assumed.

It didn't really surprise her that he had been in the military. She lapsed off into thought. His poor wife.

It was extraordinary to her that he had so much sympathy for her. Sure, she might not know the whole story, but it seemed like he was still protecting his ex-wife, regardless of the fact that she wasn't here with the kids. No. He wasn't a beast. He might do a great job of presenting as one, but he wasn't.

The little farm stand was pretty obvious, set up on the edge of a wide driveway with the big sign above that said Four Corners Ranch. South Entrance.

There was a girl at the farm stand, wearing overalls, her red hair a riotous mass of curls.

"Hello," Belle said, approaching the beautiful spread of goodies with the wagon in tow.

The woman's eyebrows shot upward. "Hi. Aren't these Adam Winchester's little ones?"

"Yes," she said. "I'm his new nanny."

"What is a nanny?" Joe asked.

"Like a babysitter that lives there, or does a little bit more care than a babysitter would."

"I'm not a baby," Joe said.

"Well, that's why I'm a nanny," she said, doing her best to smooth it over. She had to make an ally out of that one. Otherwise he could make her life miserable. She could sense that.

The farm stand had an impressive spread of fruits and vegetables, and she cheerfully chose the right ingredients for making pasta—she had noticed that he at least had dried pasta noodles, and she could make something filled with veggies, which would be healthy and delicious. She paid, and put the items in the wagon with the kids and trundled them back home. She brought the wagon into the house and unloaded it, and the kids.

"Would you like to help me make dinner?"

"No," John and Joe said at the same time. Imogene just looked at her.

"How about this. I'll start the pasta sauce and the cake, and then I'll read to you all."

She found dry ingredients, and eggs, oil and milk, thankfully, and put together her favorite easy cake recipe, mixed it all up and put it in the oven. Then she sliced vegetables, and put them all in a pot to stew. She would make a sauce with the tomatoes, but include all of the other yummy vegetables that she'd gotten.

As they simmered, she went and chose a book for the kids.

She chose one about a good fairy who gave gifts that sometimes had unintended consequences. The boys pretended not to listen, jumping around the room, but Imogene was rapt, her attention on all the beautiful pictures, and on the words. And by the end of it, Belle thought that perhaps she had an ally in the youngest child.

"Now I need to check dinner."

She stirred the vegetables, and kept them simmering, adding garlic and other spices, and then she started the noodles. Then she took the cake out and stuck it in the freezer to cool it for about fifteen minutes while she whipped up a quick vanilla buttercream frosting.

By the time it was dark and Adam came through the door, she was just getting everything put into serving bowls.

She was unprepared for him. It didn't matter that she vaguely knew what he looked like already; the sheer presence of him was overwhelming. He was broad and tall, and imposing. And his face was a storm. But perhaps the most beautiful storm she'd ever seen. Beautiful.

Was he beautiful?

His shoulders were broad, his jaw square, his nose straight. He had that intimidating look in his eye, and that scar. Dark brown hair pushed off of his forehead carelessly—she could see that, now that he didn't have his cowboy hat on. Dark stubble covered his face, evidence of the long day. There was something compelling about him, even as he was beastly. Something beautiful about him, even as he was frightening.

She had no experience with men. Her life hadn't lent itself to being in close quarters with them, and especially not a man like him. A man who was so…intimidating. Who was so…male.

That was ridiculous. Men were male. It was just that he was…a lot of whatever he was. It was like he radiated it. Testosterone or whatever.

She'd once liked a man who had often come into the bookshop. He had been tall and lean with hair that fell into his face. He had glasses a lot like hers, and had worn trousers and scarves.

She had thought he was the perfect sort of man to sit and read books with. To drink tea with. Adam was not like that at all.

And yet…he made her whole body feel like it was frozen. Like her heart couldn't quite handle itself. And there was no room for that.

That was so…ridiculous. To even remotely… It was ridiculous.

"Dinner's ready."

"Oh," he said. "Great."

The kids sat down at the table, and he followed. He looked between the bowls of pasta and the big bowl of salad. "Is there meat in this?"

"No. I didn't get any meat. I only went to the farm stand today."

He huffed.

Huffed.

"I'm sorry, I take it you are expecting the finest frozen lasagna."

"Hey now."

"Well. I've made you a homemade dinner, and it is nutritious. You might behave with some gratitude."

"I'm not ungrateful," he said. "It's just… I'm accustomed to having meat with my meal. That's all."

"Well, it's nice for your kids to have some vegetables."

He snorted. "I'm not suffering from a lack of vegetables."

"You say that now, but scurvy can come for any man."

He stared at her from across the table. "Scurvy."

And she realized that she had sat down at the dinner table like she was part of the family. And suddenly she felt uncomfortable. She got up slowly, and took her plate and melted into the kitchen. She didn't know why she had done that. Why she had taken that spot.

She should leave him to spend time with his kids. Her primary function was to help when he was gone. Thirty seconds later, he also came into the kitchen.

"Are you hiding from me, or are you finding me a steak?"

"I realize," she said, standing and holding her plate, "that I was not invited to sit at the table. And I am sorry for my presumptuousness."

He laughed. "Oh, that was presumptuous to you. Taking a spot at the dinner table. Hell and damn, girl. You moved into my house without so much as a by-your-leave. Because my mother-in-law told you to, and you're worried that sitting down at the dinner table was a bridge too far. I'm not going to make you huddle in the corner of the kitchen."

"Well, maybe I don't want to sit down if I'm just going to get scolded for the lack of meat."

Imogene came into the kitchen then, and she was carrying the fairy book. "Book," she said. "Read to me."

She pressed the book against Belle's legs.

"Oh," she said. "You liked this book. But you need to finish your dinner first. You don't have any sauce on your face, so you can't possibly have eaten."

She laughed, and set her plate down on the counter, then picked Imogene up. "Let's go back to your seat."

She turned and saw that Adam was following her, holding her plate. She put Imogene back down in her booster chair, and then took her seat next to her, still holding the book. "Yep, and then we'll read."

She noticed that John and Joe had cleaned their plates and gone back for seconds, and she felt somewhat triumphant, particularly given the grief she had gotten from Adam. After they were done eating, she took the book into the living room, and Imogene climbed on her lap. John and Joe circled the perimeter of the room again, pretending not to listen even as they listened.

"You can go to your room now," Adam said. And it took a minute for her to realize he was talking to her. "I mean, you don't have to. But I don't think the deal was that you were supposed to be working twenty-four hours a day."

"Likely not. But I don't mind reading to the kids. I love books. That's why I brought so many. I think she does too." She patted Imogene's head.

"Yeah. It seems so."

"I should get the dishes."

"No," he said. "I've got the dishes."

And she couldn't tell if he was being nice, being a martyr or wanting to dismiss her. But, she decided to go ahead and let him do them anyway.

She went into the little bedroom, with the full-size bed

tucked into the corner. It was a simple room, small, but there was a dresser, and a bookshelf, so she was able to put her own collection of books away.

Mostly historical romance novels, and she had to stare at them for a minute and interrogate herself. Was she romanticizing him, his scars and his pain? Was she romanticizing this choice because part of her longed to believe that she could have a place in a story like that?

Her heart beat a little faster.

No. She loved stories. But she knew they were stories.

She was just here to help. She obviously hadn't taken the job having any idea that he would be…everything that he was. He was compelling. And yes, wounded in such a way that made her want to…fix him. Fix things.

She changed into her pajamas and realized that she was going to have to sort things out with showering and what bathroom she was supposed to use and all of that. And she could use a shower, but everything felt a little bit too tenuous tonight, so she huddled in her room and did her best to dry-brush her teeth, and went to sleep, because she just needed the space.

She had made a huge change today, and whatever she had been expecting, it wasn't this.

From the fact that she was had been a total surprise, to everything that he was… She had no idea how to contend with it all.

But tomorrow was another day, and maybe by tomorrow she would feel a little more firmly rooted.

The kids were wonderful. So there was that. John and Joe might have been a little wild at first, but she felt like she had already won them over. And that was no small feat.

She was well on her way to success. And she was feeling good about that.

CHAPTER FOUR

WHEN ADAM GOT home from the ranch the next day, he could hear chaos long before he saw it.

It sounded like a war zone, and granted, that wasn't entirely unusual, but Imogene was there, and that was unusual. Also, he had figured that since there was theoretically a responsible adult in residence it might be a little less...

He flung open the door.

Imogene was sitting in the middle of the floor with about thirty books around her, and the boys were hopping from couch to couch, shooting each other with water pistols.

"What the hell is going on?"

"We're in a war," Joe said.

Well. That had been his thought.

"I see. And where is Belle?"

"She's a prisoner," John said.

"She's a *what*?"

"Well," Joe said. "We got her to go in the pantry to look for some snacks, and locked her in. She's a prisoner of war."

"You did what?"

And for the first time he questioned whether or not his parenting was actually all that good. Because there were shenanigans, and then there was taking your nanny prisoner.

Nanny. For the love of God. How had he wound up with a nanny?

He stormed into the kitchen, and found a broom wedged

under the doorknob, stuck tight between the kitchen cabinet and the edge of the counter.

He unwedged it, then flung the door open. Belle was sitting in there, leaning against the back wall, her legs out in front of her, her hands folded in her lap. She looked pale, but resolute.

"Are you okay?"

"Yes," she said, getting up and smoothing her dress. She pushed her glasses up her nose. "I didn't feel that it would be a very good idea to give them any satisfaction by hollering."

"Well no. They would probably just consider that a win. How did you lose control?"

"I didn't realize I had lost control. I asked that they not use the water pistols inside, which did not go over well. But, I thought that I had perhaps won the battle, particularly when I took the guns and hid them away. But, sadly, I was tricked. And that's how I ended up in the pantry."

"But you didn't yell."

"No. I think they would've enjoyed distressed quarry. I decided compliance would deny them satisfaction."

"Dammit. You're probably right."

He looked her up and down, and he felt…furious. Absolutely furious that the kids had done that to her. And… slightly in awe of how unshaken she seemed. Maybe she was stronger than she looked.

He stormed back into the living room. "Give me the water guns."

"No," Joe said.

"Joseph," he said. "You give me the water gun right now and you'll only be grounded for a week."

"What's going on?" John asked. "You never get mad at us."

No. Because he'd been checked out. Because as long as

the kids didn't make waves to him, he considered that...
Well hell, he didn't know what he'd been considering it.
Fine? But having another person in the house, and realizing how things had gotten out of hand, he could see it more
clearly. He had not been an engaged dad. He had been letting things coast along, because it had been easy. Because
it had been...the only thing he could manage. But this was
like having blinders ripped off of his eyes.

"You're going to start behaving like human beings and
not like wild animals."

They were doing the exact thing that he thought they
would. They were gearing up to scare her off, but it didn't
actually please him. Mostly because it showed him what
he'd been doing wrong. Mostly because it showed him exactly where he had fallen down on the job.

"Grandma said we were half-feral," Joe said. "I want
to go all feral!"

"Sit down!" He didn't often put on his military voice,
but when he did...they listened. "Now you listen to me,"
he said, after the boys had dropped down to the edge of
the couch, hands in their lap, their eyes rapt on him. "Belle
is here to take care of you, and you are to respect her the
same way you respect me, understand?"

"Yes, sir," both boys said at once.

"Imogene?" he asked, looking down at his tiny daughter.
She nodded.

"And you are not to lock Belle in anything. You are not
to throw water balloons at her. You are to listen when she
tells you to listen and do what she asks you to. You understand me?"

The three kids nodded.

"Now you are all grounded for the week. No water guns.
No TV..."

"No TV!" John shouted.

"Nope."

"That's not fair!"

"Locking the nanny in the pantry isn't fair."

The boys stormed off, leaving Adam with Belle.

"I appreciate that," she said. "Thank you very much for standing up for me."

"Of course."

"But you know, your manners aren't much better."

"Excuse me?"

"You're gone almost all day, and when you do talk to me or to the kids you're usually growling."

He frowned. "I don't growl." Except he did growl that and he couldn't deny it.

"You also haven't done much to make sure I know what I'm allowed. For instance, I really need a shower."

There was something about how she said that that hit him, and lingered.

A shower.

Of course she did.

But of course that made him…that made him actually look at her and think of her as a human being, then as a woman.

He was thirty-five years old. He didn't automatically picture a woman in the shower just because she mentioned a shower. But he did suddenly look at her and realize she was a woman. Not a mouse. Not a prop. Not an inconvenient accessory his mother-in-law had brought him.

A woman.

And dimly he remembered, at one time, he'd been a man with some manners. A sense of chivalry even. And that man would be appalled by the way he'd treated her.

Of course, he was not, and never could be that man again. He'd seen friends die, he'd been shot at, had shrapnel blown up in his face. He'd been married, become a father and watched his wife rip his kids' hearts out while she went down a path he couldn't get her back from.

But he could show her to the damned shower.

"Come on this way," he said.

He could let her use the kids' bathroom, but lord... It was a hazard. So he opted to show her through his bedroom to his bathroom.

The house was modest, but nice. He'd had a new one built to move his wife into. And he'd made sure it had all the bells and whistles. He didn't much give a shit about any of it. But he had spent a hell of a lot of money on a very, very nice shower and if there was any one thing of his wife that remained in this house—other than the kids of course—that he loved, it was that shower.

She looked timid, and mousy at the entry to his room.

"Come on," he said. "I'm not going to bite you."

As soon as he said that he realized that this might look bad. But he was just so out of practice with people it hadn't occurred to him that bringing her to his room could look bad until he'd done it.

"Just... Shower's through there," he said, pointing forward. "Feel free to make use of it."

She nodded mutely, her eyes too big behind her glasses.

"And I'll handle dinner tonight. You take the time to get yourself settled. After dinner...we'll talk. I'll make you an official schedule and time off and all that."

She nodded again.

"Enjoy your shower."

Then he walked out of the room, slamming the door behind him.

Dammit all. Now he had to make dinner.

CHAPTER FIVE

OVER THE NEXT few days they created a routine. More or less. There were aspects of her involvement in their lives that the boys definitely resented—like being made to take baths every night, and eat vegetables at every meal—but they liked being read to, whether they chose to acknowledge it or not, and they hadn't tried to lock her in anything again. So there was that.

Imogene was a delight. She was bright and sunny—unless she had just woken up—unreservedly loved story time and even enjoyed helping pick up toys around the living room. She was usually glued to Belle's side, and Belle thought it was adorable.

Of course, then there was the matter of Adam.

After she had taken him to task the other night over his hospitality, she had expected him to throw her out on her rear, and instead he had ushered her into his bedroom, and into the nicest bathroom she had ever seen. It had a huge bathtub, a large window that looked out over nothing but wilderness and a shower that could comfortably house two people, and in fact had two showerheads. Just thinking about it made her feel prickly.

She was certain that she was imagining it. The strange thread of tension that had stretched between them when he had brought her into the bedroom. There just... There had been a bed in the corner, and it was very large, and she had looked at him and...

The problem was, she did so much reading.

But the thought hadn't entered her mind, until now. She had cast herself in a fairy tale. One where she was supposed to break a curse on a man who was tragic and poorly, beastly. And while he wasn't unbeastly, her imagination had taken a sharp turn into a different genre altogether. One where she imagined her taciturn boss taking her roughly into his arms and...

As if you know anything about such things.

She didn't.

And he did. He had children. An ex-wife. A shower built for two.

She banished that thought from her head. It was in fact her shower time, and she was eager to take it.

There was an unspoken schedule that the two of them had settled into and that included her having access to his room, and the bathroom at a certain time each day.

The kids had been rowdy today, and she was feeling a little bit harried. But the shower... the shower was wonderful. That moment was an indulgence, and she was ready to settle into it. She turned on the steam, and let it roll over her. She sighed. It was difficult to believe that five days ago she had lived in Seattle, and she had never met these children, or Adam. Not that she knew him. Not really.

Their conversations had been kept to a minimum.

She gave him a rundown on what the kids had done with their day, every night after dinner. Then he did the dishes and she went off to have her shower.

When she woke up in the morning, he was already gone, and she made breakfast for the kids and they got about their day.

It was a comfortable routine. Her mind started to wander as she stood there in the shower, smoothing her hands over her skin. And she realized that the only thing she was really thinking about was a montage of Adam. Scowling. Appraising her with that slow, steady gaze of his. And those rare smiles—only ever reserved for when he was looking at his children. Yes. Those smiles.

They did something to her. She gasped, when her fingers brushed over her nipples, and a zing of sensation shot through her body.

It was time to get out of the shower.

She toweled off quickly, her hair still wet, her skin flushed from the heat, and put her pajamas on. She started to walk out of the bathroom, but as soon as she did, Adam walked into the bedroom.

She was fully dressed—though she was wearing a shirt with no bra beneath it—but there was still something horrendously embarrassing about the moment. About being caught in his bedroom. About being freshly warm and damp from the shower.

And she froze.

And so did he. His eyes locked on to hers, and her vision was just a little bit blurry because she wasn't wearing her glasses but it was enough. Oh, it was enough. She clutched her previously worn clothes to her chest. Which contained her bra and underwear, and that made her face feel hot.

"Sorry," he said, the word short.

But he didn't move out of her way. She was going to have to walk around him.

She swallowed hard. "No problem."

She skirted around the edge of him, and there was something about…him, that swamped her senses. He was glorious. Gorgeous and huge and…

She stopped, looking up at him. And he looked down at her. And suddenly her heart beat so hard it was more of a throb, it hurt so bad. And she examined him closely, the hard ridge of scar tissue on his face, the dark whiskers on his jaw, the way his eyes glittered almost with intense...

And she thought of the two showerheads.

But it wasn't even the two showerheads that held her there now; it was the desire to reach up and see how the scar felt beneath her fingertips. How his whiskers felt. His skin. If he was as hot as she thought he might be...

She gasped. Audibly, and she knew that he heard it, and she was reasonably certain that he knew why. And rather than standing around waiting for the fallout of that, she ran away. Completely without dignity. She ran quickly down the hall, into her bedroom, and closed the door behind her, blocking it. Not against him. Against herself.

She had never—not once in her life—had a thought like that before. She liked men, but her thoughts about them had extended to things like...sitting in a sun-drenched room reading books together, companionship. Walking around holding hands. Not...running her fingertips along their jawline. Not touching. Not...two showerheads.

She pressed her hand to her chest. She couldn't afford to do this. She needed to take care of the kids; she needed to give them stability. They were happy. She was happy. Her life felt like it had purpose, and the fact was, she was just romanticizing the situation because she had never been in such close proximity to a man before.

That was all it was. It would be childish and silly to do anything in response to these feelings.

And anyway, Adam thought she was ridiculous. He didn't even want her here. In twenty-five days, it was entirely likely he would throw her back out.

And she didn't need to give him many reasons to do that. She had to be careful. She had to keep her distance. And she was determined to do just that.

CHAPTER SIX

As MUCH AS he didn't want to admit it, Belle made his life easier. The kids were happy; they were well taken care of. She got the boys off to school in the morning, which meant that he didn't have to go out for two hours only to come back and get them ready for the day. Imogene still came with him to work occasionally, but there was also the option for her to stay home, which made working the ranch a simpler endeavor, and honestly, meant that he could finish up earlier on a given day.

And he chose not to think about the moment that had happened in his bedroom. He had been much more careful about walking in around the time she was supposed to be showering. For some reason, he'd thought that he'd heard her go back down the hall and into her room. He had probably just heard the boys doing something, but he had barged on in there, and seen her coming out of the bathroom…fully dressed. There was nothing racy about what she was wearing, nothing sexual about her at all. At least there shouldn't have been.

He had been walloped by it. The clean scent of her skin, the way that it was flushed rosy by the heat from the steam in the water. And it could be argued that the issue was he hadn't been with a woman in nearly three years, sure. It would be easy to write it off as that. His life had been devoted solely to his kids these last few years, and sex had been a distant memory that he did his best not to think about.

But it was more than that. It was her. There was something soft and inviting about her, something for him. Something that he had never been exposed to, something he had never been interested in. Something he'd never wanted. He tended to like a harder edge to his women. Be that from athleticism or cynicism, he didn't really care. But there was nothing hard about Belle at all. Which was another reason it seemed so strange that she fit so easily into this life. Into this household.

But it was like she was bringing that softness of hers into this place. And Lord knew the kids benefited from it.

He just didn't need to ponder it too closely.

It wasn't for him. It was for them.

He'd decided to come home for lunch that day, and when he walked into the house, there was a dramatic commotion happening in the living room. But this time, it wasn't a war. The boys were wearing paper crowns and were riding on stick horses. Imogene also had a paper crown. And Belle was standing in the center of it all, wearing a long, flowing dress, holding a book in her hand and reading it with a flourish. Every time she read something about a princess, they all sighed dramatically, and whenever she mentioned gallant knights they all pantomimed riding horses. Imogene made an adorable, high-pitched whinnying sound.

And they all laughed.

He just stood there, completely floored by the sight. How had he thought that everything was fine? How had he thought it was all right for the boys to be here by themselves, for them to be apart from Imogene all day? For everything to run on autopilot? They were so much happier when they had somebody involved with them. Somebody involved with their lives. And...

He just stood and stared at Belle, who was laughing freely, her brown hair swaying with the emotion brought on by her laughter. And he couldn't figure out how he thought it was dull or limp when she had first arrived. How he'd thought she was dull. Or mousy or anything of the kind. She wasn't mousy at all.

"Dad!" Joe shouted.

And Belle turned more fully toward him, her eyes widening behind her glasses. "Oh," she said. "I didn't realize you were there."

"That's fine. I didn't want to interrupt."

"Do you want to be a knight?" she asked.

"That's okay."

"We have an extra crown."

"Why are the knights wearing crowns?" He couldn't help but ask.

"Because paper helmets are too hard to make," she said.

Then she walked over to him, and took his hat off his head, and reached up, depositing a paper crown there. It brought her face within an inch of his, and he was struck by the scent of her. Delicate and lilac and tempting. And he was suddenly not thinking of a pretend child's game. In fact, it was difficult for him to remember the kids were in the room. Up close like that she was...exquisite. Those glasses... He even thought they were hot. Maybe it really had been too long since he'd gotten laid. Maybe he needed to go down to Smokey's Tavern to find a woman. Hell, Debbie and Belle could keep track of the kids for a weekend. It would be the better part of valor. It was wrong to be hanging around lusting after a woman that he employed to take care of his kids.

Her lips curved upward slightly, and his eyes dropped to her lips. They parted, and she gasped. Like she felt it. Like she definitely felt it too.

Yeah. He was going to go down to the bar tonight. See if he could find somebody else.

She might not end up making it past thirty days. If he was going to make hay, he'd better do it while the sun was shining.

She took a step away from him and smiled. Yeah. The sun was definitely shining right now. He needed to make the most of it.

"I might be away tonight," he said at dinner. "I can call Debbie to come up if you want."

"It's always nice to see Debbie," she said. "But no worries. If she isn't available, fine."

"Thanks."

He could tell that she wanted to ask, but definitely didn't think it was her business. In fact, her whole frame vibrated with it. She got up, and started fussing with debris in the living room. "You don't have to clean just because I'm going out," he said.

"Oh. No. It's not… Thank you though." She inclined her head. "Where are you going?"

And he didn't know why he found it satisfying that she hadn't been able to help herself. "Down to the tavern. I might be gone all night."

"Oh. As in…" Her cheeks turned bright red. "It's not my business. I'm sorry. It's not my business to ask you…"

"So why did you?"

"I don't know," she said, her voice suddenly becoming thin. "I'm sorry."

"No need to be sorry."

She bit her lip, and looked up at him, and she looked…

upset. His heart twisted. How long had it been since a woman cared at all what he did? Ever? Maybe at one time his wife had.

They hadn't been in love. That was the thing. They hadn't even pretended. They had met up at a bar during a military reunion thing and had gotten talking. They'd been attracted to each other, and they'd hooked up, and it had turned into a conversation about what they wanted, and how neither of them were all that close to having it. They'd decided to give it a try with each other. Kids. Domesticity. Something normal.

After all the horror of war, it had seemed like a worthy pursuit. A step toward something…healing. A step toward something normal. But they hadn't cared about each other like that. They'd liked each other, and for his part, he'd been totally faithful to her. In the end, he didn't think she had been to him, but, there were circumstances. And he didn't hold that against her.

But all that to say, she had certainly never looked at him with a mixture of fear and hope and possession that shouldn't be there. No. It definitely shouldn't be there.

This sweet girl that had worked for him for two weeks shouldn't be looking at him any kind of way.

And that was why he really needed to go out. He needed to make sure that his body understood the score. Belle was—loath as he was to admit it—a gift. One he hadn't known he'd needed, but one he'd needed all the same. And he couldn't afford for anything to mess that up.

"See you tomorrow sometime," he said.

He got in his truck and drove down to the tiny town of Pyrite Falls. Smokey's Tavern was packed full, the parking lot filled with junky old pickup trucks. And he pulled his own right alongside the others. He was basic. He didn't care. It was what it was.

He got out of the truck and went into the tavern, which was loud. Filled with voices and music, and clanking beer bottles. Some of the Four Corners gang was in attendance, Wolf Garrett and Hunter McCloud each chatting up a woman over by the jukebox. Normally, Sawyer Garrett would have been out, but he'd been scarce the last nine months, because one of his hookups had gotten pregnant. Rumor was, he'd offered to marry her, and she'd decided she didn't want anything to do with him or the baby. He went up to the bar, and waved to the bartender.

"Whatever you have on draft," he said.

The men nodded. "You hear about Sawyer Garrett?"

"That he has a kid?"

"No. That he put an ad out on the internet for a mail-order bride."

"He did what?"

"It's true. The news station went out to Four Corners just this afternoon."

"Well. No shit."

He thought of Belle back at home… A mail-order bride. Maybe Sawyer wasn't an idiot.

No. That wasn't in the cards for him. He was never getting married again. That was… The very idea was idiotic. Just because he was a little bit hot for the nanny, did not mean that he needed to think about marrying her. Or anyone. What he needed was to get laid.

He took his beer and looked around the room. There were plenty of beautiful women. Smokey's Tavern was kind of a destination for women who had a thing for cowboys. Four Corners was the largest ranching spread in the state of Oregon, and that meant there were a lot of cowboys in

Pyrite Falls. And if Western sex tourism could work in his favor, he was all for it.

There was a particularly pretty woman with black curly hair and ample curves out on the dance floor with a group of friends, and he looked at her for a good thirty seconds, which was enough to get her to look back at him.

She smiled, her dark eyes glittering with interest. And for some reason, in his mind, all he could see was light brown eyes behind a pair of large glasses.

He gritted his teeth, and walked forward. He was going to do this. He was bound and determined.

He did not do it. He had tried. The woman was beautiful, and he had wanted to feel a spark with her. But he just couldn't. He also wasn't going to go home. He'd said that he was staying out all night, and dammit, he was staying out all night. If he couldn't deter himself he would deter Belle. That little bit of attraction that he had glimpsed earlier, that hint of possessiveness...

Well. He would just let her think that what he'd said would happen had happened.

He drove his truck down to the bottom of the driveway, and parked in an outcropping in the trees. It was fine. He didn't mind sleeping in his truck. He had done it a few times when he was in a fight with his ex-wife. And he would do it again.

Anything was better than slinking home announcing that he'd failed at hooking up.

Of course, Belle might not know, but he knew that what he'd really failed at was getting rid of his attraction for her.

CHAPTER SEVEN

THEY DIDN'T SPEAK about that night. And Belle found it best. Because she was…outrageously wounded by it. And she had no reason to be. He was a grown man, and if he wanted to go out and…slake his animal lusts, that was his business.

He'd come home around five in the morning. She was angry that she knew that. Angry that she'd been half-asleep for the entire night, on tenterhooks, listening for his return.

And then she had been…she had been completely devastated by the idea that he had been with another woman. Which was ridiculous. He had never touched her, and he shouldn't touch her. She was his employee. Well, she supposed that since Debbie was paying her, technically she was Debbie's employee, but functionally, she was his, and it was actually…downright chivalrous of him to not acknowledge those strange, sparkly moments that had come up between them.

So they didn't speak of that night. She did her best not to think of it.

She tried not to think about it every night when they sat down to dinner. And slowly, she decided that maybe it wasn't the best idea if she ate meals with him. She started eating dinner in her room, and he didn't question her on it. She felt resolved in that decision when she came inside from playing with the boys to find him lying on the floor in the living room with Imogene, the sleeves of his T-shirt tight on his biceps as he moved a doll around like she was walking, much to the amusement of his daughter. And smiled.

When he smiled it was like the sun coming out from behind the clouds. When he smiled, it was a little bit like the beast had transformed into a prince. But was still also a beast. Which honestly, was better. The prince had always seemed a little bit insipid to her.

But she had found a way to keep some distance. Not having those meals with him, not falling into the trap of believing that she was part of the family. That they were much of anything.

And before she knew it, thirty days had come and gone. And they had never discussed it. She knew that it was going to be up to her. Because they really did need to talk about it.

She approached him one morning before he left for work, and she had woken up unreasonably early. As if she didn't know why. As if she had started rising earlier and earlier because she liked to listen to the sound of his cowboy boots on the hard floors, the sound of him getting his coffee, leaving the house for the day. As if she didn't find him the best part of waking up.

"It's been more than thirty days," she pointed out, reaching around him and losing her breath as she did, but grabbing a mug and beating a hasty retreat to the coffee maker, pretending that moment had not occurred.

"So it has," he said, as if it had just occurred to him.

She looked at him. And she could see that he was actually well aware of it. "I guess I'm staying."

He leaned back against the counter, his coffee mug in hand, his other hand braced on the counter, making the muscles in his forearm shift. She caught herself staring for a moment, before she forced her gaze back to his. "I guess so."

"Should we...make it official?"

"Sure. What do you need to make it official?"

"Should we do...an official schedule?"

"Sure. Works for me."

"So..."

"I'm going to work. Why don't you do something and present it to me? We'll have a talk about it."

"Yeah. I can do that."

So she had worked on that when the kids were occupied— the boys at school and Imogene down for her nap—and presented it to him when he came home.

She handed him the paper, and he looked it over. "Looks good to me. And it's essentially what we've already been doing?"

"Yeah. I didn't really... I didn't really change anything. I just thought that maybe it should be official." She pushed her glasses further up on her nose, and immediately felt annoyed that she had done it. They hadn't even slipped. It was just a nervous habit to touch them, and she did it especially when she was near him.

"Can I ask you something?"

"Yes," she said.

He rarely asked her anything.

"Why are you doing this? Because when I was twenty-four I was in the military, and I was drinking heavily every weekend when I wasn't in a combat zone, and essentially using it as an opportunity to sow every wild oat it ever occurred to me to sow. You've been living with me for a month, and all I know about you is that you used to run a bookshop."

Nobody ever asked about her. She didn't have any practice telling her life story. She had been the weird girl at school, and nobody had been all that interested in her.

They'd definitely been more interested in making up stories about her than actually asking. She had given the details to Debbie, but obviously Debbie had never passed them on.

Standing here in the darkened kitchen, with the kids gone to bed, it felt like a strangely intimate thing, and it shouldn't. He was asking as an employer.

So she just needed to tell him like it was an interview.

Except she looked up at him, and her heart did something. He wasn't just an employer. She had been living with him for the past thirty days, watching the way that he interacted with his kids. Watching the way that they loved him. She had been taking care of his kids, kids that she knew he loved more than anything.

And he trusted her to do that.

She knew a little bit about his relationship with his wife, and the way that she had left, enough to know that he was a good man, no matter how gruff he seemed.

"I was raised by my grandmother," she said. "I never knew my father, and my mother was in and out of my life for the first few years. She had drug problems. Probably mental health problems as well."

Her eyes met his, and there was something sharp there. Recognition. "I know how that is."

"I know you do. And… I love my grandmother. I had a wonderful childhood. I spent all my spare time in her bookshop, reading. I didn't have a lot of friends—they thought I was very strange. As far as I know, I don't have any wild oats to sow. But I didn't have anyone in my life, and I was really lonely. After my grandmother died, I tried to keep the store going, but there was just a lot of debt, and I couldn't manage it. It's the thing that hurts me the most. Because she loved it. I feel a little bit like I let her down. Like I didn't pay her back for all the time she spent taking care of me. But…it felt like I could come here and do something worthwhile. And that's what I want. Knowing a little bit about your kids, and their story, I wanted… I'm just an abandoned kid too," she said. "And they have you. Just as I had my grandmother. They have you and Debbie, actually, and that's a wonderful thing. It's way more than I had. But I actually understand what it's like. I know what it feels like to have a parent not be in your life, even if the reasons are complicated. Even if it's not just because they're bad or don't love you, it's difficult, and it is something that takes healing. I'm not sure that I've done all the healing there is to do, but…my life was at a crossroads and this seemed like a good road to go down."

"I'm sorry. About your mother. And I'm really damned sorry my own kids have to deal with it. I'd rather that they didn't. I wish that…" His face looked tense. And she wanted to walk over to him and comfort him. To put her hand on his face like she had thought about doing weeks ago in his bedroom. All right, it wasn't the only time she'd thought of it.

She thought about touching him a lot, at night, when she was alone in bed. In the morning, when she heard the sounds of him getting up and getting ready to go out and work the ranch. She thought of it more often than she should. Which was…thinking about it at all.

"They're really good kids." She smiled. "Hellions. But I think that's a good thing. They have their spirit. You know…it's actually a testament to what you've given them that they're not afraid to be kids. They're not afraid to be wild. I've always been afraid of it. Because I was afraid that…the one person in my life that took care of me wouldn't be able to handle me if I ever talked above a whisper. That wasn't her fault—my grandmother was a lovely woman. She was very serene and calm, and the environment of the bookstore was very serene and calm, and I was afraid to ever disrupt that. Because my mother made me feel like I must be existing on a trial basis. And somehow with her I failed. But you've given your kids a sense of security. So secure that they aren't afraid to throw water balloons at me. Or lock me in a pantry."

"Please tell me they haven't done that recently."

"The pantry, no. The water balloons are bit of a recurring motif, but I do have them trained to not do it in the house."

"If you ever need nights off. You know. If you ever need to…go down to the tavern…"

Her cheeks flamed. But when she imagined going down to a cowboy bar and approaching a man there…the only man that she could imagine was him.

"I'm good," she said.

He grinned. And she was pretty sure that was the first time he had ever genuinely smiled at her. It made her stomach go into a free fall.

"Well. Just let me know if that changes. This is a good schedule. I think this is going to work."

And right then, she felt a terror that she hadn't felt for quite a long time. A sense that it had to work. Because if it didn't… If it didn't, and she lost him, she lost these kids… it would be like losing everything.

It was the strangest thing, because she wasn't here on a trial basis anymore, and yet it all felt more high stakes than it had before.

She felt like a kid again. Desperately afraid to lose the one good thing in her life.

CHAPTER EIGHT

THE SUMMER BLED into autumn, the leaves began to turn yellow and the mornings became misty and deliciously haunted. She had always loved the rain. She was from Seattle, so you either made your peace with that sort of weather or you moved. She had enjoyed the relative warmth of the summer, but she was pleased to get back to this wonderful sort of reading weather. Though, the kids fell into a sort of cabin fever if it rained too hard and too long.

Initially she had been a little bit hesitant to let Joe and John out in a total downpour, but they became wild enough that she eventually gave in, after bundling them in a rain coat and rain boots.

Adam had given her a budget to help clothe the kids, and feed them, and she spent a fair amount of time ordering adorable clothes for them on the internet. Adam might not have a computer, but she did. And an internet connection was another thing that she—along with Debbie—had managed to convince him to get over the last couple of months.

They had spent the afternoon out in the rain on this particular Saturday, and they'd been freezing when they came inside, and she put them in a very warm bath, gave them bowls of soup and then set them in front of a movie. With the internet had come streaming services, and a whole lot of great cartoons. She was a big fan of books, but when it came right down to it she was a big fan of stories in general. So she would take them in whatever form they came.

Debbie came to take the kids for a while, and Belle decided she'd have a walk. She loved wandering around the property, and even with it raining lightly, it was still beautiful. Of course, the light rain didn't last, and midway through the walk, it began to become a true downpour that tested the resilience of her raincoat.

She started to walk quicker, and keep her head down low so that the rain didn't splatter her face, and that was when she ran smack into Adam. Literally into him. Her face connected with the solid wall of his chest, and he grabbed hold of her, his strong hands holding her steady.

She looked up at him.

Rain poured down off the brim of his cowboy hat, his afternoon whiskers grown in thick. His eyes were fierce, his mouth firm. In her heart… Oh her heart.

She had done her best not to get this close to him again. She had done her best to keep their conversations neutral. To keep them about the kids. They had both been careful. So very careful. He hadn't gone out to the bar again, and maybe he should have. Maybe that would have done something to rid herself of this… The stupid, painful hope that existed inside of her chest. Because it had become more than fascination. It had become more than attraction. It was that bright, hopeful seed that lived inside of her chest that wanted to believe that when he looked at her he saw the same thing that she saw when she looked at him.

Someone beautiful. Someone desirable. What was the point of it? What was the point of any of it? There was a part of her that wanted him, but separately from the thing that they had already. Separately from her position as nanny. A part of her that wanted this to be some kind of great fantasy that she might read about in a book. For they could get carried away by passion, and her bosoms would heave and the flowers that were blooming would be magical and lovely, and misty and perfect. But she knew... She was old enough to know, realistic enough to know that that wasn't how it would be. That in the end they would have to contend with reality; they couldn't do that and keep it separate from everything that they were. From the connection that she had to the kids, from being an employee in his house.

From the fact that she was needy and sad, and eleven years younger than him, terribly inexperienced, and he was a jaded divorcé who had a hardness to him that would break her if she hit up against it too hard.

But he was still holding on to her. And he was still looking at her. And it made her feel like maybe her fantasies weren't so far-fetched. Like maybe they weren't wrong. Like maybe all this time he had felt the same thing. Like maybe he really was just holding himself back. And she had run into him and it had been like a thunderclap. Breaking the barrier that they had erected between the two of them.

Still he held her.

And she found herself reaching her hand out, pressing her hand against his damp, warm chest, and she could feel his heart raging hard beneath her touch.

"Don't," he bit out.

And that single syllable expressed more than whole rafts of poetry ever could. He did feel it. He had been avoiding it. It was why he had never broached the topic of her eating dinner with the family again. It was why he was happy to keep things as distant as possible. Because there was this thing there. This thing between them.

And it was something she could barely understand, something she could barely put into words.

But she didn't need to. Because he had just done it.

Don't.

It spoke of restraint tested. Restraint about to break.

She was testing his restraint. And she had never felt…

Truthfully, she had never actually felt like a woman until this moment.

Here she was, a woman who could push against a man like him. He was such a man. The beast. A mountain. A soldier, a father, a cowboy, a brick wall.

He was everything.

Everything she had never known to want.

It would've been better if she had never known this. It would've been better if her fantasies could've been confined to sunny reading nooks and tall, slender men with glasses just like hers, because those fantasies didn't test her. Didn't push her. Didn't put her at risk.

And this one did.

This would jeopardize everything that she had built. Everything that she wanted. Everything that she was. This one, she might not be equal to. This one, she was almost certainly too weak for. Unqualified for. And yet here she was.

And suddenly, his large hand came around, cupped the back of her head, and she found herself being roughly lifted up on her toes, his mouth meeting hers.

And it was…an explosion.

She had never been kissed before. And this was beyond anything she had imagined. Real life, and actual exposure to men over the years had not prepared her for this. The only thing that had ever come close was her romance novels. Because it was a storm. It was too much and not enough all at once. The firmness of his mouth, the heat of it, the friction of his tongue as he parted her lips and tasted her deep, it was everything.

And yet it was still not enough. She wanted... She wanted. She wanted there to be no layers of clothes between them. She wanted to be skin to skin with him. She wanted to give herself over to him, body and soul. She wanted to strip him naked, wanted to strip herself naked, wanted to expose them both, down to layers that they had never revealed to anyone before.

Of course, he had though. He had been married. He had been in love.

This wasn't new to him. But it also wasn't normal.

And she was on dangerous ground. She was the one who pulled away, shaking, trembling. She was the one who came back to reality, and with shaking hands, managed to stop.

"Sorry," he said.

"Okay," she said.

"It's not. You should feel safe living with me, and not like I'm going to take advantage of you."

"I would never... You would never... I know that. I gave you a clear invitation. Please don't feel bad about it. I wanted to kiss you. It's just that... I shouldn't."

"Definitely not."

"It won't happen again," she said.

"It won't," he said in confirmation.

And that should have made her feel pleased. Because she was the one who had stopped it. But instead, that heavy confirmation only made her feel wounded.

She wanted him. She wanted him so much. But she wanted this family, the security more.

And she wondered why she always had to choose. Between herself and security. Between what she really wanted, and a sense of happiness.

There would always be that tension in there. That she could never truly have all that she wanted.

And on the way back to the house, she cried, because there was no way to tell the difference between the rain and her tears.

CHAPTER NINE

HE KEPT HIS distance from her. For Thanksgiving, they went to Debbie's house, and she had the whole meal catered, and they put on a pretty good front. Belle spent her time with the kids, and Adam allowed them to take as much of his focus as possible. As long as they could keep the children between each other, it was fine. But he kept reliving the kiss.

There had been an innocence to her kiss that called to him. That had shocked him. Except, of course, she had told him how she was raised; she had told him all of that. It stood to reason. It was also another reason he should never touch her again. She might have a little bit of experience with men—it was impossible to say—but he knew it wasn't a whole lot. Certainly not the vast level of experience he had with sex and hooking up. He had learned to treat it like a casual thing, just another appetite to be satisfied. He knew for a fact that wasn't how she saw it.

As if that's how you'd see it with her...

The rain gave way to snow. Christmas was his favorite time of year with his kids. It had always been a magical time in his own childhood, and after his parents had died, it had just seemed sad. But once he had gotten married, once they'd had kids, meaning had been brought back to all the proceedings, and it was like part of him had been brought alive again.

The day after Thanksgiving, they always went out and got their tree.

He loaded the kids up in a sled, and they walked up the side of the mountain to the edge of their property to choose a tree. This year of course, Belle went with them.

She looked like an angel, bundled up all in crimson against the bright white snow. Her cheeks were pink, her lips a berry red, her glasses looking extra gold and shiny and adorable. And when she laughed and pushed them up her nose as she chased after Joe, who was running as quickly as possible—which wasn't very—in the snow, his heart did something he didn't particularly care for.

It felt something.

It felt something big. Something deep. Something it never had before.

She had been soft, when he kissed her. Two months since that kiss, and he hadn't been able to get it off his mind. It haunted him when he slept. He woke up hard and sweaty and desperate for her in the middle of every damned night. And there was nothing he could do about it. Absolutely nothing. Because he couldn't offer her anything.

He wasn't sure he knew what to do with a long-term relationship in general. He had failed to protect the first woman he married. He hadn't been able to help her. And she had been tough. Not the sort of soft... Whatever Belle was.

No. He couldn't take the chance. Couldn't take the chance that he would crush her.

But he noticed that since she had come into his life things had felt lighter. He had felt lighter. He drank less; that was for sure. He was a better dad to his kids. It was weird how having help almost made him more involved, not less.

"Okay," he said when they got to the top of the hill. "Which tree?"

He stood next to one that was tall but sort of sparse, and gestured to it, then to another one that was about half a foot shorter, but a bit rounder. "We have this tall stately tree here, or this thick little guy here."

"Taller!" John said.

"Fatter," Joe said.

"Tree!" said Imogene.

"I think you're going to have to be the tiebreaker," he said to Belle.

"Choose mine," Joe said.

"No, Belle. Choose mine." That came from John, who was sounding indignant.

"Well now," Belle said. "This is a very difficult decision. Because both trees are beautiful, and each have something to recommend them. So I'm going to have to do this very scientifically. I'm going to have to spin around and see which one I point to."

And she did. She closed her eyes, and spun herself around with her finger pointed out, and when she stopped, she landed very clearly pointing at the tall thin tree, and then fell backward into the snow. She laughed riotously. "Which did I choose?"

"Mine!" John shouted.

He hooted and hollered and hopped around in the snow and Adam went over to help Belle out of the snow trench she had managed to fall into. He reached out, and her mittened hand wrapped around his gloved one, and he was damned grateful that they weren't skin to skin, because even like this... Even like this...

And suddenly, a mischievous grin crossed her face, and she pulled down hard, bringing him over the top of her, down into the snow. Her glasses fogged, and she laughed, but then the laugh seemed to get swallowed up in a gasp when his body made more intimate contact with hers.

"Oh dear," she said.

His heart was ready to gallop straight out of his chest, and he could see by the pulse beating at the base of her pale throat that she felt the same.

It wasn't a secret that they were attracted to each other. Not between the two of them. They were both painfully aware of it. They just did their best to ignore it.

"You're playing dangerous games," he whispered. The kids were shrieking and making mayhem all around them, but it was fading into the background, a fuzz of white noise that didn't matter in the face of the current moment.

"I know," she whispered. "I'm sorry. I didn't really mean to."

"Didn't you?"

"Adam..."

"Later."

He got up, and hauled her to her feet as well, before going over to the tree with his axe. "All right. Let's get this show on the road."

They trundled down the mountain, two aroused adults, a Christmas tree and three children, and went back to the house, where they set the tree up, and each had cider that Belle had put on the stove prior to them going out.

They had a completely wholesome Christmas-tree-decorating party, a stew for dinner, and the entire time, the conversation that lay ahead of him and Belle seemed to hang in the air between them.

He expected her to retreat to her room once the kids were in bed, but she didn't. Instead, she stood there in front of the Christmas tree, her expression stubbornly resolute.

"Yes?"

"I came to a decision," she said.

"And what's that?"

"I want you a whole lot. And you asked me why I wasn't out sowing my wild oats. Well, it's because I never wanted to before. Until you. And I don't want anything to compromise what we have here. I love your kids. I love them so much, more than I ever thought possible. I feel at home here. And I don't want to leave. But there's something between us, and I can't ignore it. I don't want to ignore it. My most torrid fantasy before meeting you was… Well, it just wasn't. And you make me want things…things I never have, and I'm afraid that if we don't… But if I don't…"

He took a step toward her, his heart beating heavily, like he had never done this before. Like he was the one who was inexperienced. "Let me tell you something. Sex is pretty cheap. You could go down to the bar right now and find a good-looking guy who wanted to take you home. I promise you that. He would probably be experienced enough that he could make you enjoy it."

"You went down to the bar and found somebody easily enough…"

"I didn't. That night. All I could think about was you, so I didn't pick anyone up. I camped out in my truck at the end of the driveway because I didn't want you to know that you are all I could think about. Because I didn't want you to know that you were the only one that I wanted. Because I shouldn't, Belle. That much is true. What I just said… about sex, that's always been true for me. It's never mattered. It's never meant anything. Who it was with…didn't matter at all. But you're different. And the way that I want you is different. But I don't know what the hell that means."

"I know that you loved your wife…"

"I didn't. I had an arrangement with my wife, and I thought that would be good enough. My time in the military... I think it killed whatever was in me that might've been able to love. The things that I saw. The things that I did. PTSD might have affected her in a particular way that it didn't me. But I'm not unaffected. It makes you hard. And I hoped that by making a family I could do something...to bring myself back to something that looked like normal. That looked like the kind of childhood I'd had. Because I had good parents. I had a good life here."

"You're a great father."

"I've been doing better. Lately. But I'm just trying to make it really clear to you, that I've never had...romance in me. I just think that part of me is broken. And worse, I... I think I might be bad for women. In that kind of relationship. She was doing just fine before she married me. Before the kids. And it isn't the kids. The kids are great."

"Don't blame yourself," she said, taking a step forward and putting her hands on his face. Her fingertips were soft as they trailed their way along his jawline, over his scar. His scar...

"I had a couple deployments to Afghanistan," he said. "I saw some pretty terrible things. I lived. Other people didn't. And I saw the way they met their end. I don't know why I survived and they didn't. Those things haunt me. That reality. That was one reason I decided to try the marriage-and-kids thing. Because kids, having kids, that felt like a way to make me surviving matter. And it's weird, because then you figure out really quickly that kids don't exist for you. They're their own people. You might make them but... I don't know. It changed something in me—that's for sure. But I don't know that it gave me any answers. If anything, it gave me more questions."

"I'm sorry," she said. "I'm sorry."

"There's no need to be sorry. Everybody goes through things. I signed up for the military. Nobody made me. When you're young, you think you're bulletproof. And it turns out, I might be."

"How did you get your scar?"

"There are more. You just can't see them."

"Oh, Adam."

"I wasn't speaking metaphorically. They're just on my body."

Except, there were others. The ones inside. And he couldn't really deny that. Especially not in light of all the things he'd just said.

"I want to see," she whispered.

He wasn't fueled by alcohol, just spiced cider. And his desire for her. He couldn't blame it on anything else.

But he took her in his arms, lowered his head and kissed her.

CHAPTER TEN

HE WAS KISSING her again, and she felt like she could fly. She felt like everything had finally come together. When she had pulled him down on top of her in the snow she had questioned her own sanity, but... She didn't now. The truth was, she was willing to take the risk.

Because she had been thinking about this endlessly since their kiss in the rain. Why did she have to take half? Why wasn't she allowed to have things that she wanted? And she had decided that she wasn't going to live that way anymore.

The truth was, she loved Joe and John and Imogene. She loved them like her own children.

But she also loved Adam. And over the course of living with him for the past few months she had fallen in love with him. She loved how he loved his children, the way that he took care of them. She loved his smile, rare as it was; she loved living in the same house as him. He was a good man, good to his soul, and steady in a way that she knew few people were. Dependable. Trustworthy.

He made her feel safe. And at the same time, he felt dangerous. And there was something that spoke to her soul in that. That call to the wildness that reading had always tapped into, and made it feel real.

She had fantasized about sitting and reading books with a man, but instead she had found a man who made her feel like she did when she escaped into those pages. And that was something even more thrilling.

Something she hadn't known was possible.

And as his kiss went on and on, as his kiss went deeper, she surrendered herself to this. To him.

He picked her up off the floor, holding her against his chest as he continued to kiss her, long and deep, sensual. It thrilled her. Unwound the tension that had been consuming her these last months and flooded her with a river of need.

She was slick between her thighs with desire for him, and she thrilled at understanding those descriptions in her beloved books in such a personal way. Yes, she had been aroused before, but never in the arms of a man she wanted.

It was different. This was different.

Maybe she was different.

Braver now, stronger. Because before she had never taken a risk. Before, she had never chanced showing all of herself for fear that she might be rejected.

But here, with him, she almost felt as if she had no choice. That she had to surrender to it. To wave her white flag in the name of truth. In the name of need.

He hadn't loved his wife. He had taken half a dream, hadn't even thought that a full dream was possible for him. He still didn't.

And had she been doing the same? But she didn't want to. Not anymore.

Not with him.

She wanted everything. All of this.

He carried her into his bedroom, and then into the bathroom.

"Two showerheads," she murmured as he set her down and began to remove her clothes from her body.

"Damned straight," he said.

He turned the water on, and let it get hot, and she wrapped her arms around herself, staring at him. He was still fully clothed.

Slowly, very slowly, he began to remove his clothes. His chest was broad, covered in dark hair, and it made her mouth dry. He was the most beautiful man she had ever seen. And she had never seen a naked one in person before.

He undid his belt, the button on his jeans, the zipper, and took his boots off, jeans and underwear, everything.

She didn't know where to look first. It was like a sensual feast and she wanted everything.

He took her hand and led her inside the shower, letting the hot water run over their skin. And then he took her into his arms, his skin slick against hers as he kissed her, consumed her. He soaped up his hands and ran them over her curves, his thumbs skimming over her nipples, tracing circles down her torso, her hip bones, and then he put one hand between her legs, stroking her, taking her to the brink.

"Adam… I've never… I haven't…"

He looked at her, his gaze fierce. "You sure? Are you sure you want this? Are you sure you want me?"

She looked at him, at the scars on his face, on his body. This man had lived things that she had only ever imagined. She felt every inch of her inexperience right there. Except… Except… He had told her that for him sex didn't mean anything, and in this moment she could see that it did.

So all of his experience didn't matter. Not now. Not in the face of this. Because she was special. They were special.

And if she didn't risk herself, both of them would be doomed to live only half a life.

"I'm sure."

"Good."

He continued stroking her as he kissed her, and her climax hit her in a wave, sweet and sharp and overwhelming. Stealing her breath.

He held her limp body against him as he rinsed her clean and turned the water off, taking her out of the shower and wrapping her in a fluffy towel, drying her.

That he took her over to the bed, all warm and boneless, and pulled her against his naked body, kissing her as he laid her on the mattress.

He kissed her, all over, moving between her legs and pleasuring her there with his mouth. She had never understood why, in all those books, they always protested, and yet grabbed his hair to keep him there. But she did exactly the same. Embarrassment making her feel like she should beg him to stop, desire demanding she urge him on.

Desire won.

By the time he positioned himself between her thighs she was desperate with need. Ready for anything. And when the thick head of his arousal was there, at the entrance to her body, she wasn't even nervous. He thrust into her, sharp, stinging pain lasting for but a moment before it gave way to yet more need.

He began to move, pushing them both to the brink, driving them both to the edge.

He lowered his head, and he growled. Her beast. And then they both came apart together, finding their release. And she wondered, hoped, that maybe she had broken the spell. The curse.

But she knew there was only one way to find out. And it wasn't by staying safe.

"Adam. I love you."

CHAPTER ELEVEN

HE HAD MADE a mistake. He had known that the moment he'd taken her into his arms. She had been a virgin, and he'd had her anyway. And now she thought she loved him.

"Belle…"

"To be clear," she said, "I loved you before this. This just made me brave enough to say it."

"I can't. I…"

"You had a convenient marriage before. Can't you have one with me?"

The way she looked at him. With so much hope. And he wanted to say yes. He really did. But she didn't understand.

"I ruined Laney's life. I did."

"Why do you think that?"

"Because I didn't help her. I didn't… All this did was hurt her."

"Just like you don't blame her, you can't blame yourself. What happened with her… It wasn't up to you to fix it."

"I'm not strong enough to do it. And you… You're so soft. So sweet."

"Don't underestimate me like that, Adam. I am soft. And I care very deeply about you, and about your kids. I love them. I really do. I'm soft enough that regardless of what I've been through, I have room in my heart you. For them. More than enough. But I'm not weak. I know what it's like to be abandoned. I know what it's like to feel like

you weren't enough. I know what it's like to fail. To lose
things that you love. To lose people that you love. I picked
myself up and I came here anyway. And I decided to try to
make something better with my life. To make something
new. I met you. I started to fall in love with you and I told
myself that I couldn't have this position here and love you
too. Because I told myself I wasn't allowed to have everything. I'm done with that. I'm over it." She shook her head.
"I want everything."

"I can't."

"You won't."

"All the same. Isn't it?"

"What are you going to do when your kids need you to
drop all those barriers? Because little kids take you like
you are. But when they get older… Adam, you're not going
to be able to avoid being vulnerable."

"I love my kids."

"I know you do. But I actually think you love me too.
And the issue isn't love… It's what you feel like you can
show people. You've seen a lot of really terrible things.
You've been hurt." She traced her fingers over his scars
again. "You had to be strong even while all that was happening. Did you…did you forget how to show your emotions because you were trying so hard to protect yourself?"

"Belle…"

She rolled out of bed. "You're not at war anymore. I
don't pretend to know what you went through there. But
what I do know is that you're not there anymore unless
you choose to be."

She left, and closed the door behind her quietly. He just
lay there for a long time.

And he had to wonder if she was right. If he was still

living in a self-imposed war. Right now, he couldn't imagine a way out of it.

Except…

What was the alternative?

He had to fight his way out. Because the alternative was going down the road like Laney had. The alternative was…

She was right. Eventually, it would cause problems. He could pretend that he had a handle on it all. He could pretend that everything was going to be okay, but…it was going to hold him back from the kids.

It was going to hold him back from her.

He needed her. It wasn't the kids who needed her. He needed her.

He got out of bed, wrapped a blanket around his waist and went down the hall, and barged straight into her room.

CHAPTER TWELVE

SHE WAS CRYING, and trying to get dressed, trying to decide if she was going to stay or if she was going to go. She couldn't go. She couldn't leave him. She couldn't abandon the kids. She couldn't abandon Adam. Not when he needed her, whether he believed that he did or not.

And then the door opened, and he was standing there. Wrapped in a blanket, looking ferocious.

"Don't cry," he said, closing the distance between them, shutting the door firmly behind him.

He wrapped his arms around her and pulled her close. "Don't cry."

"I'm sorry. I can't help it. I just… I love you. I really want you to love me."

"I do," he said.

She froze, and everything got so quiet she was convinced that she could hear the snow falling outside. "You do?"

"Yeah. These past few months… This is the happiest I've ever been, actually. Even while I was holding myself back from you. But you're right. I've been trying to keep myself from fully feeling…the bad things. And by doing that I kept myself from feeling a lot of good things. I love you. And I think a little bit I was trying to manage my guilt of what happened with Laney by not letting myself… I told myself that I couldn't love. And that was what had gone

wrong with the two of us. I just didn't love her. I love you.
I really love you."

"Why?"

"Why?"

"Yes. I'm going to tell you, I really love romance novels. And you just gave me a very good example of the sex
scenes being…much more realistic than I anticipated. But
now I want to know why you love me. Because this is the
part where you give me a really good speech about what
I've done for you." She squared her shoulders and looked
at him. "You have made me brave. You made me brave
enough to stand up and demand it all. You've given me a
family. You've given me a place that feels like home. You
taught me to kiss, and you taught me to make love. And
you gave me the fantasy."

"Wow. That is… That's a lot. And I can only hope that I
live up to it in the years to come. That's what you gave me,
Belle. You're making me look forward to those years. I've
been lost. Drowning. I had a lot of good things—my kids
are blessings—but I didn't even really know how to enjoy
them. Because I was keeping myself so closed off. Because
I was so isolated. You gave me joy. Laughter. You make me
want to sit and listen to you read. Though, I'm thinking I
should let you read some of those romance novels to me."

"Gladly," she said, though the idea of reading some of
the dirtier words out loud made her blush. But it also made
her feel warm. And she had a feeling they were definitely
going to do that.

"I think you're making me brave," he said. "You know,
I always thought that I liked people who were hard like
me. That I liked women who were hard like me. I thought
that was what made you strong enough to deal with things.
But…your softness humbles me. And it's a hell of a lot

409

braver than anything that was ever in me. It's easy, when you're young, to think about going out and dying like a hero, a soldier's death. What's terrifying is this. Living. Loving. Being vulnerable. But dammit, you make me want that. You make me vulnerable. And that terrifies me, and thrills me all at once."

She sighed, love making her heart feel three times bigger. "That was a great, great speech."

"Did I do okay?"

"You did amazing."

"Good, because I meant every word."

Then he pulled her into his arms and kissed her again, and soon they were both in her much smaller bed, and when he took her to the heights again, this time, he was the one who said it.

"I love you."

And when she curled up against him, she smiled.

Because they had both broken the curse. It turned out, all those stories she'd read were true.

Love really was the answer.

EPILOGUE

THEY GOT MARRIED up at the house with only the kids, Debbie and a pastor to officiate.

John and Joe were in suits, and Adam spent the morning continually catching them stuffing water balloons into their pockets.

It was totally different to his first wedding. Because he was in love. Because he wasn't getting married to try and fix himself.

He was in love, and that had fixed him. He was whole, and so he could make a life with Belle.

Debbie pulled him into her arms right after the ceremony, tears streaming down her face. "I'd love to claim credit for this, Adam. But even I had no idea it would end quite this happily."

"Thanks for being happy for me," he said.

"You're a son to me, and you always will be."

Love seemed like it only got bigger when you gave it freely. It didn't get more scarce. That's what he was finding, and he liked it.

Imogene looked like a fairy in her floaty white dress. She was a flower girl, and extremely proud of herself.

She lifted her arms up to him. "Daddy!" He picked her up off the ground and kissed her cheek. And then she reached over to Belle. "Mommy."

She'd never said that word before.

She'd never had a chance.

Belle looked at him, her eyes shining, and she took Imogene into her arms. "Yes, sweet girl. We're a family."

John and Joe came over and hugged Belle's skirts, and his eyes stung a little bit.

Debbie took a quick picture with her camera phone, and they ended up with a print of that picture hanging in the hall. And anyone who came to visit saw a beautiful, happy new family.

But if you looked closely, you could see the water balloon hidden behind Joe's back.

And only those who had attended the wedding knew, a family melee had broken out after.

And Joe and John might have ended up locked in the pantry, while Belle, Imogene and Adam declared victory.

It had only been for ten minutes.

But it had all started with water balloons, so it seemed pretty fitting that it ended with them too.

Water balloons and love. A whole lot of love.

* * * * *

SPECIAL EXCERPT FROM

(H) HARLEQUIN

DESIRE

*Attorney Alexandra Lattimore isn't looking for love.
She's home to help her family—and escape problems
at work. But sparks with former rival Jackson Strom
are too hot to resist. Will her secrets keep them from
rewriting their past?*

*Read on for a sneak peek at
Rivalry at Play
by Nadine Gonzalez.*

"Mornin'," Jackson said, as jovial at 6:00 a.m. as he was at noon.
He loaded Alexa's bag into the trunk and held open the passenger
door for her. "Let's get out of here."

Alexa hesitated. Within the blink of an eye, she'd slipped back
in time. She was seventeen and Jackson was her prom date, holding
open the door to a tacky rental limo. There he was, the object of her
every teenage dream. She went over and touched him, just to make
sure he was real.

"Are you okay?" he asked.

"No," she said. "I was thinking… If things were different back
in high school—"

"Different how?"

"If I were nicer."

"Nicer?"

"Or just plain nice," she said. "Do you think you might have
asked me to prom or homecoming or whatever?"

Jackson went still, but something moved in his eyes. Alexa
panicked. What was she doing stirring things up at dawn?

"Forget it!" She backed away from him. "I don't know why I

said that. It's early and I haven't had coffee. Do you mind stopping for coffee along the way?"

He reached out and caught her by the waist. He pulled her close. The air between them was charged. "I didn't want *nice*. I wanted Alexandra Lattimore, the one girl who was anything but nice and who ran circles around me."

"Why didn't you say anything?"

"I was scared."

"You thought I'd reject you?"

"If I had asked you to prom or whatever, would you have said yes?"

"I don't know," she admitted. "Maybe not…or I could have changed my mind. Only it would have been too late. You would have found yourself a less complicated date."

"And end up having a forgettable night?"

"That's not so bad," she said. "I would have ended up hating myself."

Alexa wanted to be that person he'd imagined, imperious and unimpressed by her peers or her surroundings, but she wasn't. She never had been. She'd lived her whole life in a self-protective mode, rejecting others before they could reject or dismiss her. She now saw it for what it was: a coward's device.

His hand fell from her waist. He stepped back and held open the car door even wider. "Aren't you happy we're not those foolish kids anymore?"

Alexa leaned forward and kissed him lightly on the lips. "You have no idea," she whispered and slid into the waiting seat.

Don't miss what happens next in…
Rivalry at Play *by Nadine Gonzalez,*
the next book in the Texas Cattleman's Club:
Ranchers and Rivals series!

Available July 2022 wherever
Harlequin Desire books and ebooks are sold.

Harlequin.com

HDEXP0522

Get 4 FREE REWARDS!

We'll send you 2 FREE Books plus 2 FREE Mystery Gifts.

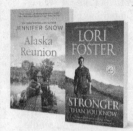 

Both the **Romance** and **Suspense** collections feature compelling novels written by many of today's bestselling authors.